# ZEBULON'S OATH

a novel of the Carolinas in the Revolutionary War during 1780-1781

## David R. Dowdy

DBD Publishing 

This book is dedicated to:

William Beck, a Private in the North Carolina militia whose service from 1780 to 1782 inspired me to write *Zebulon's Oath*

and

My Patriot ancestor Mathias Houx, a Private who mustered in Capt Henry Hardman's company of the Maryland Flying Camp on July 19, 1776

Cast of Characters ...................................................................................i
Maps.....................................................................................................vi
Part I.....................................................................................................1
Map of Zebulon's World.........................................................................2
One ~ A Chance Meeting ........................................................................3
Two ~ Turbulent Times...........................................................................8
Map at the Fall of Charles Town in Spring 1780 .................................11
Three ~ The Convoy .............................................................................12
Four ~ Stepfather..................................................................................17
Five ~ Ambush......................................................................................22
Six ~ Friends Meeting ..........................................................................27
Seven ~ Moravian Brotherhood ...........................................................33
Eight ~ Abraham ..................................................................................39
Nine ~ For King or Revolution?...........................................................43
Ten ~ Invasion......................................................................................46
Eleven ~ Catharine ..............................................................................51
Twelve ~ Find My Loyalists .................................................................54
Thirteen ~ His Excellency.....................................................................59
Fourteen ~ Are You Afraid?..................................................................63
Fifteen ~ Flattery and Loathing ...........................................................67
Sixteen ~ No Greater Task....................................................................69
Seventeen ~ Bach Has a Plan ...............................................................75
Eighteen ~ Gov Nash Calls ..................................................................83
Nineteen ~ Conspiracy .........................................................................86
Twenty ~ Breakaway .............................................................................92
Twenty-One ~ Scourge ..........................................................................98
Twenty-Two ~ Rahel ...........................................................................102
Twenty-Three ~ God Keep Us .............................................................106
Twenty-Four ~ Disconcerting .............................................................110
Twenty-Five ~ Off to Enlist.................................................................113
Twenty-Six ~ Zebulon's Oath..............................................................118
PART II................................................................................................125
Twenty-Seven ~ Neal Calls.................................................................127
Twenty-Eight ~ Taking Command.......................................................133
Twenty-Nine ~ Salem Laboratory.......................................................141
Thirty ~ The Benefactor......................................................................146
Thirty-One ~ Ammunition ..................................................................152
Thirty-Two ~ Longing to Return.........................................................156
Thirty-Three ~ Detour.........................................................................161
Thirty-Four ~ Greene's Agent.............................................................168
Thirty-Five ~ A Mission ......................................................................173
Thirty-Six ~ Camp Cheraw .................................................................180

Thirty-Seven ~ Lil Daisy .................................................................. 186
Thirty-Eight ~ Shocking News ......................................................... 191
Map of Army Routes After Cowpens ............................................... 195
Thirty-Nine ~ Second Invasion........................................................ 196
Forty ~ A Special Convoy ............................................................... 201
Forty-One ~ Besting ....................................................................... 204
Forty-Two ~ Cornwallis Pursues ..................................................... 209
Forty-Three ~ To Wachovia ............................................................ 214
Forty-Four ~ Salem Tour ................................................................ 219
Forty-Five ~ Attack ........................................................................ 225
Forty-Six ~ Council of War ............................................................. 230
Forty-Seven ~ Bugle Boy James ..................................................... 235
Forty-Eight ~ Race to the Dan ........................................................ 238
PART III ......................................................................................... 243
Forty-Nine ~ Late Again ................................................................. 245
Fifty ~ Loyalists and Provisions ...................................................... 249
Fifty-One ~ Rally Forces ................................................................. 257
Fifty-Two ~ Battle Erupts................................................................ 264
Map of the Battle of Guilford Court House ...................................... 269
Fifty-Three ~ The Day Has Come .................................................... 270
Fifty-Four ~ Cannonade .................................................................. 276
Fifty-Five ~ Clashing on the Field.................................................... 280
Fifty-Six ~ First Line Panic ............................................................. 284
Fifty-Seven ~ Defensive Nerve ........................................................ 288
Fifty-Eight ~ Holding the Line ........................................................ 293
Fifty-Nine ~ British Success............................................................ 297
Sixty ~ A Separate Battle ................................................................ 301
Sixty-One ~ The Continentals ......................................................... 305
Sixty-Two ~ Humbled ..................................................................... 310
Sixty-Three ~ Ruthless Fighting ...................................................... 314
Sixty-Four ~ Waning Battle............................................................. 318
Sixty-Five ~ Retreat and Repair ...................................................... 321
Sixty-Six ~ Renewed Outlook ......................................................... 327
Sixty-Seven ~ Grieve the Heroes...................................................... 332
Premise .......................................................................................... 339
Chapter Notes ................................................................................. 341
Bibliography ................................................................................... 345
Internet Bibliography With Links...................................................... 349

# Cast of Characters

(*f*) = fictional

## Quakers
Zebulon Mitchell (*f*) — stepson of Michael McMurray
Michael McMurray (*f*) — stepfather of Zebulon, father of Sara
Olivia McMurray (*f*) — mother of Zebulon and Sara
Sara McMurray (*f*) — daughter of Michael and Olivia McMurray
Thomas Bourne — son of Nathan Bourne

Minor players
Elders (*f*): Darlington, Haines, Folger, Mendenhall, Starbuck, Mills, Milhous, Hunt
Youngers (*f*): Starbuck, Harrold, Gardner, Canaday, Thornburgh
George Fox — founder of the Religious Society of Friends (Quakers)
Nathan Bourne — planter

## Moravians
Maria Bach (*f*) — daughter of Traugott Bach
George Heider (*f*) — son of George Heider, Sr
Yohanna Heider (*f*) — daughter of George Heider, Sr
Traugott Bach (Bagge) — Salem authority and trader
Johann Michael Graff — Moravian bishop; Salem diarist
Abraham Hellerschwarz (*f*) — Black man; elder slave
Jacob Meyer — Salem Tavern landlord
Rahel (*f*) — Black maid at Salem Tavern; female slave

Minor players
George Heider, Sr (*f*) — father of George and Yohanna
Mila Bach (*f*) — daughter of Traugott Bach
Tycho Nissen — Salem wainwright
Johann Stockburger — Salem planter and cowherd
Christof Vogler — Salem gunsmith
Johann Reuz — Single Brother, apprentice
Peter Yarrell — Salem tanner
Abraham Steiner — Salem miller
Samuel Stotz — Salem trader
Brother Zillman — Salem watchman
Samuel Benjamin Vierling — Salem doctor

## American and Allied Statesmen

Benjamin Franklin — minister to France, inventor, pamphleteer
John Adams — ambassador to the Dutch Republic
King Louis XVI — king of France
Thomas Jefferson — Gov of Virginia
Samuel Huntington — president of the Continental Congress
Joseph Reed — president of Pennsylvania
Thomas Lee — Gov of Maryland
Abner Nash — Gov of North Carolina

## British Statesmen

King George III — king of Great Britain and Ireland
King Charles II — 17th c. king of England, Scotland and Ireland
Josiah Martin — ex royal governor of North Carolina
Lord Dunmore — ex royal governor of Virginia
Lord George Germain — Secretary of State for America
King George I — early 18th c. king of Great Britain and Ireland

## Continental and Allied Army Figures (including Militia)

Maj Gen Benjamin Lincoln — Southern cdr, Sept 1778 to May 1780
Lt Gen George Washington — CIC Continental Army
Maj Gen Nathanael Greene — QM Gen; Southern cdr from Dec 1780
Lt Col/Brig Gen Francis Marion — Cdr of SC militia
Col/Brig Gen Andrew Pickens — Cdr of SC militia/NC militia
Maj Gen Horatio Gates — Southern dept cdr from July to Dec 1780
Col William R. Davie — Cdr of NC Cav; new NC Commissary Gen
Maj Gen Friedrich Wilhelm Baron von Steuben — Greene's 2IC
Maj Ichabod Burnet — aide-de-camp (ADC) to Greene
Col Martin Armstrong — Cdr NC militia, Surry Co Rifles
Col Christian Febiger — quartermaster 2nd Virginia Regiment
Lt Col Edward Carrington — Greene's quartermaster; Makers Co cdr
Sgt Matthew Vinyard (f) — Makers company NCO
Capt Abercrombie Hawkins (f) — Makers company cdr
Brig Gen Edward Stevens — Cdr of Virginia militia, 1st Brigade
Pvt James Gillies — Lee's Legion bugler
Lt Col Henry Lee — Lee's Legion cdr
Col Tadeusz Kosciuszko — Polish military engineer
Brig Gen Isaac Huger — Cdr of Virginia Brigade
Lt Col John Gunby — Cdr of 1st Maryland Regiment
Brig Gen Daniel Morgan — Cdr of light infantry, militia, and cavalry
Lt Col William Washington — Cdr of 1st & 3rd Continental Cavalry

Col Thomas Polk — Cdr 4th NC Regt; NC Commissary Gen
Col John Green — Cdr of the 1st Virginia Regiment
Maj Joseph McDowell — Cdr of NC Militia, Burke Co Regiment
Lt Col James Jackson— Cdr of Georgia Militia
Capt John Smith — Co Cdr 1st Maryland Regiment
Col John Paisley — Cdr of NC militia, Guilford Co, 2nd Regiment
Col Otho Holland Williams — Cdr of Maryland Brigade
Lt Col John Eager Howard — Gunby's 2IC
Col William Campbell — Cdr of Virginia Rifle Corps
Capt James Armstrong — officer in Lee's Legion
Brig Gen John Butler — Cdr of NC militia, Hillsdale Brigade
Brig Gen Robert Lawson — Cdr of Virginia militia, 2nd Brigade
Capt Robert Kirkwood — Cdr of the Delaware Regiment
Col Charles Lynch — Cdr of the Bedford Riflemen
Capt Anthony Singleton — Cdr 1st Bn, 12th Co, 1st Cont Artillery
Pvt Sam Houston — Rockbridge Co, VA militiaman; memoirist
Maj Alexander Stuart — Cdr of Augusta/Rockbridge Co (VA) militias
Maj St. George Tucker — officer in Col John Holcombe's Regt; diarist
Col Peter Perkins — Cdr of Pittsylvania Co, VA Regiment of militia
Maj Henry Skipwith — 2IC of VA militias: Brunswick, Mecklenburg
and Powhatan Counties
Doctor James Wallace — surgeon attached to 3rd Continental Cavalry
Lt Col Samuel Hawes — Cdr of the 2nd Virginia Regiment
Capt Ebenezer Finley — Cdr 1st Bn, unknown Co, 1st Cont Artillery
Pvt Pedro Francisco — 3rd Continental Cavalry

Minor players
Brig Gen Thomas Sumter — Cdr of SC militia
Col Abraham Buford — Cdr of 3rd Virginia Regiment
Brig Gen Henry Knox — Cdr of Continental Artillery
Col Timothy Pickering — new Cont. Army Quartermaster General
Col Christian Febiger — quartermaster of 2nd Regiment of Virginia
Brig Gen Mordecai Gist — Cdr of Maryland Line
Maj Micajah Lewis — officer in NC militia, Surry or Wilkes Co
Marquis de Lafayette — French military officer
Marquis de Bretigny — French military officer
Daniel Deshon — Capt of the privateer General Nash
Brig Gen William Davidson — Cdr of NC militia, Salisbury Brigade
Maj Ferguson Taylor — fifer
Col John Holcombe — Cdr of VA militias: Brunswick, Mecklenburg,
and Powhatan Counties
Col Beverly Randolph — Cdr of VA militias: Amelia, Cumberland,

and Powhatan Counties
Lt Col Benjamin Ford — Cdr 2nd Maryland Regiment


Unsung American Soldiers
Capt Arthur Forbis — North Carolina militia
Pvt William Beck — North Carolina militia
Pvt Henry Ingle — Virginia militia
Pvt Lewis Griffin — Virginia Regular


## British Army Figures (including Militia)
Lord Charles Cornwallis, Lt Gen — Cdr of British Southern Dept
Sir Henry Clinton, Lt Gen — CIC British Army in America
Lt Col Banastre Tarleton — British Legion cdr
Capt Henry Broderick — aide-de-camp (ADC) to Cornwallis
Maj Gen Leslie — Cornwallis' 2IC, Cdr of 71st Regiment
Brig Gen Charles O'Hara — Cdr of 2nd Guards Bn and Grenadiers Bn
Maj Johann du Buy —Cdr of Hessian von Bose Regiment
Capt Thomas Miller — officer in Tarleton's British Legion
Col James Webster — Cdr of 23rd and 33rd Regiments, Light Infantry
of the Guards, and Yagers Company
Lt John MacLeod — Cdr of Royal Artillery
Sgt Roger Lamb — Irish infantryman of the 23rd Regiment; memoirist
Col Chapple Norton — Cdr of 1st Guards Bn
Lt Col James Stuart — Brig Gen Charles O'Hara's 2IC


Minor players
Lt Col Nisbet Balfour — Cdr of 64th Regiment
Sir William Howe, Lt Gen — ex CIC British Army in America
Maj Henry Craig — Cdr at Wilmington, NC
Maj George Hanger — substitute Cdr British Legion
Maj John André — British spy
Maj Gen Benedict Arnold — American traitor; deserted to British army
Maj Patrick Ferguson — Cdr of Loyalist militia
Lt Gen John Burgoyne —North American campaigns field cdr
Capt Tavis Burns (f) — 71st Regiment co cdr
Capt Angus Mackenzie (f) — 71st Regiment co cdr


## Patriots
Catharine Greene — wife of Nathanael Greene
Martha Washington — wife of George Washington
Mary Spurgin — wife of William Spurgin

Johnny Spurgin — son of William Spurgin

Minor players
Emily Geiger — daughter of John Geiger and Ann Murff; messenger
William Smith (*f*) — planter
William Bingham — Philadelphia merchant
John Custis — father of Martha Washington's first husband
Frances Parke Custis — mother of Martha Washington's first husband
Col John Fitzgerald —friend of George Washington; retired
Squire Charles Bruce — North Carolina landowner and planter
Thomas Paine — activist; writer
Elizabeth Maxwell Steele — proprietor of Steele's Tavern
Joseph Hoskins — planter
Jonathan Jessop — son of Thomas Jessop; battlefield map artist
Thomas Jessop — planter

## Loyalists
Capt Arthur Neal (*f*) — Cdr of Loyalist militia
Lil Daisy (*f*) — Neal's collaborator
Col William Spurgin — Cdr of Loyalist militia
Col John Pyle — Cdr of Loyalist militia; MD

# Maps


Zebulon's World     p. 2
Spring 1780, Charles Town has fallen     p. 11
Southern Campaign post Cowpens     p. 195
Battle of Guilford Court House     p. 269

# Part I

# Map of Zebulon's World

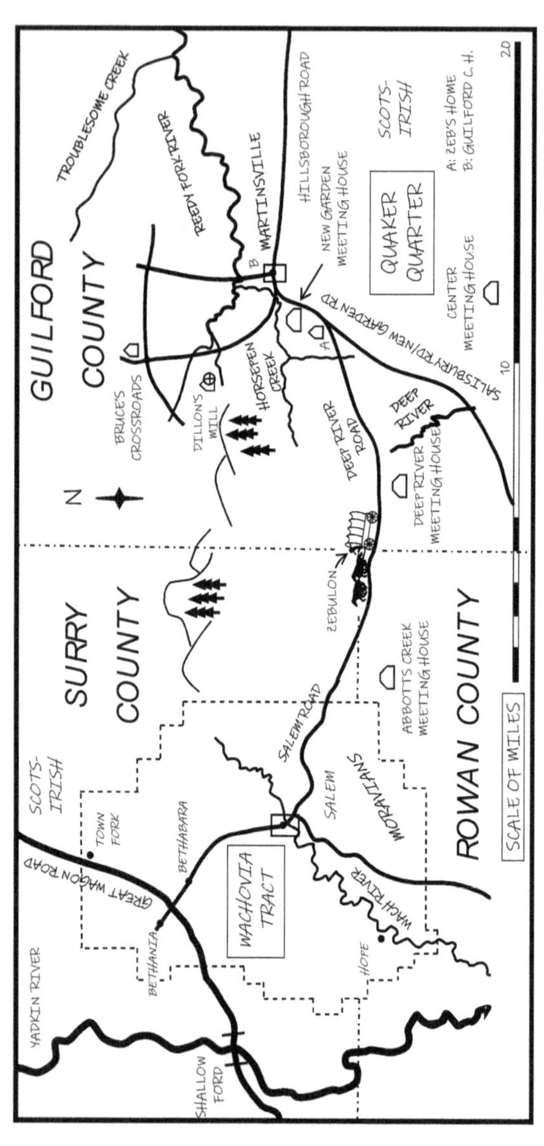

# One ~ A Chance Meeting

— June 15, 1780, Wachovia, Central North Carolina

Zebulon turned his wagon onto Bethabara Road. Phew! The journey to the Moravian town would soon be over. He grinned, thinking about the usual friendly reception he'd receive in Salem.

A commotion arose in his wake and shattered his contemplation. Heavens! Hoofbeats pounded in a crescendo as six men on horseback charged out of a grove and overtook him.

"Whoa!" Zeb winced and brought his team to a rest on the verge.

A half circle of outlaws formed around the left side of the wagon. The apparent leader pointed a pistol to the sky.

"Get down from there!"

"Sir?"

"We're taking your wagon!"

"I don't want any trouble, mister." Zeb surveyed the determined man who like his gang dressed in a drab red jacket. The rest didn't show guns, but cartridge boxes hung from straps slung across their chests and their pockets bulged with steel.

The leader fully cocked his pistol. "I won't tell you again!"

Ahead came a young man driving a cart from Salem. When Zeb's wagon came into view, he stopped fifteen yards away, baffled at the standoff.

A young woman beside the cart driver reckoned the gist of the scene. "Tories!" she yelled.

Zeb somersaulted backwards into the cargo box of the wagon dodging a ball of lead that tunneled through the side board of the driver's box.

Hoofbeats rose behind the Tories. Out of the same trees came a company of Surry militia on horseback leveling pistols and rifles. They chased the marauders away and the short skirmish ended.

Zeb climbed down and doffed his hat to the backs of the militiamen riding off in a cloud of dust toward the Tories.

The young woman who'd signaled the Tories' presence hailed Zeb. "Hello. Aren't you the Quaker wainwright's son?"

"Zebulon Mitchell of New Garden."

"I'm Maria Bach." She spoke English with a German lilt. "We're united brethren of Moravians from Salem." She pointed to the cart driver and a young woman seated to her right. "This is George and Yohanna Heider."

"Pleased to meet you." Before covering his head, he bowed to the three Moravians. "I might have lost this wagon if you hadn't made the enemy flinch. I might have died."

Maria motioned to Zeb's wagon. "Would you have given your wagon to save your life?"

Zeb's eyes blinked. "I would have held out as long as possible."

"Is that wagon so important?"

"Making wagons is my stepfather's livelihood."

"Well, thank God you have your life."

Zeb mused at Maria's logic and nodded.

"That was smart of you to get out of the way."

"Had to. I'm too young to die. My God, I'm not yet married."

Maria whispered in Yohanna's ear and turned to Zeb. "Why not?"

He caught Yohanna's smile and touched his hat. "Excuse me. I must be on my way." Zeb reckoned Maria, sitting next to George to be his wife or intended. Didn't that make the wholesome Yohanna his sister?

Zeb shook the reins and pulled away northward.

"Wait," Maria called.

Zeb didn't turn. Far ahead he saw the road converge to a point. They couldn't see the grin on his face from Maria's apparent matchmaking.

Whether stunned by the near tragedy or fatigue from driving the wagon, for the first time in a dozen journeys the final leg to Salem appeared unfamiliar. Duty snapped him alert. He cracked the whip and the beasts bore down against their collars.

While the respite had been both unwelcome and charming, Zebulon's backside still felt numb on the hard wooden seat. The reins attached to the bits of four muscular horses may as well have been in someone else's hands and the pulsing hoofbeats droned in his ears like his eighth-grade schoolmaster. There was no getting around the twenty-four miles and four hours of drudgery it took to drive a new freight wagon to Salem.

The ride from New Garden in the Quaker Quarter of Guilford County would soon be over. He rolled over the cambered Wach River bridge. The Moravian town rose past fields of ripening barley, rye, and winter wheat waving their plump golden heads from curved, narrow stems.

Beyond the distant point, Salem Tavern stood where the road improved into a graded, wide street. The wainwright arrived full of anxiety as he drove down the hill in the rear of the establishment. He jumped down from the wagon and stretched his six-foot lean body and doffed his black floppy hat to wipe the brow sweat before any more ran into his eyes tired from over-focus. A full hairline drew back into a black tail queued in a black ribbon.

In the tavern meadow amid a small wood, he pressed the round dome of the hat on his head and waved a stable boy over to help unhitch and water the team. Zeb untied a single horse from the side of the wagon and led her to the water trough. All horses were God's gift yet he treated this one with special kindness as she would carry him on her back when he returned to New Garden in the morning.

Before going inside to register, Zeb poured dried kernels of Indian corn into the feed box on the back of the wagon and spread a bale of hay on the ground under a nearby tree. He rubbed the neck of each lathered horse making sure they all got a place at the box. The boy who was already brushing one of the team caught a pewter Continental dollar from Zeb.

Traugott Bach looked up from the big table in the reception room and set aside a pottery mug of beer. "Good day, Zeb!"

Mitchell turned around. Though tinged with the man's German accent, the rich Salem trader's voice brought a smile to his face. It was the second time he'd been in anyone's company since sunrise. "Good day, sir! I've come with your new wagon."

Bach gazed at Zeb. "Are you sure you're not Moravian?"

"Huh?"

"Dependable, pleasant to obsession, and dressed in plain clothes, you could be." Bach grinned.

Zeb compared his clothes to Bach's. Both wore black felt hats made of upside down bowls with wide, round brims. Their neck cloths both simple white wool. Each wore black waistcoats, frocks, and breeches. Stockings covered their legs from the knee down, Zeb's black and Bach's white. His shoe buckles pewter and Bach's polished silver.

"Never mind, Brother. Tell your stepfather I need five more wagons as soon as possible."

"Yes, sir, I will. Thank you for your custom."

"Not at all." Bach winked. "Someday I hope our wagon maker can match your stepfather's productivity."

Zeb pressed Bach with a humble gaze before begging the wealthy trader's help. "Will you come out back and help me unload the wagon?"

"Check in and eat lunch. When you've settled in, we'll inventory your delivery and I'll write a receipt for the goods. Then I'll find someone to assist you."

Zeb remained standing in front of Bach long enough for the trader to fathom the young man's concern. "Mr. Bach, I beg of you a question."

"What's on your mind?"

"After turning on Bethabara Road, I passed an encampment. Are soldiers occupying the Wachovia tract?"

Bach chuckled. "No, my son. The North Carolina militia from Surry County is maneuvering."

"With that many, war is now more than a rumor."

"The camp bothered you."

Zeb chuckled. "A little."

"With the British so near, militias all over the state are on alert." Bach picked up his mug and slurped.

"There's something else." Zeb wouldn't reveal meeting three young Moravians, but he had to explain the hole in the driver's box. "A group of Tory horsemen accosted me."

Bach set his mug down hard, sloshing beer on the table. "Oh, my Quaker friend! What happened?"

"The leader said he was going to seize my wagon; I mean your wagon. Out of the woods came a company of militia and chased them off. But the rogue fired a smart little hole in the wood."

Bach sighed. "Thank God you're okay. Thank God the Surry militia were patrolling. I hope the Loyalists didn't scare you."

"I won't stop delivering your wagons, sir. My stepfather depends on me to keep his business profitable."

***

Zeb returned to the tavern yard. Hearing the horses munching the hard corn and hay warmed his heart. Sold with the wagon, the horses raised by farmers along Horsepen Creek in western Guilford County came with every sale.

Heavy goods lay under a canvas cover. Not to make the new wagon stable or break it in. McMurray made a bit of money on deliveries and helped Quaker Friends get their products to customers in Wachovia.

Baskets containing ten bolts of creamy linen and eight bolts of black wool for the Salem tailor came. Two barrels of nails came for the Single Brothers workshop.

A dozen flintlock hunting rifles for Bach's store came from the gunsmith. Quakers put a stipulation on the bill of sale that the Moravians would not allow military use of the guns.

***

Later that night in the tavern Zeb bought a mug of tea and drank in reverie as he marveled at the changes in Salem. No matter Brother Bach playing down the militia, everywhere he looked further signs of war had come to the South. Broadsheets and pamphlets left on the cold mantel contained opinions of eminent Americans describing the peril of the new British strategy. Upstairs he found uniformed and armed officers of the militia occupying the large boarding rooms.

They were non-Moravians and their English offered him a chance to overhear their topical conversations about the war and conditions in the South. When they mentioned faraway posts in South Carolina and Virginia, their knowledge of the world awed him.

Sleep tossed an initial net of drowsiness over Zeb. Though North Carolina entered the conversation of the military men, he fell further into repose. Before he fell asleep, Yohanna Heider lit the fires of his dreams. Whether it was right to picture himself beside her in the context of civil upheaval, she'd flattered him.

# Two ~ Turbulent Times

While Zeb slept a heavy midnight storm washed the Wachovia tract from tiny Bethania in the north of the one-hundred-thousand acre settlement down to the town of Salem. Cylinders appeared on walls as ribbons of white light flashed through gaps in the shutters and across doused tapers inside the modest structures. For twenty minutes gusting winds whipped the sweet gums in the central clearings.

Moravians took the rolling thunder as an exclamation of the Almighty and He'd never screamed louder. They lay awake listening to rain pelting from the black heavens knowing the storm, as all storms going back to their tumultuous Czech and German past, brought salvation. For as they sought religious freedom in America without fear, they believed the Lord would conduct His plan for peace.

***

In the morning, sunshine would light the muddy clay ground beset with red rivulets around the homesteads. The star-shaped leaves of the sweet gums, scoured like washing against rocks, would litter the land as always after a storm. Waking settlers would step outside amongst the debris hoping to see Mr. Franklin's lightning rods had spared the buildings, fences, and woods of fire.

Benjamin Franklin's brave tampering with God's power worked miracles. How could one not admire him for understanding the mystery of lightning? Moravians took comfort in safety, but they left magic for others.

God's will sometimes meant storms and His reasons for stirring up the winds and dropping rain needed no explanation from mortals. Though He swept the air in great whirls and thunder that frightened the modest believers of the tract, it was a bargain with nature. Destruction was inevitable but storms also brought vital water and nutrients shouted from the air.

Storms of another kind whispered through the colony of Wachovia and her unique villages spread up and down the tract. Salem, the largest of the settlements, where a magnificent taming of the wild forests led to a prosperous civilization little seen in central North Carolina, regretted the changes blowing up from South Carolina.

Physical wrath of mankind versus mankind loomed. Bodies might soon litter the ground in their own neighborhood. War was as inescapable as howling winds displacing a quiet night and it was nigh.

***

Weekly and daily accounts via grapevine and letters and gazettes carried by Express to the Moravian settlements brought news Lt Gen Cornwallis camped in South Carolina waiting for the right moment to enter North Carolina. In the meantime, he was amassing stores of ammunition and other war materials.

Bishop Johann Michael Graff, keeper of the Salem diary, woke early. By candle light he opened his log book and perused the deluge of stories while holding their plausibility at arm's length. Warnings of the British invasion became so regular the diarist soon rejected them.

Though Graff's smirk belittled the idea of Cornwallis coming to Wachovia, he admitted the British sieged Charles Town, a fact not inconsequential to the Moravian brotherhood. Give the British credit for keeping their word to their Loyalist friends in South Carolina. If Cornwallis, the British second in command in the South, promised to invade North Carolina, there should be no doubt it would happen.

The bishop recalled how events unfolded in the first half of 1780. In late February, lookouts spotted British naval troop carriers near Charles Town. Word from South Carolina in March brought Salem more dire news. A Royal navy armada of tall ships neared the coastline, each aiming their multiple rows of cannons. Overall, the navy had hundreds of guns threatening the Continental battlements and its dozens of transports lurked with thousands of infantrymen, cavalry, and artillery ready to come ashore.

Maj Gen Benjamin Lincoln hadn't seen anything so ominous for a long time. Though he'd once repulsed the British, it was four years on, and again they'd turned their attention to Charles Town in the face of a stalemate in the Northern Colonies. Led by British overall commander-in-chief Sir Henry Clinton, who'd been in the Colonies since the siege of Boston five years earlier, the invasion would begin with the British hoping to get a toehold in the South.

Lincoln rushed the information of the first signs of the British return forward. Apprised of the situation, Lt Gen George Washington wrote Maj Gen Nathanael Greene in late March from his headquarters in Morristown, New Jersey, enquiring how to send troops to save the city.

Greene, serving as Quartermaster General of the army—the man Washington entrusted with acquiring and disbursing war materials throughout the Colonies—outlined a route taking troops from Pennsylvania through Maryland. From that point Greene's sureness of getting the Continental army through Virginia, North Carolina, and South Carolina waned. Short on knowledge of magazines and stores available south of Maryland, he feared troops would starve or go unarmed.

Graff had recorded in the Salem diary rumors of the fall of Charles Town in early March and derivative unrest leading to the Continental dollar losing half its value. Buyers, not knowing how far domestic currency would fall, brought larger quantities of Continentals to Salem to ensure they'd be able to purchase goods.

Though the early speculation of Charles Town's fall proved false, by the middle of May the latest invasion news became cold reality as commissioners in counties surrounding Wachovia made ready to confiscate the land of those holding out to English rule.

Graff always believed man could do nothing. What He ordains is worthy of praise and glory. Leave to Him choice and action. God is a Prince all-wise. On the last day of May hard news arrived that Charles Town had indeed fallen, showing the earlier reports had been lightning before the rumble of thunder. Like people caught in a long-running storm, his was a confused and worried congregation.

## Map at the Fall of Charles Town, Spring 1780

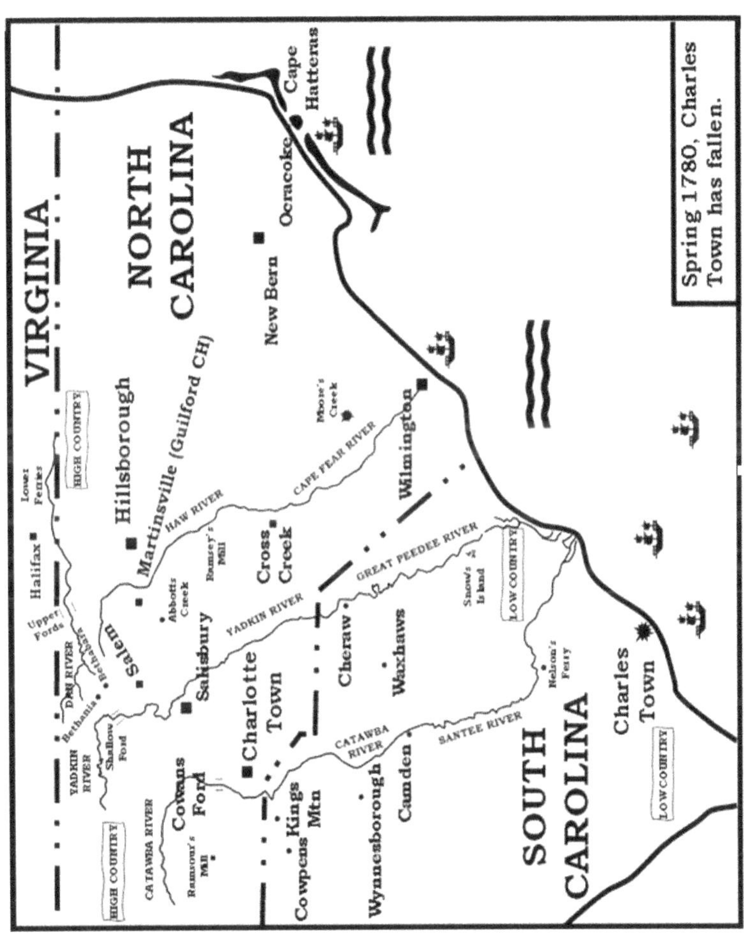

# Three ~ The Convoy

— Nelson's Ferry, Santee River, South Carolina

In South Carolina, where the storm of the Revolution had snatched the colony's peace, sleepy Rebel insurgents waited for the arrival of a secret convoy of Redcoat wagons heading north seventy miles above Charles Town.

The premises of Nelson's Ferry slept peacefully, where wind, lightning, and rain had spared the area north of the great port city. That was fine with the Rebels as they hoped to execute their plan.

Fog shrouded the banks of the Santee. Through the mist came the sound of undulating water lapping against boulders and impediments upstream of the crossing route. Massive water flow dragged past the banks creating eddies at the river's sandy and pebbled edge.

The business of transporting people and goods across the Santee River wouldn't start until dawn. Spanning one thousand feet at the crossing point, fear of the unknown kept wise souls off the black river at night. Nor did normal people approach the swamps adjacent to the ferry until daybreak as the mires craved human flesh, horses, and any man made thing.

In early morning, curved-beaked curlews often sang in drawn out peeps that resembled screams. So lifelike, the tremolo and stutter of the curlews chased strangers from the boggy ground to safety. If one listened, the songs broadcast cautions to keep away from the soupy soil.

Along both sides of the causeway leading to the dock four-hundred militia had bed down with their muskets standing upright upon bayonets thrust into a patch of drained, soft ground claimed from the low country. They lay on mats of whatever dry vegetation they could find but left curtains of tall Indian grass standing along the road and took sanguine sleep on the ground. Outsiders might mistake low snoring and breathing of the commandos for croaking bullfrogs calling females to mate in the gray light of a shrouded moon.

Intermittent whispers came from the edgy militia.

"What's taking so long for the Redcoats to get here?"

"I don't know. I'm dying to bury my bayonet in a British belly."

The keeper of the ferry stayed away while the militia formed on each side of the causeway. The crossing served as a vital link from Charles Town to Fort Camden. Any actions harmful to the British tied to the keeper would get his head on a pike in full display of the locals.

***

While misfortune deprived the Southern Continental army of provisions, arms, and uniforms, British surpluses grew. Lt Gen Cornwallis, a lord and member of the upper house of Parliament, aimed to get the supplies taken in the fall of Charles Town to Fort Camden before invading North Carolina.

Nothing showed the stark difference between American and British fortunes in the South more than their gunpowder stores. The British, after confiscating fifty thousand pounds of powder from the Continentals in Charles Town, dominated the supply.

When gunpowder could be found, Patriots couldn't get it to the field due to shortages of wagons. Lack of paper and lead to roll ammunition cartridges compounded the problem. Thin American supplies rendered academic the question of whether they could keep the British out of North Carolina.

***

"Swamp fox" Lt Col Francis Marion paused a moment before instructing the Patriot officers arrayed in a half-circle. The power of gunpowder to destroy sobered him. Wasn't it a magical alchemy of humble materials from Hell itself—niter, sulfur, and charcoal—discovered long ago and perfected for hundreds of years to kill better? He worried that fighting the British exposed his young men to death.

After the British burned his plantation, Marion made a base camp at Snow's Island in eastern South Carolina hidden between Little Carr Creek and the Great Pee Dee River and shared hearty meals of meat and sweet potatoes with destitute commandos. Sometimes luxurious whole brown rice heaped in their pottery bowls care of local Patriots.

Marion appeared meek to strangers, but the short, lanky forty-eight-year old who served in the South Carolina militia during the French and Indian War would pull himself up on a saddle and command the best local intelligence and authority throughout the low country. He sprang from Snow's Island and collected his minutemen when he got notice an extraordinary convoy was due at Nelson's Ferry from Charles Town. His men skirted the ring of British protection, looking forward to embarrassing the enemy.

Marion pushed aside any reservations of his abilities. "Brigadier General Thomas Sumter's regiment will be on the other side of the causeway," he said. "Our company will attack the first wagon after the forward guard is on the Santee. Fight with bayonets and the butts of your muskets as long as you can. Avoid gunfire unless necessary. We don't want the rear guard on our tails until we have control of at least one powder wagon."

A captain squirmed. "Won't a squad of the forward guards stay behind to cross with the wagons?"

"Kill them."

Marion slipped through a curtain of Indian grass to the narrow causeway where a convoy would soon march down the defile to the ferry dock. He crept to the other side and slipped through another curtain of grass to meet with Brig Gen Sumter.

"Morning, gamecock," Marion whispered.

Sumter mocked scorn and whispered. "Don't call me that."

Sumter, another veteran of the French and Indian War, had made a name for himself defending Charles Town with rooster zeal when the port city threw off the first attack by the British in 1776. After Lt Col Banastre Tarleton's Legion burned his house in the spring of 1780, Sumter wanted revenge.

Col Andrew Pickens arrived with a company from the western reaches of the swamp and joined Marion and Sumter. The hero of Kettle Creek, Georgia who put down Loyalists dreaming of the return of British authority tiptoed to the brush row along the causeway and peeked through the Indian grass. The colonel studied Sumpter's troops with an owl's consternation before joining Marion and Sumter.

"Why have your men fixed bayonets on their muskets? Ever hear of powder and lead?"

"I'm sorry you didn't hear the plan. Gunfire is the last thing we want. They'll have forward and rear guards. We won't do anything until the forward escort is on its way across the Santee on the ferry. We also don't want the rear corps joining the party when we attack." Marion gave Pickens an awkward grin. "Anyway, our powder might be too moist to fire.

"So, how can I assist you gentlemen?"

"Keep an eye on the British guards at the rear of the convoy while Sumter and I attack the front."

"With your boys in the front and mine in the back, we'll squeeze them."

"Me and Sumter are going to attack the wagon in front as soon as the forward guards are on the river. I'll send a guide to signal our forward action. Hold your fire unless the rear guard reacts."

"Don't get too jumpy," Pickens said. "Give yourself away early and you'll die."

"Worry not, sir. I might have missed the Battle of Charles Town with a dislocated ankle, but I'm determined to get back the gunpowder we lost."

***

The gunpowder train left the magazine at Charles Town a day earlier and was due on the same road via Nelson's Ferry at Fort Camden northward where Cornwallis was amassing supplies in anticipation of invading North Carolina.

Out of the darkness came sixteen-year-old Emily Geiger, the daughter of Swiss-born parents John Geiger and Ann Murff, riding a swift horse up the causeway. She stopped long enough to shout, "Convoy! Convoy!" and rode away. The Partisans had ample time to make their final preparations.

From afar screeching hubs and clip-clopping teams announced the convoy advancing toward Nelson's Ferry in the gray early morning. Soon, the British 64th Regiment of Foot, would come down the narrow road and reveal the prize. If the cargoes equaled the ones brought up the road three previous times, Patriots would celebrate throughout the Carolinas.

The day's first crossing soon began at Nelson's Ferry. A long, wooden flatboat with low sides slipped away on the water with all but six forward guards who stood at attention next to commanding officer Lt Col Nisbet Balfour on the dock area.

Balfour clicked his tongue. The horse raised her head and walked the short distance back to the wagon train. A captain commanding the wagons raised a sword in salute and Balfour returned the gesture.

"Close order—March!" Balfour said. The drivers drew their wagons up the causeway toward the dock to wait for their turn.

Each wagon and four-horse team spanned thirty-three-feet. With twenty feet between the three team-wagons, a mere one-hundred-and-thirty-nine feet separated the forward and rear guards.

On either side of the causeway, rows of five foot butterfly weed and Indian grass concealed the scrawny, filthy insurgents crouched in readiness. Bayonets spiked from the ends of their muskets at right angles to the clusters of yellow and orange flowers and tall green shoots. Including an incredible number of teens, the youthful militia consisted of white, black, and native men and mixtures of white and black and native and black standing an average of sixty-six inches.

They emerged from the edges of the causeway, feet squishing in the dewy undergrowth and parting the Indian grass. Staid infantrymen in the army of King George III gazed in dread as dozens of militiamen flew to them wearing rags on their bony frames, brush in their hair, and carrying musket cartridges in handkerchief bags tied to rope belts. More shocking came weird, piercing wails accompanying the points of bayonets.

"Ee-hah! Ee-hah! Ee-hah!"

Tiger moths and monarch butterflies took flight from milkweed as the guerillas rushed out of the cover to converge on the wagons. Their bayonets pointed forward with an audacity dwarfing the meek militia.

# Four ~ Stepfather

— New Garden, Guilford County, North Carolina

"Ye are my friends, if ye do whatsoever I command you." (John 15:14 King James Version)

Since Friends first gathered and trembled in the presence of the Lord, they have been known as Quakers. He laid down a set of commands: Keep an austere piety within the self and maintain a Society where Friends can find release from the impositions and teachings of men; find inspiration to dispense universal love and goodwill for each other; and take refuge from ungodliness and worldly lusts.

***

Zeb woke before the tavern cock crowed. Breakfast would have to wait until he rushed home headlong in gray. At sunrise he rushed into the McMurray Wainwright shop in New Garden on Horsepen Creek looking for his stepfather. Wheelwrights rubbed their eyes and prepared for a day of shaping wood and assembling wheels.

Michael McMurray, himself a wheelwright, often said wheels formed the most important part of a wagon. Any carpenter could join boards into a rectangular cargo box. Making wheels took skill. Wheels provided motion.

In a large shed, the sounds of wood and iron undergoing change by the craftsmen filled Zeb's ears as the various subassemblies of a wagon took shape. Like hoofbeats on soft ground, a wheelwright pumped the treadle of a small lathe to turn rough sticks of wood into spokes. Another tradesman joined spokes to hubs.

Shaping hubs required a massive lathe powered by a waterwheel sitting in Horsepen Creek to spin and cut a rough oak stub into a balanced, round core. Once hollowed, an iron ring would be inserted for turning on an iron axle. Later, the hub and spoke assembly would be joined to the felloes of a wheel.

A racket rose from a back room where a blacksmith rotated and pounded a long glowing bar heated in a furnace of coals. He beat the softened metal on an anvil to form a wear-resistant wheel collar. Sometimes while waiting for a brazed metal patch to weld the ends, he'd plunge a red hot rod into a kettle to heat water for tea.

Zeb had apprenticed, but building wagons meant little to him. Though the humble labor of wheelwrights, blacksmiths, and carpenters working together provided contentment, nothing could surpass the joy of delivering a McMurray Wainwright wagon. Pride might corrupt his soul like dry rot in a wagon wheel, but each happy customer taking ownership of a wagon motivated him to drive another.

Zeb found his stepfather greasing the millwheel's main bearing and described the militia's presence near Salem. Hearing of the near disastrous encounter with the Loyalists would only worry his stepfather, so he held that piece back. Nor did he want to trouble the old man with his romantic titillation from a woman outside of their faith.

"The state is taking matters too far," McMurray said.

"Has delivering wagons to Salem become too dangerous?"

Practiced glumness steadied McMurray. "Stay clear of the militia and you'll be fine. They won't trouble a Quaker."

"I've never heard you speak so kind of the military."

"Don't mistake discretion for kindness when we're paying a four-fold tax to exclude ourselves from militia service." McMurray stowed the grease and wiped his hands on a linen rag. "Come, Zeb. It's time for the weekly Friends Meeting."

***

Zeb and his stepfather started walking. A drunken man lay on the ground outside New Garden Tavern, sleeping off a night of debauchery. Zeb and McMurray delayed their walk to the meeting and stopped at his feet.

The short McMurray and his tall stepson wore plain black Quaker frocks, waistcoats, breeches, and hats distinct from the fallen man who'd modified his otherwise similar clothing with foppish colors and frills abhorred by the Religious Society of Friends. A Friend banished from the Society, the man had tied a red cotton band around the dome of a plain Quaker hat and stuck goose feathers in it. A green lace cravat wrapped his neck.

From any angle, the devout Quakers stood in silhouette. Their clothes proclaimed them to be Children of Light, separate from the world. Zeb frowned and bent down to check on the inebriate.

"Leave him. We must be on our way to the meeting."

Zeb's empty stomach groaned. "Look at this man, father. Don't the demonic effects of drink worry you?"

The drunk stirred and gained enough sobriety to sit up. "Worry not. I'm on my way as well." Hiccup! "To recovery."

The man rose. He wobbled and leaned against the whitewashed tavern, gaining a white stripe across the back of his frock.

McMurray shook his head. "Drink marks your reputation, sir. Straighten up and remove the decorations from ye clothes. What are the prospects of your good wife and children if you drink ye wages?"

Zeb studied the man with more practical care. "You threaten your security by drunkenness. Whether your heart be Rebel or Loyalist, the other will see your state and take advantage."

"Go to the meeting, son. I'll take care of this foolish man and catch up."

Zeb departed. A well-dressed man stepped out of the tavern. His dark suit exhibited none of the plainness of the upright Quaker McMurray's clothes. He wore shoes with silver buckles and a narrow brimmed hat with an oval dome. The similarity of the drunkard's clothing to Quakers' caught his eye.

"Why do you bother this man? Isn't he a Friend in your Society?"

"He's a wastrel just coming out of the tavern."

"Sir, I've just stepped out of this establishment. I'm not a wastrel."

"I have no argument with you. Only this man polluted by spirituous liquors and beer."

"Can this man argue in his state? Otherwise, with whom would you argue?"

"The Quaker tavern owner," the drunkard said. "If not for him, I wouldn't drink to excess."

"If you had a relationship with the divine, you wouldn't drink to excess," McMurray said.

"Oh, to be a Quaker," the drunk man said, "who resists spirits while serving them. That's a fine thing."

"It's more complex than that."

"Double standards always are to the beneficiary."

The bickering ended when the drunk man laid on the ground and fell asleep.

"I've never known of such an insolent Quaker as you. Mr.—"

"Michael McMurray, Quaker wainwright."

"William Smith. I've purchased land for planting. Must you harass this poor man?"

"Before getting certified into the New Garden Friends Meeting, I was in the Philadelphia Meeting. Despite losing much in fleeing, I was never happier than when the Crown took that intemperate city. Alas, demonizing spirits are bad here."

"Do you claim loyalty to the Crown as well?"

"You're confused," McMurray said.

"I'd be careful espousing the King in these parts."

"I never said that."

The planter looked hard at McMurray. "You implied it. If I'm wrong, will you thus arm against the King and his Loyalists?"

"Quakers abhor arms. You must know that."

"I only know if you don't resist Loyalists, then you're for them."

"I've shown you no particular animosity. Why do ye challenge me?"

"You challenge this man who's taken too much drink. Will you swear to help his kind?"

"My conscience forbids saying oaths. This is God's realm. He makes the promises."

The man's eyes flared. "Very well. Don't swear."

"I'm not helping him until he renounces the drink."

"Fine thing, sir, letting your fellow man fall."

"The drunkard isn't my problem."

"Nothing is your problem. Not the man's welfare. Not the legitimate government in Philadelphia the King's troops came to destroy."

"Making and destroying kings and governors is God's prerogative."

"There is no better time than now to fight for our independence. General Cornwallis will be here soon."

"Quakers shall not be busybodies."

The planter looked past McMurray, appealing to his memory. "Quakers led the War of the Regulation, fighting excessive taxes when North Carolina was a Royal province! Long before the Revolution came!"

"That was before I came to North Carolina."

"Too bad. You would have been on the right side."

"What did that get except bloodshed?"

"So, you strive to be loyal to King George III?"

"I support the legitimate government which the Rebels stole from the Crown."

"Then you'll be happy the King who, rather than protecting the Crown's citizens, is coming after them with guns."

"I don't support the King's army!"

"You can't separate the King from his army."

McMurray's face reddened. His eyes threw anger at the planter. "I must go."

"Goodbye, sir. Change your mind and support the Revolution."

The planter lent a hand to the drunk now awakened and struggling to his feet.

McMurray seethed and headed to the Friends Meeting. He settled when he remembered King Charles II. Great is the debt we owe him for freeing Quakers to practice our beliefs going on a hundred and twenty years! My God, how could I ever turn my back on the Crown?

# Five ~ Ambush

A sergeant of the **64**[th] Regiment disregarded the screaming attackers and searched for a firework in the toolbox attached to the side of the first wagon. In an instant he lay on the sandy causeway oozing blood from a muddy bayonet wound in his neck. He released an unlit squib while his blood ebbed.

Roused British guards formed a cordon around the wagon. From both sides of the narrow approach to the ferry, Marion's force attacked the **64**[th] Regiment skeleton crew in overwhelming numbers. All around the insurgents jabbed bayonets with ruthless verve, unusual action from militia.

Powder barrels lay on their sides three across and ten down filling the holds of the wagons. Bold, red *FFg Bedford* stencils indicated they held fine-grained gunpowder milled in Bedford, Virginia, meant for the muskets and rifles of the Continental army.

Small militia boys patted and rubbed down the four uneasy horses harnessed to the lead wagon. While the riotous scuffle unfolded, they murmured in soothing, vernal voices. The beasts steadied and quieted, their lips quivering and curling when the boys pulled small, green apples from their pockets.

The guerrillas attacked the driver and the **64**[th] Redcoat guards. The driver feigned death then righted himself and killed the militiaman trying to take his place. Another militiaman shoved a bayonet in his neck, pushed him to the ground, and prepared to drive the wagon.

The vanguard of the convoy ferried across the black Santee. The commotion brought them to their feet in horror. They squinted at the chaos and heard the din of violence but couldn't help.

A guard major held an oil lamp to an assistant ferryman's face and bellowed. "Turn around!"

"I can't do that, sir. We're on taut ropes fore and aft and we're on our way across."

The vanguard troops held their fire and steamed with rage.

Meanwhile, a guard on the lead wagon dodged a bayonet and pulled a firework from the toolbox. He tussled with militiamen while snapping a flintlock tinder lighter under the fuse. The rocket hissed and showered white sparks into the gray sky before exploding. A fire burned mounds of trampled dry grass along the causeway and threw flames next to the wagon of volatile powder. Soldiers and militia shuddered.

All the better for the Rebel driver who dipped and slapped the reins with his left hand and exhorted the horses with a whip in his right hand. The wagon rushed forward, went around a bend, and flew down a service road. The road circled back to the main road a quarter mile from the causeway.

The streaming firework alerted Col Pickens and the enemy rear guard who made a bastion with six men around the last wagon. The remainder formed columns and marched forward double-time. Hordes of Pickens' militia charged the marching Redcoats with bayonets while musket men prepared to take pot shots.

Lt Col Marion had gone to the rear. He watched a private make a clean aim and squeeze his musket trigger. Though the flint struck the frizzen and opened the pan, the sparks failed to light the gunpowder. Others tried without success. They kept trying until six militia got their muskets to fire and turned back the Redcoats.

An insurgent driver escaped from the causeway with the second wagon of gunpowder and joined the first in dawning light on the main road. From a byway came a Patriot cavalry to escort the two renegade wagons. British horsemen took to the road but fell back under withering militia fire.

Back at the ferry launch, a sleeper Loyalist operator reversed direction on the payout line. The ferry prow line snapped and before long, the ferry boat of vanguard troops disembarked nearside too late to aid their countrymen.

Two gunpowder wagons had been taken. Charred Indian grass and milkweed covered the ground all the way to the wettest swamp in the distance. Dead 64th Regiment troops littered the causeway in heaps. Flies swarmed in the morning sunlight sipping their warm blood.

***

Smoke billowed up the hot fireplace in the study of Cornwallis' Fort Camden headquarters. The general was burning sensitive documents. When Lt Col Banastre Tarleton revealed the news, the lord threw a tumbler of brandy against the brickwork, sending blue flames racing to the mantel.

"When?"

"Two hours ago, my Lord."

British forces held tenuous control of the lower districts around Charles Town. Since they began transferring surplus supplies from

Charles Town to Fort Camden, shipments had gone from safe to insecure.

Tarleton watched the alcohol fire burn out and waited for the lord's reply.

"Where on the Santee was the boat taken?"

"At Nelson's Ferry. We changed our transport of late. Partisans attacked river boats relentlessly and forced us to use the road and ferry."

"We threw too much security at Fort Camden and too little to the river."

"Most correct, my Lord."

"This is bad timing. Sir Henry Clinton expects me to invade North Carolina! You told me you put down the most violent Rebels? Now this!"

"My Lord."

"Parliament is anxious!"

Tarleton snapped his head to reply, his fine, fiery red hair shaking like wheat in a gust. "All summer the inhabitants in this quarter due to their constant breach of paroles and perfidious revolts have overstretched the Legion. With the cavalry on constant detachments, I have no reserve. We're on the edge of breaking."

"What did you expect from your ruthless behavior? At Waxhaws you incited the Rebels by giving Colonel Abraham Buford no quarter."

The young, green-jacketed leader of the British Legion of Loyalist cavalry and infantry had come south having burnished his status as an aggressive, ruthless leader in Northern campaigns. His eyes wilted under the stare of Cornwallis who despised his junior's tactics for the retribution they wrought. "We had to do that, my Lord. Please evaluate my actions in light of the horrible Partisans."

"While a good tactic, you went far beyond reducing the Patriots. You gave their gazettes reasons to attack us and turn the people against our mission."

"You once ordered me to attack Brigadier General Thomas Sumter like a rat wherever I could find him. Sumter, Buford, Francis Marion, and the Partisans are all vermin."

"I suppose we should get used to those disrespectful animals." Cornwallis rubbed his red eyes. "How many gunpowder wagons did they take at Nelson's Ferry?"

"Two, my Lord."

"That's six-thousand pounds. Enough to make—" Cornwallis sat down with quill and paper and jotted figures. Sixty-thousand musket cartridges for a major battle. Two-hundred grains of gunpowder per cartridge. Seven-thousand grains per pound of gunpowder. The lord stood. "That's enough gunpowder for three major battles."

Tarleton studied the floor.

Cornwallis wrung his hands. "I hope you get at Mr. Marion. We can't let the Rebels retrieve any more gunpowder." Cornwallis closed his eyes and massaged the bridge of his nose.

Tarleton's snapping heels brought Cornwallis out of his musing. He removed the black cocked hat and bowed low. "My Lord, I'll root out Mr. Marion."

"Will you do the same for Mr. Sumter, another of our greatest plagues?"

Tarleton's eyes strayed from the floor to Cornwallis. "May I be so presumptuous as to suggest a way out of these plagues?"

"Very well."

"If you seek Loyalists—"

"Good God that we might get some."

"They're scarce here, my Lord, but a vast majority of North Carolina citizens are loyal subjects. They don't accept the so-called free constitutional government that replaced Royal power."

The lord grabbed two fresh tumblers and poured plentiful brandy.

***

Lt Gen Cornwallis mulled the choice before him. Keep swatting the Partisan flies of South Carolina and continue to suffer setbacks and lose soldiers or invade North Carolina. The prospect of cooler weather augured a bountiful harvest. Excuses to delay—the last to avoid the summer heat—were losing validity.

The invasion to the north that Sir Henry Clinton expected and Cornwallis wanted induced the lord to write a cautionary letter. He hoped the commander-in-chief of British forces in America would see that if he invaded North Carolina, the Partisans would remain a threat to British interests in South Carolina.

"Dear Sir Henry: Lieutenant Colonel Marion, Brigadier General Thomas Sumter, and Colonel Andrew Pickens have so wrought on the minds of the people by the threat of cruel punishments and plunder that friends between the Santee and Pee Dee are scarce. Partisans have crossed the Santee to terrorize the gates of Charles Town.

"My first objective was to reinstate matters in that quarter, from which Fort Camden gets supplies. I have therefore ordered Tarleton to pursue Marion to convince the 'swamp fox' of our superior power …"

Cornwallis couldn't finish the sentence. Superior power? That was a lie. Nowhere in the low country was safe for the British. The

Partisan scourge mobilized guerrilla units to attack British units with abandon. South Carolina only enraged him. Cornwallis wanted nothing more than to leave the awful place in exchange for an easy run through North Carolina.

# Six ~ Friends Meeting

The focal point of the Quaker settlement came into Michael McMurray's view. The New Garden Friends Meeting House stood in a wooded fifty-acre site down New Garden Road. Behind the plain building, Horse Pen Creek splashed over rocks as it made its four mile run north to Guilford Court House in Martinsville.

Beside the wood-framed Meeting House lay a graveyard surrounded by oak trees. Austere stone tablets etched with initials and birth and passing dates marked the dead without distinction. Epitaphs had emerged on fine cut stone in nearby graveyards where non-Quaker farmers, millers, potters, tanners, and hatters seeped into the settlement.

Summer weather chased the weekly Quaker Meeting to an outdoor meeting room. Split logs served as pews. A dirt path divided men and women into their own sections. The men assembled minus the women. The Clerk of the meeting and the Minister on his left sat at rustic tables facing the Friends.

Behind the clerk and minister dappling sunshine filtered through branches of bordering trees. In front, rows of plain-clothed elders gazed through sober eyes, some bent over canes. McMurray sat halfway back. After him, younger Friends like Zebulon Mitchell filled the seats followed by boys in the last rows.

As the meeting progressed, the Sun would sweep from the men to the boys burning each in his black hat and clothes like a daily cross to remind them Hell punished ungodliness and worldly lusts. Plain clothes and plain speech—which rejected all honorary titles and the swearing of oaths—manifested unbending Quaker refusal to go the way of the world.

The clerk inked a quill. To avoid the taint of heathen names for the days of the week and months of the year, he wrote, 'The sixteenth Day of the sixth Month of the Year 1780' at the top of the minutes.

"Dear Friends," the Minister said, "let us take time in silence to connect with the divine before taking up the business of the meeting."

The meeting commenced with the men dwelling in contemplation in keeping with the sacred Quaker ideal of unrestricted divine worship leading from the spirit within each of them. Elder Friends stirred as they came out of their private worship.

"Friends," the Minister said, "wherever we gather may we appear as one family into a Religious Society for the instruction or direction of each particular member in regard to the rules laid down. We meet today and always to establish the wisdom of truth among friends. We foster an individual relationship with the divine with a strong element of conscience without aggressive preaching of the gospel message."

The clerk put a stack of folded papers on the table between him and the minister. The minister touched the stack. "We will hear the Queries submitted since our last meeting. Let the Rules of Discipline shine a pure and holy measure of light to guide us as we consider our errors. As we walk and abide in the light may the spirit fulfill us. Think of Queries not as letters of law but from the light of the spirit. For the law killeth conscience and the spirit giveth life. Hear every Query read aloud and search your consciences so we may resolve these questions as a society."

The clerk took the top paper and unfolded it. "Friends, the first query. With respect to New Garden, will we continue to thwart the Rule of Discipline that Friends avoid tavern ownership?"

"Let us accept the query," the Minister said, "and voice any concerns. Afterwards, I will issue Advices based on the Rules of Discipline and your concerns.

"The Rule in 1737 advised Friends to avoid the vanity of idle company that attends the sipping and tippling of drams and strong drink. Those in that evil practice may not become drunk, yet they often become ground fitted for the seeds of the greatest transgressions.

"Pertaining to taverns, the Rule issued in 1777 in Philadelphia citing the corrupting influence of beerhouses advised our members to avoid engaging in such employments for a livelihood and listen to pure wisdom for that end. Friends, contemplate the Query in silent introspection."

After allowing the light to move the Friends, the elder Darlington stood. He'd examined his conscience and wished to speak. "I have a Concern."

The clerk inscribed the Friend's name and looked up from the minutes.

"The meeting recognizes the elder Darlington."

"George Fox, our Religious Society of Friends founder, stayed at taverns during his travels. We have no knowledge he complained about tavern keepers."

The Friends made space to consider the Concern. The room fell quiet as the men contemplated. The Clerk recorded the Concern.

The younger Starbuck rose. "I have a concern. The elder Haines keeps New Garden Tavern. He's a pious and temperate Quaker landlord. Who'll regulate drinking if not a Quaker?"

Time to reflect passed and the clerk recorded the Concern.

"I have a concern," the elder Folger said. An ache shot up the old man's spine. He'd refrained from stretching lest he appear not suffering the cross. Relief came when he stood to speak. "Raucous taverns are shut down even by non-Quaker societies, however New Garden Tavern is a respectable establishment."

After a fair amount of reflection passed, Michael McMurray rose. Frustration etched his forehead. "I wish to respond to the concerns voiced."

"Friend McMurray is recognized," the Clerk said.

McMurray had fled Philadelphia with a wife and two children after Sir William Howe seized the city in 1777. Escaping Chester, Pennsylvania to the western shore of New Jersey, they halted as British troops stopped and searched flat boats crossing the Delaware River. They came down to North Carolina carrying all their plain goods in a wagon McMurray had built.

They found refuge in New Garden's Religious Society of Friends with the expectation the Rules of Discipline spouted in Philadelphia governed Quakers everywhere. Yet New Garden's isolation in the backcountry of central North Carolina had loosened Quaker advice on spirits of liquor.

The process of considering a Query often came to the point where the Friend who brought it unmasked himself. McMurray needn't feel shame as the Friends respected the Query-makers. It was the last thing on his mind. Yet he trembled thinking of his naive New Garden Friends.

"I visit Salem Tavern in Wachovia for my wagon business," McMurray said. "The Moravian tavern keeper regulates customers to prevent drunkenness. Let him and other non-Quakers operate taverns. Friends must avoid such employment lest it ruins our good names." McMurray's voice rose and his body lurched. "If we tarnish our character, religious toleration on which Friends depend might vanish!"

"Stop, Friend!" the Minister said.

"In Philadelphia the Religious Society of Friends frowns on Quakers owning taverns."

"Stop! You are out of order. I will render advice on the Query."

"When will rules good enough for the Friends in Philadelphia take root here?" McMurray paused for effect. "Someday…strong drink will make a Whig threaten a Tory and a fight will break out in New Garden Tavern. To what violence will it lead? Maybe a battle…that draws Lord Cornwallis to settle the dispute."

McMurray sat down. The minister stood and eyed him with breathless anger for preaching, hogging time, and breaking the politeness of the meeting.

"Even in the best Quaker Meeting," the Minister said, "we do not conduct a perfect or profitable style of business that omits unnecessary matters and ordinary human indiscretions. We admit the Meeting is not the most formal of endeavors. It is without plan and therefore disposed to confusion. It is not my place to castigate specific Friends, however lack of decorum and dignity is immoral. We are equals here. Do not talk too much and disregard one another's sentiments or the purpose of the Query."

Before sitting down, the minister nodded to the wainwright. "Non Quakers revile and persecute us for our beliefs. Let the minutes show Friend Michael McMurray and his stepson Zeb Mitchell are pious and in good standing. They have become profitable businessmen and Quaker stewards of propriety in New Garden. My advice will answer The Friend's Query." The minister sat down and nodded to the clerk.

***

The clerk unfolded the next paper. "Friends, the second query. In this time of rebellion when war may sweep up the entire populace, shouldn't we eliminate disownments for aiding the combatants?"

"The Rules of Discipline are clear," the Minister said. "We must tenderly deal with those who aid war, and if they do not acknowledge their error, we'll read to testify disownment. The individual may appeal, but the rules are as unbending as the spirit. Listen to your conscience and we will hear your concerns."

Following a period of contemplation, elder Mendenhall stood. "We Friends are losing majority status. God told me we Friends should stick to our beliefs lest our influence in civil matters shrinks to nothing."

Younger Harrold: "If we give in to war, we have no reason to exist."

Elder Starbuck: "Our refusal to bear arms against the Indians or steal their property has returned two generations of security from them. Combat is not the answer."

Younger Gardner: "We're called cowards for not serving. We should advertise conscientious objection takes more courage."

Elder Mills: "If we measure success as keeping our boys out of the war, then we've missed the point. There is something bigger than us."

Elder Milhous: "I am a parent and God forbade me to indulge my children in liberties with the Rules or else I would see them disowned. Take heed or you will lose your children from the Society."

"Any others? Alright," the Minister said. "That is the query. I will issue advice based on the Rules of Discipline and your concerns."

***

The clerk unfolded the next paper. "The third query. Friends, we're in a tenuous position. Whether the pro-independence people call themselves Whigs or Patriots and the anti-independence people call themselves Tories or Loyalists, the middle is alone. If we don't aid the Whigs, they say we oppose the American cause. If we don't aid the Tories, they say we oppose King George III. How can we avoid these extremes?"

The Minister cited the Rules of Discipline. "The Rule of 1762 calls us to show forth to the world in life and practice the blessed reign of the Messiah the Prince of Peace and we doubt not will proceed till it attains its completion in the earth when, according to the urging and prophecy of Isaiah who said nation shall not lift up sword against nation, neither shall they learn war anymore. Is that not clear? Now contemplate the Query in silent introspection."

While the Friends contemplated in silence, the minister couldn't deny the rebellion had ripped the fabric of central North Carolina. On one side are Patriots and on the other Loyalists. In between are the tattered edges of indecision. Young men in the Society face troubling questions from the public. How can you refuse to fight tyranny? Will you give up your freedom to choose worship and work?

He'd cover his ears if that would smother the palpable rips in the flesh of elder and young souls alike, formulating their concerns. One wants to take sides. Do you defend authority and lose your home? Why do disownments happen when the Rules of Discipline are clear?

Elder Hunt: "Friends may not so much as provide a wagon to combatants. Loud disagreement and taking up guns to kill fellow humans begets revenge. War is unthinkable but we won't withhold aid to the wounded or leave the dead unburied."

Elder Darlington: "Our conscience does not allow the overthrow of an established government and we are obedient to nonviolence."

Younger Harrold: "Our silence to the world on matters of war puts Friends in an awful position. From my short experience with God,

He would have us push the center of the argument and negotiate for peace."

Younger Canaday: "Blind support of the Royal government strengthens the Anglican Church which despises Friends. By not opposing the Crown, the King abuses us. He will silence us after the war."

Younger Thornburgh: "We can't support either side. Rebels despise our conscientious objection. As for the Loyalist camp, we are not a Tory sect."

"We have taken up the query," the Minister said, "I will issue advice based on the Rules of Discipline and your concerns."

Elder Friends sitting at the head of the meeting stirred and the clerk and minister acknowledged the cues. Without uttering a word, they found the queries had aired Friends' feelings. Everyone shook hands and brought the meeting—neither rushed nor held to a predetermined schedule—to a close. The New Garden Quakers walked out of the Meeting their consciences clear.

# Seven ~ Moravian Brotherhood

— July 1780, Salem, North Carolina

George Heider rose from a straw mattress in the Single Brothers House on Bethabara Street where the young, unmarried adult males lived in Salem. For Moravians the choir system specified Wachovia's settlers of similar age, gender, and marital status slept, ate, and worshipped together to develop strong bonds of brotherhood.

While dressing, George dreamed of being in the choir of marriage after taking holy vows with a Single Sister. He went downstairs to breakfast. After a meal of bacon, brown bread, and tea, he grabbed his clean set of clothes and walked west to the wash house on Peters Creek.

He stood in a dim stone room with a lifeless hearth rubbing a wet, rough bar across his skin. The caustic-rich soap was the price of once-a-week cleanliness. Like magic, all dirt and foulness left his body. While a bucket of cold rinse water was nothing to look forward to, no longer smelling like a stable was worth it. He shivered as the water fell.

He emerged from the washing room and dabbed a towel over his hair and skin and reached for the folded clothes. Consistent with the plain clothes of Moravians and his choir, George dressed in a white linen long-sleeve shirt, twelve-button black waistcoat, white linen breeches, black wool leggings, black buckled shoes, and brown frock. Before leaving, he clapped the dome of a broad, floppy-brimmed black hat over long hair dried, combed, and queued with a plain brown ribbon.

At Salem Gardens, his father put the last baskets of onions, cabbage, spinach, broccoli, cauliflower, and snap beans on a one-horse cart as George approached, which meant he was late. His resourcefulness often rising to meet demands, he embraced George Heider, Sr., kissed both cheeks, and apologized. As the father seized his son's eyes with faux anger, George hopped up onto the seat and shook the reins to start the deliveries.

Seventeen-year old Sister Maria Bach, a pretty miss one year younger than George, occupied his thoughts. He didn't know the cart had stopped on Gemeinhaus Street until Betsy raised her arrogant nose in protest, neighed a loud complaint, and shook her head in fury. George rose from deep thinking. A brethren's small herd of escaped cows blocked the road.

"Surely you've been milked. Go on! Git!" After a stubborn linger, they moseyed away.

George gave a gentle lick to the old mare. The blinders kept her from seeing the cows leave, but she sniffed the air, elevated her head, and trotted. A bed of clean pebbles on the main thoroughfare pleased her old hooves and she took her time, expending five minutes longer to get to the Gemeinhaus.

George tied Betsy to a hitching post. The horse slurped from a trough kept filled with water running through hollowed-log pipes all the way from the Wach River. The settlement had its own waterworks.

"The British are coming! The British are coming!"

George rotated and found little Mila Bach, sister of Maria and the youngest of the two fair-haired offspring between the great Salem trader Traugott Bach and his late wife Elisabeth, staring at him. Arms folded across her chest projected resistance to the intruders. From beady eyes came an urgent stare.

"You're too late. They're already here."

She panned the small part of Salem before her eyes. "Where? Will they get me?"

"Not here in Salem or North Carolina. In nearby Colonies."

"I'm afraid."

"They won't hurt a young miss such as yourself."

Mila smiled and let a relieved George go to the door of the Gemeinhaus. Six leather fire buckets hanging on each side of the entry drew his admiration as he walked in. A large room provided a congregation room on Sundays and the Saal civic meeting room on other days. A fireplace on the south side dominated the room. At the back ran a hall and Bishop Graff's office occupied the last of three rooms. George stood at the shut door and knocked.

"Bishop Graff. It's me, George Heider." The name, pronounced locally as *hi-dare*, drew howls from the English-speaking neighbors who came to Salem for trade.

Bishop Graff finished the Salem Diary entry for the previous day. At the knock, he punctuated a line and put the inked quill in its rest. "Come in, Single Brother Heider."

The room was free of flies which explained the closed door. As a result, it was also hot and smelled of Graff's sweat. George despised his awareness of the world's smells and said a short, silent prayer as a reminder brotherhood allowed no space for hatred of body odor.

"Good morning. I'm here with your onions and green beans." He laid the bishop's produce in a basket on a sideboard in the congregation room and entered. "Bishop Graff, if I may—"

Graff swatted a fly. "Speak your mind, Brother."

"Something's bothering me. When I deliver vegetables to the Moravian village in Hope, I hear them speak English. How do I accept them when they speak the tongue of the invaders?"

Bishop Graff rose behind his desk and pushed back the drape and looked at the alley. He spun around. The worry lines on George's forehead had hardened.

"Do not confuse language with heart. Our Hope brethren are good Americans from Pennsylvania. They're not here to invade."

"Are they not Loyalists?"

"What's bothering you? That they don't speak German?"

"I hate hearing about Whig Rebels and Tory Loyalists killing each other. Each side is loyal to their own place whether it be a King's realm or a free government. Are there no brothers, either by blood or community outside of the Moravian settlements who believe in unity for its own sake?"

"We are different," Graff said. "Impartial to politics. Partial to peace. Naming this town Salem after the Near East word for peace was no mistake. We are a united brotherhood never splintered nor taking up arms against men."

"Then we're alone in this world."

"Brother George, John Adams says Americans are divided into three groups: Loyalists also known as Tories; Patriots also known as Whigs; and pacifists or neutrals like us."

"I know of no other pacifist people. May I beg to repeat myself and say we're alone in this world?"

"Not quite. Pacifists are few in the Southern Colonies. Still, we can count ourselves among other pacifist groups. For one, the Quakers in Guilford County."

"Have you been there?"

"I've passed through the Quaker Quarter on my way to visit the non-Moravian Germans in Stinking Quarter. Maybe two-hundred Quakers live in New Garden."

"More travelers and militia than that get off the Great Wagon Road and find food and accommodation at Salem Tavern every week. Coarse people, however."

"Unfortunate, yes."

George shuffled his right foot in an arc. He watched the toe of the shoe stop each time it reached a maximum and moved in the opposite direction.

"You have something else on your mind, Brother Heider?"

George watched his rocking shoe come to a stop.

"We keep hearing the British are invading North Carolina yet they never come."

"You shouldn't worry. To Him leave choice and action. He is a Prince all-wise. Worry about your future. Have you ever thought of a trade?"

"I want to continue growing and delivering vegetables."

"Consider apprenticing under Brother Tycho Nissen. He makes fine wagons, though too few. That is why we buy so many wagons from Michael McMurray, the Quaker wainwright in New Garden."

"He is coming today to deliver a wagon."

"No. His stepson Zebulon Mitchell makes the deliveries. The proprietor is too busy for that."

George's eyes invited more explanation. "Their enterprise is profitable," Graff said. "You could make a comfortable life for you and your family as a wainwright once you decide to marry."

"I know nothing of making wagons."

"Learn. If we want to grow as a settlement, then we must have wagons to carry our goods to the markets on the Great Wagon Road."

"So, what's the problem?"

"Even after McMurray Wainwright fulfills the current wagon contract, we will need more." The conversation had gone on longer than the bishop expected. His lack of friendliness shamed him. "Please take a seat, young Brother, and listen to what I have to say. Have you proposed to Single Sister Bach?"

George's face reddened. "You know I fancy her?"

"It's my job to know these things. The reason I ask is I have two suggestions to help me get a positive response from her father should I bless your proposal for marriage."

Sister Maria Bach's privileged status and worldly advantages had never stopped George's longing. He never intended to grow as rich as Brother Traugott Bach. If God had intended the Heider's to attain great fortune, it would have happened by now.

Still, a vegetable man knew if the bishop proposed Bach's daughter marry him, the trader might oppose the idea. "Of course, Bishop Graff, tell me what I need to do."

"For starters, I want to see a more loyal and outward appearance in your Christian faith."

"But I'm loyal, Brother Graff."

"That's what I mean. Show more piety. Your ability to maintain relationships among brothers depends on your personal understanding of Christian beliefs, one of which is fealty to your elders."

George sank in his chair, hoping Graff would feel elevated. "Understood, Brother. I mean, good Bishop."

Graff's eyes narrowed. "Sister Bach's standing alone commands a worthy marriage."

"I'm not worthy?"

"The betrothed often bring complementary personal worth and skills to a marriage. She's a well-educated Sister. She can write! Apprentice with Brother Nissen and gain skills."

"Why can't I go to Guilford County and apprentice with Brother McMurray?"

At least he didn't reject the command. "Your place is here in Salem."

"What's wrong with Quakers?"

"For one thing, they do not understand German."

"I know a dozen English words. That wagon man's stepson will teach me more and I'll teach him German."

"Don't become too close to Quakers."

"Why?"

"To them, we're pagans. We celebrate God and believe He is bigger than us. They believe God is inside each of themselves."

"That's not such a terrible thing."

"Breaking God into bits is blasphemous. One piece in every man and woman? To leave everyone to his own device and spiritual guide is confusing. There's no place for hierarchy or a Bishop in that religion."

"Brother Graff, I'll bet there's a bigger wainwright shop in the Stinking Quarter."

"Heavens, Brother George, Stinking Quarter is twice the distance of New Garden!"

"Beg your pardon Bishop, are there not Germans living there? Brother Bach said they pay high wages and don't bind their apprentices for years."

"He told you that?"

"I overheard him saying it."

"Brother Heider! It is a sin to listen to private conversations."

"Still, don't you agree the Germans there must pay handsome wages? I'll bet they're worthy people."

"The Germans of the Stinking Quarter don't believe in a united brotherhood. Their Loyalists and Rebels are troublesome. Though it's their choice, either one is as bad as the other. I forbid you to go there."

George absorbed Graff's wish. He'd also stay near Sister Maria.

"Anyway, George, between here and there lies disturbance. Wait until the Rebellion is over."

George scowled. "I must continue my rounds."

"I'll arrange for another boy to take your vegetable route and ask Brother Nissen to take you on. Are you ready to take a step closer to marriage?"

George looked at Bishop Graff, but Maria Bach's chestnut eyes appeared. "Oh, yes. I'm ready."

# Eight ~ Abraham

— "Knowing that whatsoever good thing any man doeth, the same shall he receive of the Lord, whether he be bond or free." (Ephesians 6:8, King James Version)

Zeb Mitchell got to Salem with another new wagon for Traugott Bach. He jumped down from the driver's seat. George Heider, through with the day's vegetable deliveries, waited on him.

"Hello, I am George. Do you remember me?"

Zeb pained to understand the German-inflected voice. No wonder George let Maria do the talking after the Loyalist bandits conducted the ambush. "Um, yes."

"We help you unload."

Mitchell soon found himself in a strange and enlightening situation. Normally, Zeb unloaded the goods with a quiet laborer supplied by Bach. The "we" George mentioned was himself and a strong, yellow-skinned man with black eyes and black frizzy hair who came with a two-wheeled handcart.

"He's Abraham," George said.

Zeb stared, confounded at George's thick utterance and handed down the first parcel. He stopped and scratched his head. To communicate all three would each have to use his own knowledge of the other's language. Zeb recalled a bit of the German phrasing Bach and others taught him. It was a struggle, but an inquiry to George of the helper's identity came out. "Wir ist…das?"

"Mein Helfer."

"Do you own this black man?"

"Sorry. Mein English, it is poor."

Abraham grasped George's shoulder. "Ich werde übersetzen." He faced Zeb. "I will translate. The answer is no. Black Moravians belong to the church but they're lent out to the white Moravians." He translated back to German for Heider's benefit. "Der Kirche gehören die Schwarzen."

"Huh? You speak English?"

"Yes. Are you surprised?"

"Well, yes." He offered his hand. "I'm Zebulon Mitchell."

"Brother Abraham. I learned English from my first owner. My second owner, Bishop Graff, taught me German."

"Huh? You're a slave?"

Abraham shrugged. "They say I'm a spiritual equal in the congregation."

Zeb recalled a recent Friends meeting. "Are you equal as a person?"

Abraham didn't answer but a myriad of emotions lurked in his face. Wide-open eyes and pursed lips expressed humility and embarrassment in the inescapable truth of his situation. His dark, beady pupils reserved a small amount of contempt for the foolish question.

"You don't object to slavery?" Zeb said to George.

"Sie haben nichts gegen Sklaverei?" Abraham echoed to George.

George folded his arms. "Ich bin nur ein junger Mann."

"A young man has no place to object," Abraham translated.

"Doesn't George know slavery is wrong?"

"Ist Sklaverei schlecht?"

George considered the question and gave a firm reply. "Wir schenken ihm christliche Freundlichkeit."

Abraham smiled at George's spin. "Abraham is treated with Christian kindness."

Abraham's simple, eloquent voice brought Zeb's admiration. Treated kind or not, Abraham was under George's authority owing to his race. Though George's youth and inexperience paled against Abraham's gravitas, rather than stupid, he appeared jealous.

"Who in God's name are you?"

"Abraham has survived. He's tough," Abraham said, appreciative of Zeb's inquiry. "I'm twenty-eight years old and have less authority than George but I don't think begrudging being under charge of an eighteen year old man would help. An English-speaking man sent me from West Africa to America as a boy in a slave ship. Nine years ago, the Moravians bought me."

On Zeb's second meeting of George, the young man's authority had grown from modest cart driver to modest slave master. Abraham was under George's will only for the small unloading job and the body language between Abraham and George revealed an awkward slave-owner relationship.

Abraham smirked at George's immature directions. George's frustration made the atmosphere tense. Abraham laughed it off.

"Don't worry, Zeb. Abraham is a good Moravian brother."

"I know little about Moravians."

"We, I mean they, left Germany because the state church bound them in too many rules. Here, we have a plain united brotherhood."

"Then Moravians are like Quakers. We are also independent and cherish brotherhood. However, ours is a strict, personal religion. Our Rules of Discipline don't allow any diversions from a pious life." Zeb looked at Abraham's skin. "Such as ownership of another man."

"Don't you know the Bible states God's approval?" Abraham said.

"No, sir. I don't believe that." Zeb's sure gaze at Abraham wilted into deep mystification. "Huh? Does it?"

Abraham looked away for a moment to access his memory. "A verse in Ephesians says, 'whatsoever good thing any man doeth, the same shall he receive of the Lord, whether he be bond or free'. I'm often reminded of that passage."

"That may be true for Moravians, but Quakers abhor slavery."

George may not have known what Zeb said, but he blushed at the Quaker's gesture of denial. He whispered in Abraham's ear.

"George says you fancy his sister Yohanna and want to marry her."

"I never said that."

"I beg your forgiveness." Abraham reached for another item Zeb handed down. "What's your real problem with marriage?"

Zeb dismissed Yohanna's fair skin and full lips. She's Moravian and German. There's no way he could marry her. "Nothing. I haven't found a bride. Anyway, as a Quaker, I must avoid lustful matters."

Abraham winked. "What else do Quakers avoid?"

Zeb laughed. "Long conversations on worldly matters. I must get back to Salem Tavern to eat and sleep. I have an early ride home."

***

From that point on, George exerted less power over Abraham and rushed to unload the wagon and leave. The last Zeb saw was George sulking beside Abraham as they left, the latter straining to power the laden cart.

George stopped Abraham. He whistled and waved. When Zeb returned, George put Abraham in the middle to translate.

"I've never been out of Wachovia. How does it feel to be away from home?" George said via Abraham.

"The world is large and free."

"I would do anything to journey afar."

"My travels may soon end if my stepfather's wagon business dies."

George gazed into the distance then turned and spoke to Abraham who relayed the question. "Why would it die?"

"Four-fold taxes keep me out of the militia but they're eating my stepfather's profits. "

"What are you going to do?"

"If we pay the taxes, we'll go broke until we have no money to pay. Then, they'll take our property because we aren't paying our taxes. We won't owe additional tax if we give in, but we could die serving."

"Besides paying taxes to stay out of battle, Moravians aid the militia. Why can't you do that?"

"Quakers can neither fight nor aid hostile factions."

"If you lose everything, you might die. If you fight, you might live."

"I could die fighting. Are you planning to fight?"

Abraham had had enough. Mouth tight yet not angry, he looked at the young white men one at a time with eyes chiding the tremble of their conversation. "You're afraid to fight. I see that. Slavery has crushed Abraham for a lifetime. It's time for me to lose my fear and maybe time for you men as well."

***

At noon the following day Zeb Mitchell rushed into the McMurray home to tell his stepfather about Abraham.

"I've always suspected they were slave owners."

"Should I stay away from Salem?"

"I wouldn't go that far. Deliver my wagons."

"How can we deal with them knowing what they do?"

"They're not our people and we can't disown them. Deliver the wagons and keep the Discipline in your heart."

"Abraham wants to be free. Aren't we against slavery?"

"Son, it's none of our business."

# Nine ~ For King or Revolution?

— August 16, 1780, Salem

Zeb Mitchell delivered the sixth McMurray Wainwright wagon to Traugott Bach in three months. As he drove across the Wach valley toward Salem, the once green and floppy sword-shaped leaves of corn shooting up from the red clay in June had wilted. They'd soon yield one or two ears to the harvesters shearing their golden cane stalks to the ground.

Bach looked up from an account book at a table in the dining room and greeted the young wainwright stepson. In addition to outright ownership of Salem's general store, Bach owned minority shares in Salem Tavern which often brought him to the establishment for a check of the accounts with primary shareholder Brother Meyer.

"Good day, Zeb. Brother George Heider will come soon to take possession."

"Good day, Brother Bach. George? That will be fine."

"As Salem's new apprentice wainwright, he's becoming familiar with wagon plans. One must understand the basic components of a wagon before building one."

"Is Mr. Nissen trying to build more wagons?"

"Business is growing, and wagons are becoming harder to get with the military competing for them. Don't worry. Nissen is far from matching your stepfather's industry."

A young man came up behind Zeb Mitchell.

"Hello."

Zeb recognized George's voice and turned around. "Hello, George. Come out to the yard and help me unpack the wagon. Then I'll explain wagon-making."

Bach translated for George and the young men hurried outside.

***

When they finished unloading, Zeb described how to build a wagon. George lost interest and fell into introspection. Zeb, thinking the heat of the day and a lack of English had lulled George, excused himself to take supper before settling into a mug of tea.

Traugott Bach nodded to Zeb as he left the dining room on the way to Meyer's office. Zeb blew on the tea, took a burning sip, and sat the mug down.

A stranger at the next table murmured. "Whose side are you on?"

"Beg your pardon."

The man moved his beer mug and himself to the place across from Zeb. "Are you for the King or the Revolution?"

Zeb leaned back to avoid the man's spirited breath. "Neither."

Zeb appraised the man to be a patron. He excused the man's forwardness and gave him the courtesy of his attention.

The man spoke in a low tone. "Arm against the British or be known as a Tory."

"Sir, I'm a Quaker. A pacifist."

"Men have been beaten for not taking up the cause of liberty."

Zeb shot to his feet. "Leave me to myself, sir."

"Take it easy, son. You don't want to start a fight. Remember, you're a Quaker."

Zeb sat down, tight brows and mouth persisting. "Must you anger me?"

The man continued speaking in an understated voice. "Whose side are you on?"

"It doesn't matter. I can't go against my stepfather."

The stranger eyed Zeb. "Like father, like son?"

Diplomacy was over. "My stepfather's wishes are none of your concern." Zeb's voice rose but he didn't shout. "Please, sir, leave me in peace," he enunciated in clipped tones.

Traugott Bach rushed out of the office and approached the table. "Get out of here!" He followed the man to the door and returned to the dining room. "Please forgive us. Outsiders help business, but their trade carries risks. What did he want?"

"He wanted to know whose side I'm on. I told him I'm a Quaker and a pacifist."

"Some of our guests try to provoke involvement in the conflict."

"The Revolution is confusing and anyway my stepfather told me not to take sides. Knowing I'm on neither side is embarrassing."

Bach studied Zeb's face. For a young, pacifist man to feel guilty for standing in the middle was something to behold. "Do you want to know what I think? I don't take either side when the question only concerns war."

"But that's the question."

"The question to me is whether Quakers or Moravians are free to control their destiny or worship God the way they want."

"So, you're on the side of independence."

"Yes, if that's the only question."

Zeb looked askance then sidelong at Bach. "You're confusing me. Aren't you neutral?"

"Of course." Bach patted his chest. "Yet in my heart, I feel our right to produce for ourselves will disappear if we lose the Revolution."

"You know my stepfather's reputation. Americans can out-produce the British any time."

"My exports to England are vast. Should the British win the war, they'll manipulate trade and flood our markets. Even with capital goods."

"My stepfather's wagon business would fail."

"Think of a nobler question. What would you do to support your father?"

Zeb gazed. "My God, you've made my choice clear."

"Upheaval is necessary. Don't fear it."

Zeb finished his tea and climbed the stairs to the common guest room crowded with beds. He lay under the covers and fell asleep.

# Ten ~ Invasion

— October 11, 1780, Charlotte Town, North Carolina

North Carolina backcountry humbles whoever ventures there. Such a place forsaken to bears, mosquitos, and impassable swamps God never created for comfort. Somewhere between oven-hot summers and cold, rainy winters you can make a tolerable life. Caution to frivolous wanderers and hunters: Go there to chase the wild goose and she will make you a misery. (Anonymous)

King George III detested the plodding conflict in the Northern Colonies from 1775 through 1779 that wrought the battles of Lexington and Concord, the siege of Boston, the New York and New Jersey and Philadelphia campaigns, including Brandywine.

After massive victories on either side, the war came to a draw. The Patriot victory at Saratoga, New York in late 1777 drew France to the Rebel side followed by Spain, yet from that point a series of limited battles couldn't shake the status quo. Washington's inability to find enough gunpowder to wage a large campaign hardened the stalemate which continued two more years.

George III sought a move that would break the deadlock, something better than America's alliance with France and Spain. Something dramatic and decisive to upset the balance. He decided to divide the southernmost colonies from the North.

Though Charles Town, South Carolina repelled a British attack in 1776, in 1780 the British sent Sir Henry Clinton and five times the infantry forces they had four years earlier and a sizeable Royal navy presence. By the end of May the port fell. The war had turned.

The King had followed Benjamin Franklin's advice. A clipping tucked in the cushioned throne since 1773 had come out warm and wrinkled in his hand. Rules by Which a Great Empire May Be Reduced to a Small One: "A great Empire, like a great Cake, is most easily diminished starting at the Edges. Turn your Attention therefore first to your remotest Provinces; that as you get rid of them, the next may follow in Order."

Such fantasy. I shall turn this insult upside down into a sweet plan to deny the Colonies their independence. Beginning at the Southern frosty white edge I will slice away Georgia and South Carolina and place them back into the Royal fold. Then, North Carolina exposed, I shall devour her and eat my way through Virginia and Maryland and continue north to Canada.

***

Georgia and South Carolina having fallen, Cornwallis marched to North Carolina. Away from the swamps and Partisans, he breathed in peace. Yet the northern tier of South Carolina was no Charles Town. The comforts of British imports, clear urban vistas, and improved roads lay behind.

The British army progressed north during the hottest months of the year. Camden, a critical supply post after the fall of Charles Town and cemented to British claims after the Continentals and militia under Maj Gen Horatio Gates gave up the nearby battlefield, lay in their wake.

After two-hundred miles, His Majesty's forces neared the Old North State. Vanquished Charles Town and the secure Camden fort became specks. Though British Maj Henry Craig controlled the coast of North Carolina with an army corps at Wilmington, the lord was on his own.

Forest walls grew up thick and tall in the vast backcountry of North Carolina and made for a close horizon. When the army arrived at the border, according to Loyalist guides, Cornwallis should expect provincial conditions. Hillsborough lay a hundred-forty miles away. In between, Charlotte Town, Salisbury and the odd hamlet offered less. Still, the baggage train held plentiful provisions and war materials. He hoped to find fodder for the horses and beef cattle along the way.

***

The British army arrived at Charlotte Town, North Carolina, in late September and made camp at the Mecklenburg County Court House. Artillery pointed from the courthouse square to the village corners and beyond to hotbeds of Continental troops and North Carolina militia. The Rebels couldn't fight general or full-scale warfare, but their spirit was growing.

Cornwallis hoped Loyalist North Carolinians would look to the capture of Charles Town and Maj Gen Gates' rout at the Battle of Camden, South Carolina and spur them to collaborate. He couldn't wait to trample North Carolina.

Sir Henry Clinton's strategy foresaw Cornwallis invading and obliging Gates to quit North Carolina. Signs of Gates regrouping and resupplying the Continental army of the South moved up the timing. By advancing and getting into formation across from Gates, Cornwallis envisioned another battle victory—this one in North Carolina. Could he get a general uprising of the Loyalist population to help?

***

Two weeks after Cornwallis took Charlotte Town, his aide-de-camp Capt Henry Broderick announced the arrival of North Carolina Loyalists at the Mecklenburg County Commissioner's office. "My Lord, the Royal Governor of North Carolina Josiah Martin. And Captain Arthur Neal."

Martin and Neal bowed. Cornwallis offered chairs. "Governor, didn't we meet after Sir Henry Clinton's invasion of Charles Town."

Four years prior when the Second Continental Congress in Philadelphia adopted the Declaration of Independence, Gov Martin had been deposed as the North Carolina free constitutional government took power. "Yes, my Lord."

"What business occupies you?"

"I've reinstated Royal authority to myself and will soon return to the governorship."

"Very good. We'll need you as soon as we flush the Rebels from North Carolina."

"How was Charles Town?" Martin said.

"Equal to the repugnant low country north of it. Even here the Rebels sting like hornets."

Cornwallis failed to mention it was Maj George Hanger of the British service, substituting for Lt Col Banastre Tarleton ill with a violent fever, who precipitated a stinging response from Col William R. Davie and his Partisan cavalry of North Carolina militia. Though losing the Battle of Charlotte Town near the end of September, the North Carolinians scattered and refused to surrender their arms.

Between the close proximity of Davie's cavalry and Major Patrick Ferguson's demise in the Battle of Kings Mountain, the situation in Charlotte Town proved tenuous.

Cornwallis' eyes met Arthur Neal's. "Now, captain, state your credentials."

"Nearly five years ago, I led a company of Loyalist militia to counter a Rebel incursion in North Carolina. We came under ruthless attack while crossing Moore's Creek bridge near Wilmington. Sad but the Whigs defeated the Crown's men."

Cornwallis gazed at Martin, the Royal governor at the time of the defeat, and Neal. They noticed his rising derision. Martin flinched but Neal remained steady. "Have you been active, Neal?"

"Yes, my Lord. After the Continentals paroled me from a Philadelphia prison, I joined Sir Henry Clinton in the Charles Town victory."

"I missed seeing you."

"Duty engaged you, my Lord."

Cornwallis pivoted to a sideboard and retrieved two documents rolled and tied with red ribbons. "I have warrants for you."

Martin erected himself in his chair and flattered the general with a fawning nod. "We're at your Lord's service."

"Governor Martin. I desire you to raise a battalion called the North Carolina Highland Regiment for His Majesty's service under my command in North Carolina with you in the rank of Lt Col Commandant."

"My Lord, I most graciously accept."

"Very well. Waste no time forming. I'll call on you soon to go with the King's troops to defeat the oppressive Rebels in this state."

"Most humbly, I'll honor your wishes."

"Neal, I convey upon you the title of Colonel of Loyalist Militia."

"Thank you, my Lord. I'm at your service." Neal smiled knowing he outranked Martin. "How may I help, my Lord?"

"I need intelligence about North Carolina. Where are the King's friends? Where is the Rebel gunpowder and ammunition?"

"My Lord, you skinned the Rebels of ammunition after capturing Charles Town."

"Alas, when we routed Major General Gates at Camden of late, we found the Rebels had more."

"Was it the ammunition taken from the ambushed convoy?"

"No and that's why I need you to infiltrate the Rebels. They're rearming and I don't want to go through the same hell I went through in South Carolina."

Horrid memories of the hazards everywhere in South Carolina haunted Cornwallis. Before setting the army in motion to the interior of North Carolina, he wanted to be wise to Rebel peril.

"I need shrewd operatives in the field to learn the enemy's strength, favorable routes for maneuvering, places where the enemy might take refuge, and locations of Rebel provisions and war materials."

Lt Col Tarleton's Legion wouldn't do for scouting and intelligence. Their brute force unmasked themselves.

The Great Wagon Road offered access to towns for operators who could model themselves as Patriots using forged enlistment papers and letters of commendation any Patriot or Whig would accept.

"Colonel Neal, being from the coast of North Carolina and unknown in the central part of the state, will find easy access," the former Royal governor said. "He has a good history of discovering useful intelligence from local Rebels and Loyalist contacts."

"That sounds encouraging. Does the King have friends in this province?"

"Not so many as he once had, my Lord," Neal said.

Martin wanted to claw Neal's eyes. "My Lord, many Loyalists consider themselves subjects of the Crown."

Neal continued. "Friends? They're citizens of a state that declared itself free. They don't hope for rescue by the King's forces. Considerable numbers are turning neutral or changing their allegiance."

"Why, Colonel?"

"Moore's Bridge schooled them and Lt Col Tarleton's lightning quick bloody revenge at Waxhaws so near Charlotte Town make them vigilant."

"Explain yourself."

"Moore's Bridge was a total Loyalist collapse and the massacre at Waxhaws took unwarranted advantage. Only honorable successes will induce wobbling Loyalists back to the bosom of the Crown."

# Eleven ~ Catharine

— Continental army camp, West Point, New York

Crisp fall air, colorful leaves, and ripe apples graced New York. Catharine Greene reclined in a stuffed chair in an army marquee. Maj Gen Nathanael Greene sat behind a field desk in the roomy tent. He'd been holding an inked quill over a sheet of paper for the last five minutes.

He shuddered as she lamented the depravity brought by the Revolution. Shortages of food and clothing. Before that it was the exploitation of poetry, newspapers, and music to advocate this or that political belief.

"Do you know what I miss most, Natty? Dances until the wee hours."

"When the revolution is over, we shall hop on the dance floor."

"How's your asthma? Can you dance?"

"My tricky knee burdens me more. Still, bivouacs offer little opportunity for merriment. Patience, my dear."

"Hopefully, you'll dance all night. Your father's Quaker aversion to frivolity won't bar you."

"Somehow I think he watches from heaven."

The quill moved toward the paper. The force of Caty's conversation keeping it aloft vanished.

"It's such a shame letter writing is restricted to government business and the military."

The quill stopped and hovered. Nathanael responded as much to interrupt her flow as to disagree. "Caty, anyone wishing to communicate may send their letters by Express."

"Only the rich can afford fast riders."

"There's nothing anyone can do until the war is over."

That brought her snort. "All the more reason for winning this war so Mr. Franklin can move the regular mail again."

"If we can lure him away from Paris." Nathanael shook his head. "There's an expense for you."

"For heaven's sake, Natty, Ben is our Minister to France and my friend. *You* spend money."

Greene tapped the quill on a blotter, released the old ink, and refilled it. Again, it hovered.

"My dear Caty, I'm doing the business of the Continental army."

"You're wasting paper and ink on three letters to the same correspondent in one day."

"I'd never do such a thing."

"Two letters addressed to General Washington sit in your mail tray waiting for a rider."

"What does that have to do with anything?"

"Isn't that another one you're writing to him?"

"You can't expect me to remember everything in one sitting. Anyway, a pertinent request of our commander came to mind after I wrote the first two."

Catharine shook her head and howled.

Nathanael swiveled his eyes with chagrin. "If there's any consolation, dear, his Excellency writes multiple letters to the same person on the same day as well."

"That's his prerogative as commander-in-chief. I doubt he *reads* three from the same person every day. What do your letters say?"

"One letter thanks him for the appointment, a second says I'm beginning to make plans to go South—"

"I'm glad you'll oppose Cornwallis on the battlefield in North Carolina."

"I hope to honor the Colonies."

"Careful, Natty. Heroes can take bad turns."

"What do you mean?"

"Benjamin Lincoln surrendered Charles Town in one of the largest, most crucial falls of the war. Horatio Gates the decisive victor of Saratoga, New York surrendered Camden in a rout."

"Don't you have confidence in me?"

"You've won no major battles on your own."

"That hurts."

"Okay, I'll concede your successes under Washington in the New Jersey and Philadelphia campaigns. But you gave up Fort Washington and Fort Lee in the disastrous New York campaign."

Greene faced the tent wall and consoled himself by reliving the rout of the Hessians at Trenton, New Jersey with Washington on Christmas day in 1776 after a daring overnight crossing of the Delaware River.

"Look at me, Natty. Washington relegated you to the Quartermaster Department because he was desperate."

His eyes fixed on her simple beauty. "Is that your way of trying to make me feel better?"

"That department used to be chaos. May I tell you of the countless battles you've waged and won as the Quartermaster?"

"Now, you're flattering me, dear."

"Field battles with shooting they weren't, but challenging Congress for aid and merchants for contracts to procure uniforms, provisions, and war materials took guts."

Nathanael gazed at Catharine and grinned. She'd done it again.

"What are you going to say in your third letter?"

"To beg a visit with Washington at Passaic Falls, New Jersey should the general be obliged."

# Twelve ~ Find My Loyalists

Former Gov Martin wanted to lash Neal's lips. "The situation isn't dire, my Lord."

"Governor, where are these friends?" Cornwallis said.

"On the coast."

"My bloody luck."

"Why, my Lord?"

"The Continentals and North Carolina militia are decamped in the central part of the state."

"In that case, my Lord, you'll be near the Scots-Irish." Neal dared not use "Ulsterites" to describe immigrants who left lowland Scotland for Northern Ireland then America. No term could be more profane to Cornwallis.

"Dear God! More haters."

"If it helps, the Scots-Irish are independent and decry governmental regulation."

"Can any of the wretches be made loyal?"

"They're wary of British overtures. Make your presence too strong and they might turn rebel."

Cornwallis sat back in his chair and threaded his fingers. "Parliament has agreed to continue the war on the pretext a pool of Loyalists have cemented themselves to Britain. Where are they in North Carolina?"

"I suggest you call on disaffected cults," said Neal.

"Cults?"

"Religious sects, my Lord. Quakers and Moravians. Zealots who often shun public service in order to maintain their principles."

The colonel stood and pointed to a map of North Carolina on the wall. "Moravians are situated in the Wachovia tract northeast of Charlotte Town. Quakers are located at New Garden and other areas in the western part of Guilford County on the road to Hillsborough."

"Are they promising?"

"The Quakers have set themselves so far apart from the norm, some might break away if given a chance. They're a most dismal bunch of devout people who congregate in a meeting house."

"Still, if they serve our cause…What about the Moravians?"

"They're less rigid but that's what makes the Quakers more suitable."

"Sit down and explain."

"Occasionally, Quakers turn their back on the starkness of Quakerism."

"Can we hope for more of that?" Cornwallis said.

"Quakers might sooner turn to the Rebels when they break."

"What's a Meeting House?"

"A dark, unadorned building. Something between a church and a cottage and tending to the latter."

"That's a wide range."

"It's not a high-minded place given to priests and confessions. Certainly not for loose talk and hoisting pints of ale. Rather grim and suited to people who love showing off their piety."

Cornwallis curled his lips. Should he ever desire to confess his atrocities, it wouldn't be there.

"You can wear a sword and pistol at times in a church. The Friends never allow arms in their Meeting House."

"So, are the Quakers useful or not?"

"Quakers appreciate the Royal decrees over the years giving them religious rights and they strongly believe constitutional authority was stolen from the Crown."

"You didn't answer my question."

"They disapprove of violence, but they might fight for religious rights."

"Forget the Quakers. What about the Moravians?"

"They might be open to trading with the King's forces."

Cornwallis rubbed his palms together. "Good, so far. Do they abhor violence?"

"They're not above profiting from it."

"Which side are they on?"

"Though they claim neutrality, they're known to assist the Rebels."

"Military aid?"

"Not military per se. Let's say you're unarmed. You can't kill your enemy with a loaf of bread, but food will suffice until you get a gun."

"Who do they supply?"

"They do good trade with travelers on the Great Wagon Road. I understand they sell to the Rebel militia."

"Spy on the Moravians and report back to me."

"At your service, my Lord, but in this instance I cannot help." Was Neal hedging? Maj John André's fresh capture and execution must have sent shivers up the spines of anyone spying for the British.

"Why?"

"I don't speak their language."

"My good Colonel, you must take advantage of these people who are so kind to my enemy."

"My Lord," Gov Martin said, "Colonel Neal will accede to your wishes."

"I've learned who I can count on in North Carolina. Thank you for coming."

Martin and Neal got on their feet.

"Wait, Governor. Tell me the situation respecting Blacks."

"Free or bonded?"

"Either. I can always use more foragers to seize livestock, provisions, and horse fodder."

"Slaves are mostly in the eastern part of the state on the numerous plantations. In this backcountry, farms are smaller and usually run by families."

"How many Blacks might be recruited?" Cornwallis said.

Gov Martin consulted a brown leather journal. "Of the four-hundred thousand inhabitants of North Carolina—"

"Get on with it."

Martin risked a harsh gaze on Cornwallis before turning back to his book. "One in four North Carolinians are Black. Half are men and half of those may be suitable. That's twenty-five thousand."

"Colonel Neal, distribute a proclamation inducing Blacks to join His Majesty's service in North Carolina."

"How do you know Blacks will join your cause?"

"My dear Colonel, in South Carolina all the Blacks upon the approach of any detachment of the King's troops, thought themselves absolved from their masters."

"They quit the plantations and followed the army?"

Cornwallis stared at Neal and intoned candor. "I admit it proved detrimental to cultivation and occasioned property disputes between Loyalists and the army."

"You separated them anyway."

"They attached themselves to us."

Martin wriggled at Neal's enmity. "Colonel, can't we agree freeing up His Majesty's combatants from foraging is a good thing? If Blacks revolt, we may as well put them to work."

Neal allowed a soft nod. "Well, Blacks, being from that insufferable hot part of Africa, are used to working hard in the climate whereas soft European men suffer fatigue."

"Well put," Cornwallis said. "I'll issue the proclamation."

"How will you pry them from their masters?" Neal said. "Revolt is one thing. Securing their safety thereafter is another thing."

"I shall do like Royal Governor Lord Dunmore who incited a slave revolt in Virginia and offered amnesty." Cornwallis gave Neal a confident grin. "Don't worry about the farms and plantations. The growing season is over. Now, explain the situation with Blacks in the central part of North Carolina."

"Quakers have dissolved ties with slavery, so recruiting in the Quaker Quarter of Guilford County is pointless. However, as Moravians employ slave labor, I could advertise your proclamation adjacent to and within the Wachovia tract."

"Go there and distribute it while spying."

"Of course, my Lord."

"Do you know how to develop intelligence?"

"By guarding my real intent and thereby engendering trust by those I want to deceive."

"Recruit independent men whose goals align with the King's."

"My Lord, I will determine their fealty when I recruit and train them."

"Who will you recruit?"

"Volunteers as they're less likely to desert or collude with the enemy. I won't employ Continental or militia deserters for sensitive or undercover work, but I might use them to ascertain information. Slaves too are privy to the goings on and often know more than their masters about the operation of a mill, plantation, or other enterprise."

"You'll have little time."

"That's to our advantage. Quick missions deployed without notice catch the target off guard."

"Excellent. I'll put you in contact with my intelligence officer."

"How will we communicate with security?"

"Use one of the code books you'll be given." Cornwallis smiled. "The Rebels won't be able to read our messages without it."

"Will you provide an Express rider, my Lord?"

"No, you must recruit a rider, but never share the code with him. If I don't hear from you in a reasonable period, then I'll assume you used a dead drop point given with the key."

"Yes, my Lord."

"I must learn of Rebel ammunition and wagons."

"Shall I attack their ammunition supplies as I find them or wait for your orders?"

Cornwallis didn't hesitate. "Don't attack. I only want intelligence."

"My sources know of a Rebel lead mine in southwest Virginia. It's vulnerable to attack."

"Patience, Colonel. Any attack must come from my detachments. Rebel supplies must not slip away because of a failed mission."

"Yes, my Lord."

"My ADC will put you in contact with the intelligence officer for the code and dead drop points. Never leave the code unattended."

# Thirteen ~ His Excellency

— October 16, 1780, Passaic Falls, New Jersey

Lt Gen George Washington stood in the doorway of his headquarters; twisted gold threads of the epaulets fell like waterfalls from his shoulders. Between each shoulder and the gold-faced collar of the commander-in-chief's indigo coat lay three silver stars stitched into the wool. He waited for Maj Gen Nathanael Greene to step down from an army stagecoach.

"Good morning, your Excellency." Greene steadied his gimp leg, stood tall, and touched the band of his black three-cocked hat above his ear with the outstretched fingers of his right hand. Two silver stars adorned his dark blue coat.

"You've just displayed one of the ideas under consideration for salutation protocol." Washington gave Greene a sideways glance. "Are you well?"

Greene knew Washington wasn't referring to the gimpy leg he'd had since his youth. "Not well, though better. A fever ailed me the past few days."

"Come in, my dear friend and we'll drink a cup of tea before getting to work."

***

Greene's cup clinked against his saucer. "How's Lady Washington?"

"As well as ever. She has her hands full with the duties cried by the homestead. And your Catharine?"

"Well by health if not by temperament."

"Oh?"

"She's restless about the war. Isn't it strange how the revolution has shifted our complaints? You hardly hear people anymore complaining of taxation without representation. Deprivations dominate conversation."

Washington placed his cup and saucer on his desk. "King George III was wise to attack the South. We have no choice but to fight there." Washington was never calmer. An easygoing person, he hid his yearning to secure victory and return to his Virginia home. "South

Carolina is in thrall. We must stop Cornwallis before another state plunges to Britain. If North Carolina falls, Virginia may be doomed."

"Your Excellency, I'd like your opinion of me."

"Anything specific?"

"How did you rate me as a quartermaster?"

"You took the department from chaos to order with rapid deployment of stores when the army took to the field, carrying out orders with integrity and to my satisfaction."

"How do you apprehend my ability to acquire honor in the field?"

"Didn't I nominate you to lead the Southern army?"

"I only wish to be more competent."

"You excel my modesty. Still, humility doesn't hurt a commander in the field. There will be embarrassments in the South. It's better to go there not promising the world so you don't look like a failure every time something goes wrong."

"Your candor and advice are most appreciated, sir. I won't disgrace your appointment. May I bend your ear with respect to supplies?"

"Bend, pinch, or punch it, I can't promise you anything."

"The Continental troops in the South won't fight without considerable supplies. They have no clothing or blankets. They're unsupplied for any kind of service."

Washington grimaced. "We're down to crumbs."

"We'll only fill the hospitals and sacrifice valuable lives if we throw men into battle. Musket ammunition,—"

"Stop right there. Ammunition?"

"You'll not find a more dire situation. We don't have enough to fight one battle."

"We'll be toothless wolves."

"Notwithstanding the losses at Charles Town and Camden, I hoped we had untapped magazines of it." Greene's face tightened. "There's a rumor we've taken some back."

"Let me deal with it. We must have supplies available somewhere."

Greene noted the permanent worry lines in Washington's face. Shouldn't the bigger problems of coordinating military actions with the French, obtaining more cash and loans, and finding an endpoint to the revolution concern the general?

"Supplies in the South are so wanting. Congress cannot provide the money nor seem willing to raise it. I beg your Excellency to urge them with every rhetoric in your power to send supplies to the South or show them we may lose Georgia, South Carolina, and North Carolina forever."

"Your appointment to the Southern army empowers you to call upon the Southern states for supplies and support. Make Thomas Jefferson see your needs. Virginia is a rich state. It's obvious General Cornwallis plans to take North Carolina and the lower part of Virginia. Make the Governor see how easy the enemy can take the land and all the valuable property upon it."

"I shall write to Governor Jefferson to supply the Virginia Line."

"Oblige Maryland as well. You'll have their Old Line under your command."

"I'll put that request through Governor Lee."

Washington nodded. "The South has been living on borrowed time, and I've had no money to do anything. I always express our embarrassed state of finances in the strongest terms to Congress. My God, I had to obtain a loan from King Louis XVI of France before we fell to complete ruin."

"Congress will get an earful from me. Yet as soon as I leave Philadelphia, they'll forget my needs."

"Don't take it to heart. Congress has little money. Though the Colonies flourish, there's a scarcity of willingness without compensation. I can promise no arms or uniforms until they arrive from France."

"The merchants of Philadelphia will hear from me. We shall see whether they desire to defend liberty or deserve to be slaves."

"Excellent." Cheered by Greene's knack for perseverance, Washington changed the conversation to the military situation in the South. "I'm sorry to say after a five-year absence from my beloved Mount Vernon, my knowledge of affairs southward is lacking."

"That you've been a ghost to Lady Washington except for winters when she stays with you at off-war encampments only demonstrates your resolve to put out the fires between New York and Philadelphia. No wonder the Colonies below don't occupy you."

"Without knowing the forces Cornwallis has available for an invasion of North Carolina, I can't instruct you. Have you considered a strategy?"

"With only a little force, I'm considering how to respond if the King's forces attack Virginia and North Carolina at once. First, I want to equip a flying army of eight hundred horse and one thousand men of infantry."

"Very appropriate and I approve."

"News of the Partisans harassing the British in South Carolina is encouraging. My aim is to keep the British on their toes in North Carolina until I have a force large enough to stand and fight in general warfare."

"That's a wise approach. I recommend, should Cornwallis harass those parts of North Carolina and Virginia intersected with large navigable rivers, that you build large flat boats and transport them on carriages."

"For moving supplies? I've heard the rivers in southern Virginia and throughout North Carolina might be useful considering wagons are in short supply and overland travel takes such effort."

"I was thinking of *crossing* those rivers otherwise impassable and taking safety from the enemy."

"Carry boats in my baggage train for crossings. Understood. I apprehend the wisdom of your idea."

"I've written to Governor Jefferson on the strategy. You may hear from him about how to procure boats." Washington assumed a warm and pensive gaze. "As for yourself, your reputation is strong. Your abilities and exertions and everything in your means will enable you to effect great honor."

"Thank you, your Excellency."

"You're the last astute general I have left to save this war. Remember what you told me four years ago when General Howe moved against us in the City of New York."

"I recommended a speedy retreat to secure us from disgrace. With our great disadvantage in infantry and naval forces, by obliging ourselves to fight the enemy we would have submitted to defeat."

"Retreat is not inglorious if it means preserving our army to fight another day. You showed honor then and will be correct again if you maintain the security of your corps. I rely upon you and it's with satisfaction I know you'll not submit to general warfare before you're ready."

The commander-in-chief stood and walked around his desk to Greene who stood, a solemn semblance chiseled in his face.

Washington put his right hand on Greene's left shoulder. "Keep me advised of the state of your affairs. My warmest wishes for success accompany you. I wish for you nothing but health and happiness."

A dour Southern campaign lay ahead; Greene regretted leaving Washington's sturdy company.

# Fourteen ~ Are You Afraid?

— October 21, 1780, Salem

Zebulon Mitchell drove a new wagon behind Salem Tavern. Abraham met him in the yard.

"Hello, Abe! How are you?"

"Doing well, Zeb."

"Where's Brother George?"

"Apprenticing with Brother Nissen."

"How are things in Salem?"

"News of the Battle of Camden has died down. This heat is the issue." Fall's delayed arrival in central North Carolina was evident in the parched land and the same day in and day out stifling heat and humidity. Weary flies opted for shade rather than fresh horse manure.

"If Cornwallis intended to defeat North Carolina, he'd have done it by now," Zeb said.

"Bishop Graff said we should look to God and wait for what He will do with us." Abe wiped the sweat from his face and pulled a blade of straw sticking from under his neck wrap. "But mark my words, Brother Zeb, war will come."

"I don't see you joining."

"Nor you. Are you afraid of dying?"

"My stepfather should be afraid."

"Because he's a Quaker?"

"He could lose his only son. Why do you stare? I deliver his wagons."

Abe shook his head in contempt. "You talk but don't hear what you're saying."

"Huh?"

"Few are brave enough to leave the security of home for days at a time and drive all over God's great earth not knowing who or what is out there."

"I drive during the day. Nobody causes trouble in daylight." The Loyalist ambush in June had faded away.

"We've known each other since early summer. War is coming. Will you only deliver wagons?"

Zeb opened his mouth and hesitated. Abe meant well but didn't understand. "I've given the Revolution consideration. It's not for me to pick up a musket."

Abe shrugged and studied the myriad of goods in the cargo box of the new wagon. "I suppose you need my help." Abe wiped more sweat from his face.

Zeb nodded and walked to the toolbox on the side of the wagon. The stable boy watched and threw his eyes like a lasso around the half jar of honey Zeb held up to the light. "Will you water these horses?"

The filthy, ragged boy nodded, and filled the horse troughs from a barrel one bucket at a time. Zeb gave him the honey and made a devilish grin. "Wait a minute." Again, the boy watched as Zeb went to the toolbox and pulled out something the size of two fists wrapped in a rag. "You'll need bread."

With the horses sated, Zeb pulled himself up to the driver's seat. "Come on, Abe."

***

Zeb drove to the southern end of Wachovia to show Abe the listless Surry militia camp. They turned around, crossed the Wach River bridge, and dropped off a barrel of nails at Brother Johann Stockburger's farm for a new split-rail worm fence.

When they drove back up Bethabara Street, Zeb noticed a posting on the front of Salem Tavern. A tattered, yellow page printed in German detailed the devastating Patriot loss at the Battle of Camden only two months on.

Abe translated. Upper hundreds each of American casualties and captured. All of the field ammunition seized. Between the fiascos of Charles Town and Camden the British had gained more than a hundred barrels of gunpowder from the Americans.

"My Quaker brother, we may have no choice whether to fight."

"There's talk in New Garden about emergency actions and George Washington sending a new general to the South."

Abe pointed at the posting. "There's nothing here about Moravian flour wagons seized at Camden. Maybe your stepfather's shop made them. I reckon you could go to Cornwallis' camp and find wagons labeled *McMurray Wainwright*."

Zeb shook his head. "No, thank you. Your word is good enough."

***

"Next stop is Brother Traugott Bach's to deliver a cabinet made in the Quaker Quarter."

Zeb continued down Bethabara street but slowed the wagon as he addressed the militia's predicament. "Did the Battle of Camden take a toll on the Surry regiment? Back there when we passed their camp, they only sat and laid around."

"I apprehend Camden cooled their fire. Besides, troops aren't happy being back in Salem for inglorious defense from Loyalists and outsiders coming to stir up patriotism."

"One instigator tried that with me."

"How?"

"By demanding to know on whose side I'm on." Zeb shook his head. "I won't be accused of being a Tory."

"Whose side *are* you on?"

"The side of the Revolution. Brother Bach threw out the troublemaker and said having a reason to aid the Revolution is more important than favoring it."

"Brother Bach is a wise man," Abe said.

"I thought so too at the time. But what qualifies me to be a soldier? I'm a wagon jockey."

"Again, whose side are you on?"

"I'm still on the side of doing something to help the Revolution."

"That sounds mushier than cold porridge."

The wagon reached Traugott Bach's grand house.

"Abe, I'll do my part."

Abraham smirked. "Won't being a Quaker get in the way?"

Zeb roused the trader-merchant. "Hello, Brother Bach. I've just come from New Garden to deliver a wagon."

"Apologies for not meeting you at the tavern. I'm working on something important."

"Your cabinet from the Quaker furniture maker has arrived."

Bach leaned over to look at the wagon. "You and Brother Abraham must fetch it."

Abe and Zeb set a graceful wooden crate in Bach's study. The rich trader studied the box. If the cabinet was like the package, it had to be fine. Once they opened the crate, Zeb and Abraham removed thick blankets and bracing that surrounded the work.

Bach inhaled the aroma of wood and varnish and exclaimed the cabinet's beauty. "Oh my!"

A five-foot high chest stood on s-shaped cabriole legs and trifid feet carved with elegant webs and toes. The honey oak finish glowed with hints of red in the grain. A curved pediment and finials crowned the piece. Three spacious drawers lay below a cupboard. The decorative brass pulls and knobs glowed.

"Such high American craftsmanship in wood I've only seen in Bethlehem, Pennsylvania," Bach said.

Zeb wiped a hand on his woolen breeches and let it glide over the smooth wood. "My God, the furniture maker has done a superb job. I reckon he scraped, burnished, and rubbed this wood awhile. I wonder if he knows he's connected to the war effort."

Bach sharpened his eyes. "Explain yourself."

"He's a Quaker and must profess pacifism if he wants to remain in the Meeting of Friends. Yet you, Brother Bach, who profits from selling to the militia, purchased the cabinet."

Bach gazed at the young Quaker. "Don't twist things."

Zeb feigned surprise at Bach's resentment. "That was unkind of me, sir."

"Be the craftsman who lets his labor go out to the world."

Zeb shrugged. "Did he let it go?"

"For a high price, I should say!" The regret on Bach's face affirmed Zeb's case. "Brothers, continue your rounds."

Zeb and Abe carried the crate and dunnage to the hall. The door to the study clapped shut.

Abe tossed the crate and packaging into the wagon. He shook the blankets and folded them before turning his attention to Zeb. "You insulted the most powerful man in Salem."

"Men of the Surry militia and others will become the objects of lead balls while Bach enjoys a fine cabinet."

"Don't make it so personal. Mistreating Bach is counterproductive. Anyway, I thought you'd made up your mind to support the Revolution."

# Fifteen ~ Flattery and Loathing

Lord Cornwallis gathered letters written by his superiors from late Spring through Summer of 1780. Sheafed in a leather portfolio on his desk, the messages held more rhetorical than strategic value. As sweet as the King's fictitious cake, he embraced them with foolhardy belief in his superiors. He needed no other material to justify his actions and indulge his vanity.

The lord reread the first letter. Clinton related that Loyalist populations could be found in North Carolina backcountry. That lifted Cornwallis' spirit and hopes that the British army need only go to the frontier and those British subjects would flock to the Crown's side. Clinton teased an inducement. If Cornwallis would get Loyalist backing, he might send a small expedition up Cape Fear River to aid them.

Britain hoped for a final conquest of the Colonies. Parliament, desperate for a resolution of the war found a diplomatic solution unpalatable. They accepted the refocus of the King and his advocate Lord George Germain—Secretary of State for America in Lord North's cabinet—on victory by opening a new campaign in the South.

The Southern campaign had been risky. Military resources in the Northern Colonies thinned when Sir Henry Clinton sent half of them to conquer Charles Town. After a successful campaign, Clinton returned north leaving Lt Gen Earl Cornwallis with a modest army and a mandate to take the rest of South Carolina and conquer North Carolina. Pressure to enlist Loyalist support in the South increased.

Loyalist numbers in the South had never been substantiated. The highest levels of British military and political leadership blithely viewed the situation from afar. Sir Henry Clinton was back in New York and Germain remained in London. If Loyalists in the Old North state were to help crush the rebellion, then it was up to Cornwallis, the titular head of England in the American South, to find and persuade them.

Never mind the theories of deposed Gov Josiah Martin and Col Arthur Neal, sizable Loyalist backing in North Carolina remained generally elusive. Nonetheless, British leadership had expressed a singular faith in Cornwallis, exaggerating his capability to enlarge his forces with Loyalists and win the South. Flattery warmed his heart but the desperate position he'd been placed ached his head.

Cornwallis turned Clinton's letter over. A subsequent message from Germain expressing wonder over Cornwallis' ability to march with speed in the South thrilled the lord. No British warrior had driven so fast through American opposition and progressed with such spirit and skill. It was no less than astonishing to Europe and the American Rebels. Germain spoke for the King who looked forward to the fulfillment of his utmost expectations.

In the next letter Clinton enclosed a copy of a letter he'd written to Germain. He was persuaded Cornwallis would act under his instructions to avoid making a halfhearted move into North Carolina without a force sufficient to protect them or provisions to support them.

Invited by proclamation, the Loyalists will join him, Clinton said, and he won't quit his friends of that province before giving them a fair trial. The lord's movements will be rapid and decisive and, should any unforeseen unhappy consequences occur, Clinton would endeavor to stop him. No man was more fervent than Clinton to see a British victory brought to the most burthensome war.

Clinton's follow-up to Cornwallis came next. It espoused a high opinion of the lord's military talents, leaving him at full liberty to do the King's service. Clinton would aim for none other than attending to Cornwallis' wants and send large detachments southward whilst remaining in New York in a defensive nature.

Cornwallis wavered over including the last message in the sheaf, another copy of a Clinton-to-Germain communication. Taken as a whole, it expressed Clinton's clear confidence in Cornwallis. By accident Cornwallis laid parts of two other documents on the margins of the letter. The "unmasked" section in the middle said Clinton had no power to assist him anymore; the burden of the Southern campaign was on Cornwallis. The lord shuddered that Germain knew the letter contained a hidden message and had a key to reveal it.

The American commander-in-chief had just nominated Maj Gen Nathanael Greene to lead the Continental army in the South. It was only a matter of Congress to approve Washington's choice and they would because they were down to a few generals. Cornwallis had experienced Greene's talent for employing a mixture of conservative strategy and radical tactics in the New York, New Jersey, and Philadelphia campaigns. Pressure from the lord's superiors was high. Greene doubled it.

Depleted and forlorn, Cornwallis closed the portfolio.

# Sixteen ~ No Greater Task

— October 26, 1780, Philadelphia, Pennsylvania

The Pennsylvania State House spire poked the sky like a church steeple. Maj Gen Nathanael Greene, settled in nearby quarters, eyed it as he neared the red brick entrance on Walnut Street. He dismounted and admired the building up close, throwing his head back to glimpse Ben Franklin's lightning rod atop the hundred-and-seventy foot tower. The crook in his neck reminded him people with lofty goals don't succeed without pain.

In the Assembly Room, Greene laid two letters before the Second Continental Congress, Washington's appointment to command the Southern department of the Continental army and his acceptance.

"I am ignorant of Congress' intentions with respect to the plan and extent of the war and how the men are to be paid, fed, and clothed, but I endeavor to make the most of the means put into my hands."

Greene beamed with pride upon getting Congress' blessing four days later. Prussian émigré Maj Gen Friedrich Wilhelm Baron von Steuben, approved by Congress as Greene's second-in-command, didn't smile from his mouth but from his august eyes and high cheekbones.

When von Steuben first arrived in the Colonies he saw a ragtag, undisciplined army, far from the British ideal. Under Washington's behest he wrote a pamphlet of guidelines for everything from how to march in formation to keeping camp kitchens and waste pits separated. Titled Regulations for the Order and Discipline of the Troops, it became known as the Blue Book.

Congress granted Greene all the powers given to Maj Gen Horatio Gates and extended to him all the instructions and resolutions framed for the Southern department in the interim. Subject to the commander-in-chief's approval, Congress authorized Greene to employ the army according to his own judgment. Congress urged the states within the Southern department to comply with requisitions for men, money, clothing, and arms.

***

Greene's late two-year presence in Philadelphia as Quartermaster General echoed in the state house. Who couldn't appreciate the battles he'd waged to procure clothing, provisions, and arms? His good agency served the musket-toting men as well as Congress. He took a personal interest in meeting their needs and getting good terms from suppliers. Leaving the Quartermaster Department doused a fire in his chest.

Greene wasted no time convening a meeting with Congress President Samuel Huntington, Joseph Reed the President of Pennsylvania, and Col Timothy Pickering the new Quartermaster General.

Greene lamented the Patriot loss at Camden in the middle of August. He scanned his notes and glanced at the men across the table, resting on Pickering. "The enemy captured nearly two-hundred wagons. I need half as many to forward stores South."

"I don't have many wagons," Pickering said.

Reed interrupted. "I'll try to raise a hundred."

Greene, apprehending Reed's reach too great, rotated back to Pickering. "How about forty covered wagons?"

Pickering let his blank face answer for him.

"Send what you can with the stores you round up."

"Do you need artificers? I can send a dozen."

Greene stared at Pickering, startled by the seeming substitution of artificers for wagons.

"Forgive me. I don't mean they're the same, but artificers can maintain what wagons you have."

Greene nodded hard. "Order them on."

Greene still wanted wagons. "If you can detach a small number of wagons from ordnance or any other branch of the army, it would afford us great relief."

Pickering again let a blank face answer for the impoverished Quartermaster Department.

Greene gave Pickering a cool gaze. "I'm aware of your difficulties, and the impossibility of providing." He turned to Reed. "Let's discuss arms. If you'll lend me four or five thousand muskets, I'll have them replaced out of the Continental magazines."

Reed whispered to Pickering while the latter quilled notes on the margin of a broadsheet.

"Together we can give you fifteen-hundred," Pickering said.

Greene shrugged. "I'll take what I can. By the way, in between sessions of Maj John André's trial I asked Brigadier General Henry Knox for artillery."

The late news of Maj Gen Benedict Arnold's treachery shadowed Continental army quarters. In September, Greene and Knox served on the court martial that convicted British officer André for conspiring with Arnold to surrender Fort Arnold at West Point, New York.

"Henry promised a company of artillery, four field pieces, and two light howitzers." Across the table Greene's colleagues waited while he consulted his notes. "I've been unsuccessful in obtaining uniforms. The merchants in town refused to take bills on France's future payment for five-thousand suits."

"What excuse did the merchants offer?" Huntington said.

"Having engaged more than they could perform."

Huntington grimaced. "Congress has no clothes to give you."

"I intend to beg Maryland and Virginia for clothing. Whether it produces any good, I shall have satisfaction of doing my best. If the people decline to defend their liberty, they deserve to be slaves."

"Is that all?" Huntington said.

"No, that isn't all. Carrying unclad men into the field for a winter campaign will do violence to humanity."

***

Southward the scene was setting. Cornwallis had been chased back to South Carolina but his army was still within a two day march of the border. Before going to North Carolina, Maj Gen Greene reviewed his plan for the Southern command to counter the lord. With the fall of Charles Town, the disastrous loss at Camden, and the poor effect to garner supplies, the means of the Continental army was shaky.

Blocking Cornwallis from marching all over central North Carolina was out of the question. Any confrontation with the British could result in unrecoverable defeat. Against a strong, aggressive army led by Cornwallis, what options did the Continental Army have?

Greene's initial concept envisioned equipping a flying army by converting some infantry to cavalry. Five-hundred miles south of Philadelphia the Partisan horsemen that harassed Cornwallis in South Carolina found Greene's esteem and he looked to co-opt Lt Col Francis Marion's tactic of shifting his ground often to prevent surprises and total losses of his party.

Washington, being familiar with the methods of guerilla warfare, agreed. An infantry stands, fights, and suffers the slow attrition of human life while a cavalry goes in fast, menaces the enemy, and escapes intact with their lives, arms, and a little less ammunition. A flying army had to take precedence as long as Greene was destitute. The infantry would stay in the background for the present and only come to the fore when supplies amassed and an equitable footing found for general warfare.

*****

The Continental army's ability to prevent Cornwallis taking North Carolina depended on how its supply issues shook out. Between the rout at Camden in August and Washington selecting Greene in October, a flurry of efforts to resupply the Continentals needed time.

Greene gathered from the Philadelphia gazettes that crushing losses of Southern gunpowder supplies threatened his ability to fight. The British seized three-and-a-half wagon loads of gunpowder at Charles Town and one wagon load at Camden. In addition, the Americans had removed and secreted ten-thousand pounds of gunpowder from the Charles Town magazine behind St. Philip's Church and wouldn't be able to access it under the eyes of the British.

Two repossessions provided hope. Only known in private was Marion's capture of two wagon loads of gunpowder from the British at Nelson's Ferry in June. News of a full gunpowder wagon recaptured from Maj Patrick Ferguson's Loyalist militia at the Battle of Kings Mountain, South Carolina in early October headlined Philadelphia news sheets.

Maj Gen Gates commanded a decisive victory at Saratoga, New York only to lose big at Camden. But Gates was getting back on his feet and, while Maj Gen Greene was in Philadelphia pleading for aid, he undertook rebuilding Continental army supplies in North Carolina.

The day before Greene wrapped up business in Philadelphia Gates ordered four-thousand pounds of lead from Fort Chiswell, Virginia for delivery to Col Martin Armstrong in Surry County which surrounded the Wachovia tract's northern border in safe backcountry above Charlotte Town. He pledged the state's faith and honor in payment. Gates had no money.

*****

George Washington would soon get the pathetic letter Greene wrote on his fifth day in Philadelphia when he came away wanting again after lecturing and begging the Continental Congress for wagons, arms, and clothing.

Two days later Greene ran into Danish-American Col Christian Febiger of the 2nd Regiment of the Virginia Continental Line who was in Philadelphia hoping to procure stores for his forces. Both served in the Battle of Germantown and knew well how to purchase and distribute war supplies.

"General Greene, this is quite an honor!"

"My dear, sir!"

"What business brings you here?"

"I've been assigned to command the Southern army."

Febiger winced and shook his head. "Oh, my dear friend, things are much in disorder in the South."

"I'm departing soon to join my new command."

Febiger smiled. "I'll divide the few items I've obtained for the Virginia troops and send part of them in wagons to your army."

"Are you sure? That's very kind." Greene clapped Febiger's shoulder. "You are indeed a fine Patriot. Consign them to me in Charlotte Town, North Carolina."

"Give me a detailed list of your requirements before you leave Philadelphia. I shall report to you from time to time the prospects of executing your orders."

*** 

Days before, Greene had sat in drafty quarters reviewing the high feelings swimming in his head following formal appointment to lead the Southern army. He sobered when it dawned on him getting a great command didn't guarantee Philadelphia would send him south flush with war materials.

Febiger rejuvenated his hopes when he promised war materials and the wagons to transport them. Will Congress find supplies? Will they also furnish wagons? Greene imagined a great rush to get them to North Carolina. He couldn't erase Washington's boat idea from his head.

Though I respect his Excellency, using boats to cross rivers runs counter to my thinking. Rather, once supplies come down to North Carolina we should transport them in flat boats down the rivers to cut the shipping time and reduce the need for wagons.

It's the scarcity in wagons that drives me to value boats for transportation. Why shouldn't I look to river transportation? Are the rivers not as navigable as the Potowomut River of my youth? It would be easy to build ten or twenty flat boats and ship clothing, arms, and provisions from Continental stores behind the lines to my encampment.

The flames of the idea flickered and burned down like the wood in the fireplace. The room turned colder and darker.

I can count on Colonel Christian Febiger, but the Continental Congress and the new Quartermaster of the army won't deliver uniforms or wagons. If I'm going to repair wagons and build flat boats, I'll need more artificers than they're sending.

Greene wrote a letter to Maj Gen Gates waiting in Charlotte Town to be relieved. He asked him to post a recruiting advertisement to draft a Makers company of Artificers, Wainwrights, Blacksmiths, Boat

Builders, Carpenters, Armorers, Saddlers, Harness Fitters, and Farriers consisting of men from southern Virginia and the Carolinas.

***

Greene dined with William Bingham, a successful Philadelphia merchant of twenty-eight. Afterwards, Bingham asked the general to see his carriage house. An invitation to examine a stinky barn seemed unusual. Greene indulged him. When a stable boy pulled the doors back a magnificent golden-yellow stagecoach appeared.

Greene circled the vehicle taking in the elliptical under-carriage springs and folding stairs below the compartment doors on each side. Glass-encased candle lights, two facing benches with cushions, glass windows either side, leather door-pulls, and carpeted floor.

"You're welcome to take it south."

"What? The coach?"

Bingham nodded.

"Your country thanks you for securing my journey to the South. You're a fine Patriot."

In the morning, after a nine-day stay in Philadelphia, Greene and his young aide-de-camp Maj Ichabod Burnet set off with Maj Gen Friedrich Wilhelm Baron von Steuben three days into November for the first leg South to Maryland.

# Seventeen ~ Bach Has a Plan

— November 3, 1780, Salem

Massive losses of Continental gunpowder headlined Southern gazettes during the fall of 1780. Mortifying Retreat! Baggage Plundered! Enemy Given Advantage!

Salem trader Traugott Bach dreamed of finding supplies to meet the demand and sweetening his strongbox. Unlike flour, ink, or leather, gunpowder was no commodity but a necessary material.

Though he hadn't fired a musket in a while, Bach remembered a portion of gunpowder and ball of lead rolled up into a paper tube as fat as his index finger constituted an ammunition cartridge. "Gunpowder" wasn't powder but black grains. As for ammunition's true value, without enough of it the British could destroy Salem.

Bach asked Salem's gunsmith how to manufacture gunpowder from scratch and learned it was seventy-five parts saltpeter, ten parts sulfur, and fifteen parts charcoal which was everywhere. From Bach's occasional brushes with science, he gathered saltpeter and sulfur came from minerals in the ground.

Bach didn't have time for mining and abandoned the idea in favor of purchasing large, pure quantities of the chemicals from the market. He wrote a series of letters to fellow traders entreating contracts.

***

That day, while Traugott Bach conceived his plan, Greene and his party departed Philadelphia. During the first long stretch in the Bingham stagecoach, Greene aired the issues of too few wagons, arms, uniforms, and provisions and the hollow promises and excuses connected to supply sources.

He stopped griping when batty faces glared back. Convinced willing suppliers would arise, he turned to letter writing, conversing with Maj Gen von Steuben about his little Blue Book, and reading ADC Burnet's textbooks from his recent graduating year at the College of New Jersey.

Four days later the party arrived at Annapolis, Maryland where he attended the legislature. Reason, Greene hoped, would oblige Gov Thomas Lee and the House of Delegates to support the Southern army.

He chided them that the army was in the field but might soon abandon it and any momentum. Greene had their attention; he laid before the legislature its quota for the army and got the same reaction as Philadelphia.

"You promise me all the assistance in your power but tell me I must place little dependence upon them. As you have neither money nor credit, it's hopeless to push matters."

Greene garnered the support of Brig Gen Mordecai Gist, the heroic commander of the Maryland Line, and made him the point man to argue needs before Maryland politicians. He assured Gist any supplies he provided would go to the Marylanders in North Carolina.

Greene used cunning to strengthen Gist's petition. "Make all your applications in writing that it may appear hereafter we left nothing un-essayed to promote the public service. If the Southern states lose to Cornwallis, we shall stand justified."

While in Annapolis Greene received a letter from Col Christian Febiger: "Ten wagons will set off tomorrow loaded with tents and camp equipage but no uniforms except shoes. All the arms I can get shall come on the first wagons. A partial company of ten artificers will march on Thursday with one travelling forge. Congress has done nothing and seems averse to draw on France. I beg to suggest the good effects another letter from you to Congress with respect to clothing would produce."

Greene had no sooner gotten over Febiger's kindness in Philadelphia than he shook his head in wonder at the unexpected assistance.

***

Bach's prospects for contracting supplies of chemicals fell flat when replies to his letters came. He learned Continental Congress-sponsored laboratories had exclusive contracts for saltpeter and sulfur and they controlled gunpowder mills.

Buying gunpowder was also out of the question. A litany of responses in Bach's mail told him the finished product was in short supply due to sparse production in the Colonies and increasing demand. No longer needed only for hunting and personal security, battles consumed twenty-thousand musket cartridges, a thousand pounds each of gunpowder and lead.

One contact laid down the facts. Few Colonial powder mills and inconsistent quality from poor raw materials or inexact recipes led to gunpowder's spotty quality. With gunpowder unobtainable from

England, the Colonies relied on other sources. France had been supplying most American needs through the war. But the French never produced gunpowder at England's rate and only sold spare supplies.

Bach put out a dozen feelers and waited. It was a long shot but a contact in South Carolina came through. He thanked God for finding a supply of gunpowder. For a large source of capital, he turned to the executive office of the state of North Carolina. Gov Abner Nash agreed to come to Salem for an emergency meeting.

Bach dropped his backside into a cushiony wingback. Gunpowder was one thing. Acquiring lead was another. Without lead shot blasting down a musket muzzle, gunpowder was unnecessary.

He shuffled through a stack of opened letters. Hadn't one contact mentioned Surry militia commander Col Armstrong was taking delivery of four-thousand pounds of lead purchased by Gen Gates? Bach wrote a quick message to Armstrong volunteering Salem's blacksmith and helpers to pour the molten metal into molds to make musket balls.

Brother Christof Vogler wrote down the process for making cartridges. "Roll a piece of broadsheet into a five-inch tube and crimp the bottom inch. Drop in a standard-sized lead ball and a measure of gunpowder and twist the excess paper on top." A healthy donation to the Single Sisters Choir House fund would entice them from their washing and baking long enough to roll thousands of cartridges.

Bach got a quick and stern reply from Col Armstrong. "You must control the diameter of lead shot and amount of powder in each cartridge. Odd diameter balls and random dumps of powder result in under-shot and over-shot balls. It's bad enough the smooth bore of a muzzle throws shots at random angles. In the hands of a nervous or inexperienced young man, a musket needs all the built-in control we can give it."

Traugott Bach found no disgrace in Armstrong's response. He wrote and asked the Colonel to supervise.

***

The Bingham stagecoach pulled up to Mount Vernon's entrance facing the Potomac River at noon in the second week of November. The general removed his cocked hat and bowed to Martha Washington.

"Lovely to see you, Lady Washington. His Excellency sends warm greetings."

"Thank you, Nathanael. Welcome to Mount Vernon. Follow me."

She took him to the Old Chamber off the central passage. Wooden packing crates covered a large part of the floor.

"I apprehend you're packing for your annual winter stay with the General."

She rolled her eyes. "I'm leaving for camp soon. Ugh! You have no idea the work it entails."

"Do you ever contemplate not going?"

She pointed mock reproving eyes. "A little bit of packing won't keep me from going." From an unsealed crate she pulled a corked pottery jug. "George said you would visit so I saved you one."

"Thank you. What is it?"

"Cherry bounce, for a special occasion. George promises to make it with his whiskey instead of bought brandy after the war."

Later, John Custis and Frances Parke Custis of Williamsburg, the parents of the Lady's first husband, and Col John Fitzgerald joined Greene and Martha Washington at dinner.

Mrs. Washington waited for Greene to finish chewing a morsel of roast beef. "My brother wrote from Williamsburg saying the enemy are still fortifying at Portsmouth."

"The Virginia militia turned out in greater numbers than expected," John Custis said.

Col Fitzgerald put down his fork. "They've never been more willing to sacrifice for the cause than at this hour."

Greene washed his pallet with claret and dabbed his lips on a linen napkin. "Yet the things necessary to equip an army are not to be had."

"Don't give up," Custis said, "I'm sure the prosperous Colonies will meet your needs in time."

"General Greene, have you heard that Lord Cornwallis is dead?" Fitzgerald said.

"We have various reports respecting his critical situation, but I don't believe them. I hope for clear information at Richmond with respect to the enemy here and in the South."

The next morning Greene brought his packed bag downstairs to the central passage.

"Well, dear Lady Washington, I must be on my way to Richmond."

"Did you enjoy your stay?"

"Your company was refreshing. I slept well and woke early to write by candle light." He made one last look into all of the rooms leading from the central passage. "Mount Vernon is one of the most pleasant places I've ever seen. No wonder his Excellency languishes not being here."

***

Three days later Greene arrived in Richmond, Virginia and met Gov Thomas Jefferson in a building housing a temporary capital isolated from British coastal attacks fifty miles inland of Williamsburg. It was their first meeting. Except for titles, they had no familiarity. Jefferson was a year younger than thirty-eight-year-old Greene. A generation younger than George Washington, they enjoyed privileges the commander-in-chief had never seen in his youth.

Classic military texts had schooled Greene. Jefferson was eighteen years out of William and Mary college, had spent the last thirteen years practicing law, and was now in the second year as governor of Virginia. His stature as the chief author of the Declaration of Independence awed Greene. Physical height worked to his advantage as well as he stood above six-feet, around four inches taller than Maj Gen Greene.

Greene worked up to the meeting by girding his nerves. This is challenging work and new ground for each of us. We require quick decisions with little time for character failing. The fate of the Colonies rests on finding material reserves and recruits in time. We need each other. Let the gravity of the occasion do my speaking.

"Obtaining supplies has been all but hopeless." Greene handed Jefferson a list. "As Congress affords me powers to call upon the Southern states. I lay before you a requisition."

Jefferson pored over the requests: Virginia's militia under brigadier generals Robert Lawson and Edward Stevens to continue in service until the Continental regiments are formed; clothing, blankets, arms, and accoutrements to equip the troops for a winter campaign; 10,000 barrels of flour and 5,000 barrels of beef and pork; 3,000 head of cattle; 200 hogsheads of rum or brandy; 100 good road wagons equipped with drivers, horses, and harnesses; recruiting stations; £5,000 to defray army officer pay and equipment expenses; 12 House Carpenters, 12 Shipwrights or Boat Builders, 6 Smiths, 4 Wheelwrights, 3 Armorers, 2 Saddlers, and 1 Harness Maker.

Jefferson looked away with a blank stare, mulling the requests. Greene imagined the governor getting input from others.

We both have countless ideas going on in our heads. There's so much to do, and we want to act on every notion in the present. This business where the Governor and I meet so many people in a short span of time leaves no room for intimacy. We must seem cold and reserved to each other.

"All well and good," Jefferson said. "Why so many house carpenters and shipwrights or boat builders?"

"To build shelters and hospitals for soldiers, magazines for food and ammunition, and prison barracks. The shipwrights or boat builders will build flat boats."

"His Excellency General Washington wrote to me about boats."

"Are you in favor?"

"They would be most useful in case of invasion. I'll give you instructions for building light boats that you can pull on wheels."

"When I get the artificers, we can start. On my arrival in North Carolina, I intend to have all the rivers examined for transporting supplies by water."

"If the situation is 'hopeless', why do you feel supplies will come to North Carolina?"

"They must or we'll lose this war."

Jefferson sensed melodrama and moved to enliven the conversation. "How was your journey from Philadelphia?"

"Dispossessed travelers carrying all their goods have clogged Richmond's roads. The entanglement will detain me for days."

The governor nodded. "The enemy evacuated Portsmouth and fell down to Hampton Roads with their troops where they remain this morning."

"What news do you have of the enemy's aim?"

"They'll leave Chesapeake Bay or continue north. I'm awaiting news."

Jefferson showed Greene a tiny silk letter. "This is an intercepted letter from Major General Leslie to Lord Cornwallis taken from a person who put it into his mouth like a quid of tobacco rolled up as small as a goose quill."

Greene read the letter and handed it back.

"What do you apprehend?" Jefferson said.

"The enemy have come here to prevent supplying the army in North Carolina. Leslie appears disappointed in not meeting with Cornwallis."

"Would Cornwallis quit North Carolina to form a junction with Leslie?"

"Not while Continental forces there are weak. I shall appoint Major General Baron von Steuben, my second-in-command, to command the Virginia troops opposing British forces in Chesapeake Bay with your approbation."

"Most excellent. I can furnish one-thousand militia."

"No body of forces harass the enemy more than a corps of militia."

"My dear General, militias not only harass. They can enlarge an army in a snap."

"But they cannot continue long in the field against professional forces who retain a proper military footing throughout the year."

"Didn't I see the Virginia militia in your requisition?" Jefferson stopped speaking as a new thought came. "Governor Nash of North Carolina told me that Cornwallis traveled to Charles Town much indisposed. Flying reports say he's dead."

Greene drew his lips into a pleasurable grin. "I only have confusing intelligence of the enemy's retreat. There's Major Ferguson's death and the hundreds of casualties and prisoners suffered under the Over Mountain Men at the Loyalist uprising at Kings Mountain. Or was it the warm fire put up by Colonel William R. Davie's militia at Charlotte Town? Either way, he's likely back in South Carolina."

Jefferson's eyes enlarged at the stunning news. Before he could reply, Greene continued. "As for the business of supplies for the Southern army, governments everywhere are at a standstill for want of money and public credit. Our supply prospects are very discouraging."

"Fulfilling your requests for supplies will take time as we can neither march our troops nor transport their provisions for want of wagons. I can get thirty. I'll send them on with stores to the depot at Taylor's Ferry on the Roanoke."

"I'm afraid from the deranged state of the Virginia quartermaster department, you'll meet with difficulty sending them on."

Jefferson eyed the general with irritation but softened when he remembered Greene's inclination to drama. "Colonel Pickering can't find someone for our department. I prefer Lieutenant Colonel Edward Carrington but he serves Maj Gen Gates. Actually, may I recommend Carrington to quartermaster the Southern army? He's an intelligent, mature Virginian who leads well."

"Excellent. I accept your suggestion. Now, what can you do to lean on your legislature? They must accept responsibility for the Virginia Line in the Southern command."

"The Assembly is meeting. I hope they will soon furnish us with money to send supplies southward. Incursions by the Royal navy are reducing trade and affecting state balances, so they'll have less than needed."

"Leslie's incursion is a small miracle," Greene said.

"Why in God's name would you say that?"

"If it alarms the legislatures of Maryland and Virginia, they might be more inclined to find money for supplies. By luck Cornwallis and Leslie are of the same ilk. The proximity of the lord and thus his ability to come to Leslie's aid should double the alarm. What serendipity."

Jefferson snarled. "Yes. How fortunate of Leslie to show up on my doorstep."

***

Greene returned to his rooms and wrote to President Huntington of Congress and the Board of War in Philadelphia saying he couldn't proceed further south without requesting the Northern army spare arms, accoutrements, clothing, and camp equipage.

# Eighteen ~ Gov Nash Calls

— November 17, 1780, Salem

The iron knocker rattled the front door of Traugott Bach's three-floor brick house. Rustling footsteps came followed by a tapping on his study door.

"You have company." Sister Maria swallowed and whispered. "The North Carolina governor."

"Tea, Sister." Bach walked out to the entrance hall. "Governor Abner Nash. Welcome to Salem and my home."

Bach led the governor to the study, giving Nash the comfortable wingback and taking the Windsor chair at a small, round tea table. Heat radiated from a tall tile heater.

Nash finished his tea and struck a high-pitched rattle placing the cup on the saucer. "Tell me more of your idea."

"I want to help alleviate the shortage of musket ammunition."

Nash sharpened his eyes. "What do you know?"

"I often get requests for ammunition from the Surrey militia."

"Our Board of war gets stacks of mail from militia across the state begging for it." Nash leaned close. "Will you reciprocate my confidence?"

"Enlighten me, sir. I wish to know the state of affairs regarding gunpowder, lead, etcetera."

Nash sneered at Bach's entreaty. The wise trader knew everything. "After taking Charles Town this May, British commander-in-chief Lieutenant General Henry Clinton returned north to New York City after ordering General Cornwallis to invade North Carolina. Cornwallis failed in his first invasion. He wants to seize Continental gunpowder and ammunition preliminary to his second try."

"Why doesn't the lord simply march in?"

"He seems to want North Carolina without firing a shot."

"I understand he's gained much American ammunition."

"Offered to him on a silver tray."

"For instance?"

"Major General Gates lost two-hundred wagons in the Battle of Camden, South Carolina including wagons of gunpowder in the field this summer. He lost fifty-five barrels of powder at the Waxhaws in May."

"That explains the militia's hardship."

"Not all of it. Of course, fortunes go both ways. George Washington with legal authorization from the Continental Congress has been sending privateers to plunder merchant vessels shipping gunpowder and other war materials from England to the King's army in the Colonies."

"Perhaps I should invest in a privateer."

Nash gave Bach a tactful grin. "Now with the war heating up in the South, General Clinton made Benedict Arnold a brigadier general and sent him on a mission to destroy Continental supplies in Richmond. When George Washington read Governor Jefferson's letter about the enemy throwing five tons of our powder into a canal, he could have wrung Arnold's neck."

The hard chair rail pressed into Bach's vertebrae as Nash pantomimed Washington strangling the traitor.

"It'll take time, but Jefferson, who has a keen, scientific mind, said the 'ruined' powder can be dried, remixed, and milled to the proper size. Can you imagine Washington comparing three hundred forty two chests of tea thrown into Boston harbor to his gunpowder? He can save the powder, but the British will never return the reddish-brown essence to the cut leaves."

Bach stoked the heater's fire chamber. "Would you be interested in buying two wagon loads of gunpowder for North Carolina?"

Nash was interested. Couldn't Bach get to the point instead of fly-baiting him like a common, ordinary trout?

"I have a contact in South Carolina who's willing to deal in gunpowder."

"Probably ours!"

"I don't ask questions."

Nash swallowed his spleen. "Alright, I'm listening."

"Who will make the lead balls? Who will roll the cartridges?"

Nash got a complete picture of the shrewd trader. "I apprehend you're proposing the service."

Bach winked and nodded. "Five-thousand British pounds—"

"My dear sir! I hope the North Carolina legislators agree. I don't have the purse to fund your extortion."

"I find that remark unfortunate. Every month a militia drafting party visits Salem. They know we choose to pay the triple tax for every man selected to remove him from service."

"What's your point?"

"Moravians have a conscientious objection to war, so we pay the tax. Still, I consider the drafts as picking our pockets."

"Are you done? Because I would—"

"No, I'm not. Few in the state support the militia like Moravians and that's on top of the triple taxes our men pay which they borrow from me."

"We're all under hardship. Will you put up collateral?"

"Governor, I mean well," Bach said. "Trust me. My Christian name is Traugott. Do you know what it means?"

God, here it comes. "Please tell me."

"*Trust God*." Bach never shifted his gaze while Nash recoiled. "I suggest we do more of that."

Gov Nash glowered. "Will *you* put up collateral?"

"Very well. I'll put up my house and store."

"You have a deal. I can send a militia force as soon as I have your contact's location. What will you do to obtain lead?"

Bach shrugged, not wanting to reveal his knowledge.

"Perhaps the lead General Gates ordered from Fort Chiswell will come your way."

"Let's draft a contract," Bach said.

They went to the kitchen. Next to a bowl of bread dough proofing under a towel, Maria shuffled through a stack of currency, at times inscribing one with black ink.

"What in God's name is she doing?"

"Marking 'counterfeit' across false bills."

"Incredible. She bakes your bread and serves as your aid as well."

"This is Sister Maria Bach, my daughter."

Nash bowed. "How do you do?"

"Good morning again, sir. I serve my dear widowed father."

"Maria will draft the contract."

"My aid is standing by. Let's sign the draft at Salem Tavern where I hope to find quick refreshment before rushing back to the legislature."

David R. Dowdy

# Nineteen ~ Conspiracy

— November 23, 1780, Salem

Zeb Mitchell sat in Salem Tavern hauling spoonfuls of pea and salted pork soup into his mouth after delivering another wagon to Salem. With a full belly, he sauntered up and down the commercial district on Bethabara Street. He stopped when a cheerful, piped music arose. Nothing like the resonant organ or brass music characteristic to Salem and it couldn't be their seasonal music of Christmas. Moravians wouldn't be honoring the birth of Christ for a month.

Mitchell occasionally stayed at the tavern with Quaker businessmen. Once, one raised the window on the second floor to hear the glorious singing and organ pipes from the congregation house across the square. Thereafter, Friends always booked it for rooms and Moravians referred to the tavern wall facing the square as the Quaker Side.

Zeb admired the Moravians who didn't believe seasons necessarily led to intemperance and levity. While they'd soon modestly celebrate Christmas, Quakers wouldn't so much as whisper their joy in public. Why do we restrain ourselves from openly cheering the birth of the Lord? We don't celebrate anything. Nothing quakes us except the Spirit of Jesus, yet we quiet, miserable Quakers don't cheer or admire Him. Nor do shiny jewelry or telltale stars catch our eyes.

Should a Quaker find another admiring a Christmas candle in the window of a Presbyterian's house, they'd show him the List of Disownable Offenses including observance of Christmas, Easter, and other days special to liberal Christians. How long before hardened Quakers bar secret musical lovers in the Society of Friends from visiting Salem?

Unlike the Moravians, I've never seen us move our bodies to music. That is a privilege reserved for the spirit. Outside of Salem a choir has never graced my ears. I've walked and rode up and down New Garden Road during the week as long as I can remember and have never heard a whistling worker or a piano recital. Ironic that we allow chiming clocks.

The music drew Zeb out onto Hope Street. He watched a parade of Surry militiamen pass in columns. High notes came from a man in front blowing through a hollow wooden rod placed across his face. A tense, organized uproar from drummers followed him. Then came soldiers, their muskets aligned vertical over their hearts.

Besides their alarming presence, Mitchell hadn't paid attention to the military activity below Salem except to notice it withered after the Battle of Camden. Since moving into town, the militia had undergone a spectacular revival.

After the parade moved out of view, he scanned to the barren kitchen and apothecary plot they marched from. He'd seen it full of vegetables and herbs during previous wagon deliveries. Now it hosted rows of tents and two wagons.

Strange. He looked closer. Why are *those* wagons staged at a militia camp? He shook his head, perplexed at the sight of *McMurray Wainwright* branded into the side boards of the freight boxes. He headed toward Salem Tavern filled with dread. His stepfather would deplore the militia impressing Quaker-made wagons.

His attention turned to traffic noise. It was George Heider driving the brand new wagon south down Bethabara Street with Abraham beside him. A load of barrels covered with canvas filled the freight box.

"George!" Zeb said. The young German looked long enough to see Zeb and flinched back to his driving. "Abraham! Wait!" Zeb waved and Abraham returned the greeting.

George studied Zeb and heeded the Quaker. "Whoa!" Abraham eyed him with panic and motioned forward. George didn't budge. Abraham conceded the wagon had stopped and looked to the heavens.

"What are you guys hauling?" Zeb said.

Abraham reached for the reins, but George pulled them away. The horses stirred in confusion.

George beamed. "We have gunpowder."

Abraham covered his face with his hands and hung his head.

Raised flaps of canvas allowed Zeb a view of the barrels on their sides. Stenciled English writing appeared on the barrel heads. A step toward the rear of the wagon helped him line up the wording. Under one flap, red block letters shocked him. *DANGER! GUNPOWDER! FFg Bedford.*

Abraham glanced at Zeb. "No one is supposed to know."

Zeb noticed a ruddy, stout man who hadn't been there a moment ago gazing at them from across the street and approaching like a curious bee searching for nectar.

Zeb spun around in place, covering the exposed warning. "Can I help you, sir?"

The stranger responded in English with a wheeze. "No…I'm…I'm sorry."

He looked at Zeb, his left eye giving an eerie tremble, and flew down an alley. Zeb looked to the ground and walked the other way toward the tavern. The team and wagon left down a side street.

***

Dismissed from ranks, militiamen dressed in long hunting shirts, some gray and others brown-checked linen, walked about town. It was hard at first for Mitchell to imagine them as troops. They exuded the youthful, sure deportment seen in young men everywhere, yet there was a seriousness to their faces and erect bearing. Salemites nodded with admiration and a bit of skepticism, paying the respect for the troops one reserves for a lawman.

Before turning in for the night, Zeb ordered a mug of tea and apple bread pudding in the tavern's main dining room. Sister Rahel, a slave woman of twenty-nine served him and dropped his pence in the cashbox. When she turned around, the stranger Zeb had seen earlier grabbed her arm and demanded to see the proprietor. She wriggled from his grasp.

Zeb got a better look at his clothes. They clashed with his rough manner. Free of stains and broken fibers, the plain fabric was too new and clean.

Rahel looked at her greasy, wrinkled linen sleeve but withheld disgust.

The stranger apprehended her lack of English and yelled for the proprietor. "Brother Meyer!"

Rahel ran to Brother Jacob Meyer's office recalling the caution ever preached by the house fathers in Wachovia. Avoid worldly talk and thoughts of foreign things. If they're so worried about worldliness, then they have committed a great error in assigning me to Salem Tavern for all the strange outside world comes here with their loud voices and demands.

Rahel lingered outside Brother Meyer's office. The guest spoke English and Meyer stopped him to repeat certain words so that he could say them in German.

"I represent a company that takes salt from the sea. Has an Express rider come for my letter?"

Salt from the sea. Salz. Meer "No Express riders have come."

They came out of the office and Rahel emerged from the spell cast by spoken English. She walked to the dining room with indifference, yet inside her head the worldliness of salt and sea buzzed.

Rahel served the guest who ordered brandy. He'd positioned a copy of Cornwallis' proclamation recruiting Blacks on the table where she'd see it.

"You can be free." He pointed at the paper.

Rahel pulled her arms to her side and stammered, "I have no English."

He sighed and jabbed the paper. When tears rolled down her face, he downed the brandy. "I'm leaving tomorrow morning. Let me know when I come back."

Rahel stuffed the proclamation in her apron. The guest pounded the stairs going up to his dorm room. Zeb Mitchell watched the impertinent stranger leave just as another man sat down at his table.

"Hello, sir. I am Major Micajah Lewis."

A veteran of the Battle of Kings Mountain, Lewis wore a hunting shirt that would have looked correct on the stranger's frame. Though cleaned and pressed at the Single Sisters laundry, a mended, red-stained hole in the shirt's linen fabric signaled a recent firefight.

"You must have seen the local militiamen gathering here, getting ready for war." Lewis considered Mitchell's pilgrim clothing. Floppy black hat, plain white neck wrapping and white shirt. Waistcoat, frock, breeches, stockings, and shoes all in black. The latter secured with dull pewter buckles. "You're a Quaker. Aren't you?"

"From New Garden Friends in Guilford County."

"Militiamen are also mustering at Charles Bruce's Crossroads in Guilford County. Near the courthouse."

"I didn't know."

"Didn't I see you driving a wagon into Salem today?"

"Delivering it for my stepfather's wainwright business."

"The Continental army of the South is far short of wagons. Major General Greene is recruiting men who can mend them."

Maj Lewis showed Zeb a poster distributed by Greene throughout the South: WANTED to serve the American army of the South—Artificers, Wainwrights, Blacksmiths, Boat Builders, Carpenters, Armorers, Saddlers, Harness Fitters, and Farriers, &c. Report to your County Militia.

"Why don't you post this here in Salem?"

Lewis shook his head several times. "Tried but someone removed it. I'd be wasting time posting it again. The Quakers won't let me post it in New Garden either."

"I'm interested, but—"

"Major General Greene needs you."

"I'm a Quaker. My stepfather would never—"

"Firing a musket wouldn't be your priority," the major lied. "Listen, I can tell you're intelligent. You probably know a trade. Militiamen will return to regular work after the war."

"I don't know, sir." Zeb blushed at Lewis' flattery. He held back a furious desire to mention the barrels of gunpowder, fearing the major's criticism and disgracing Abraham and George.

"The southern Colonies are struggling. Generals Benjamin Lincoln and Horatio Gates lost battles in South Carolina. Major General Greene enters third yet he's our best chance to save ourselves. Come to our aid."

***

Mitchell awoke from a nightmare, echoes of Maj Lewis calling roll while bleeding from multiple round holes. No matter. His stepfather would be expecting him. He dragged himself out of the bunk, dressed, and went downstairs for breakfast. A spoonful of steaming oatmeal propped in front of his face, but it was the stranger across the room he noticed. The man's clothes still made an impression. New and made in the plain dress of the Moravians, the clothes fit him but he didn't fit them. He exuded worldliness. George and Abe's wagon interested him too much.

He forgot about the man and visualized the gunpowder, determined to know the truth before riding home. Wolfed oatmeal lay in his stomach like hot coals as he grabbed his frock, retrieved his horse, and sought George and Abe at the Single Brother's House.

"Why were you moving gunpowder?" Zeb said.

Abe lay a finger on his lips and swept the alley behind the young men's home with his eyes. He pulled his frock lapels tight around his neck, unwrapped in a rush to get Zeb out of the building before anyone noticed. "Not one word."

"I won't betray you."

"The gunpowder is to be used to make musket cartridges for the Continentals and state militia."

Zeb's eyes shot open. He quelled a whistle by clamping a hand over his mouth. "On my honor, I'll tell no one."

"No one is to be trusted." Abe's jaw teeth clenched. "Turncoats are rumored to be in the midst of Salem."

George nodded at Abe with insistent eyes. "Tell him."

Abe glared at George and sighed before turning back to Zeb. "Day after tomorrow George and I are going to Charlotte Town to join the militia as three-month artificers." Again, Abe's index finger rested against his lips.

Zeb nodded before striding to the horse at the end of the alley. He pivoted and gave a warm glance. The horse galloped away as Abe and George returned inside.

George stopped halfway up the stairs and looked over his shoulder. Abe waved him on and walked to the kitchen surveying the room with furtive eyes. He laid the poster Rahel had given him on the hearth coals. It burned orange and yellow and turned into brittle, gray ashes that floated up the chimney.

# Twenty ~ Breakaway

Though groggy much of the way home, Zeb Mitchell felt guilty Abe and George had risen to take a stand. Could he bear sitting out?

He walked into the kitchen and avoided his family's eyes. He forced a greeting. "Hello everyone." His stepfather and sister Sara looked up from their lunch.

His mother Olivia poured boiling water into a teapot and turned from the hearth. She couldn't miss the pain in Zeb's eyes. "What's bothering you?"

He stood before his place at the table, gripped the top rail of the chair, and hesitated. His fiery stare fell on Michael McMurray. "Why do we protest war in public but aid the militia in private?"

McMurray squinted without fathoming Zeb's question.

Zeb persisted. "How can we be deceitful?"

Red anger flooded McMurray's face and he backed his chair out. "Excuse us, please."

Outside, McMurray stared at Zeb. "What are you up to?"

"You're profiting from war. Have the Friends not caught on?"

"What are you talking about?"

"Two of your wagons are at a militia camp in Salem." He shied from mentioning a third McMurray Wainwright wagon laden with gunpowder.

"When?"

"Yesterday."

"I don't sell wagons for the war effort."

"They were there plain as day."

"Don't be too quick to judge. The Moravians must have allowed the militia to press them into service. I'll communicate my displeasure to Traugott Bach."

"Will thee also communicate to the Loyalists?"

"Don't play with me."

"In June, Loyalists tried to steal the wagon I was driving to Salem."

"Why didn't you tell me?"

"You'd have stopped me from going there."

"That pains me." McMurray looked askance for a moment. "Didn't you deliver rifles for the gunsmith?"

"Yes, father."

"He'll want them back before the militia impress them."

"You don't know they'll be impressed."

"The military are the powers of darkness. They do what they like."

"Better the militia impress them than the Tories."

"Either way, I'll be disowned."

The Quakers of New Garden paid four-fold taxes to forgo militia service while the Moravians of Salem paid three-fold taxes. To keep themselves inviolate of the List of Disownable Offenses, the Quakers went further by withholding war materials and otherwise from the state militia, Partisans, Tory Loyalists, and the Continental and British armies.

Fabric and basic foods carried less risk to Quaker merchants. Cloth once processed into clothes and grain into flour concealed the originator. Zeb had delivered linen and wool Quaker fabrics without terms prohibiting military use. People bought clothes and food war or not.

The gunsmith sold rifles to the Moravians for peaceful use. Had Michael McMurray failed to notice the Patriot military needed wagons and teams after losing hundreds in South Carolina?

"Disownment isn't death."

"Why aren't you bothered the military has my wagons?"

"I'm bothered you don't *openly* provide them. People are dying for independence."

McMurray frowned at Zeb's gall. "Independence! The word deserves ridicule."

"That's not what people ridicule."

"What then?"

Zeb liked how the music in Salem made him move. If it was offensive to Quakers, so be it. "Quakers. Have you not heard people laugh when we pretend the spirit moves us?"

McMurray frowned.

"You know what I mean. Quaking as if we feel a force acting on our bodies."

"The spirit moves us. You're a fool and atheist if you believe otherwise."

"I believe in God. He acts on my heart. To feel the need to give my brother physical proof is deceitful."

"Our faith is neither deceitful nor shaky."

No father, the Quakers are shaky, Zeb wanted to say. The bloody iron tasted bitter.

"Are you renouncing your faith?"

"Our customs leave me wanting. I heard music yesterday and felt joy."

McMurray shook his head in disgust. "Do you side with Quakers at all?"

"A Quaker's conscientious relationship with God is good. Living an unadorned life and not keeping my fellow man bound are things I aspire to."

"You must take Quakerism as a whole. If you accept violence, you're rejecting the Society."

"I don't espouse violence, but if the King is to be regulated, it will have to be at the end of a gun."

"Is the state of the world so bad you want to change it? My profitable business will be yours someday."

"Wealth doesn't turn a young man's head. Why isn't greed on the List of Disownable Offenses?"

"Don't confuse greed with wealth which comes from working hard and pious living."

"So, it does. The market for wagons is good."

"You're starting to make sense."

"That's the point, father! The market is good without Britain. We need neither their governance nor meddling in trade."

McMurray lowered his head at the sharp logic of youth. Maybe Zeb is right. Maybe the Colonies should break away. Maybe he's wrong. "No, you're the King's subject and he's not letting that go."

"Letting go is hard. But can't you see we must defeat the British?"

"At best the present state is a stalemate."

"Give the independence movement time. War will be unnecessary once we take power."

"Why do you keep saying 'we'? Have you taken the state oath against the King?"

"No. I'm not inducted. I hope it happens soon."

"Stay away from Squire Bruce's! I've already lost a man to a week of muster. My operation suffers as he feasts and gets fat and lazy while standing on a pedestal thinking the world owes him something."

Zeb looked past his stepfather at the magnificent stand of short leaf pines still dotting the land McMurray claimed when he brought his family to Guilford County. They'd survived hundreds of years and went unmarked in the plunder to provide masts for the ships of King George I when Britain ran out of tall trees. McMurray's complaints seemed akin to chiding the mammoth trees for blocking his view. "Those are poor reasons to be against the militia."

"Then, I'll give you two more. I'm taxed against my beliefs to pay for these affairs and the militia are grabbing control."

"Yes, the militia are taking control. From Tories and Loyalists. Is that so bad?"

"Militia are an arm of a state government that usurped power from the Crown. What will happen to us if we change our allegiance from the King to the state and the King wins the war? Won't he punish us for disloyalty?"

"The King gave you nothing!"

"British kings promised Quakers religious freedom long before you were born."

"And George III abandoned us when the people kicked the Royal government out of North Carolina. Look to independence and a free constitution. They can guarantee your right to believe and compete."

"For a Quaker you take an inordinate amount of interest in the militia."

"Not long ago they defended Salem from Loyalists trying to enter at Shallow Ford. They continue to protect Salem."

McMurray frowned and shook his head. "Very well. Abide the militia. The Friends will disown you from the Society."

Zeb recalled the fallen Quaker outside New Garden Tavern. "Most families would close ranks in this situation."

"Don't you dare throw that military phrase at me. You're the one making a hard break."

"The Friends will take me back."

"You'll lose your desire to live in the faith. You've already taken ridicule to heart. Soon, you'll call yourself a Free Quaker."

"Better to be a Free Quaker than a non-Quaker."

"People who use violence to get their way then resume living by the light are not Quakers."

"Why do you despise them?"

"They poisoned the Philadelphia Society of Friends. I left the hot war over them. They can have Philadelphia."

His stepfather's argument tumbled like one of those mighty trees behind him. "You think the hot war lies in Philadelphia? How mad are you? It's almost here in Guilford County."

"You don't stand a chance against the British army."

"If I can stand up to thee, I can stand up to the King's men."

"Pay the four-fold tax and you won't be forced to serve."

"No one is forcing me." Zeb stomped away but returned. "I have another thing to say. Never did I want you to worry—." Zeb stopped to watch Michael McMurray's wagging head. "So, I've held back my feelings for a young Moravian lady."

"She's another thing out of our faith."

"Already you want to bar me from marrying. Her name is Yohanna and I love her."

"Leave. I have nothing more to say."

Olivia stuck her head out of the door. She ran to Michael, now standing alone.

"What happened?"

"I always count my blessings, but not out of pride. I showed him the error he's making."

"What is he doing?"

"Joining the militia."

"Make him come to his senses."

"After a labor of love, I'm done talking."

Her shoulder slumped against the clapboard siding and she hung her head. "The divisiveness across the land has gone too far. I never thought my own family would stop speaking to each other. I'll lose my son."

***

Zeb walked into the kitchen, gulped a mug of tea, and grabbed slabs of meat and bread. Sara followed him out the front door.

"What's going on, Zeb?"

"I'm joining the militia."

She came close with burning eyes. "You can't! The Friends will read you out of the Society."

"Good. I won't have to pay four-fold taxes."

"Where do you get your dark humor?"

"I'll be taxed to death for not serving and if I'm delinquent paying, everything I own will be confiscated."

"Father pays your taxes."

"From my wages. I can't accept that. By flesh or pocket book I'll lose blood."

"You're wealthy enough. You *want* to be at war."

"I want to be free."

Her eyes nailed him. "You'll leave your mother, father, and me at the mercy of the Rebels and Whigs."

"Quakers aren't Loyalists."

"To outsiders we are!"

"The militia needs me. General Cornwallis will come and without an army New Garden will die."

"How can you forsake the man who took you under his wings?"

"I was a baby then. I had no choice." Zeb took a step back. "Look at us. We don't resemble each other. You're of his blood."

"Is that what this is about?"

"Who am I?"

"Don't go there, Zeb." Her eyes rolled. "I know what you're doing. Try to separate us. We four are thicker than blood."

A bit of Sara's hair showed. Zeb seldom saw his own hair. The long untied ends when he washed it or a rare reflection. Did it matter if his black hair clashed with his family's?

He tucked a stray blond lock under her black wool bonnet.

"You're a Quaker. You have no business killing men over politics."

"I must do this."

"What will you do?"

"General Greene needs artificers, wainwrights, boat builders, and carpenters."

"Boat builders? Perhaps Greene is a ship captain. Will he fight Cornwallis on a watery battleground?"

"Don't ridicule, Sara. You haven't seen the great rivers in our state. American forces may need boats."

"Where will you draw the line, Brother? Will you fire a musket at a man? How long have you wanted to kill?"

"Don't waste your scorn. Cornwallis is coming. I must do what is necessary."

"You'll stain the Society of Friends. The British will mark us as enemies."

"Besides the British, evil Loyalists will bring harm. They thrive on fear and hate and find solace in division. They must not win."

"You're one man."

"I know people who are willing to help. People who want freedom."

"Wait! I'm going with you."

"You're no Jezebel. You shall not become a camp follower."

She smacked his cheek.

"You got your little bit of vengeance, though I misspoke." He stormed out the door wearing stinging red skin.

# Twenty-One ~ Scourge

— November 29, 1780, Salem

Brother Jacob Meyer looked up from the tavern reception desk. "Oh, Mr. Neal, good to see you. How long will you be staying?"

"A day or two. Look, I need to see Salem's best trader."

"Traugott Bach. Down Bethabara Street past the Gemeinhaus."

Neal stowed his things upstairs and headed for Bach's house. While walking, the encounter with Zeb Mitchell issued from his memory. No one would mistake the wainwright for a Moravian. *Is he associated with the militia or Rebel state government?*

Neal found Traugott Bach's home. Maria knocked on the study door. "A salt merchant to see you. Mr. Arthur Neal."

Traugott Bach strode to the entry hall.

Neal made a half bow. "Arthur Neal, your most humble servant."

"Good morning, Mr. Neal. Traugott Bach at your service. Please come into my study."

From the wingback chair Neal pitched a tale. "I represent a salt manufacturer in Beaufort, North Carolina."

"What's your inventory?"

"Barrels and barrels. Might I trade salt for wagons?"

"Why wagons? I don't have any available."

"I saw a man deliver a wagon here days ago. When will the wainwright return?"

"I don't know."

"Don't you want salt?"

"You ask a lot of questions."

"I need wagons to deliver your salt."

"My wagons will take goods to Beaufort and haul salt back."

Neal shook his head. "My company profits on the shipping upcharge as well as the salt. I need wagons to make deliveries."

Bach dismissed the upcharge, but loathed competition for wagons. "I don't know when the wainwright will return but it won't be Zeb Mitchell."

"Why?"

"Mr. Neal, I have a lot of work to do."

"What happened to him?"

"He enlisted in the militia."

Neal's eyes screwed dumbfounded. "Are you sure?"

"I didn't go to the induction center and watch him enlist."

"You have a lot of wagons here."

"We have a lot of trade."

"Mind telling me where they're made?"

Bach analyzed the man's clothes. Humbler than his demeanor.

"A great trader can't turn away salt."

Bach frowned at Neal's flattery. "I'm a busy man. Leave my house."

Neal started back to Salem Tavern. The militia encampment down Hope Street caught his eye. When he got near the wagons he saw *McMurray Wainwright* had added their location beneath the brand. The wainwright is a New Garden Quaker.

* * *

Bach' shoes echoed on the irregular polished boards. He took the backless seat at the head of a simple long table in the Gemeinhaus. Members of the Board of Elders sat on bench seats along the sides.

"Sorry. Detained on business."

The Gemeinhaus on non-religious days served as the Saal, a spacious community room. Arched plaster alcoves projected morning light into the room. Heat thrown from oak logs in the fireplace took the chill out of the air.

Bach, the sixty-one year old merchant from Sweden, held the reins of all non-ecclesiastical decision-making in Salem. Guided by his pro-Moravian, pro-growth approach, Salem and Wachovia had become one of the most successful private enterprises in North Carolina.

As with all meetings between the united brotherhood of Moravians, this one started with the chairman's hands placed together and head bowed, asking for God's intercession.

"Lord, we ask You to bless this committee with a thorough understanding of the predicament we find ourselves in as the Revolution draws ever closer. Guide us to work together as brothers as we consider how to manage our war burdens. Whatever Your purpose it is for our good. We humble men thank You for endowing us with more unity of heart and more brotherly sharing in each other's circumstances. Amen."

The chairman laid a stack of papers on the table. Moravians had submitted a record number of criticisms over the last six months. Outsiders, Rebels, and Loyalists rose to the top of their concerns.

Moravians suspected Loyalists would rise as soon as the British got traction in North Carolina. Salem invited the militia's security but found their sinful influence tiring.

Bach patted the stack of papers. "These are the complaints."

"Brother, we know what the complaints are," Johann Reuz said.

Bach's eyebrows furrowed and nose flared. Tis a pity that more of Salem's manpower comes from Philadelphia where petulant young men often speak above their station.

Over a short stint as a helper under Bach and a half year of apprenticeship under the hat-maker on Bethabara Street, Single Brother Johann Reuz hadn't broken. That Reuz had snared one of the two at-large board of Elder seats rotated amongst the Single Brethren increased Bach's desire to be rid of him.

"Brother Johann, we must approach our work with order and not lose our temper." Bach made a mental note to speak to the head of the Single Brother's House. He picked up the first complaint. "In June Rebel outsiders came and spoke evil of us as Tories and threatened to burn the town." Bach's eyes panned the boardmen. "We're not Tories or Loyalists nor are we Rebels or Whigs. We're a neutral people." He slapped the complaint upside down in a new stack. "Besides, no one will be able to burn Salem unless our Lord gives His consent."

Bach summarized the next complaint. "A week later a rumor was heard that a party of soldiers had come to seize all the food they could find so the English wouldn't take our plentiful stores."

"Nothing was taken," tanner Peter Yarrell said. Yarrell's white leather belts found favor with the state militia for carrying cartouche boxes. Business had fallen when the gunpowder shortage obviated the need to carry ammunition.

"Yes, Brother Peter," Bach said, "because we committed ourselves to the care of our Father."

Next Bach restated a complaint often heard. A North Carolina company of infantry left the Wachovia tract less than two weeks into August for the Continental Army near Camden, South Carolina with flour ground at Brother Abraham Steiner's mill. Before leaving, the captain paid for his own food and board at the tavern albeit with devalued Continental dollars. For the soldiers he wanted to pay with worthless North Carolina currency but gave a bill against the public account.

Brother Samuel Stotz, himself still agitated after Reuz' testiness, interrupted. "Is it any wonder the British routed the Americans at the Battle of Camden? They don't pay for our hospitality."

Stotz chafed at Brother Reuz' disobedience. An upcoming Salem trader, Stotz had seen the same bad temper displayed throughout Wachovia from certain single brothers and militiamen. Rude, un-Moravian behavior and declining Christian values grew rampant.

"Today half of the Surry County Regiment marched from Salem to forage grain," Stotz continued. "Before they departed, they stole butter and bread for their breakfast."

"Well, we are lodging soldiers," Bach said.

"Lodging soldiers isn't the point."

Bach viewed the upstart competitor and made his mouth small and sour. "Is that all, Brother Stotz?"

"Last week, when silver shoe buckles and clothing from a washtub went missing, Colonel Armstrong of the Surry regiment said he couldn't answer for the soldiers."

Bach's hand and forearm supported his head while Stotz droned.

"Then, all the militia but the colonel marched to the Quaker settlement in Guilford County to thresh grain. Quiet returned. But when they returned, the soldiers found a keg of wild grape wine, drank it, and refilled the keg with water. One drunk man was beaten."

Stotz nodded to Salem watchman Brother Zillman across the table for help. "I told the militia to go home to Surry County."

"What happened?" Bach said.

"They claimed to be hungry, so I told them to get food from the Salisbury militia stores. They refused saying the stores were empty."

Bach shared a look of concern between Stotz and Zillman. "I know for a fact the militia created that depot so that the regiments and horsemen would leave us alone."

Stotz shook his head and stared at the chairman. "Brother Bach, can we believe them?"

Brother Peter Yarrell interjected. "Well run out of food. Brother Steiner can't get help with so many outsiders gone to the militia."

"Have you asked Bishop Graff for labor?" Bach said.

"Brother Meyer needs the Blacks to work in the tavern in place of absent Brother Abraham the negro," Yarrell said. "Steiner's three day laborers from the English settlement at Hope refused to work because of the false news the English were coming. We shall have to pitch in and help him ourselves to eat our daily bread."

# Twenty-Two ~ Rahel

Rahel cleaned the dining room and washed breakfast pots and dishes. She brushed the hearths in Salem Tavern and put the ashes in a bin outside for the soap maker. Before cleaning the guest rooms, the maidservant shook the dust from her blue gingham apron and pulled her blue bonnet tighter to cover her black, frizzy hair made into a bun.

She struggled to climb the stairs with her heart crowding her feet. Most days she could quell the loathing. She had let down her guard, however. Every bother accumulated until life didn't seem worth living.

For whom do I work? For my master, Brother Meyer? For all manner of people on the Great Wagon Road who come to the tavern to eat and sleep?

Good people come. Sinister and moody people also come. God, unburden my mind. Every time I climb these stairs, the same lustful leers of the same rude men burn right through me. Never did I feel free until they fetched their black men from the tavern shed and left.

Hadn't I hoped with my kind heart and took the masters to be fair? What made them dismiss my rightful refusal and turn on me? Why did they complain and curse me in English? To their eyes I'm stupid. Though I know but few foreign words, I derive the hate in their downturned lips. Why didn't my sweeping tell them I paid no interest?

Even Brother Jacob Meyer belittles me in my presence. Did I cost him a hundred pounds when an ox costs two-hundred-and-fifty pounds and the state taxes an eighteen-year-old German Single Brother at the value of a thousand pounds?

Rahel dragged herself up the stairs hoping to plunge into work and forget everything. Of the guests in the largest room, only the one using the single to the side of the window on the front wall had made his bed. A grin widened her face as she imagined a mature military man tucking in the sheets and blanket.

She smoothed the pillow on the handsome bed but jumped when something inside poked her. She retrieved a thin book filled with numbers and words in tables similar to Brother Meyer's account ledgers.

With the book tucked in the pocket of the apron, she descended both flights of stairs with stealth. Trembles came from every nerve knowing the corners of the book gave it away behind the gingham.

In the cool cellar, her forehead chilled under perspiration. The book opened in the middle. Confusion clouded her brown eyes as she scanned the small incomprehensible English text. A creaking floor joist startled her.

Fearing the book's owner would catch her with it, her heart pounded. From the officials and traders visiting Salem to the various people stopping for meals and drinks, the entire building stirred at times and she never knew when somebody might come down and reproach her.

Negativity crept back. Our guests bring good profits to Salem, but may God protect us from the robbers and thieves, the spitzbuben who have nothing better to do than prey on the innocent. More lone travelers come who seem to have no genuine business. Though projecting innocence, they're watching.

Rahel saw rough guests as the predators that escaped the haus fathers of Wachovia attempting to rid the wolves, bears, and big cats from the forest. Now that the human predators have entered our space, how long will it be before we're devoured like a building in an unstoppable chimney fire?

Teamsters and militia are rough in this tavern. Horses turned out into a small corral after a long haul behave better. Their cursing drives children of visiting families to the Choir lodgings in the Single Sisters or Single Brothers houses for proper care in gentle surroundings.

The tavern serves hard-drinking guests. As the night wears, quarrels and fights arise. Brother Meyer has tried everything to keep the men calm. He vowed to serve brandy in meager amounts. Any delay pouring a fresh portion would regulate the rowdiness. If necessary, he would erase brandy from the slate to stop the drunkenness.

Alcohol alone doesn't bear civil conflict. A Patriot captain rumored to have skirmished with the English sent his underwear to the Single Sisters House for washing. The blood stains showed the engagement was true. Another soldier had his putrid healing wounds bandaged.

Military men don't always bring horror. Col Martin Armstrong of the North Carolina militia is always well-mannered and attends worship service. Same for the company of cavalry who camp in the tavern meadow.

This book brings too many worrying thoughts. I'm going to get help never mind the book gnawing at me and demanding its return to the pillowcase.

As she flew up to the first floor three men entered the tavern dining room. She froze and watched.

"Whose chestnut mare is that tied up in the meadow?" the leader of the trio said.

A voice came from a table where two white men, sharing the looks of a father and son sat with a black boy. "Mine."

The three men approached. "That's my horse," the leader said.

Scuffling occurred when the three men prevented the "father-son" pair from running. Rahel's eyes, already jumpy from the strange book, gaped.

"Empty your pockets," the leader said. "Both of you." His hand lay at the edge of his side pocket bulging with a pistol.

Paper money and counterfeit silver and gold made an impressive pile.

"Where are you from?"

"Georgia," the evident father said.

"The boy?"

"We got him on the Catawba River."

"Everything you have is stolen or fake." The leader motioned to his partners. "Collect this and bring them. We're going to Shallow Ford for a proper questioning." He headed for the door.

The leader left last. He was going thru the door when Rahel touched his sleeve and pointed at the boy.

"Watch over him."

Rahel gave him a cup of milk and a hunk of bread and ran out the front door with the book. In two minutes, she was knocking on Traugott Bach's front door.

The door opened and Rahel pushed the book into Maria's hands.

Maria thumbed through the pages amazed at the hundreds of numbers and words. Rahel spoke only German. Maria spoke fluent German and English. In German she said, "Where did you find it?"

"In the pillowcase of a guest. What does it mean?"

"We'll worry about that later. Go back to the tavern. I'll copy and return this within the hour."

***

Maria brought the book to the tavern kitchen where Rahel was kneading dough. While Rahel returned the book to the pillowcase, Maria wrote a sentence using the copy as a guide.

Rahel took a deep breath and sighed. "No one was upstairs, thank God."

Maria showed Rahel the sentence. 150-42-15-566. "These numbers stand for words. Can you guess the meaning?"

Rahel shook her head.

"150 is 'I am'. 42 is 'going'. 15 is 'to'. 566 is 'Salem.'" Maria read the sentence aloud. "I-am-going-to-Salem. Try it."

"No. I understand."

"You're brave for sharing the book. It's for writing secret letters."

"How do you know that?"

"My father and I can speak English. You don't speak English. Let's say you're with us and he speaks English to me. You don't know what he said, but I do."

"That book allows writing that nobody knows without it?"

"Right. It has a secret code and a list of dead drop points."

Rahel shuddered. "Drop dead points?"

"Places to hide a secret letter. The *dead drop point* in Salem is the tavern dining room."

They found a fan-folded letter wedged between the supports of the big round table. Maria copied it and stuffed it back in the table.

Maria and Rahel warmed their hands at the kitchen hearth.

"What does it say?"

The converted letter was short yet detailed:

November 23, 1780, Salem
To General Cornwallis

Sir: Apprising you of events in Salem. Large Rebel militia camp. Bound Blacks are happy. Miscreant removed proclamation poster. Moravians serve the enemy. No prospect of recruiting Blacks or Whites. Eluding notice as a salt trader. Staying longer may draw suspicion. Awaiting your command.

Your very obedient and humble servant, etc, etc, etc
Colonel A. N.

P.S. While waiting for an Express rider, I learned a wagon load of powder barrels marked FFg arrived.

# Twenty-Three ~ God Keep Us

— "Except the Lord keep the city, the watchman waketh but in vain." (Devotional text for the day, Salem Diary, Psalm 127:1, King James Version)

Hosting the Patriot military had put Moravians in a predicament. What could the Board of Elders  do?

"We can't let this go on," Peter Yarrell said. "The militia is irresponsible. They and the Patriot army abandoned the field in the Battle of Camden and left ten wagons of Brother Steiner's flour."

"As for Patriot wagons and horses," Traugott Bach said, "I prefer we say 'impressed'. They're borrowed, not taken."

"I call it seizure, Samuel Stotz said. Anyway, it hasn't been long since Colonel Armstrong returned with wagons loaded with powder and lead. Providing food and light goods for the militia is one thing. Storing ammunition in Salem makes us direct military targets."

"At least they didn't lose those wagons," Bach said. Before reading the next complaint, he scanned the large room. "Now," Bach whispered, "I want everyone at this table to swear they won't gossip about the gunpowder and lead."

The boardmen touched the Bible in the middle of the table and swore. Bach picked up the next complaint. On a Sunday two weeks into October, Friedland church dismissed early to feed a militia detachment camped at the settlement. Word came out in the rain-soaked feeding lines next to Friedland Tavern why the hungry soldiers had come.

Hundreds of Surry County Tories hiding under state militia colors had shown their loyalty to Gen Cornwallis, who'd occupied Charlotte Town, by rising up at Shallow Ford on the Yadkin River. To protect Wachovia east of Shallow Ford, hundreds of militiamen from Salisbury, Charlotte Town, Guilford and Surry counties, and Virginia routed the insurrection in a hearty fight that killed fourteen Loyalists and a Patriot militiaman.

"Five-hundred troops descending on Wachovia is intolerable," Brother Zillman said.

"Would you call God turning away the enemy intolerable?" Bach said.

Stotz sneered. "One of the Whig soldiers was so wounded he couldn't be treated and for that another Whig soldier threatened to burn Salem."

"It didn't burn," Bach said. "Look at the bright side. The uprising induced the Tories to lay down their arms."

"Have you not heard the rumors?" Stotz said. "The Tory label has fallen on Moravians as we don't serve in regiments."

From the center of the table Bach opened a writing box and laid a sheet of paper in front of him. He uncorked a bottle of ink and primed a goose quill. "The Brethren will be instructed not to permit the hated name 'Tory'. We've proved the contrary by paying the three-fold tax."

The three-fold tax amounted to sixty shillings, enough money to pay for up to a week of lodging, eating, and stabling at a tavern. Men who served paid five shillings tax.

Stotz patted the table. "If your instruction was worth anything, you wouldn't need the Patriot militia turning Salem into a military post to convince the world we aren't Tories."

"Why are you upset?" Bach said.

"At the beginning of the month six Virginia officers came from Salisbury to Salem Tavern for a rest. Instead of payment they gave the tavern a draft on Virginia's treasury."

"We can't go through every issue." Bach stacked the complaints, spending an inordinate amount of time evening the edges. "Brother Meyer and I have losses. Sometimes the regiments don't pay at all."

Bach hoped the board would see the war burden spread out and make them lay aside their individual concerns. He realized from their angry faces he'd whipped them up.

"What do the regiments say? Have you confronted them?"

"Colonel Armstrong gave me written protection from promissory notes for the store and Brother Jacob Meyer received written authority to arrest anybody leaving bills at the tavern and send them on as prisoners."

Stotz cottoned to Bach's tactic and pounded the table. "Is that it?"

If Bach didn't soon convince the board to be even-handed, they might lead a pitchfork-toting, torch-burning mob running soldiers and non-Moravians out of Salem. He tried a small smile.

"Please, Brother Bach."

"What's on your mind?" Bach said.

"Wachovia has prostrated to the military. They're ruining us with their immoral behavior and debts."

"I don't like it either." Bach restrained himself. "But can you deny Colonel Armstrong and the militia regiment provide for our safety by making a presence here? Who but the Whig militia could put down hundreds of Loyalists at Shallow Ford intent on destroying Wachovia?"

Stotz hung his head and shrugged while avoiding the chairman's eyes. The board followed the submissive gesture and listened to Bach.

"We're the King's subjects, but he has left our side. This board, as need arises, will consider the best interests of the congregation, and in that spirit will be our agents in the war affairs that concern us. Brothers, we're no longer immune to the strains of war. It's coming."

Stotz came back to life. "Can't we at least have order?"

"Who do you want to cast out? Customers of the tavern, the store, and the mill? Let us not be too bitter toward neighbors who are jealous because God has blessed us so well. Someday the war will be over. Do you want everyone to turn against us then?"

"You know I don't want that," Stotz said. "Why can't we stop the soldiers drinking and their thievery and noise at night? If we don't, our boys will see their fearless antics and start bending cocks into their hats!"

Bach played it well by throwing up his hands. "Alright. We'll increase the night watches." He wrote a neat sentence then stilled himself and searched the whitewashed wall across the room. "This board will assign four single brothers with trumpets far enough from town and near the main roads to alert Brother Zillman the watchman of drunks and vandals."

"Brother Bach," Yarrell said, "will you tell Brother Zillman not to blow the hours? It upsets the officers in the tavern when he blows his conch shell like a bugle."

Half a smile crept into Bach's lips. "Do you, Brother Zillman?"

"Yes, but I wouldn't if we had a clock bell."

"We must get one," Bach said while scratching ink on the paper.

"Unless the Lord keep the city the watchman waketh but in vain."

Bach's head still faced the writing paper and his eyes rolled up. "Of course, Brother Stotz. We'll always call on the protection of the Lord first."

"Will God keep the city?"

"Brother Reuz! One more outburst and I'll no longer welcome you on this board."

Reuz persisted. "Will the single sisters help by sounding the alarm? Or will they take on other chores?"

"That's insolent and petty. The single sisters may soon be doing extra work to pay into the fund to build a girls' school."

"Doing what?"

"Making musket cartridges," Bach said. He leaned toward Reuz. "Not a word." Bach straightened his back. "Now, as for night watches—"

"Night watches alone won't save us," Stotz said. "Like rolling musket ammunition, evil works in the daylight hours as well. Our innocence is ending. The Lord is coming."

Zillman nodded. "Evil works all year outside our settlement. Innocent ones go into the thickets to gather wild foods but find evil men and women awaiting."

"We should tell the congregation not to forage alone so they may not stray into the hands of the fallen ones," Stotz said.

"There's no need to forage the woods," Bach said. "The store sells everything we need."

"Don't you intend to share your list with the congregation?" Stotz said.

"Yes, of course."

"Then add avoiding the woods by oneself to it."

Bach didn't want to control every moment in Moravian's lives until it occurred to him the less foraging the more business for his store. "Wise, Brother Stotz," Bach said as he added to the list.

Chairman Bach blotted the goose quill and laid it on the writing stand and corked the ink bottle. He gathered the complaints with his list on top and stood.

"Good day, my brothers. That's all until we meet Sunday for the love feast and communal singing to celebrate the beginning of advent."

# Twenty-Four ~ Disconcerting

Traugott Bach walked out the front door of the Gemeinhaus and stopped to embrace the late fall chill. He continued west down Hope Street past the Square and stopped at Bethabara Street to admire Salem, laid out so well. Against a blue sky the steep pitched tiled roofs and brick and half-timber structures lining Bethabara Street conformed to the standards of staid, modest order and presented nothing outlandish in design or color to assault the eyes.

Across Bethabara Street the Single Brother's House was the tallest, grandest building in Salem, bursting from forty-eight young single brethren lodging and working in its rooms. Sunshine gilded the ochre bricks fronting Bach's general store further south where bonnet-clad women scurried in carrying empty baskets and others exited lugging laden ones.

He faced north and the townscape blurred. Unsettling visions of the future gave him a momentary shudder. He grabbed a hitching rail. After this war is over, Salem and the Wachovia tract must lean on our strength. A distant second to praising the Almighty, our congregation and vast one-hundred thousand acres will prosper. We shall erect true borders and keep out the non-believers.

Bach walked with care over icy patches. He couldn't wait for Christmas and the simple seasonal ornaments of green boughs and red ribbons tied to door fronts. Alarm duty yet to come, a quartet of soprano, alto, tenor, and bass trumpets would assemble in old world charm near the clock tower and play a Christmas chorale.

He imagined the congregation amassing in the Gemeinhaus and lighting candles on Christmas day and raising their voices accompanied by the horns in a harmonious hour of singstunde for Holy Lord God.

***

Maria put down the letter which revealed a writer loyal to Gen Cornwallis who'd spied on the gentle Moravians.

Rahel tapped the copy. "Salt. Please point to it." With the word singled out, Rahel nodded. "I heard a man in the tavern mention salt and the sea. He asked Brother Meyer for an Express rider."

"The 'salt trader' Arthur Neal has no genuine business in Salem. He wanted to spy on us."

"Everybody's hiding something," Rahel said. "This hidden book itself hides words."

"I must tell my father."

"How will he take it?"

"Bad. He's already upset with George Heider and Abraham who left to muster with the militia."

Rahel contemplated the circumstances of George and Abraham. "I wonder if the book has anything to do with their secrecy."

"I didn't sense secrecy, only a hurry to get to camp."

"We shouldn't have let our men leave."

"They were determined."

"Without us?"

"Do you think we should have followed them?"

Maria looked down and pinched the bridge of her nose. Why would we follow the militia? We'd be a nuisance. Still, they wouldn't turn down our cooking, cleaning, and nursing. We might sew their uniforms, perform errands, and soldier.

It's not such a mad concept. Women aren't stupid. We see the work men do. We're as capable. We've seen Tory and Whig women driven from their homes hoping to join their husbands. What do they do? They come to Salem for bread, meat, brandy, and candles for whatever camp they can set up.

The single sisters make gloves and wash clothes. The money goes to their proper financial accounts. A single sister presently keeps the Friedland Diary. A man's job.

How could I be so stupid? I don't know Martha Washington's face, but I see her ladling stew onto tin plates for the troops.

Rahel stared. "Are you okay, Maria?"

"Oh." Maria left her thoughts. "Yes, I'm fine. In my mind I saw a woman feeding soldiers."

"Why did you imagine that?"

"My father works all day at a desk finding new ways to bring trade to Salem. Working hard and feeding him is my job."

"Try feeding a tavern full of men."

"You work hard, Rahel. Of course, you do." She touched Rahel's hands. "Do you ever wonder who's feeding Brother Abraham?"

"Please, I'm trying not to worry."

"I fret over Brother George as his sister Yohanna does."

The camp came back in Maria's thoughts. Why do women join up with militia and army regiments? They don't have to. Are they motivated by fear of starving at home? Are they escaping lustful eyes watching them in their village? Do they seek the protection of the military? Don't they do it for love?

"Maria?"

"I was thinking. Our brothers need us."

Rahel scowled. "We can't follow them to camp."

"Why not?"

"Keep the Lord our Savior in your thoughts. Don't put His will far from your busy mind."

"I'm not an evil woman. It's for the sake of Christ and with my entire heart that I'd go. I want to serve and please Him."

***

The "salt trader" returned to Salem Tavern.

"Excuse me, sir. My name is Arthur Neal. I'm looking for someone."

"Good day, sir. I'm Captain Micajah Lewis. Who are you looking for?"

"Zeb Mitchell.

"What's your business with him?"

"I need wagons."

"You're too late. He went to Charlotte Town for induction with two Moravian friends."

Neal recalled seeing Zeb Mitchell with Abraham and George who drove the gunpowder wagon. "Thank you, sir."

Neal packed up to leave Salem Tavern. He pushed the Bethabara Street door halfway open but, hearing  Rahel's footsteps, he turned around. "You evil woman!"

Brother Meyer heard the commotion and appeared. "Sir, please calm down."

Neal ignored him and glared at Rahel. "Why didn't you tell me Abraham went to Charlotte Town to enlist with the German and the Quaker? You'll never see them again."

# Twenty-Five ~ Off to Enlist

— November 30, 1780, central North Carolina

Zebulon Mitchell, George Heider, and Abraham bounced on the driver's seat. The wagon Zeb "impressed" from his stepfather moved down the uneven Hillsborough-Salisbury Road toward the south central border of North Carolina. At Salisbury the Trading Ford ferry took them across the Yadkin River. Ahead the Great Wagon Road continued to Charlotte Town.

Often, they met American military traffic. Worn and faded indigo uniforms identified Continental soldiers. Militiamen wore plain backcountry neutral, brown, and black hunting clothes of linen and wool.

The three young men looked for signs of friendliness on the road. Once Zeb hollered, "God save Washington!" A group of men clad in green jackets yelled back from horseback, "God save the King!" Zeb held his tongue thereafter.

George had crawled into the cargo box to nap. Abraham had the reins. Zeb said, "I read a pamphlet in Salem Tavern by a man called Thomas Paine."

"Who's that?" Abraham said.

"A man who wrote about common sense."

"When was sense ever common?"

Zeb grinned. "Paine put it simply; people will fight for change if they feel the future holds something better."

"Moravians are afraid of the future."

"Quakers too," Zeb said. "Why fear living in a free country?"

"People don't want to be sewn together into a quilt."

"You've lost me."

"We're isolated. Quakers have their place and Moravians have their place. Rebels have their place and Loyalists have their place. If we can't come together now, how will we after the war?"

"We'll come together."

"Quakers don't accept slavery. Moravians don't accept Quaker austerity and contemplative worship."

"We both believe in non-violence."

Abe stared sidelong. "Zeb, we're joining the militia."

"Maybe that's what Paine meant. We're accepting change now for a better future."

"Our peoples separate from the world. We frown on liberal ideas and shudder at disrespect for law and authority."

"Our people will come around to the world and vice versa."

"I'm a black man. I stopped waiting for the world to come around a long time ago."

"You've accepted being carved from your family?"

"Have I?" Abe grinned. "A motherless, fatherless slave is miles worse than a stepson."

"You got me."

Abe looked down the road without blinking. "I got over the break long ago."

"I can see that it hurts you still."

"Fine, my son. I'm a slave. I hurt."

"Someday society will question what it has done to you."

"Don't bet on it."

"Heavens! Doesn't the militia accepting Blacks mean anything?"

Abe guided the team around a bend in the road. "My answer is what your Thomas Paine said. The coming change is better than what I have."

"Nobody can blame you for putting your back to Traugott Bach."

"Perhaps he enlightened me to the militia when he ordered that gunpowder."

"That doesn't sound like you're all in."

"Slaves fear leaving Salem as if they owe their lives to Moravians. I gave up security."

"The British are promising freedom after the war."

"You're so innocent. A boy knows what happens to the cattle he leads to the slaughter house."

"Didn't you see the advertisement?"

"See it! I saw the man tack it up."

"Did he see you?"

"Mmm hmm. I read it and he asked if I was interested."

"Well?"

"I told him yes but went back later and destroyed it. Rahel gave me another one and I burned it."

"Why?"

"The posters contained English. Anyway, the Salem slaves can't read."

"You could have read them a translation."

"Bishop Graff would have put me in chains."

"Would he?"

Abe shrugged. "Doesn't matter. The British would have sent me back to Salem."

"To resume being a slave?"

"This is a war about America's future. Not mine."

"I wish you could live in New Garden. Quakers are living up to the Discipline that disavows slavery."

"Bishop Graff would never let me."

"You could have run away."

"What do you call this?"

"I don't mean joining up. Why don't you run for good?"

"What are my chances of freeing Rahel and bringing her along?"

Occasional rain fell. Was it raining in Salem? Did Rahel, the sister arranged by Bishop Graff to marry Abraham, realize by now he'd left to join the militia?

They stopped to erect the steel hoops and canvas cover.

Back in the flow of traffic, Zeb steadied the reins and glanced at Abraham hanging his head. "Are you okay?"

Abraham deflected the question and gazed ahead. "I've been thinking. If anyone asks why you're travelling with a black man, tell them I'm your slave."

Zeb shuddered. "Are you deranged? I can't do that."

"The authorities will haul us in. They'll think I ran away."

"The militia won't care."

"I'm talking about civilian laws. Anyway, you'll be in trouble too."

"Never thought of that."

"You better start being a master."

Zeb's eyebrows furrowed. "Don't you start."

Abraham fell over laughing. "I'd ask you to write a note for me but I'm afraid of your anger."

"What kind of note?"

"Quakers are so innocent. A black man must always carry written orders from his master."

Zeb's face soured. "That's awful."

***

An official jotted their names on a register at the Mecklenburg Court House in Charlotte Town. He told them they'd be in the Makers Company after each had his particulars recorded, submitted to a health check, and gave the oath of allegiance.

*Makers Company* sounded fortuitous to Zeb. Blacksmiths, carpenters, wheelwrights, wainwrights, and harness men numbered few. He knew only a handful of wainwrights. No more than twenty out of a hundred working men made things. Together they would make a mighty group.

He gazed at Abraham and George talking. They seemed distant speaking German. But he was part of them. Thrown into a room as big as the one in the New Garden Meeting House, Zeb and the two Moravians sat in their own little group.

Why are we in Charlotte Town? Freedom for the Colonies and ourselves. I want more. George has had none. Abraham's need is a different kind.

All three of us are distinct from each other and from others in the room. Differences sort people into groups of their own kind where they remain isolated unless they can change and fit into other groups. I imagine changing will be difficult for us three. Our strict, disciplined lives have caged us from the world. Abraham has the extra difference of his skin color caging him.

Zeb came out of reverie. Abe was speaking to George, switching from German to intone certain English words in a tutoring session. At one point, Abraham said "Stinking Quarter" in English. George echoed him and, although his German inflection carried, an English speaker might not notice with all the dialects present in North Carolina.

The lesson continued as Zeb surveyed the room. Pit against the others, my group is different. Abraham's difference is as plain as the color of his skin. It's easy to feel compassion for him. Do the other boys look at our plain clothes and round, floppy hats and see how different we are? We're far from Macaronis but we stand out.

Nearby, young men from the frontier wearing stained and torn buckskin shirts and breeches and beaver hats stood out in their own way. Town boys stood out as well in their tri-corner hats like soldiers already kitted out for war. Other boys wore modified floppy hats. One had an edge of his brim buttoned to the dome of his hat. Another made sharp folds in his brim to create a poor-man's cocked hat.

Our biggest differences have nothing to do with our clothes. Maybe it's the temperament of our lives that sets us apart. No, that's not right. Neither the backcountry harness man nor the village wainwright is any less calm or mature than the others.

Not that the frontier boys are cold-blooded killers but killing to eat is central to their lives. George, Abraham, and I aren't strangers to hunting, but we depend on others tending husbanded and cultivated farms to feed us. Of course, the world doesn't afford the frontiersmen days with nothing to do except hunt game. They might hoe a garden and farm wheat and corn and tend livestock.

At that moment the one true difference came to Zeb. To them we live in a strict, austere world where our beliefs disavow malicious taking of a life. We must look idle and soft. My God, we won't join the militia without giving the oath to defend North Carolina. If it comes to it, we'll pick up a musket and aim at our fellow man.

# Twenty-Six ~ Zebulon's Oath

The wait ended when a man sporting a splendid indigo uniform with red facings and a red epaulette on his right shoulder entered. A buzz erupted as the recruits awed his uniform. They followed with their eyes as he went to the head of the room and froze.

"Atten-shun!" Stern and erect, he waited for the din to cease. "I'm Sergeant Matthew Vinyard of the Makers Company," he bellowed. "You'll each visit with me so I can register your name, father's name, where you live, and your occupation. Then a doctor will examine you. Last, Captain Abercrombie Hawkins will swear you into the militia. Do you understand?"

A handful mouthed "yes" or "yes, sir". The main body nodded.

"As you were!"

A gray-haired civilian man and a dashing commissioned officer entered and headed to the front of the room. Everyone watched them set up their places behind a long oak table. The doctor took a chair in the middle. He donned a pair of spectacles and put a quill and bottle of ink on the table.

At the end of the table on the doctor's left, the officer laid down a Bible. His uniform surpassed the glory of Sgt Vinyard's. A gilt epaulette adorned his right shoulder and similar shades decorated the facings of the blue frock and the saber hilt on his left side. The tri-cocked hat shimmered with a border of gold.

Sgt Vinyard approached Capt Hawkins, threw up his right arm and touched his hat band with extended fingers. The commissioned officer reciprocated and sat down. Still at attention, Vinyard spun about-face.

"Atten-shun! I'll call you one at a time. Remain silent while waiting. Understood?" After a lackluster response, Vinyard bellowed. "Louder!"

"Yes, sir!"

"File up six feet in front of me."

Zeb, George, and Abraham jumped to the first three places while Vinyard placed a writing set and a stack of forms on the table to the right of the doctor and sat down. He eyed Zeb.

"You, come forward." Vinyard took a blank record from the stack and held an inked quill over the paper as he read the first inquiry. "Name?"

"Zebulon Mitchell."

The sergeant inked Zeb's name in the box. "Your father's name?"

"Michael McMurray."

The sergeant stared.

"My father died when I was a baby. Michael McMurray married my mother and took me in."

Vinyard gave Zeb an uplifting smile as false as teeth. "Well, isn't that a touching story?" He gazed at Zeb's clothes. "What are you?"

Religion wasn't part of the official inquiry but Zeb knew from experience what he meant. "I'm a Quaker."

"Quaker? Aren't you people loyal to the King?"

"It depends on whether the smoke blows toward you or away."

"That's a daft thing to say. Men that don't side with the Patriots side with the King."

"Men that don't side with either might be neutral."

"What are you?"

"Patriot."

"Residence?"

"New Garden."

"Your work?"

"Wainwright."

"Good. We've nothing but broken down wagons needing repair." Vinyard handed the form to Zeb and shouted. "Next!"

Doctor James Wallace took the document from Zeb. "Step back here behind the table."

The doctor examined Zeb from the neck up and jotted his findings. Black hair, mahogany brown eyes, fair complexion, no smallpox scars. He pulled a glass disk from a leather box and held it between his thumb and forefinger in front of Zeb.

"Open your mouth." Healthy. No missing teeth.

"Step back here against the wall and I'll measure your height." The doctor read a scale marked on the wall. "Six feet. My, you're tall." The doctor shook his head.

Zeb gave him a perplexed gaze. "Is that bad?"

"A tall soldier can see over the fray, but he's easier to spot."

"I'll take that as advice."

"Age?"

"Eighteen."

"Birth date?"

"March 31, 1762."

"Strip to your breeches and I'll weigh you."

The doctor noted Zeb's frame. Normal posture. Scar on right knee. Then he added the Quaker's height, birthdate, and one-hundred fifty-five pounds to the document.

"Dress and stand before Captain Hawkins. He'll administer the oath."

Hawkins eyed Zeb. "Do you belong to the Quakers, Moravians, Dunkards, or Mennonites and have conscientious scruples against taking an oath?"

Zeb mulled the hypocrisy of taking the oath. It meant disavowal. "Quakers. Prepared to take the oath, sir."

"Read the words on this paper and say 'affirm' instead of 'swear' and drop 'so help me God' if you prefer."

Zeb placed his right hand on the Bible and swore loyalty to the independent State of North Carolina and to renounce any allegiance he may have borne to King George III of Great Britain so help him God. He'd do the utmost to support, maintain, and defend North Carolina against King George III and his heirs and successors, abettors, assistants and adherents.

"You're hereby validated as an able bodied man for service in the North Carolina militia."

Decorated with gold epaulettes on each shoulder, an officer strode into the room making quick glances before stopping in front of his junior Capt Hawkins. They exchanged salutes and spoke. He studied Mitchell's fresh paperwork and nodded before leaving.

George's turn came. "Name?" Sgt Vinyard said.

"George Heider."

"Hi dare?"

"Ya, Heider, Heider!"

Vinyard chuckled. "You sound like a salutation. Hi there! Hi there!"

George stood on his toes. "Heider!"

"Don't get testy, my son." Vinyard stared at George and put down the quill. "Are you German?"

"Ich bin ein Amerikaner!"

Vinyard slammed the table. "I'll have you digging privy holes!"

Abe came to George's side. Eyes piercing, Sgt Vinyard menaced both by turns. Mystified by their similar plain dress, the sergeant could have mistaken them for each other if not for their race.

"Who are you?"

"Abraham." He put his hand on George's shoulder. "This is my friend George Heider. We're from the German settlement of Haw Old Fields in the Stinking Quarter and they speak the language, but he's American."

"Ich bin ein Amerikaner."

"There he goes again."

"He's nervous."

"I am George Heider. Yes, not ya. No, not nein. Hello. I want to join militia."

Vinyard shook his head in frustration. He cast doubt on Abraham. "Are you a runaway?"

Abraham nodded.

"Stay here," Sgt Vinyard said. "I need to talk to the captain."

Vinyard huddled with Capt Hawkins and pointed at Abraham. "Sir, that black man claims to be a runaway. How do I know if he's telling the truth?"

"Let me speak with him."

Hawkins listened to Abraham's life story altered to conceal his true Moravian identity. The officer heard Abe's references to carpentry skills and knowledge of two languages and knew the foolishness of not recruiting him.

Vinyard's estimation of Abe's value grew as well. Interrupting the captain, the sergeant said, "He's already used to subordination. Don't you reckon he could guard a baggage train and tend horses?"

"Don't be stupid. I apprehend this man to be valuable. He's healthy and speaks well. Either we take him or the British will."

"He won't return to his master after the war."

"War has consequences."

Sgt Vinyard faced away to hide his anger.

Hawkins looked at Abe. "Are you running from your master?"

Abe patted his pockets. "I don't have a note."

Hawkins sprang into Abe's face. "Does your master support the King?"

Abe put on an honest face and nodded.

"Do you swear your master is loyal to King George III?"

Abe raised his right hand and looked into Capt Hawkins' eyes. "With all my honor."

"Why do you wish to join the state militia?"

"To keep North Carolina free."

"Why shouldn't the King bind the Colonies to his realm?"

"Neither man nor land can be bound by two masters. I wish to be rid of both, but the King is most damnable because he brought me here."

Capt Hawkins glanced at Vinyard. "Finish inducting these men."

"Yes, sir." Vinyard squinched and leaned in. "Are you a runaway slave?"

"I'm a carpenter."

"That's not what I meant."

Abe, still facing Vinyard, glanced sideways at Capt Hawkins, who'd returned to his place at the table. "Why do you persecute me? I told your boss I ran."

"I'm your boss now. Tell me."

"Do you want me to join the British?"

Vinyard's indignant face caved. "Let's get you inducted." He took a blank form and inked a quill. "Your name?"

"Abraham."

"Surname?"

Abe looked into Vinyard's inquisitive eyes and paused. The German Abrahams of Wachovia—Steiner, Loesch, and Leinbach—had a last name given at birth, but he was Abraham "the negro". He racked his brain and said, "Hellerschwarz" which translated as *light black*.

"Father's name?" Vinyard winced and drew a line through the box. He entered "Hawfields" and "carpenter" in the last two boxes.

Finished with Vinyard, the doctor studied Abe's features. Black hair and eyes. An impressive, well-made man in his prime. Free of pock marks, though he'd never warrant "fair" or "fresh", typical for an unsullied complexion.

Nor would his looks garner a poetic "swarthy" or "ruddy". Neither black nor white. Somewhere in the middle regarding complexion, he wasn't native American and there was no mistaking the black, frizzy hair. The doctor scratched "yellow" on the form.

***

Abraham took the oath of allegiance. George Heider sat before Vinyard and answered the questions with Abe's help, then moved to the doctor's place at the table. George's well-built physique and middling height matched Abe's. His face scarred from the pox, eyes blue, hair light brown and wavy. The doctor noted his face as "fresh".

When the group passed induction, Sgt Vinyard took the Makers company outside where ten Northern artificers joined them. The company numbered ninety. Vinyard taught them to march in a single file taking two steps per second. Then he marched them in two files of forty-five. When they'd graduated to six files of fifteen ranks, the sergeant looked pleased.

"You're going to march to Camp New Providence, partake in rations, and learn to fire a musket to army standards."

"Excuse me, Sarge," Zeb said. "Can I take my wagon?" He pointed to the McMurray Wainwright wagon and team he'd driven from New Garden.

"We'll press it into service, Private Mitchell. Captain Hawkins will write you a claim for the property or monetary compensation after the war."

Vinyard ordered the company to follow in two files while he drove the wagon in the company of Zeb, George, and Abe to the camp.

The sergeant couldn't get over Abe sitting on his right. "Why did you run away?"

"Leave him alone," Zeb said from the freight box where he sat with George. "He's here to help you."

"I have a right to know."

George called out Vinyard's demeanor. "Du bist ein Dummkopf."

"What was that?"

Zeb chuckled. "I have no idea. Why don't—"

Vinyard raised his left hand to interrupt Zeb. He pulled the reins to turn the wagon down a side road then hollered, "Gee-up!"

Zeb started up. "Leave him alone. Can you speak two languages?"

Abraham Hellerschwarz took his cue. "Mein Vater ist Englander. Meine Mutter kommt aus West Afrika."

Vinyard scratched his head and tightened the anger points on his face. Meanwhile, the wagon sped over the rough road. The right wheels ran across a tree root and bounced the sergeant to the left side. Before an oncoming wagon could take Vinyard's head off, Abe took the reins and pulled the sergeant in. Vinyard finished driving to camp.

With the wagon halted and the company marching up, Vinyard hopped down and made a blank gesture to Abe as if wanting to thank him but unable to grovel. He settled for a faint nod.

# PART II

# Twenty-Seven ~ Neal Calls

— December 1, 1780, British army camp, Wynnesborough, South Carolina

Arthur Neal caught up with Cornwallis who indeed had snapped back into South Carolina. One of the pickets dotting the wooded security perimeter heard a noise in the distance. Through the darkness, he sensed an apparition. As Neal got closer his shape became clearer and his horse on lead clopped louder.

"Halt! Identify yourself."

"Colonel Arthur Neal, loyal friend of General Cornwallis."

"Advance to be recognized."

Neal closed in. The picket surmised by Neal's provincial clothes the so-called Loyalist might be a Quaker.

"Halt! Give the countersign."

Neal slowed his approach due to the musket leveled at him. "I don't know it."

"Throw down your weapons and step towards me with your hands raised over your head."

Neal lowered a musket and a linen knapsack to the ground and raised his hands. "My warrant is in the knapsack."

The picket found the warrant and waited for a roving guard to come.

***

Aide-de-camp Capt Henry Broderick peered into Cornwallis' office. "My Lord, Colonel Neal."

A feeble voice. "Come."

Cornwallis lay balled up sweating in an armchair. The colonel took the furthest chair.

Cornwallis raised his head. "What news do you bring?"

"Are you okay, my Lord?"

Cornwallis looked through lifeless pupils floating in miasmas of chaotic white mass. "Another fever. Give me a moment." The lord let his strength accrue. "I've had to endure the cruelest torments and suffer the most violent oppressions…"

My God, how sick the lord is!

"…and yet I'm not unlike His Majesty's subjects in these provinces who have great affection to the cause of Great Britain."

No, he judges the King's people to be sick. "My Lord, can you help them?"

"Ha! My poor North Carolina friends bear with patience the most oppressive and cruel tyranny ever exercised over any country."

"Don't they deserve our care?"

"Not if they don't learn to fight for the King!" Cornwallis shuddered and mopped a linen rag over his red brow. "Why are you here? You could have messaged me."

"Alas, no messenger came."

"Haven't you raised any Loyalists?"

"No, my Lord."

Cornwallis mumbled. "Undoubtedly, Maj Patrick Ferguson's destruction at Kings Mountain has stifled them. Don't go acting on your own."

"Understood, my Lord."

"And don't promise to hang Patriot leaders and lay their country to waste with fire and sword."

"My lord?"

"Oaths of the late Ferguson."

The major's death quelled the conversation, further spoiling the room's air already sick with the lord's disease. Cornwallis couldn't release Ferguson's calamity.

"The Over Mountain Men took Loyalist officers captured at Kings Mountain to Wachovia and cut them with swords." Spasms jerked the general. "Humiliating them, charging for food and drink in captivity."

Neal wagged his head. "I'm unaware of that happening at Salem. Though nobody commits those acts absent of extreme injustice done to them."

"Perhaps they were kept in another Moravian town."

"How do you know this, my Lord?"

"Some escaped Wachovia the fifth of November and arrived at my encampment on the twentieth. You didn't see any of the hundreds of Loyalist prisoners in Salem?"

"My Lord, I can hardly tell an American Loyalist from an American Patriot. But I saw a wagon carrying gunpowder."

"Gunpowder!"

"The cargo box of a wagon brought into Salem contained barrels of gunpowder."

"How do you know it was gunpowder?"

"By the copper barrel hoops and the *FFg* markings."

Cornwallis recalled the convoy raid at Nelson's Ferry. "Not two wagons of powder?"

"I saw but one, my Lord."

"Did you raise Blacks in Salem?"

"No interest."

"So much for recruiting thousands."

"They aren't amenable to His Majesty. By way of example, I understand a prime slave ran from Salem to join the rebel militia with two young white men."

"You disappoint me."

"If it pleases your lordship, might I command a detachment of His Majesty's troops to investigate the Moravians?"

"My Regulars are tied up fighting Rebels here in South Carolina."

Cornwallis, debilitated with fever, might not push back if the colonel pressed him. "Don't you want to put North Carolina on defense?"

"They're defending themselves too well, committing the most shocking cruelties and horrid murders on our friends. It's worse than the South Carolina low country."

"It's rumored General Greene is expected to relieve General Gates."

"More's the pity. I was beginning to like the coward."

"I apprehend you'll be acting before winter."

"Winter isn't the problem. I'm waiting to hear from Major General Leslie."

"With a body of troops, my Lord, I might—"

"Out of the question. I need them when I march back into North Carolina."

"My Lord, I can attract Loyalists to my side with a company of troops."

"Tell me more about the powder."

"It was conveyed in a wagon made by a New Garden Quaker wainwright."

"So, the Quakers have turned."

"I suspect it. Two other wagons made by the same Quaker wainwright lay in a Rebel encampment in Salem. The Quaker's son joined the Rebel militia."

"Spy on the wainwright then return to Salem and watch for ammunition wagons."

"Yes, my Lord. I'll advise him against aiding the Rebels."

"Do nothing violent."

"My Lord?"

"I admire Americans as long as they're committed to the King."

"My Lord."

"I'm not fawning over them. Their disloyalty rouses my contempt. Use caution with the Quaker. And leave the powder alone until I've detached a larger force. I want it."

The general's forbearance irked Neal. He'd either lost his mind to fever or wanted to save the egregious Rebels for the uniformed wolves of his army. "Will you lend a detachment, my Lord?"

Cornwallis closed his eyes and groaned. He called Broderick and told him to detach eleven Loyalist forces from a company of the Royal North Carolina Regiment Cornwallis had been fortunate to recruit on his own.

***

Col Neal traveled to New Garden with the provincial horsemen emblazoned in a green jacket like theirs. As he rode, he pondered how to manage the Quaker wainwright. If McMurray abided his Quaker tenets, he'd be neither Loyalist nor Rebel. Which side would he favor if roughed up?

Neal couldn't agree with Cornwallis' admiration of Americans. A weak voice in the straits of fever reached into Neal's head recounting the treatment of Loyalist prisoners in Wachovia under Rebel swords.

How long will the King's subjects accommodate the cruel Rebels? Cornwallis can't expect restraint from me. I'll disavow it.

***

Neal found Michael McMurray. "One of your wagons was seen hauling gunpowder in Salem."

"They weren't sold for that purpose."

"Don't deflect." Neal panned the wainwright shop. Wagon assemblies in various stages of build lay about. Hammering, sawing, and metallic odors from the blacksmith's forge filled the air. "Are you selling to the Rebels?"

"It's against my conscience."

"Your conscience is moth-eaten wool."

"My conscience is whole!"

Hot blood pressured Neal's brain. "You're Quaker in dress only."

The Loyalists made a semicircle behind Neal. Michael McMurray and his craftsmen sized up the pistols, swords, and axes hanging from their belts. "Destroy my business. I'll maintain the testimony."

"That won't be necessary if you cooperate."

McMurray smirked.

"Where's Zeb Mitchell?"

Fright ticked McMurray's eyes. "I don't know."

Neal lunged at the wainwright, grabbed his throat, and pulled him to the ground. "Surround them!"

Olivia and Sara entered the shop and shouted in unison. "Stop! Stop!"

Neal jumped on McMurray's chest and beat his face. McMurray said nothing until Olivia and Sara approached.

"Get in the house and arm yourselves!"

"Who are they?" Neal said.

"My wife and daughter."

Neal shouted to a pair of Loyalists. "Hold them!"

McMurray struggled to free himself.

"Your son is in Charlotte Town joining the militia. Boys, destroy this shop!"

When the destruction began, Neal pushed McMurray outside on the ground with Olivia, Sara, and his workers already under guard of a horseman bearing a cocked pistol and gleaming sword.

Sara approached the guard and hounded him to let her and Olivia go. A second Loyalist broke away from destroying the shop long enough to tie and gag her.

After a half-hour of breakage and ruin, Neal and the horsemen came outside.

"Is this how you treat a loyal subject of the Crown?" McMurray said. "The King is dead!"

***

Neal sent a coded message to Cornwallis with one of the horsemen:

December 2, 1780, New Garden
To General Cornwallis

My Lord: I have the honor to report to your Lordship the events in New Garden. I found the Quaker wainwright Michael McMurray guilty of aiding the Rebels. My men destroyed a waterwheel and the gears and driveshaft used to power a large lathe. We set fire to the gear shed, threw all the smith's anvils in the creek, and ruined the hearth. We are going to Charlotte Town to question the wainwright's son, then to Salem to reconnoiter the gunpowder.

Your most humble servant &c, Colonel Arthur Neal.

Cornwallis crumpled the letter and threw it into the hearth. "Idiot!"

Broderick took a fresh sheet of paper and wrote the general's coded reply for the Royal North Carolina horseman to carry back to Neal:

December 2, 1780, Wynnesborough, South Carolina
General Cornwallis to Colonel Arthur Neal

Sir: You intimated evenhandedness but did the opposite in New Garden. Your dishonor harms my ability to recruit Loyalists in North Carolina. Gather intelligence of the enemy's position and supply movements but take no extreme action. Otherwise, you will hang.

I am &c, Cornwallis.

# Twenty-Eight ~ Taking Command

Diverted to North Carolina via the Upper Road, Maj Gen Greene had left Richmond three weeks into November with Lt Col Edward Carrington and aide-de-camp Maj Ichabod Burnet after the six-day stop. Five days later the Bingham coach stopped in Hillsborough, North Carolina where Carrington parted company.

Further down the road at Martinsville, Greene passed the Patriot magazine and landscape surrounding Guilford Court House. He learned scores of men had stopped there in August after running a hundred-and-fifty miles from the rout at Camden. Now the village lay quiet and absent of military forces.

As the general and Maj Burnet boarded the coach, taking them on the last leg to Charlotte Town, Greene wondered if sending supplies down rivers was fanciful. Common practices like a well-regulated army once existed as concepts, but that hadn't stopped Maj Gen von Steuben from authoring the *Blue Book*.

On the road to Salisbury, Burnet woke from a nap when the general blurted out, "Why shouldn't the rivers be employed to transport supplies?"

Burnet's book fell from his lap. He peeked through bleary eyes at Greene sitting across from him. "Sir, don't let it eat you."

"Very well, write down this letter to Brigadier General Edward Stevens. Dear Sir. Go up the Yadkin River until Hughes Creek five miles west of Bethania in the Wachovia tract." He waited for Burnet to draw fresh ink in his quill. "Explore the river, its depths and currents, and every obstruction that might impede the business of transportation."

***

Greene looked up from the *Blue Book* when the footman let down the step and opened the door on a warm mid-morning, December 2, 1780. The four-week trip to Camp New Providence in Charlotte Town was over. The General would take command in two days.

***

Maj Gen Nathanael Greene met with Maj Gen Horatio Gates in a brown canvas marquee. Gates' shaky and ragged folding chair reflected the

Southern army. Ten minutes earlier, Greene's world sobered when he took authority and responsibility for the welfare of the small, fifteen-hundred man Southern Continental army.

Formed in ranks and sporting cocked hats, the lean troops resembled upside down crescent moons atop poles. Greene took heart in the impoverished scene. Though in dire condition, the rows exhibited neat lines in the style promoted in Baron von Steuben's *Blue Book*. Arrayed behind the assembly, Camp New Providence also made impressive visual geometry though the small rectangular plots placed on a grid had pitched tents for but a quarter of the men.

Spirited fife and drum music still played in Greene's ears in the private meeting with Gates. The agenda began with Greene performing an initial probe into the disastrous rout of Gates at Camden. Tension sapped the atmosphere.

"General Washington instructed me to hold a court of inquiry into your conduct. Can you produce evidence supporting your actions?"

"Should a formal inquiry be held today, I couldn't defend myself as I'm deficient in it."

The new commander looked for a beneficent tone. "You want to put this matter behind you."

"Could I but justify myself to the world."

Greene halted Gates with his hand. "Don't bother. An inquiry right now isn't practical though it's the tenor of my instructions."

Gates' shoulders relaxed. He never expected a reprieve.

Getting the army's support was crucial. If leniency with Gates risked condemnation from the political and military leadership, Greene accepted it. Cornwallis invaded North Carolina and pulled back. There was no guarantee his strategy would remain fickle. Any fool could see a change at the top of an American corps presented a vulnerability.

"Besides, an inquiry would require Baron von Steuben's presence which would be imprudent as I need him to defend Chesapeake Bay and Richmond from Major General Leslie."

Still feeling dishonored, Gates hung his head. "I did all that could be done."

"Understood." Greene scratched notes and looked up. "I'll put my recommendation to rest the inquiry before General Washington and other heads above me and wait on their decision."

"You have my gratitude."

Greene laid down the quill and threaded his fingers atop the desk. "Now, respecting preparations for Cornwallis, I beg you to inform me of our readiness."

"Coming from the North, you may be unaware of the great exertions to procure provisions at the local level."

"Is anyone aware? General, the men are of poor physical constitution. They're in rags and shoeless."

"The evidence is scant but feeding them and replacing their clothing has been my first priority."

"What bills have you drawn and for what purpose?"

"The Committee of Clothing of the Continental Army and the Board of War in North Carolina have been covering this state like locusts ordering provisions. I've pressed Maryland and Virginia to supply their troops."

"Show me your quartermaster's reports."

"My young quartermaster preferred to oversee supplies rather than an account book."

"When did you expect to be feeding and clothing the men and replenishing the magazines?"

Gates at fifty-three years old, reddened with humiliation as if returned to adolescent embarrassments. "When the great unwilling people comply."

Greene paused to let Gates' torment dissipate. "I understand you assigned Lieutenant Colonel Edward Carrington to study the Roanoke River for supply storage between Richmond and Hillsborough."

"He's setting up a magazine at Taylor's Ferry, locating flat boats, and building a battery."

"Excellent. I'd hoped to set up such a facility."

"Carrington moved five wagon loads of Continental provisions from Hillsborough to Taylor's Ferry. Two-hundred-fifty muskets have arrived from Richmond."

"Impressive. He's my choice to serve as quartermaster for the Southern army."

"He has a mind for details and figures."

"I beg you to forward him all your supply orders. Also, send him reports of the arms and ammunition we possess and give him an account respecting the way and manner you get lead from the mines. Who's in charge of this business?"

"It's time to bring in Colonel Martin Armstrong of Surry County militia to apprise you of a gunpowder and lead situation in the Wachovia tract."

Gates stood before William Henry Mouzon's 1775 *Accurate Map of North and South Carolina With Their Indian Frontiers, Shewing* *in a different manner all the Mountains, Rivers, Swamps…*on the tent wall and circled Wachovia with an index finger.

"We have an opportunity in Salem, not quite a hundred miles northeast of here. It's a Moravian town. Though conscientious objectors, they're not against supplying provisions. Colonel Armstrong is here. Let him explain."

Gen Greene hung his head outside the door flap. "Major Burnet, fetch Colonel Armstrong." He turned on his heels. "Thank you, sir. I wish you good health and happiness. Are you going north?"

"Within the week."

"Let's discuss the Southern situation tomorrow." Greene pulled back the tent flap. "I will ready William Bingham's private coach for your travels."

***

Col Armstrong apprised Greene of Traugott Bach's plans to manufacture musket cartridges.

"Odd but welcome," Greene said.

"Dangerous as well. Cornwallis has a man named Arthur Neal who learned of Bach's gunpowder. A Moravian lady copied Neal's letter to the lord as well as a code book found stashed at the tavern."

"Is Neal still in Salem?"

"No, and we haven't discovered a single body of Loyalists meddling around the settlement."

"Take precaution, Colonel."

"We have pickets guarding Salem and a heavy guard around the gunpowder. Bach has yet to roll ammunition."

"What's the problem?"

"He can't spare any labor to build a laboratory for fashioning cartridges. I have artificers but no carpenters."

"I've formed a company of artificers including carpenters. They may be in camp."

Greene held the tent flap for Armstrong. "Major Burnet, do you know where the Makers company is?"

"On the parade ground, sir."

Before reaching the Makers, Greene and Armstrong met a teenage bugler standing alone blowing battlefield calls with expertise.

"What's your name, son?"

"James Gillies, sir."

"I'm General Greene. We need buglers like you."

"I'm promised to Lieutenant Colonel Henry Lee's Legion."

"That's fine. Cavalry can't hear orders without a bugler."

Greene and Armstrong resumed walking and neared a small corps in rapt attention to their sergeant. "They might be the Makers," Greene said, "as they have but ninety men."

"Two of the Makers are from Salem," Col Armstrong said.

"If they help build a laboratory in Salem, do you reckon they'll return to us once they're done?"

"That's not the problem. Traugott Bach and Bishop Graff maintain firm control of Salem. They'll hate to see their men return and fly off again."

"I'll write a message for you to carry to the elders. I need every Maker I can get, and I don't want to displease the Moravians."

They approached the parade ground. Lt Col Carrington and Capt Abercrombie Hawkins stood on the sideline waiting for the Makers to resume drilling after taking a short break. Zebulon, Abraham, and George huddled in conversation. They wore cocked hats but dressed in their usual plain clothes.

Sgt Matthew Vinyard faced the Makers, oblivious to the officers assembling behind him. When Carrington and Hawkins joined Maj Gen Greene, Carrington touched his cocked hat. Greene shushed him with an index finger to his lips.

A copy of the *Blue Book* stuck out of Vinyard's frock pocket. From the sergeant's ease on the parade ground, he was versed in Maj Gen Friedrich Wilhelm von Steuben's guidelines for the instruction of recruits.

"Makers company—Fall in!"

Vinyard brandished a cane. "If you hear 'fall in', you'll form two neat columns and come to attention." Thwack! The stick resounded against his boot. "Otherwise, I'll wallop your backside."

"If I say 'attention', stand firm, silent, and steady. Move neither hand nor foot until I say 'rest'. Do you understand me?"

The recruits offered a variety of replies and body language.

Thwack! "Don't prattle. The proper response is 'yes, sir'. Say it loud, you dead meat!"

"Yes, sir!"

"Rest! Fall out!"

The company fell into disorder, sitting on the ground or roaming.

"You bunch of ignoramus bumpkins. I'll give you credit. You've taken 'fall out' to heart. Now listen. When you hear 'fall in', make two neat columns and come to attention."

Seconds passed. Their stony faces crumbled with anxiety.

"Fall in!"

The first trial failed. Thwack! A lash moistened the eyes of three oafs. Some boys got more.

"You lice don't hear well. When you hear 'fall in', make two neat columns and come to attention facing the man ahead." He drew two columns on the ground with his cane. "Do you understand?"

"Yes, sir!"

"Fall in!"

Two dunderheads faced him instead of forward. Vinyard made his face small. "You should be seeing the back of a man's head!"

They turned. The sergeant reviewed the Makers company still in formation, rotating his eyes back and forth.

One soldier motioned with his head at Maj Gen Greene while whispering to another in the file on the right. The second one snickered. Sgt Vinyard ran to him.

"Fall out, wretch!"

The sergeant rapped the cane on the palm of his hand. Gen Greene cleared his throat and elbowed Carrington. Vinyard looked over his shoulder and jumped at the expanse of gold insignia.

"Makers company—Atten-shun! To the left—Face!" Sweat tickled Vinyard's ribcage.

"Good afternoon, men. I'm Lieutenant Colonel Edward Carrington. Welcome to the Southern command of the Continental army. We serve under Major General Nathanael Greene."

"Makers company—Rest!" Greene said. "Come here, son."

The snickering recruit turned grave, feeling the general's hand on his shoulder.

"Was something funny?"

The recruit hung his head. "Yes, sir. No, sir. Sorry, sir."

"Thank you. Now, get back in formation." Greene glanced at the officers before turning to the sergeant. "He's the first soldier I've seen here taking a notion to levity. There will be times in this cause when he won't have a reason to smile. Cheer is lacking."

Sgt Vinyard stiffened. "Yes, sir!"

"Dismiss your company, Sergeant and join us." Striding on his left leg and letting his halting right leg catch up, the general called to the officers. "Come to my tent to plan a laboratory."

Vinyard yelled. "Makers company—Fall out!"

***

Gen Greene prefaced the meeting with a warning. "We all apprehend our dire state of ammunition. Salem is critical. Carrington, I beg of you a laboratory plan."

"Colonel Armstrong, how big does the laboratory need to be?" Carrington said.

"I need ten Moravian single sisters each working at a table around the clock. We'll need temporary space for storing gunpowder and finished cartridges."

"You're planning on a huge undertaking?" Greene said.

Col Armstrong watched Carrington drawing a layout. "About sixty-thousand cartridges."

Greene's eyebrows arched. "That amount of ammunition could decide the South and the war."

Carrington laid down his quill. "Twelve feet by fifteen feet."

Armstrong studied the drawing. "Begging your pardon, the work tables need space. The powder won't explode using non-sparking tools, but a fire would flourish in close quarters. The sisters will need aisles to get out fast."

"Wise of you," Carrington said. "Let's make the laboratory twenty-four by thirty. Do the Moravians have lumber?"

"They have trees. Bring all your saws, hammers, and nails and we should be fine."

"Capt Hawkins," Greene said, "you're hereby ordered to take Sgt Vinyard, and ten Makers experienced in wood construction. Find two wagons and all the sawyer and carpenter tools and nails you can collect and depart soon."

"Yes, sir. I'll conduct a wagon myself one of the recruits brought."

"Very well. Take a travelling forge to make nails and mold lead balls."

"Understood, sir."

"Keep your Makers on site until you've finished rolling the ammunition. Can any of the remaining Makers sew duck?"

"I have a tailor and a sailmaker."

"Make those two corporals over the rest of the Makers company. Round up all the duck and canvas and heavy thread and order them to make tents while you're gone."

Greene sat down as the meeting broke up. He reached for a quill and halted midway. "Oh, Colonel!"

Armstrong stuck his head in the tent.

"Sit down while I compose a message to Traugott Bach and Bishop Graff."

The general lit a sealing candle and wrote the message. With the paper folded, he dripped a button of hot wax to the paper's edge and licked the seal before pressing.

"I beg of you to carry this letter and send Arthur Neal's letter and code book with Captain Hawkins when he returns."

"It'll be done." Armstrong dashed off to find the others going to Salem.

Greene wrote to George Washington informing the commander-in-chief of the cartridge-making operation. He hoped the news would help lift his Excellency's burden.

# Twenty-Nine ~ Salem Laboratory

Vinyard found Zebulon Mitchell, Abraham Hellerschwarz, and George Heider scraping parade ground mud from their shoes. "You're going up to Salem."

Zeb and Abe glimpsed at each other. "Up to Salem" made George smile. Abe came alongside and patted the shoulder of his dubious master.

Zeb was going to Salem! Yohanna in the flesh would again fill his eyes. He could no longer subscribe to Quaker disbelief in luck.

The sergeant saw Abe shrugging at Zeb. "Pay attention, Private Hellerschwarz. We're going to put up a building. His eyes swiveled over all three. "Come help search for sawyer and carpenter tools."

The three privates followed Vinyard. Abe and Zeb fell back a bit behind George.

"Remember," Abe said, "if anyone asks, you're my master."

"Abe, I—"

Abraham glared. "I don't want to do it."

"Fine." Zeb looked away then rotated back to Abe. "What are you and George going to do about Salem?"

"Huh?"

"You better hope Sergeant Vinyard doesn't figure out you're not from Stinking Quarter."

"My God, I forgot."

***

Arthur Neal hid in a thicket with his Royal North Carolina horsemen until a convoy of two wagons and a body of men departed Camp New Providence at Charlotte Town. Pickets monitored the far edges of the site. Torches brightened the camp's entrance in the settling dusk.

Camp guards paraded three hundred paces in front of the tents in regular thirty-minute intervals. The thick security cautioned Neal to turn his green jacket inside out to sport the dull black lining before approaching the gate.

"Good evening, fellow Patriot."

The guard showed no emotion. "Identify yourself."

"I'm a wheelwright from Guilford County."

"State your business."

"A most dreadful misfortune has befallen the father of a militiaman. I need to speak to Zeb Mitchell who's said to be in this camp."

"Sergeant of the guard!"

Neal sat down and waited.

"I don't know Zeb Mitchell," the sergeant said.

"He's a wainwright."

"The one who came by wagon with German messmates?"

"Yes, my friend."

"What's the problem?"

"His father was attacked at New Garden."

"Well, sir, I'm embarrassed. Mitchell has gone to the Moravian town to build a laboratory. His squad must be over the Yadkin River by now. You won't get past Salisbury until the ferry runs again in the morning."

Neal mused. I came to confirm Mitchell's whereabouts and I'm leaving with an unsolicited gem.

"Thank you, Patriot. You have been most kind."

***

Had the militia or Continentals ever doubted the resolve of Moravians to bear their share of the public burden in North Carolina, they believed when Salem's Board of Elders consented to host an ammunition laboratory. With one caveat. It had to be built away from the town. The boggy wasteland on the north bank of the Wach River seemed perfect.

Salem's founders named the river Wach. Far downstream in the village of Hope the English speaking Moravians translated it to Awake. The Wach drew the first Moravian settlers for its cool, clean drinking water. That it could provide a safe place to assemble musket cartridges was another sign of God's providence.

Bishop Graff spotted Abraham and George with stunned eyes. Yet it was true. The single brothers have returned. He could cement the marriage proposals of Abraham to Rahel and George to Maria.

I prayed to God to ask Him to help Salem and all of Wachovia in these troubled times and He heard me. This is His answer, for everything is an answer to our prayers. He sent our boys home. He will take the ammunition away from Salem. I asked for God's safety and He brought it.

As for their feelings toward George and Abraham, the Board swallowed their bitter anger when they read Gen Greene's letter begging for the release of the single brothers at the completion of the mission.

George Heider, Sr. invited to the meeting by Traugott Bach took the news as fate and neither damned young George nor took issue with Gen Greene or Col Armstrong.

Brother Samuel Stotz, however, raised his eyebrows and wrinkled his nose at the worldliness befalling Salem and its young people. That Salem was becoming a garrison and a target for Cornwallis meant the Savior's forgiveness had run out. He would judge the people soon.

***

On the first day, the Makers company went into the great untouched northern woods of the Wachovia tract and cut down three giant short leaf pines. The mill nearby on Town Fork Creek sawed the logs into planks. Later that night, to the mighty relief of the Salem townsfolk, the militia moved the gunpowder from the shed behind Salem Tavern to Brother Zillman's house.

Over the next two days Col Armstrong impressed wagons to haul planks south over twenty miles of poor roads to the building site. A frame grew in three days on the northern bank of the Wach between the Makers and extra labor from Salem single brothers who didn't run to the militia. Finished in the rain, the large laboratory would soon host cartridge-making.

***

Arthur Neal left Cornwallis' Loyalist dragoons in the woods at Shallow Ford and slipped into Salem where he planned to circle the town on horseback starting in the northeastern quarter at the end of Gemeinhaus Street.

"Gottesacker." A rough pronunciation of a sign had no sooner rolled off Neal's lips than he realized it meant God's Acre. He guided the horse over the sacred ground. Indistinct gravestones, each side the length of a forearm, dotted the ground. Drying spikes of Indian grass, lupine, and milkweed grew between the stones. Though the cemetery entranced Neal and delighted the horse, he left before turning maudlin.

Outside of the burial ground the wind howled as he rode west and south. Down in the lower part of Salem, expansive garden beds lay barren and flattened by the regimental tents of Surry militia away on maneuvers. In the next lot fruit trees stuck out their black skeletal branches waiting for spring.

Circling behind Salem Tavern and other buildings, eerily lifeless Salem impressed Neal as someone holding their tongue. The gunpowder was past news, so it had to be something else. Then, along the Wach in the far distance, he saw Zeb standing next to the large new building.

***

The Board of Elders, notwithstanding their suspicion of single brothers Abe and George and the outsiders who'd come with them, put the Makers up in Salem Tavern. While the laboratory was under construction, the men worked among single brothers at the site. When cartridge-making started, they would cross paths with single sisters.

At Salem Tavern, Rahel and Abraham met during the laboratory construction phase but refrained from speaking. Modesty had kept them from talking in public before and they remained tight-lipped in their reunion. Over the next few days they often spoke in public.

During a supper Sgt Vinyard noticed loud conversation at the Maker's table across the room whenever Rahel served them. Abe found Vinyard standing at the table beside him.

"Something wrong, Sergeant?"

"How come you're so chummy with the people in this town?"

"They like me."

"Sergeant, he speaks—"

"I didn't ask for your opinion, Private Mitchell."

"You said you're from the Stinking Quarter."

Abe measured his response. "The people of Salem and Stinking Quarter are German. Here people feel comfortable hearing me speak the language."

Vinyard felt Abe was fibbing. "Well, remember, we're here on militia business."

The two-shilling supper of roasted venison, stewed apples, bread, and cider had recommenced without Vinyard's company when a heated conversation erupted across the room at a table in front of the hearth. Zeb looked over his shoulder. Traugott Bach was arguing with the man who'd haunted the gunpowder wagon driven by George and Abe.

The stranger's back was to the fire. Bach ignored him but the stranger grabbed his sleeve and made him stop drinking beer.

"Let go, swine. You're not a salt merchant. I doubt Arthur Neal is your real name."

Bach's tormentor begged in a deceitful, drunk voice. "What's wrong?"

Bach pulled free and stood. "State your business and leave Salem." From Bach's new perspective, orange flames spiraled and whirled behind Neal's head and shoulders.

"You won't be getting any wagons from the New Garden wainwright in a long time," Neal said.

Zeb froze. A knife and fork jutted from his fists resting on the table and his eyes crossed as he listened.

Bach returned a look of surprise. "What happened?"

"His shop was destroyed by Loyalists."

Bach exploded over the gleam in Neal's eyes. "Take your cold blood out of my town!"

***

The Makers trudged upstairs and drew straws for the privilege of bunking two to a single bed. Zeb, having no stomach for games, didn't participate and slept with the losers on the floor where vermin visited them in the night, drawn to the smell of food arising from the snoring mouths. Zeb wouldn't have known had they not aroused him from shallow sleep. He watched them in moonlight streaming through the window. They skittered on the wooden floor and fought over morsels stuck on the men's clothes.

# Thirty ~ The Benefactor

— December 6, 1780, Camp New Providence, Charlotte Town

Maj Gen Greene leaned over a small iron stove filled with hot coals, rubbing his hands. His head turned to avoid the asthma-inducing smoke. After a quick lunch he warmed his hands again before reading the daily commissary record.

Developed during the New Jersey battles, learning how well his soldiers ate became a habit to sense their morale, not to mention their health. They weren't getting enough daily rations in Camp New Providence.

The army allowed troops one pound of bread per day in camp or three-and-a-half cups of flour or cornmeal on the march. Actual portions halved that and, whether leavened with brewer's yeast, pearlash, or not at all, too little bread made an incomplete meal.

Rum rations were equally crucial to a mess meal. Troops call it kill devil for a half gill brings heaven to their minds. So too having something to toast the other five men in their mess unit raised their spirits. If the two ounces a day didn't come, they'd leave the security of camp to obtain it.

Greene had written every military and government official begging for supplies of everything. Words can leverage only so much. Neither portraying his command as the most wretched nor making outright demands made a difference. Shortages of food and everything else stole his mind from conducting the army.

From Charlotte Town, potential benefactors in the war-stricken state ranged three-days or less by stagecoach. Greene hoped the imploring letter written to North Carolina Governor Abner Nash during the ride from Richmond to Hillsborough would get attention. Four days into his command, he received word Nash, the second executive of the free constitutional government in the state, was on his way.

***

Gen Gates apprised Greene of Nash's charmed life. "He grew rich with a mill in Hillsborough and used his fortune to oppose the King at the start of the Rebellion. Shots at Lexington and Concord still resounding, Nash and others ran off Governor Josiah Martin in 1775.

"When I came to North Carolina in 1780, Governor Nash had a cache of arms and provisions waiting. When Camden fell, the Governor began a campaign to rebuild the lost stockpile."

***

Aide de camp Maj Ichabod Burnet announced Abner Nash at Nathanael Greene's marquee. The governor set a wooden valise on the straw covered floor and offered his hand. He attempted to show Greene a genial manner amid the chancy Rebellion but the general saw a dispirited, feeble man.

"I haven't been at full strength and working from sunrise until late by the light of an oil lamp to answer your needs is taking a toll."

It was easy for the general to associate Nash's anxiety with South Carolina's precipitous fall after the Patriot defeat at Camden. Nash must have seen the gaunt soldiers on his way to the general's tent. How Greene would get help from the weakened governor was impossible to know.

"How can I help you?"

Aghast that Nash dared ask the question, Greene recited the speech he'd been giving in written appeals.

"My knowledge in the art of war is small. But were my abilities and experience much greater, I could exert to no advantage without men and supplies. A general without an army, or an army without supplies, can give no protection to the country. You and the North Carolina legislature must lay the foundation for your own security. On your exertions your political existence depends."

Nash hugged himself wishing to be closer to the stove. Rubbing his torso and arms would have to suffice. Still, Greene's reply got his attention. "Whatever force is committed to North Carolina will have my full support."

"We need fresh and salted meat, flour, and rum. Our bellies are empty."

As if to underscore the Southern army's plight, a soldier's woeful plea rose as he paced outside Greene's marquee. The commander of the Southern army and Gov Nash listened to the soldier's plaint.

"Two Continental dollars for one hoecake of bread! Two Continental dollars for one hoecake of bread!"

"Two Continental dollars for one hoecake of bread. Four years ago, one Continental dollar would have purchased twenty hoecakes. Worse than that, Governor, cornmeal can't be found."

Greene debated using a fresh letter from Gen Washington warning of a possible landing of the British army on North Carolina's coast to deepen his appeal. The debate was short. If Greene were ready to lead himself and his men into battle, then using a little deception on the governor was fair. He leaned in until his cocked hat touched Nash's forehead and whispered.

"I've received confidential information from a reliable source."

"You don't say."

"From a person employed by the Marquis de Lafayette who speaks from his own knowledge—"

To fuel the drama Greene shushed and rolled his eyes across the tent. Nash stopped rubbing his shivering torso and rolled his eyes in concert.

"Royal navy troop ships just left New York."

"Enough to transport an army?"

"Indeed, sir. A battalion each of British and Hessian Grenadiers and a regiment each of British Light Infantry and Infantry. A total of twenty-five hundred men." The major general halted and waited for the governor to beg the crucial question.

"Well? Where are they heading?"

"The destination, the informant says, is kept a secret, but suspects it to be southward."

"That's unwelcome news."

"What's more, Governor, I have another account that Major General Alexander Leslie is landing at Cape Fear."

Nash turned white. "Not Charles Town?"

"No. All public property upon your seacoast and all the horses and cattle of the country and rum, salt, clothing, and provisions of all kinds should be removed to the interior at once."

"Interior meaning Charlotte Town?"

"Yes, Governor."

Nash fought a smile. His cheeks turned rosy. "I know two reasons why you shouldn't count on it."

Greene interrupted. He sensed the governor would claim a journey from Cape Fear to Charlotte Town too far, so he framed it in two legs. "Cross Creek is a one-hundred mile jaunt on a flat boat up the Cape Fear River. From there, it's but a one-hundred-forty mile ride over land to Charlotte Town."

"Too distant. That's the first reason."

Greene frowned, imagining all the horses, cattle, rum, salt, and clothing that wouldn't come to the interior of the country and was miles away when Nash started speaking.

"The second reason is the state of North Carolina has come into a godsend."

Greene scooted to the edge of his seat. "I'm waiting."

"Soon after General Gates lost Camden, a privateer called *General Nash*, captured two English brigs off Ocracoke Island and ordered them up the Cape Fear River. The cargoes including rum and sugar are worth £50,800."

Greene erupted into a huge smile. "Rum?"

"Yes. Enough kill devil to keep your men in good spirits for the better part of a month."

"Dear Governor Nash! Kill devil, grog, or demon water. Whatever you call it, soldiers need it to tolerate conditions like what you heard outside this tent. Such good news!"

"In October three more brigs fell."

Greene grabbed a pair of iron tongs and pushed the heater near Nash. "I've not heard of these prizes!"

"Subscribe to *New Lloyd's List*, sir!" Nash warmed his hands. "I wrote to Lieutenant General Washington yesterday how privateers have also troubled the enemy off the coast of Charles Town. During this summer river boats of men took everything that came their way."

Greene burst into laughter. He rose and limped to a drinking chest and pulled two small tumblers and a bottle of rum.

"May I offer something, sir?"

Nash removed a bottle of red wine from his case. "Let's open one of the many bottles of port found on one of the brigs."

"Amazing, Governor."

They raised their glasses.

"May our privateers forever have such magnificent designs!"

Gov Nash put the port to his lips and swallowed the pleasing liquid before exclaiming. "Also, the Marquis de Bretigny reached New Bern bringing four-hundred stands of arms including pistols, saddles, accoutrements, and forty-two barrels of powder."

Would Washington's privateers relieve the gunpowder shortage? "You're answering my prayers, dear Governor."

"I'm afraid, when Captain Daniel Deshon of the General Nash conveyed his prizes to Ocracoke and Old Topsail, the manifests listed no uniforms or shoes."

"What then?"

Nash unfolded a list of the privateer hauls. "£10,800 prime lots sterling, three-hundred barrels of flour, a large quantity of bottled porter and claret, one-hundred and fifty hampers of cheese, a large quantity of teas, rum, sugar, fruit, all sorts of dry goods, hardware, old horse saddlery, three-hundred-fifty bolts of canvas, and a large quantity of osnaburgs."

"My God! Osnaburg."

Nash sneered. "Osnaburg is sackcloth."

"Have you seen my ragged men?"

"We'll have flour, rum, and arms in hand and money to buy uniforms, shoes, and salt when they're available."

"Deliver the uniforms when you get them. I'll have the sackcloth made into clothes."

"Everything is under guard. Transport depends on the availability of wagons. Actually, we're driving beeves and horses to safe places in this upcountry. Don't refrain from foraging the land if you must."

"I've never been ashamed of eating off the land."

Nash handed Greene the paper.

Greene glanced at the list. "Are you promising everything listed to the army?"

"Yes, with the exception of two glasses of port." Nash knocked his back and set the glass down. He threw a grin at the general. "May I beg your complete candor."

"What for?"

"Your skillful begging."

"I'm telling the truth."

Nash observed Greene's two chins. Either his neck cloth came up a bit too high or the man's flesh exceeded the normal. "Perhaps you've decorated it."

Greene winced. "Perhaps."

"You have the art of compelling others to do their duty. Trust me, I won't betray your confidence."

Greene had met few people who had the audacity to critique his methods. "I apprehended early in my career not to claim my supplies satisfactory. Otherwise, my troops would have run out. The militia on Breed's Hill—"

"The Siege of Boston?" Nash said.

"That's right. Lacking a small supply of powder and lead, they ceded the hill."

"To be without is one thing. It's another matter to have it offered in exchange for a fortune."

"The men on Breed's Hill would have paid a fortune."

"Yes, but it reminds me of a North Carolina merchant who won a lucrative contract from the state to supply ammunition."

"I apprehend you're referring to the Moravian."

"He had no legal rights to sell me my own gunpowder, though he's skilled at asserting moral obligations to authorities in states of peril."

"We need the gunpowder."

"He portrays himself as a humble servant doing the state favors."

"What would you have him do?"

"Use persuasion. You seem to have good rhetoric for showing your destitution."

"I didn't pay that hungry man to walk by my marquee hollering."

"Why aren't you doing any better at this? You should have all the supplies you want."

"Claiming poverty doesn't bring supplies."

"We're in a war. To not meet your needs is immoral."

"It's not that simple. You heard the boy crying for bread. Merchants can neither profit from our worthless money nor pay it to the producers."

***

After the governor left, the major general considered the haul's significance. He calculated the flour and rum could see the army through thirty days of rations. Too little time for the Continentals to prepare for Cornwallis.

As for the beeves, he hoped for them because the confiscated brigs had yielded neither stores of salted beef and pork nor peas and beans, the other mainstays of the army diet.

Greene called Maj Burnet and dictated a letter to Lt Col Edward Carrington, the new Quartermaster. "Sir: We will soon be in possession of a large quantity of osnaburg. I want you to engage the women of the country to make shirts and overalls for the soldiers. Pay them in salt if you cannot do better. Finish sewing the camp's tents with three-hundred and fifty bolts of canvas coming. You know the distresses of the soldiery, and I flatter myself you will make every effort to follow my orders. I am your humble servant &c, Nathanael Greene."

# Thirty-One ~ Ammunition

— December 9, 1780, Salem

Doom pounded Zeb Mitchell's forehead. As the news of his stepfather's ambush taunted his thoughts, sleep came when he admitted he could do nothing. When the tavern cock crowed, visions of the attack resumed.

Maybe opening my eyes in the light of morning is for the best, to keep them occupied with real sights so my mind will be powerless to conjure the unreal. Can I be so daft as to believe I could start the day without the questions coming?

Why was the shop destroyed? Did the Loyalists learn the militia pressed his stepfather's wagons into service? While bothersome, the questions never asked how Zeb felt.

How could I have deserted my father and family? Were they hurt? What will happen to them? If we win this war, will it have been at the expense of our families and values?

Zeb abhorred the consequences of his actions, depressed that he couldn't turn back the calendar and walk out of the induction center before swearing the oath. Besides the Quaker objection to violence, he abandoned other Rules of Discipline. He should have maintained universal love and goodwill and exercised tender care over his stepfather. Why hadn't he guarded against weakening the bond of Christian brotherhood?

The boys in the company are dressing. Half want to eat right away, and the others want to wash first. None of us have a change of clothes. Pathetic. We're too polite to say it aloud, but never can we deny our bodies smell as awful as the decadent notions we have around the Moravian ladies. What's the use of bathing?

Upstairs, Zeb didn't see Arthur Neal nor did he appear in the dining room. He gobbled a bowl of porridge and slurped a cup of hot, sweet tea before going to the tavern yard to groom the horses.

The gaunt stable boy had fed the team corn and filled the water trough. He'd been pounding a meager portion of blue and gold kernels into meal between rocks but froze at the sound of steps. Zeb offered a hunk of bread. The boy grabbed it with a dirty hand and shoved it in his mouth.

Zeb dug gear out of the wagon toolbox and threw himself into grooming the horses. One at a time, he picked stones from their hooves and checked their shoes. The four gentle beasts rubbed their noses against him as he combed their manes and brushed their coats. Satisfied with his work, he smiled at having been free of worry the whole time.

***

During the course of building and working at the laboratory, the Makers traveled along Bethabara Road between Salem Tavern on the town's high ground and the site in the valley. Moravians long ago cleared the dense wilderness. The smooth, sloping land exhibited the sophisticated cultivation of plantations, grazing lots, and pens rolling to the River Wach.

Once, on their ride from the tavern to the laboratory, the Makers halted their wagons while Brother Johann Stockburger sent his cattle across Bethabara Road to an upper pasture. One of the boys recited talk overheard in the tavern that Stockburger had asked a non-Moravian man to lend him money without notifying congregation officials. Bach and Graff would decry Stockburger's scandalous behavior.

The Makers didn't seem to be interested in that particular story, but another disobedient act pricked their ears. Stockburger had a late summer corn-shucking and invited teen Moravians. Town fathers told him he must not do it again for there was danger of frivolity. Though unsaid, the Makers got the impression a mingling of single brothers and single sisters at the event had led to conversations between the sexes.

Preoccupation in Salem and across the land with keeping the sexes apart to prevent hurt and danger, secret connections, and engagements of marriage made without proper order was unmistakable. When it comes to his cattle, Stockburger doesn't buck the elders. He keeps his heifers and cows separate from the bulls, lest offspring arrive out of season.

***

Belabored with a father's concern, Bach worried the Makers company would linger at the finished laboratory. Col Armstrong promised that once he taught the single sisters the methods of rolling cartridges, he— not the young Makers—would supervise them. The colonel assured Bach the Makers wouldn't mix with the single sisters. The young ladies would not leave his sight until the company left for Charlotte Town.

Before starting a tutoring session, the colonel set up an array of wooden non-sparking dowels, funnels, spoons, and spatulas on the table nearest the laboratory door. He poured small black grains of gunpowder the size of the coarsest cornmeal from a barrel into a powder horn using a funnel.

One by one, he recited each step and paused. While Maria translated, he demonstrated the method and moved on to the next one.

"Sisters, I've cut old news sheets into pieces shaped like the side of a saltbox. Start with the long end and roll it around a wooden dowel the diameter of a lead ball. Leave a little paper past the end of the dowel."

Meanwhile, George and Abe cast lead balls on the travelling forge. Armstrong stuck his head out of the door and called Abe.

"Bring me the balls you've made so far."

Armstrong carried a wooden box of lead balls to the work table.

"Crimp the excess paper against the end of the dowel and dip it into the pan of melted tallow and beeswax to make a good seal. Take the dowel out, insert a lead ball, pour in gunpowder leaving two inches of the tube unfilled. Twist the end and seal it. Do you understand?"

The single sisters nodded. One pointed to the black grains. Maria Bach translated the question. "Is it dangerous?"

"This powder lying on a table without a fuse won't explode. However, it can burn fast. If there's a fire, file out with calm."

The single sisters went to work under the meagre light of candle-lanterns hanging on the walls. The flurry of their nimble fingers added up as production numbers accumulated and stacks of pine crates filled with cartridges mounted at the end of the long room. Col Armstrong often checked the constitution of the cartridges by ordering militiamen to fire rounds into woods across the Wach.

***

Quartermaster Lt Col Carrington rode into Salem on horseback. He dismounted outside the laboratory and lay prostrate on the ground.

"Are you okay?" Armstrong said.

Carrington opened his eyes and sat up. "Tired. I've been on horseback the past four days. As soon as your party left Charlotte Town, I headed to Irwin's and Boyd's ferries on the Dan River. Charlotte Town to Virginia to Salem is three-hundred and fifty miles."

"What did you find?"

"The ferries are operating well."

"I reckon militia forces are mustering up there."

"You apprehend well. General Greene ordered me to find a way to get the cartridges to safety at Halifax Court House in Virginia and look for barns and sheds suitable for magazines."

Armstrong invited Carrington into the laboratory. The quartermaster gazed at the stack of ammunition boxes. "That's all?"

"The rest are in the gunpowder magazine. Three times a day we send finished ammunition to the magazine and bring powder back to the laboratory."

"This is taking longer than I thought it would."

"We're doing the best we can. Give us another week."

Carrington stood and stretched. "Alright. I beg of you to secure wagons to haul this ammunition northward. Put teams on grain. It's a long, hard journey. They'll need strengthening."

"How soon do you reckon to haul it to Halifax?"

"I don't apprehend it will be soon with Cornwallis still repairing in South Carolina. You never know, so best be ready."

***

Traugott Bach and Col Armstrong stood outside the laboratory. They watched Private Zeb Mitchell put an empty barrel on a wagon.

"Wait a minute, Private Mitchell," Armstrong said. He caught Bach's eyes. "We need to do something with the empty barrels."

Bach's eyes fixed on the empty barrel. "I can sell them off."

Single Sisters Yohanna and Rahel approached the laboratory to begin their shift. Zeb balanced the barrel on his shoulder and tipped his hat, paying particular attention to Yohanna's fancying eyes. To glimpse her up close soothed his heart. Her nearness brought palpitations.

Yohanna empathized with Zeb's frustration holding the barrel and appealed to Bach. "The barrel must be heavy. Isn't it filled with soil?"

"Why would it be filled with soil?"

"So that it won't bounce off the wagon."

"My dear Sister Yohanna, the barrels will be secured under canvas and rope."

Rahel folded her arms and hung her head in boredom. She panned from the wagon of empty barrels to the wagon of fresh barrels and grinned. "The full and empty barrels are identical."

"What's going on?" Armstrong said.

After Bach summarized the conversation in English, he and the colonel watched Abe and George heft an untapped barrel of gunpowder into the laboratory.

"Privates, when you're done," Armstrong said, "unload the empty barrels and fill them with soil."

Bach put on a show of agitation. "Huh? Why?"

Armstrong returned a sly face. "A bandit won't know them from the real thing."

Bach shrugged.

# Thirty-Two ~ Longing to Return

— December 15, 1780, Wynnesborough, South Carolina

Safely back in South Carolina, Lt Gen Lord Charles Cornwallis lay submerged up to his neck in a tin tub warmed by a hearth fire. The lord's shaved head rested on a small pillow attached to the back of the tub. A horse hair wig powdered in flour and jasmine talc rested on a wax dummy head in a cool corner.

The lord shut his eyes and pondered the state of war in the South. Built for battle, the British army thought nothing of lining up across from their adversary and fighting. Cornwallis itched for true battle. Yet after Gates' ill-conceived decision to fight at Camden, getting the aching Continentals and their new general to meet on the battlefield looked impossible.

A hornet's nest of insurgents chased the British commander out of North Carolina before the first invasion had gotten above Charlotte Town. Given no peaceful interlude by the Americans, the lord found the Continentals neither ready to accept a battlefield challenge nor quit their stinging attacks.

The lord regretted not planting the King's standard across the border. It wouldn't have restored order but it may have dared the Rebels to challenge him on the field and given the British resolve to stay and defend it. As for a recruiting symbol, it couldn't have done any worse acquiring Loyalists than Col Arthur Neal.

Cornwallis would give Maj Gen Greene little time. If the Continental commander of the South wouldn't appoint troops to the battleground soon, the lord would have no choice but to invade again, plant the standard, and pursue him.

Brig Gen Benedict Arnold had taken command of a magazine-destroying mission in Virginia, allowing Maj Gen Alexander Leslie to reinforce Cornwallis. Leslie hadn't landed at Cape Fear as rumored but at Charles Town and was marching north with a force of fifteen-hundred men to join the lord.

The British would have their day and invade North Carolina a second time. The lord couldn't stop ammunition production in Salem or prevent Patriot troops getting back on their feet. It was time for the British to employ their current advantage. The lord would soon put South Carolina behind him and hope it stayed locked down.

While waiting on Leslie, Cornwallis acquired daily intelligence of the enemy and the nature of the country in the vicinity of his army. Local scouts lined up to take British specie for information about the state of the roads and provisions from the Wateree River ten miles east and to the Broad River ten miles west.

***

The water quaked as Cornwallis sat up in the tub and called Lt Col Banastre Tarleton and aide-de-camp Capt Henry Broderick to the bathing room.

"How can I get the Continentals onto the battlefield?" Cornwallis said.

"Unleash Loyalist dogs on the heels of the Rebel people and they'll implore the Continentals and militia to stand and do battle."

"What Loyalist dogs? Haven't you noticed our efforts to recruit are going nowhere?"

"My Lord, let me pursue the Rebel forces and cut them to pieces."

"Your foes ever bleed, but now is not the time to detach you."

The Lt Col eyed Cornwallis. "What is the remedy, my Lord?" Cornwallis didn't answer straight away. After an uneasy gap of silence Tarleton smiled as an inkling of the general's plan emerged in his mind. "With my forces combined with Leslie's you'll be unmatched. Take no caution, my Lord. Put the Rebels on defense."

Cornwallis sneered. "Think of an action less impetuous for once. Recall the effect of Sir Henry Clinton's proclamation in South Carolina."

"A profound effect, my Lord. All around Charles Town substantial numbers under the direction of the late Major Ferguson fell in line to defend us."

Cornwallis wiped sweat from his face with a hand towel. "His Majesty's colonials loathe involvement in this war. By prodding they often feel compelled to return to their—"

"Senses?"

"No, allegiance. Don't interrupt me. To return to their allegiance and manifest their loyalty by joining the King's troops."

"What will you do, my Lord?"

"Return to North Carolina and erect the King's standard. I'll circulate a proclamation amongst the inhabitants inviting them…Broderick, write this down."

Broderick put a fresh sheet of paper on a mahogany lap desk and inked a quill. "Ready, my Lord."

Cornwallis soaped a rag and scoured his back. He formulated a statement behind a pensive face. "Whereas it has pleased the divine providence to prosper the operations of His Majesty's arms in driving the Rebel army out of this province…I do hereby assure them I am ready to concur with them in effectual measures for suppressing the remains of rebellion in the North Carolina province, and for the reestablishment of good order and British constitutional government."

"My Lord," Broderick said, "would you like a copy suitable for posting?"

"Copy! I want two-dozen copies."

Broderick sighed in mock death.

"We have a letter press, idiot! Give it to the printer and come right back. I want you to write the General's Orders."

Cornwallis rolled in the tub like a child, creating waves. He looked for Tarleton's reaction. "Don't you admire the utility of the rivers of the Southern Colonies for conveying supplies to the interior?"

"Yes, my Lord. But the Partisans made them dangerous in South Carolina. If we could navigate North Carolina's rivers, you might love them."

"Nelson's Ferry was quite a disaster."

"I prefer fords for crossing rivers," said Tarleton.

"You say that now after the 'swamp fox' ambushed my ammunition convoy at that ferry."

"Fords are just as good or better than ferries and more plentiful. I've never seen rivers in South Carolina that we couldn't cross at wagon and horse fords. Why waste time loading and unloading boats?"

Cornwallis held up a saturated sponge. "Indeed, during hot weather, water that might have deepened the channels stayed in the sultry air."

"That's behind us. With winter rains, crossing points will be deeper everywhere."

Cornwallis squeezed the sponge. Broderick returned to the humid room.

"I gave the print order, my Lord. Ready to write General's Orders."

Cornwallis dictated as soon as the aide-de-camp nodded. "All replacement soldiers and those convalescing from wounds, smallpox, and general fever must rejoin their regiments. Regimental officers are to order supplies of arms, ammunition, and accoutrements necessary for battle. Examine the ammunition. Dry out any wet supplies on blankets at a considerable distance from fires."

"Sorry, my Lord. Your words after 'blankets' escaped me."

"Dried on blankets at a considerable distance from fires. Return damaged rounds to the supply depot. At that point each soldier will be issued enough musket cartridges to make sixty." Cornwallis rose from the water. "How are you doing?"

Broderick inked the quill, finished the sentence, and inked again. "Ready, my Lord."

"Collect and purchase enough horses to mount the cavalry and pull the wagons during the expedition. Fit the clothing of your brigades and dress your battalions as uniform as possible." Cornwallis watched Broderick writing and reinking the quill.

"Put the Camden miller on notice to lay in an amount of threshed wheat to supply four day's needs of flour."

"Anything else, my Lord?"

Water dripped from Cornwallis' pink, shriveled body as he stood in the tub. "Hand me that towel." The Lord patted his face but stopped when the sound of rain tapping on the headquarters roof surpassed the water tinkling into the tub. "What do the scouts predict for the weather?"

"Naught but rain until mid-January."

Never did the Lord suffer news worse. He lowered himself into the water and closed his eyes. Cornwallis rose after five minutes. "You have my orders. Now, go communicate them to the King's officers. First, tell the printer to cool the press."

***

ADC Broderick crept into the printing room. One case of relief type occupied a shelf above the bench and another sat behind the chase the printer was loading. Setting the last line of the proclamation, the printer gathered capital letters from the upper case and small letters from the lower case. Meanwhile his devil grasped the handles of two leather-covered balls coated with soot and oil waiting for the finished chase.

Broderick's sorrowful face loomed. "What! Don't tell me the lord wants revisions. I'm almost done."

"He wants to cancel it."

"Do you know the work it took me to set this proclamation?" The printer's face twisted. He loosened the chase and let the metal type rain onto the bench. "What made the lord decide against the proclamation?"

"Drops of water falling from his pink body."

"Huh?"

"My guess is the lord doesn't see Loyalists flocking to the King's standard in all this rain. What difference would a proclamation make?"

***

Broderick dispatched the lord's orders to the officers. Fresh clothes and wig donned Cornwallis as he opened a message from Col Arthur Neal offering more proof of the gunpowder supply in Salem: "Soldiers built a shelter away from Salem town then often for the next week fired many musket volleys to proof their cartridges. I was on the other side of the woods and they gave me no peace."

So, they're making ammunition. That means the Rebels have a supply of lead. Good. They're stronger. I hope they chance general warfare so we can move closer to victory.

Cornwallis read further: "The Loyalist provincial horsemen positioned to watch the entrance to Salem have seen no signs of the ammunition leaving."

There's hope. If that fool had attacked with his small force, the Continentals might have spirited the ammunition to safety and used it against me.

# Thirty-Three ~ Detour

— December 17, 1780, Salem

The Makers' mission completed, they drove to Salem Tavern to pack their belongings and feed the horses.

Zeb fell into daydreaming. What did he know about the "salt merchant" Arthur Neal? Had Neal witnessed the violence or committed it? Only a Loyalist would destroy a shop making wagons needed by Patriots. How is my family coping? I'm killing myself with these questions. Only with my eyes and ears will I get answers.

Zeb asked Sgt Vinyard if they could divert to pick up a wagon at his stepfather's wainwright shop. Vinyard put the question to Capt Hawkins.

"Do you apprehend Private Mitchell will follow through?"

"Mitchell can be trusted to gain a well-needed wagon."

"Permission granted. Muster the men outside the tavern in a half hour. We're going to the laboratory to gather our tools and take nourishment before travelling." Hawkins opened the tavern door, heading to Bach's store to buy ink and paper. He stopped and turned. "Have your men load my trunk before I get back."

***

"Zeb Mitchell. Zeb. Zebulon?" Abe gave up and left the Quaker to his thoughts.

The ride to the laboratory had stirred Zeb to distant reflections in the cargo box behind Abe and George. Arthur Neal seeped into his head. No, Zeb. Arthur Neal isn't the one who should fill your mind.

Zeb came out of his musing when they arrived at the laboratory. He watched the single sisters carry platters and bowls of food and jugs of milk and cider into the laboratory.

Yohanna admired him and his heart panged knowing the spark between them persisted. He'd miss her company. When this Revolution ceases, I'll marry her smile and gorgeous eyes!

***

The Makers set off on the road to New Garden. Abe held the reins beside George. Among the wooden crates of tools and the Makers' sundry belongings, Zeb sat wrapped in a blanket behind the driver's seat. In the warm and comfortable place amid the dim light and rocking wagon he fell asleep.

Maria Bach sat in the back of the wagon. The hinges of Hawkins' trunk screeched as she opened it looking for writing materials.

Zeb snapped awake and glimpsed Maria through a gap in the crates holding the copies of Neal's coded letter and key.

Zeb parted the crates. "Maria! What are you doing? By what rights did you choose to stow away?"

"The same rights my father and Colonel Armstrong chose to put the single sisters to work rolling musket cartridges. The same rights you, George, and Abraham assumed when you ran to the militia."

"Don't yell at me. It's not my fault." Zeb hung his head but soon gazed into Maria's eyes. "I beg to apologize, Maria. Loyalists destroyed my stepfather's shop. You may apprehend my distress."

"George told me the news. I'm sorry. What will you do?"

"Go to New Garden and check on my family."

"Who would destroy a wagon shop?"

"Arthur Neal." Zeb eyed the packed cargo box where Maria squirmed for room between trunks and a jumble of items. Black iron tripods, skillets, kettles, Dutch ovens, spoons, forks, knives, ladles, bowls, candles, sewing boxes, blankets, towels, and rags and scraps of linen and cotton.

Two familiar Moravians leaned their heads around the pile of goods. Rahel and Yohanna, themselves jammed in a mire of goods, threw modest smiles. Rays of light found a way through gaps in the canvas covering the wagon and danced in the latter's eyes. Zeb let the issue of Arthur Neal slip away as his hope and confidence soared.

***

At New Garden his stepfather's bruises and the wainwright shop destruction broke Zeb's heart. He shouldn't have been surprised that below his purple and yellow face Michael McMurray's outlook on the world was never more sanguine.

The Makers helped the shop workers rebuild the waterwheel and the main gear. Zeb and his stepfather sat on a workbench chatting. The shop crew and the Makers joined them.

"I have a spare wagon if you promise to return it when the war is over."

"Thank you, father."

"Don't thank me."

"You're doing a generous thing."

"To repay the kindness you all have shown."

"We felt sorry for you."

McMurray shook his head. "I don't need your pity or your Revolution."

Zeb lowered his eyes. Silence cut a two-minute gorge between him and his father. He stirred and studied the shop. "Did Arthur Neal bring this ruin?"

"A group of ruffians on horse came. The leader didn't identify himself."

"Was he of average height, barrel-bellied, and ruddy-skinned? Wheezing like a—"

"Bellows?"

"Yes."

"His left eye trembled. His general restlessness reminded me of a bee."

"That's uncanny. I thought the same thing. He appeared all of a sudden in Salem in plain dress."

"These all wore green jackets. Rather impulsive and aggressive men."

Sara cleared her throat. "Sorry to interrupt. Would you like tea and bread?"

"Yes, of course. Thank you, dear Sister. How long have you been outside the door?"

Sara trembled. "Long enough to hear Arthur Neal enter your conversation." She stuck her head out the door. "Come in ladies."

Sara's left arm wriggled for all to see until she forced it against her waist. She held a tray of cups pressed against her right side. Was it for balance or to calm her nervousness? Maria, Rahel, and Yohanna followed with trays of bread and butter and more cups and a kettle of steaming tea. Their mouths gaped at the destruction.

Zeb hung his head at the shock of the Moravian women, ashamed for having felt less surprised. "My God, I feel guilty."

"Examine your conscience," McMurray said. "That's all I ask of you."

"I feel as if I pointed you out to Arthur Neal. I can do nothing until my three-month enlistment is up."

McMurray shook his head. "Don't do any violence in my name."

"Perhaps the militia can do something. They've been going after Loyalists."

McMurray returned to restoring the shop without another word. The shop craftsmen and Makers followed his example.

Zeb finished his tea and bread and put the cup on a tray. "Father's amazing. He's worn the destruction of his shop well."

Sara remained to pick up the odd cup while Maria, Rahel and Yohanna went to the house with the other trays. She set her wobbling tray down each time to gather an empty cup, not risking all the cups to fall. She rounded the shop and came back to him. "He agonizes over the injuries to the shop, not his bruises."

Zeb recalled a meeting for coming of age Quaker boys when the minister told them of marital vows which committed a couple with divine assistance unto each other in loving, obedient, and faithful marriage in spiritual as well as secular concerns until separated in death. "Does she still talk to father?"

"Their marriage is fine, my brother. Mother advised him to rebuild and strive to be different."

"Different in what way?"

"He takes the ruin of the shop as a reminder to deny all ungodliness and lusts. He admitted to the wasteful practice of owning a half-dozen of every tool when two or three would suffice. It bothers him that the economics of the shop wasn't meant to sustain and enrich the life of all working in it."

"I never thought father would consider them as equals. Not just Quakers work here."

"Don't make fun of him. He seeks to share his rewards. It's what you wanted."

"I wanted him to support the Revolution and thereby save his business." Zeb meditated. When he opened his eyes, his guilt lingered. If father can discard greed, why can't I stop shaming him? "Sorry, I need to put immaturity behind me."

"He's frightened of what's happening to his world."

"I see that now."

Zeb showed Sara the Salem laboratory plan, unfurling it like one of the newfangled folded maps coming into use.

"You fool!" She refolded the crisp paper using her side as a second hand. "You're meant to be a wainwright making the finest wagons in the Carolinas. You've exchanged craftsmanship for rough-hewn carpentry. Come home and work with father. You belong with your family."

"I'll return home in three months."

"Why did you come home now? Guilt? To apologize?"

He gazed at her, reluctant to speak.

She took his hands in hers. "Pay me no mind, Brother. You have your own life."

"Your worry is well-taken. You must understand I've missed you. Believe me." Zeb hugged Sara and backed away to admire her. Brightness came into his eyes. "When we return to Camp New Providence, will you come with us?"

"Would you want me along?"

"Of course, Sara."

"I'd go with you to camp but—"

She laced her fingers to arrest the anxiety that had gripped her and she caught him eyeing her shaking.

"Dear Sister, the attack has unnerved you."

She noted his pained eyes. "I'd love to serve but I'd be worthless as a camp follower."

"Are you out of your mind? I never wanted you to be a mere camp follower. You could help in a myriad of ways."

She rescued him from turning into a bigger, fawning fool. "I want to stay at home with mother and father. Give me time and I'll find my purpose."

Her internal strength revealed itself. He was sapped for words.

"Until then, there's nothing I can do."

"Don't pressure yourself, Sister."

Sara's left hand wavered. She picked up the heavy tray with her right hand and it tilted. A cup slid off and broke among the debris left by the Loyalist rampage.

"There's nothing I can do that doesn't break something."

***

At Camp New Providence, the lady Patriots made a love feast for the Makers. They couldn't wait until Christmas day next week. Rumors said Gen Greene was restless. Who knew where they'd be or what they'd be doing on the holy day?

Zeb's eyes glazed in awe hearing his Moravian companions sing a hymn to baby Jesus.

Maria and George and Rahel and Abe coupled around the campfire. Yohanna and Zeb sat apart.

"Maria," Zeb said, "today I watched you labor at the cooking fire. You and Rahel and Yohanna have exerted yourselves with love. I'm so thankful."

"This little spread? It's nothing compared to the lovefeasts the single sisters prepare throughout the year."

"Let's see," Yohanna said via Maria's translation. "There's Christmas, Easter, congregation festivals, welcomes, farewells, and on and on."

Maria gave Zeb a perplexed stare. "Haven't you ever sat at your mother's feet while she spun yarn or sewed?"

"It's been a while since I've given her work much attention."

"You need to know more of her worth."

Zeb stole a momentary return gaze at Yohanna. He recoiled thinking someone might spy his lust and moved his view from her eyes to her bonnet. "I see you got too close to the cooking fire."

Yohanna threw Zeb and Maria an inquiring sweep of her eyes. Maria translated.

"You singed your cap ribbon."

Yohanna winked at Rahel and Maria and told them how she could fix the problem. Rahel's eyes bulged and Maria gave Zeb a gentle smile.

"What did she say?" Zeb said.

Maria handed Zeb a hot drink and giggled. "She hopes to soon exchange the pink ribbon of a Single Sister for the light blue of a Married Sister."

Zeb's face reddened and he avoided the awkward moment by slurping from the steaming mug. When he recovered from burning lips and throat, he changed the subject. "I've never had this before."

"You wouldn't as you're a Quaker. It's coffee, nothing plain or moderate to conform with your beliefs."

"My tongue apprehends that. It's light brown, but what a nutty and delicious brew."

Zeb reflected on the new camp followers. Unlike the typical pathetic women in Camp New Providence, the lady Patriots of Salem stood strong in their own right while offering heartfelt company and practical support. Their presence was more than a selfless sacrifice to the war cause. Yohanna's presence gave him an additional effect which he felt in his loins.

***

Capt Hawkins neared a row of fire pits where his company lolled in the night. He fathomed music and espied the celebration. Jealousy pulled his eyes to the mixed singing. He huffed all the way to his tent where he found his trunk. Upon searching it, he ordered Sgt Vinyard to assemble the Quaker and the two Moravians.

Hawkins stirred before Vinyard, Zebulon, Abraham, and George standing at attention. "How could you be so stupid and errant? Your foolish adventure across the country exposed the militia."

The Makers offered dumbfounded faces to the captain.

"The enemy knows what you're doing, and it will bring harm to this army. Sergeant, do you have anything to add?"

Vinyard stepped forward to Hawkins' side. "They were deceitful, sir. I believed Mitchell's cock and bull story. We got a wagon but at the cost of dishonor."

Hawkins paced back and forth. "My trunk came back without the copies of a code book and a coded letter. What happened to them?"

Zeb and Abe glanced and caught sight of their eyes, each waiting for the other to answer. George was clueless. Silence stretched thin on the spot while typical camp noise droned.

"No one's going to confess? Well, I'm damned. Major General Greene wants the papers."

Hawkins believed the truth would come out when he caught George elbowing Abe and whispering. "Well, what is it?"

Abe winced. "He said the papers got left behind."

"Do you three wish to be flogged?" Hawkins shook with anger. "I think you conjured a diversion to New Garden so you could spend time with your lasses." He reviewed them. "Don't look bewildered. I know they're here and I know why."

# Thirty-Four ~ Greene's Agent

The Makers remained at attention while Capt Hawkins continued to pillory them with Sgt Vinyard at his side. Twigs snapped and a guard slipped through the darkness with a package. "Excuse me, sir. This came for you by Express from the militia camp in Guilford County."

The captain opened the package. A note begged him to forward to Maj Gen Greene the contents: an anonymous sealed letter and a copy each of Arthur Neal's code book and unsent message to Cornwallis.

***

Greene read his mail in the early morning. Of all the challenges confronting the Continentals, Neal shot to the top of the list. The Loyalist spy could ambush the Salem ammunition and silence Patriot muskets, never mind the Marquis de Bretigny's forty-two barrels of gunpowder. Gov Nash meant well but the powder hadn't arrived at Continental magazines and the army had yet to roll it into cartridges.

Neal's unsent message to Cornwallis meant an active spy had infiltrated Salem, a town the militia thought they'd secured. Might the British agent be roaming Camp New Providence? Plain costume and manner were not unfounded there. A Tory mole would be inconspicuous in such a camp poor of uniforms.

***

Quartermaster Carrington and Makers company captain Hawkins sat down in the general's marquee. Greene showed them a letter.

"Captain Hawkins, this is the letter the Loyalist spy meant to send from Salem. I decoded it using the copy of his code book. Why didn't you carry them back to me?"

"My trunk got put on a wagon diverted to New Garden."

"Unless you're wanting court martial, you won't err again." Greene turned to a table behind him and picked up a letter folded to expose only the middle section. He handed it to Carrington. "The spy is Arthur Neal. I received this letter from a Patriot friend who forwarded the copies of the Tory's papers. Both of you, read this part."

A grave face gave the quartermaster's impression of the contents. Hawkins read the letter and handed it back to Greene.

"I've no money to pay for intelligence," Greene said, "but there's value in the Patriot's letter. It's remarkable to have copies of Neal's letter and code book and his description."

Carrington nodded, welcoming Greene's approach.

Hawkins gazed at the general. "A Patriot spy found the papers and sent them to you with a letter?"

"Appears so." Greene pulled a document from a leather binder and handed it to Hawkins. "Lieutenant Colonel Carrington and I have formulated your orders. Take a small crew of the Makers to a place above Salisbury on the Yadkin River which we may use as a secret, alternate crossing point. Build flat boats there." He tapped the Patriot's letter. "Take the writer of this with you."

"I shall be most pleased. Who is the person?"

"They will remain anonymous and travel under cover on a mission for me. You must not betray them."

"What will the secret fellow be doing on their assignment?"

"Posing as a Loyalist."

Carrington mulled the order and returned a wary countenance. "Forgive me, General. Is this person safe? Might they be counterfeit?"

"We must take a chance. Tell your Makers they're going to build a headquarters for me. There will be minor damage if our anonymous friend should expose that knowledge. Better yet, keep this person away from your work and men."

"Sooner or later there will be little disguising the fact we're building boats," Capt Hawkins said.

Carrington sighed and indulged the captain with a smile. "Use your initiative. Saw the wood and meanwhile make tar to seal the gaps. Wait until the last minute to assemble the flat boats."

"Alright, sir. That will give us time to fathom whether this person's intentions are honorable."

***

Capt Hawkins left and Lt Col Carrington stayed for a council of war called earlier by Greene to announce decisions he'd made since taking command in Charlotte Town. Nineteen attendees filed in from the commands of the Delaware, Maryland, and Virginia Regulars, the Continental cavalry and artillery, Lee's Legion, and regiments of the North Carolina and Virginia militias. Polish military engineer Col Tadeusz Kosciuszko sat at Carrington's side.

"Gentlemen, I apprehend you're wondering if the Southern Continental army will obtain clothing, provisions and ammunition. With poor results I've begged everybody from General Washington to Congress to the free Southern states. Though the Colonies are productive, we must buy what we need with gold, and silver British specie. Merchants refuse script and Continental dollars. We have less than the ideal one month's provisions in the magazines at Salisbury on the Yadkin and Oliphant's Mill on the Catawba.

"Operating an army has always been difficult. Without supplies we'll crumble like mud bricks made without straw. But we have hope. Governor Nash has promised the manifests of two prize brigs. Also our Partisan friend Colonel William R. Davie has agreed to be Commissary General of North Carolina. I beg of you, Colonel, to summarize your orders from the state."

Col Davie waved a letter. "I'm a cavalryman, not an accountant. But General Greene assures me ledgers are unnecessary as there is no money." When the laughter ended, he continued. "I accept the power of the office. All North Carolina County commissioners will apprise me of their stores and I will provide the army and militia according to needs. North Carolina has supplies. Soon they'll go where needed."

Greene rubbed his dry palms together. "Thank you, Colonel. I expect daily rations through piecemeal deliveries to soon meet the promise we made to our troops. By the offices of army, militia, governor, legislature, counties, merchants, privateers, and farmers there's hope we'll survive to fight Cornwallis."

"We need ammunition," Lt Col John Gunby said. "The Maryland Line is down to two musket cartridges per man."

"Governor Nash is sending privateer gunpowder. Meantime, the single sisters in the Wachovia tract have rolled sixty-thousand cartridges." A cry of jubilation came as the officers rotated their heads to one another at the revelation. "They'll be sent to safety in Virginia."

Amid the noise Brig Gen Daniel Morgan fluttered his hands at his side. When the celebration tamped down, the veteran of the French and Indian War, head of Morgan's Rifles at Saratoga, and the eldest present spoke. "Pray that it gets secured. Now, general, what happened to Continental supplies?"

Greene went to the map of William Henry Mouzon's 1775 *Accurate Map of North and South Carolina* pinned to the tent wall and drew imaginary paths from Virginia to central North Carolina with his crop. "I took for granted uniforms, arms, and camp equipment would fall down from the North in a hundred wagons."

"You never got much of any," Morgan said.

"No, but I hoped they'd come. I envisioned wagons arriving at the Roanoke River and boats taking over to navigate supplies down the rivers of North Carolina."

Col William R. Davie wasn't acquainted with Gen Greene's life. "You have boating experience?"

Greene paused until shouting outside the marquee ended.

***

Capt Hawkins had stood outside Greene's tent waiting for Carrington to come out of the meeting. Zeb Mitchell strolled by.

"Mitchell!"

Zeb made an abrupt stop. "Yes, Captain?"

"I just had a tense meeting with the general. He near gelded me for not bringing him the code and letter of the Loyalist spy."

"Begging your pardon, sir. I didn't handle your trunk."

Red riddled the vessels of the captain's face. "Well, it was your idea to divert to New Garden that led to its disappearance. And just now you would have heard me sooner if you hadn't had trollops dancing in your head."

"Trollops!"

"Go ahead and disobey the rules but hear my caution because General Greene intends to make jam of the next offender."

***

Greene unnerved Davie. Though the stare felt centered on his forehead, the general sought a view of the distant past in Rhode Island.

"I used to sail my father's shallop down Narragansett Bay to Newport."

Morgan interjected. "Without supplies there's no need for transport boats."

Gen Greene's eyes swept over the faces of the field officer staff. "Must I continue? You gentlemen apprehend the entire story."

"Not me. I want to hear the rest," Davie said.

Greene glanced at the map. "If we were to navigate supplies by boats, we would have to know the rivers. Brigadier General Stevens, Lieutenant Colonel Carrington, and Colonel Kosciuszko reported to me the depths and widths and encumbrances on the Dan, Yadkin, and Catawba rivers. They also stated the military significance of each ford and the inventory of boats at each ferry.

"Rather than moving supplies by water, General Washington suggested carrying boats in our baggage train for crossing rivers. I hadn't been in Charlotte Town long and heard General Gates recall the embarrassments of record high waters and lack of boats that often haunted his infantry and cavalry at river crossings in late days of heavy rain.

"In short, my plan of transporting supplies on rivers was a dream. Thus, I reconsidered his Excellency's advice to bring flat boats along to cross rivers. Instead of bringing them, I want to place them at the crossing points ahead of time. We can't stop high water, but we can have boats ready."

Greene motioned to Carrington.

"The plan, however," Carrington said, "relies on positioning extra boats at critical ferries to ensure the army crosses before the enemy catches up. We'll start locating flat boats at logical river crossings and building others to supplement what the ferry-keepers lack.

"General Greene formed a temporary militia company of Makers, artificers if you will. They report to Captain Hawkins and others under me with a mission to provide vessels big enough to ford wagons, cannons, and infantry. Teams and cavalry horses can swim across.

"We have orders to place boats at the ferries across the Catawba, Yadkin, Dan, and other strategic spots. Once that's done, we'll stay in the vanguard to set up camps and assist crossings."

Carrington motioned for Col Tadeusz Kosciuszko to stand. "The Colonel designed defenses to protect a chain strung across the Hudson River at West Point to prevent infiltration of the British navy. He's also renowned for engineering fortifications at Philadelphia."

Kosciuszko waited for Carrington to sit then bowed. "I regret the chain didn't ensnare General Arnold at West Point. In the South I'm designing fortifications to secure the army supply depot over the Dan below Halifax, Virginia where the traitor may attack. In addition to boats, the Makers company will build defensive works designed by me at the Dan and the other crossings."

When Kosciuszko sat down Gen Greene moved before the officers. "Three last words. First, Patriot scouts inform me Cornwallis waits at Wynnesborough for Major General Leslie to arrive from Charles Town. Second, be on guard for Loyalist spies. One named Arthur Neal may be present in camp.

"Before we adjourn, I beg to be blunt. This army's condition is wretched. We so neglect our quarters, nobody looking in would recognize a military encampment. Expert formations and marching are gratifying, but true esprit de corps doesn't exist. On taking command, I took pity on your travails at Camden. No longer will you find me obliging.

"Hunger is at the heart of our miserable morale. We'll do better regarding food for ourselves and our beasts as Col Davie comprehends his new office. Still, we're hungry, so I'm ordering a march to Camp Cheraw on the Pee Dee River where Governor Nash is driving up supplies won by privateers and beeves and horses raised on the coast."

# Thirty-Five ~ A Mission

ADC Maj Ichabod Burnet drew back the marquee flap.

"Captain Hawkins, sir."

Greene motioned Hawkins to a chair. "I've been studying the Loyalist's copied secret letter and key."

"How may I be of service?"

"I wish to forge a coded letter or more from Arthur Neal to Cornwallis."

Hawkins squinted. "How will you send it?"

"Via a man who conducts British messages."

"A British spy?"

"Not a spy. An Express rider who knows the channels of each side. That isn't why I asked you to come."

"How can I help you?"

"I need to know how Neal formed the numbers in the original letter. Numbers are far easier to forge than handwriting, but slight differences may disqualify a false letter. Who made the copy of Neal's unsent letter?"

"Pardon me, General. If I'm to be involved in this intrigue, I beg to know about my anonymous passenger."

"I'll level with you. The Patriot who'll accompany you is a spy who goes by the name Hub. Neither you nor anyone else in your little camp will know their identity."

"I apprehend this Hub person is a non-combatant. Won't they be risking significant harm?"

"By maintaining a secret identity and working alone the risk will be diminished."

Hawkins turned up his nose. "On my mission, they may witness violence."

Greene's gaze came firm and direct. "The people in Salem didn't falter when they found and passed on the British code."

"They knew who they were dealing with. How can I trust Hub? He might expose us."

"How can I trust you?"

Hawkins squirmed. "I'm loyal to the revolution, otherwise I wouldn't risk my life."

"Don't you see? You and this citizen spy are no less Patriots. There's something else. I know Hub's identity. Take my word."

"Alright, sir, I will. I suppose any pretense of building a headquarters isn't necessary."

"No. Now, about the letters. Besides my letter from 'Neal' to 'Cornwallis', I've ordered Hub to forge one or more number-coded letters from Cornwallis to Neal. Therefore, Hub will need evidence of how Cornwallis' ADC forms his numbers."

Greene handed Hawkins an intercepted letter written by the ADC for Cornwallis and a copy of the code. "Pass these on to Hub."

Hawkins took Cornwallis' letter and the code with a grave swallow and circled around to the general's question. "Who made the copy of Neal's unsent letter? We should ask Private Mitchell."

***

Zeb Mitchell sat among wooden boxes of crosscut saws, tools, and supplies on one of the wagons wondering how best to pack them. Footsteps accompanied by the familiar sound of a dragging shoe got his attention. Gen Greene and Capt Hawkins approached. After Zeb told Greene that Maria Bach copied Arthur Neal's letter, the general sent Hawkins to fetch her.

In the meantime, the general surprised Zeb with conversation. "In what trade did you apprentice?"

"Wainwright, sir, under my stepfather. I'm a wagon jockey. I purchase teams and drive finished wagons to their destination."

"Has your father any great supplies of nails?"

"No, sir. My stepfather uses few nails."

"You'll need scores. You can fashion them but I'd rather have them on hand."

"McMurray Wainwright uses joinery."

"We don't have time for joinery."

"Sir?"

"You must make up to a dozen boats and fast. Spare any perfections."

"Understood, sir. The company has three smiths. Give them heavy wire and you shall have nails."

Greene nodded and conceded a warm smile. "I've made nails. My apprenticeship was in the forge."

"Forge work? You're an esteemed man."

"Between fabricating anchors, I found time to study. My son, read if you want to succeed."

"May I build your boats first?"

"Very well." General Greene inspected Zeb's plain clothing. "I know what you are."

"Sir?"

"You're a Quaker."

Zeb blushed at Greene's deduction. "Oh, my clothes. My stepfather was a Philadelphia Quaker."

"I'm a Quaker as well."

"You? Friends don't associate with the army, never mind generaling."

"I had to leave the Society. I know what you're going through."

Zeb snapped to attention. "I can work hard, sir."

"At rest, Private. I'm sure you can, but will you stick with us?"

"I have no plans to run."

"What did your father say about taking the oath?"

"To examine my conscience."

"He must miss you. Do you have a large family?"

"A stepfather, mother, and sister Sara."

"I've heard of New Garden. Isn't it in Guilford County?"

"Yes, sir. Near Guilford Court House. We have a good stand of short leaf pines."

"Capt Hawkins is taking your platoon to a pine forest above Salisbury."

"I passed through it on my way to Charlotte Town."

"Is it remote?"

"Wilderness, sir."

"Excellent. There'll be more large pines for a second build to replace your first boats."

"Sir?"

"I'll burn any boats I don't need to cross the Yadkin. Otherwise, Cornwallis will make use of them."

"General, mayn't you need boats in the future?"

"Keep your saws sharpened." General Greene noticed Hawkins returning with Maria Bach. "Private, I beg of your leave. Good luck."

"Thank you. Good luck, sir."

***

Later, Capt Hawkins rounded up the Makers and the Salem ladies.

"Tomorrow, we set off for camp as one of four Makers platoons with a mission to provide boats. I'll lead this platoon myself. We'll saw all the boards first so anyone prying won't know what we're building. We'll assemble the boats at a camp on a potential crossing of the upper Yadkin River near a place called the Horse Shoe.

"We'll conduct a convoy of three wagons and six riding horses to camp. Anyone not on horseback or driving a wagon will march. Drivers will rotate through the platoon. Shelter yourself from the rain with a good hat and canvas sheet.

"Though our mission will be indirectly military, it won't be trivial. We'll run a tight schedule in support of General Greene.

"We'll have two extra people along. Bugle boy James Gillies whose fever keeps him from joining his cavalry detachment. And an anonymous guest called Hub who you're ordered to keep away from."

***

The wagons set off north from Charlotte Town in icy rain toward upper Rowan County. After three days, the Makers and Salem ladies woke in Camp Horse Shoe near the babbling Yadkin River. The sun hadn't quite risen on the freezing morning but the rain was over. A changing breeze came and lifted the fog.

Smoke from the cooking fire blew in every direction. Black iron pots and pans clanged as the Salem ladies set up. After walking fifty miles on muddy roads that often sucked their feet into the mire, the camp followers shuffled their overwrought legs .

"How soon before we eat breakfast?" Capt Hawkins said.

Maria spoke in a stupor. "We'll bang pots when it's ready."

Abraham Hellerschwarz approached the firepit and sighed at the Makers idling at a wagon. "It's going to be awhile. Wipe the cobwebs from your eyes and fetch the axes, boys. Let's fell trees."

***

Following breakfast on the third day at Camp Horse Shoe, Abe and Zeb teamed up to cross cut logs to form the beams and planks of primitive flat boats. Pulled back and forth over a pine trunk, the whispering saw moved Zeb to contemplate the tensions dividing the campers.

Animosity arose from the formation of the Makers. It didn't take long before the storms came, many out of Sgt Vinyard's prejudices. With the addition of the Salem ladies the sergeant's biases extended to them.

Vinyard's stunts start small so he can dull our minds to his deceit. In Camp Horse Shoe the sergeant noticed how I lingered with Yohanna after an evening meal. Soon the small-minded man wanted to know if she was my "camp wife".

Of course, Sergeant Vinyard isn't above eating the delicious meals Yohanna cooks. Once after I told him that Yohanna isn't his maid and cook, I realized what I'd said. She's not mine either. Does someone responding to your loving overtures mean you have control over them? Did I mistake my father's love for a desire to control me?

Comments about Abe roll off the sergeant's tongue. Sometimes his prejudice is too obvious. Once he singled out Abe by jumping ahead of him in the chow line when George was first and I was second.

Rahel, dishing food, halted and glared. Rather than meek subservience to the sergeant, she made a stand. Her resistance wasn't surprising given the men had lined up to her and not the other way around. She had authority.

Did she wonder how Redcoat soldiers would treat her in a comparable situation? I imagine Rahel asking Abe whether they'd chosen the wrong side and Abe saying they couldn't let the Patriots down. Vinyard took her condemning stares to heart and shrugged his shoulders before going to the end of the line.

Repetitive swings of the saw numbed my arm until I could no longer feel the vibrations. George Heider is anything but numb to Vinyard's despise of Germans. He may not know the language, but his eyes gather the sergeant's intent. When Abe asks what he has against Germans, Vinyard says they side with the British. Abe shut him up when he explained knocking George weakened the sergeant's authority.

I'm not blameless. George is a gentle creature and doesn't compete with me. Yet in my heart I've kept elitist sentiments sure he could never work wood. After a while, I saw my behavior was no better than the sergeant's. George wants to get along. Anyway, Maria is his biggest stake in this war, not me.

The brilliant bugle boy James Gillies is recovering. He's devastated he didn't detach with the cavalry. Besides praying he will meet them, for what else does he yearn? What's at stake for him? Will he grow into manhood under a free government or a tyrant? How will battle suit him when it comes?

If we only have our meek lives, we all have something at stake. For me, I know it's Yohanna. Her yearning unmasked itself in an unsubtle way I wasn't prepared for when we met. The door is open and she's always in my thoughts.

This revolution may not go as I wish which puts my future at stake. My family is at stake. The injustice done to their lives and business was awful and I feel responsible. Whether the people live free or the King prevails, the connection to my home is fragile.

***

Gunfire divided the Makers and Salem ladies from sleep. Nothing like they'd experienced before, it lasted moments.

Rahel looked for Abe who'd been standing watch. She grabbed Yohanna's hand and they ran and found him unconscious on the ground.

Yohanna searched his eyes. She felt for his pulse when Rahel's screams entreated the Makers who came and muscled her and Yohanna aside.

A small recovery lit Rahel's face after Sgt Vinyard took charge. "Brandy!" Vinyard said. That meant Abe could drink and drinking meant breathing. Zeb ran to the rations wagon and returned with the jug. Soon the brandy stirred Abe to consciousness. Rahel, hands crossed on her chest, thanked God the blow to his head had only knocked him out.

In the light of morning everyone stuck to their business while Hawkins and Rahel watched over Abe. He'd suffered a small laceration and a half-inch knot.

Neither the wagons nor valuables in the camp suffered gunfire damage. Nothing was missing. Was it a mistake? A warning? Besides Abe's knotted skull, the attack scarred the spirit of the camp. The Salem ladies refused to cook, and the Makers refrained from working.

The camp regained footing after Hawkins and Vinyard called roll and found the Makers, the camp followers, and James Gillies present. Hawkins found Hub, still anonymous to all but him, safe. Somebody had rekindled and stoked the cooking fire.

Capt Hawkins gathered the campers around the yellow, orange, and blue flames. "You're wondering what happened last night. I apprehend mobs and bands of Tories and Loyalists are rising against us. They're trying to scare—"

Rahel prattled from her pained face. Yohanna Heider joined her, murmuring in similar distress.

The captain stared. "Hellerschwarz, what are they saying?"

Abe came to Rahel's side and held her close. He waited until her sobbing ebbed. "Rahel said the attack on me shocked her. She spoke of the recent harrowing events starting with the indiscriminate wrecking of the wainwright's shop. Yohanna's thankful that providence spared McMurray's life and mine. They abhor violence and war."

"It's a bit late for that," Hawkins said and stabbed an index finger at Rahel and Yohanna. "No one goes home."

Positioned between Rahel and Yohanna, Maria held their hands and spoke to them before translating her words to English. "War can't go on forever."

Hawkins smirked at the Moravian women.

Zeb came to Yohanna's side. "Don't doubt their fears. They have good intentions."

Hawkins ignored Zeb but his face softened as he continued to speak to the ladies. "I see now you have patriotic aims. Your service is welcome."

Zeb saw an opportunity. "I hope you apprehend changes are necessary. How are we going to stop intruders?"

"From now on," Capt Hawkins said, "two pickets will stand watch at night. James Gillies will join them and sound the warning with his bugle." He glared at Zeb. "Does that suit you, Private?"

Zeb eyed the ground and nodded.

George Heider whispered a question to Maria which she broadcast in English. "What do they know? Why do they hate us?"

The captain chewed on the question and shrugged. He clapped his hands. "Ladies, prepare breakfast. Go to the woods, Makers, and cut wood. We'll send for you when the food is ready."

Zeb waved to Abe. "I'll be right there after I get a file. The two-man crosscut saw is making more dust than shavings." He walked to the wagons and had no more gotten there than Hub emerged.

Though the anonymous person wore a hood, Zeb resisted the temptation to look. He averted his eyes and went to the toolbox on the side of the wagon. Water splashed into a bowl. It was impossible for Zeb to avoid looking now that the hood was down.

"Why in God's name are you here?" Zeb said.

"Mitchell!" yelled Hawkins. Zeb would have lingered had he not remembered the captain's threat of punishment in Camp New Providence. "Coming!"

# Thirty-Six ~ Camp Cheraw

— Late December 1780, Camp Cheraw, Pee Dee River, South Carolina

The Continental army of the South departed Charlotte Town. Every horse, pair of feet, and wagon wheel toiled down seventy-five miles in heavy rain to Cheraw, South Carolina. The marchers endured a cold cleansing, though below their knees slopping mud covered them in filth.

As he set off, Maj Gen Nathanael Greene bid farewell to Col Thomas Polk, withholding any complaints about the lack of provisions from the outgoing Commissary General. "It's time to leave. Colonel Kosciuszko has found a campsite on the Pee Dee River with good provisions. Thank you for your patriotism."

Before marching out of Charlotte Town's southern limits into South Carolina, Greene converted his forces into a flying corps, closing the promise made to commander-in-chief George Washington. Every available horse in ten miles was impressed to mount a rider.

To increase agility and unpredictability, Greene divided his modest army between Brig Gen Daniel Morgan and himself. Morgan had orders to annoy British military emplacements in northwest South Carolina and build anti British sentiment. Greene wanted no general action with Cornwallis' army.

Morgan went southwest out of Charlotte Town leading a corps of eight-hundred Continental infantry and Lt Col William Washington's 1st and 3rd Continental Cavalry to wilderness west of the Broad River and north of the Pacolet River.

Greene marched southeast with the remaining seven-hundred Continental infantry, Lt Col Henry Lee's Legion of cavalry and infantry, Brig Gen Edward Stevens' Virginia militia, two companies of North Carolina militia, and the Continental Artillery to winter quarters at Cheraw, SC.

In addition to Capt Hawkins' platoon of Makers tasked with supplying boats on the upper Yadkin River, two platoons stayed behind to provide boats at the Catawba crossings in Charlotte Town and the Yadkin crossing at Salisbury. Another platoon went to Camp Cheraw.

Rations at Camp Cheraw improved as troops subsisted on fattened, stall-fed cattle driven up from the coast, the beef hides then traded for shoes and other leather goods. A third of the militia beat out wheat at local farms. From grist mills dotting the rivers, flour and meal arrived in camp to supply daily rations.

North Carolina secured a sizeable portion of the 1780 wheat and corn crop by way of a specific tax payable in one peck of grain per £100 of taxable property. Thereby, surplus grains harvested from the vast river-fed backcountry would go to the state troops and the Continentals. Additionally, an embargo stipulated no grains would be exported from the state.

***

Cornwallis lay encamped in Wynnesborough, South Carolina within two days' march of Morgan to the west and Greene to the east. He waited to form a junction with Maj Gen Leslie's corps marching up from Charles Town. Though Loyalist scouts said the Americans intended to stay put at Camp Cheraw, the lord hoped Greene wouldn't long repair.

Greene scratched ideas on the margins of broadsheets, working on a coded letter to Cornwallis in the name of Arthur Neal containing falsehoods to lower the lord's guard and stretch his imagination of American stupidity. On his third try, his deceit soared: Hammers are flying in Camp Cheraw as General Greene builds a grand house on the Pee Dee River. He's buying furniture to fill up the rooms.

"Major Burnet!"

***

Greene called a staff meeting to address rancor hanging over camp. His upbraiding of the army leadership at the Charlotte Town council of war undoubtedly accounted for the ice in their stares. Then again, experience strengthened his assumption that some officers regretted Gates' replacement.

Greene had seen both sides of leadership change, a sadistic process in which a new commander removes attachments with the previous leader and replaces them with his own. Foremost on his mind was getting the men behind him.

"We're still soaked from the march here and I know this is no Egypt, but it has better forage than Charlotte Town. I feel for you. Still, we have everything to thank God Almighty for.

"I understand what happened after Camden. You lost all confidence in General Gates, and the regiments all their discipline. The troops terrorized the country, so addicted to plundering to feed themselves." Greene wouldn't dare say in Camp Cheraw northerners viewed the Battle of Camden different than southerners.

I've learned that few, from general officers down to the buglers, deserved any extraordinary merit. The action was short and succeeded by a flight wherein officers and soldiers took care of themselves.

I wish General Gates had halted at Waxhaws or Charlotte Town, the first sixty miles and the last eighty from the field of battle. Twenty mere miles can either make or destroy a reputation. A man labors with an honest zeal in his country's service yet the people can disgrace him for the most trifling error either in conduct or opinion. Thank God the British ran up against the Yadkin River at Salisbury or it would have been worse.

Brig Gen Isaac Huger defended the Continental men. "Among the troops that fought with courage are the Maryland and Delaware Continental regiments trained in the rigid school of Steuben."

Greene nodded. There was no part of the army more bitter over Camden than the renowned Maryland line. "Not everyone forsook Gates."

Col John Green of the 1st Virginia Regiment protested. "Are we to praise two regiments and rebuke others?"

"Of course not. You don't want or deserve it."

"That's considerate," Green said. "Gates deciding in haste to fight at Camden was unfortunate. At least we preserved a piece of the army."

"I recognize that," Greene said. "There was chaos and I know how that feels as I flew from Fort Washington and Fort Lee. Luck has given us another chance. What will we do better?"

"First, not abandon care," Green said.

Greene gave a sharp nod. "You have my word, sir. I promise not to do that."

Brig Gen Edward Stevens had led the Virginia militia at Camden. "What else do you promise?"

"To advise and listen. We've done well by coming to Camp Cheraw. We are but a small force though Cornwallis is in the middle with General Morgan on the other side."

"He can't take his eyes off of Morgan to meddle with Camp Cheraw," Huger said. "Otherwise, Morgan can attack his rear guard or raid British outposts in South Carolina."

Lt Col Henry Lee of Lee's Legion stood. "If Cornwallis needs supplies, he can't get them from Cape Fear as we stand in the way of Cross Creek. He can't go to Charles Town and leave his forts at the mercy of two flying armies."

"Excellent points." Maj Gen Greene ruminated over the last poor option for Cornwallis. "Likewise, if he chases Morgan or goes to Virginia, we will attack his rear guard. So, what should he do?"

"Divide his own forces," Lee said.

Greene nodded. "He must create two corps if he hopes to catch us. What shall our strategy be?"

"Attack before he splits his forces," Green said.

"In the present relative positions and strength of the two armies, it would be empowering the enemy to fight him."

Greene paced in front of the officers. The gimpy knee forced his right leg to drag and cut tracks in the dirt floor. He pointed at Mouzon's 1775 *Accurate Map of North and South Carolina* on the tent wall with a riding crop.

"Notwithstanding the lord's superior numbers in men, weapons, horse, and provisions, he is inferior to the country whose flowing waters march with a force unstoppable by man. We must put the rivers between us and the enemy."

Greene's eyes fixed on the map. He lowered himself to a folding stool.

"We cannot risk entanglement with the enemy, only fight him and turn."

Col William Davie countered Greene. "If we retreat, the lord will take whatever road we take and thereby catch us."

"Can our enemy cross the rivers?"

"At fords, certainly."

"If there are no fords, Cornwallis can't cross," Greene said.

"Nor can we cross," Davie said.

Greene stood and his covered stool skipped across the floor. The sleepy eyes of the officers shot open. They realized the fabric of his breeches had tangled with the folds of the canvas.

"Why be so defeatist? We have strengths. We're a flying army. We're positioned in a place that has advantages. We'll have boats." Greene slapped the crop against the map. "Consider the great, beautiful rivers of North Carolina."

Huger chuckled. "You won't say they're beautiful six months from now when the mosquitos carry you off."

Greene ended the meeting and called the officers to dine at his table where he entertained them with a camaraderie that atoned for the middling fare. No tastier than Camp New Providence's food, the portions met the army's requirements.

They toasted Lt Col William Washington's late crushing victory over Loyalists at Hammond's Store at a site west of the Broad

River and down the Cherokee Path from the Waxhaws where seven months earlier Lt Col Banastre Tarleton defeated a Continental army corps leaving over two-hundred casualties, the majority harrowing deaths.

***

Days later Patriot scouts informed Gen Greene that Cornwallis had indeed divided the British army and ordered Tarleton to go in motion toward Gen Morgan's position. Greene had been in Cheraw, South Carolina for a week. The camp's days dwindled.

Greene called a council of war. From the chaotic, half-cocked Camp New Providence to the mature Camp Cheraw, the army fancied what lay ahead. The spirits of the men had improved and they wondered what plan the commander had devised.

The general stood before Mouzon's map. The leaders of the Continental brigades of Delaware, Maryland, and Virginia and of the cavalry, light infantry, militia, and artillery again sat before him.

Irregular hammer beats interrupted his opening remarks. Nearby, the Makers toiled on a modest stockade to hold a small portion of the seven hundred Loyalist prisoners captured at the Battle of Kings Mountain in October.

Greene looked past the wall of the marquee to the Makers detachment. "While Cornwallis shackles our prisoners on fetid ships, I refuse to return one of his so help me God!"

Soldiers passing by the marquee shuddered.

"The enemy isn't giving us much more time to prepare ourselves. We'll soon be returning to North Carolina. However, I don't intend Cornwallis to drive me out of that state if I can avoid it. If Virginia deposits the requested provisions upon the Roanoke River, we'll hold one corner at all events. Perhaps we should go there via strategic retreat."

A broad moan pervaded the meeting. "Huh?"

"Who said that?" Greene scanned the officers and found no one owning up. "Well, it doesn't matter. Lieutenant Colonel Lee, explain what I mean by strategic retreat."

Already famous for taunting and raiding British forces, the youthful but capable leader of mounted infantry pivoted left and right and looked over his shoulders until he had every man's attention. "It's a strategy the Romans used to defeat the stronger Carthaginians and promoted by our commander-in-chief to goad the enemy and harass him until the army is strong enough to fight him on the field."

Greene nodded. "I've always perceived General Washington to be wise."

"Now, I see doubt in some eyes," Lee said. "The kernel of the strategy is avoidance of general warfare in favor of harassment. You must admit the approach timid. You might think goading the enemy is risky or aimless. But the enemy wastes energy going on the offense, sending large, ineffective corps but never defeating the insurgents."

The crop pat the general's left hand. "If we retreat, where would you go?" Greene pointed to a half-dozen points in central North Carolina. "Should we go here, there, or here? I say we go to our stores in Virginia."

Quiet gloom pervaded the council, still convinced retreat was meritless.

Slouching, cowering, and biting his nails, Lee mocked the pessimism. "Isn't retreat another way to describe cowards running?"

Greene slammed the crop against the map. "Cowards don't turn and take potshots at a stunned enemy."

Turn. Potshots. Kill. Stunned. Enemy. A noticeable change came over the council as the officers sat taller in their chairs.

"Enticing Lord Cornwallis away from British supply depots," Greene said, "will damage his army more than general warfare. The closer he comes, the further we'll retreat to Virginia. As long as the lord chases, we'll remain in motion."

"What does retreat have to do with rivers?" Davie said.

"If we own the crossings Cornwallis will have to go around them or find boats. He'll always be a crossing behind until we get to Virginia."

Lee added. "By then, he'll be weak, and we'll be closer to Virginia where our stores will lie in safety."

"Okay," Huger said, "let's say Cornwallis is as deranged as you say. What will it take to provoke him to chase us?"

"I suppose a mighty punch on the jaw," Greene said. "But heaven help us if we don't retreat at breakneck speed."

# Thirty-Seven ~ Lil Daisy

— January 1, 1781, Camp Horse Shoe on the Yadkin River

Late in the day the Makers had the completion of their project in sight. Six crude flat boats lay at the toes of a horse shoe bend in the Yadkin River. Laden with troops, artillery carriages, and supply wagons, a makeshift winch would be ready to tow them across the two-hundred-foot wide deep channel as soon as a cordwain finished making the rope. The simple mechanism only wanted a beast for power.

The Makers' hooded guest Hub departed camp on horseback. On their way to fetch water to clean up after supper the Salem ladies watched the rider disappear with a regular and moderate clip-clop down the path. When they returned lugging buckets, a young woman strolled into the Makers' camp from the direction Hub went.

Maria lifted a bucket to a black pot heating on the fire and sized up the approaching stranger. There was so little of her, a handful of seed corn thrown her way could have entirely missed her short, slender frame. Dressed in a green and white checked frock, the maid stopped and waited for Maria to finish.

Water sizzled and steamed as it fell into the hot pot. Maria finished pouring and looked up. "Hello. What's your name?"

The young lady opened her mouth to speak but hesitated. She reached behind her back with her right hand and grabbed her thin left arm then produced a bashful smile. "Lil Daisy."

From twenty yards, Sgt Vinyard watched the ladies preparing to wash dishes. After counting the women a second time and concluding they numbered four, he investigated and learned Lil Daisy's name. She threw flattering eyes and his leer acknowledged her company.

Capt Hawkins, who'd gotten used to Maria, Rahel, and Yohanna in camp, watched Vinyard wooing the newcomer. He rushed over and got between them. "All of our cooking and cleaning needs have been met."

Vinyard gave Hawkins a sidelong wink Lil Daisy was sure to appreciate. "Not all of our needs."

"She'll be trouble."

The Salem ladies stopped cleaning and listened with Lil Daisy while the men raised their voices in disagreement.

"How?"

"What if she gets with child?"

Maria's jaw dropped.

"She and her children will obstruct our every movement."

Vinyard craned his neck, making an exaggerated inspection of the area surrounding Lil Daisy. "I reckon she has no children." He gave a moment to consider the notorious ambiguity of George Washington's rules for conducting an army. "I can't imagine how this young lady might breach the commander-in-chief's order prohibiting camp followers not absolutely necessary."

***

At nightfall eleven outsiders walked into Camp Horse Shoe begging for refreshment. The Makers refused on the grounds they had no extra rations. Nor did they want exposure to smallpox. But the rough men persisted. They ate all the scraps and invited Lil Daisy to make a pallet by the fire with them.

Vinyard, flabbergasted by the strangers' gall, told Lil Daisy to sleep elsewhere. She refused. Fearing Lil Daisy to be a seductress, he tried to stay awake, but dozed off by the fire.

The sergeant woke in the middle of the night and discovered Lil Daisy gone. He woke the strangers and told them to leave. They refused. At daybreak he prodded them awake with a musket muzzle and said he'd shoot the last one's backside. Capt Hawkins intervened and told the men they could live if they took an oath not to threaten the Makers again. They did and he released them on parole.

The strangers set off and not much later Lil Daisy drifted back into camp. Vinyard asked why she left in the middle of night. She broke down and balled. The sergeant quit the interrogation and welcomed her back into the camp.

The strangers met their leader Arthur Neal two miles away at camp. The Loyalist provincial horsemen of the Royal North Carolina Regiment mounted their horses at sunrise the next morning. They rode toward the Makers camp and before they got there, Sgt Vinyard spotted their green jackets in the distance. He fled with Lil Daisy.

Capt Hawkins regretted giving in to Vinyard over Lil Daisy. He threw a tin cup of coffee to the ground and ran to the armory located in one of the wagons. "Master James, blow the alarm! Makers! Take a musket and cartouche box!"

The Makers platoon formed into a box defense and met the Loyalists with alternating volleys. The wet journey from Charlotte Town dampened the first ammunition pulled and nearly gave the horsemen an opportunity to approach. But the Makers found dry cartridges and fired on the Loyalists. The attackers wielded swords and pistols for a half hour but never closed in.

Zeb trained a musket at the marauders flying by the camp, his vision confined to an imaginary tunnel down the barrel. He recognized Arthur Neal. The opportunity to kill his father's tormentor chilled his spine. He squeezed the trigger. The breech explosion bucked the gun and ripped the air.

The blue smoke cleared. When Zeb's eyes recovered from the brilliant light of the musket's flashing pan, the sight of Neal and his horse laying on the ground shocked him. The poor beast pawed the ground as arterial blood spurted from a hind quarter.

As Neal pushed up from the ground and freed himself, a ball whizzed into his left arm. Zeb looked over his shoulder. George Heider had fired true. A Loyalist comrade tied a tourniquet around Neal's arm above the red hole and they rode from the camp with the others.

The Makers stripped the dead mount's saddle and dragged the beast far into the woods with a pair of horses.

***

Meanwhile, Vinyard took Lil Daisy to nearby Dutchman's Creek and held her by the feet and dunked her head in the freezing water until bubbles of exasperation and half-drowned thrashing signaled a successful punishment.

Lil Daisy woke up later and found herself locked in a shed. When released, she went home and kept silent. Vinyard succumbed to camp fever the next day.

Yohanna Heider held her tongue whether the man was good or evil and nursed him as a brother. When Capt Hawkins and the Makers intervened, she ran them off.

She rid the clothes and Vinyard of lice and stench, fed him tea from Dr. Samuel Benjamin Vierling's receipt of apothecary rose and tulip tree root, and anointed vinegar on the dull red rash.

There was no denying when she looked at him and prayed, her convalescing patient reminded her of the country where a great portion of the people and land itself outside of Wachovia wasted under civil unrest. The worldly wantonness and ruin forecast by Moravian leaders had come true. In helping Sgt Vinyard get over his illness, she realized her duty to nurse the cursed land.

***

The breach of their safety dogged Zeb. He sat down on a log beside the captain who was cleaning and lubricating his pistol.

Hawkins read the anger on Zeb's face. "No more trusting strangers?"

"No more feeding the hungry?"

"We didn't feed them, Private Mitchell. They ate scraps."

"And stole our peace." Zeb made a lengthy sigh. "My stepfather says the Colonies must reject civil violence. How can we win without it?"

"Giving quarter to strangers is impossible. Killing is immoral. A great dilemma has come to this land."

"Let's pursue the Loyalists. The more these attacks go on, the more our safety wanes."

"Our mission is to build flat boats or round them up at river crossings. I will report the attacks. It's up to Lieutenant Colonel Carrington and Major General Greene to decide our orders. The general is busy preparing the Continentals for battle, so action is remote."

"Their leader is Arthur Neal. We should find and take him prisoner."

"Was he the one who attacked your father?"

"Undoubtedly. If we're not going to act, we should call on the local Whigs and Patriots for support."

"Drop it, Private. Our mission is to build boats."

"The Loyalists and Lil Daisy may have been spying on our boat-making operation."

"They're gone. It's over."

Zeb rose from the log. "Well then, that's all right. We're bosom friends with the Loyalists." He stomped off.

Abe watched Zeb coming. "You fought bravely today."

"So did George. He used to be so gentle."

"Heard you arguing with the captain."

"The answer is right in front of us and he won't budge. Abe, what's happening to us?"

"Try not to be troubled, Brother."

"Why not? Everything wrong is happening at once."

"When emotions get pent up, all the small forces of nature crack at once like lightning. We're seeing that now in these troubled times."

***

Capt Hawkins had also noticed Hub leave and Lil Daisy arrive. Perhaps they signaled to each other. Maybe Lil Daisy was a conduit for getting false messages to the Loyalist Arthur Neal.

An Express rider appeared. Hawkins took a message from Gen Greene and went to the armory. He retrieved a code book tucked in a false panel of the gun cabinet.

Uncoded, the message directed Hawkins to remain at Camp Horse Shoe but be prepared to depart at once to Salem to guard the Moravian ammunition.

Hawkins sent a reply with the Express rider. "We skirmished with Arthur Neal and his men yet he remains alive. Hub left camp. Marching to Salem."

# Thirty-Eight ~ Shocking News

Charlotte Town Gazette

Special edition! Tarleton Cut to Pieces at Cowpens!

Charlotte Town, January 27, 1781

We have learned from men of high reputation that Brig Gen Daniel Morgan routed Lieutenant Colonel Banastre Tarleton on January 17 at the Cowpens in the northern Camden Precinct of South Carolina. Morgan, a hero of the Battle of Saratoga, offered no quarter obliging Tarleton to retire with considerable losses after the hour-long battle.

Patriot readers take note! Morgan whipped one of the world's best trained armies using brilliant tactics. With three battle lines formed—two in a flat clearing and one further back at the bottom of a small hill—Morgan egged on Tarleton.

Morgan believed deeply in the brass of his eight-hundred Regulars and one-thousand militia who joined him against Tarleton's twelve-hundred green-jacketed cavalry and redcoat infantry. The Patriot general little worried that the Broad River, being on the other side of the hill, could have prevented his corps from retreating with their lives. Tarleton, known for ruthless, quick attacks, arrived early with troops cross after a long journey and missed breakfast. Morgan's troops were fresh, energetic, and eager to abide his orders.

Daring up-close American riflemen sharpshooting on the first line launched the battle. Maj Joseph McDowell, veteran of Kings Mountain, brought his Burke County Regiment of North Carolina militia. Lt Col James Jackson joined with his Georgia militia.

Drawn into engagement, Tarleton threw every man including reserves into the skirmish. Heavy fire continued when the British met the second defensive line. South Carolina militia under Col Andrew Pickens made two shots and retreated. Tarleton's forces wanted more.

Continentals, comprised of Maryland, Virginia, and Delaware troops, put up a valiant defense then retreated. Meanwhile, Lt Col

William Washington, second cousin of George Washington, led the 1st and 3rd Continental cavalry from behind the hill and surrounded the British right flank. Pickens' militia returned to swoop around the left British flank.

With the British Light Infantry enveloped on both sides, the retreating Continentals turned and gave volleys and a bayonet charge. British forces collapsed, dying and surrendering. Tarleton fled on horse.

We post extracts of letters as testimony:

From Daniel Morgan to George Washington
Camp near Cane Creek, January 19, 1781

"Sir, the Troops I have the honor to command have gained a complete Victory over a Detachment from the British army commanded by Lieutenant Colonel Tarleton...on the 17th Instant about Sunrise at a Place called the Cowpens near Pacolet River...An Hour before daylight one of my Scouts informed me the enemy had advanced within five miles of our Camp...When the Enemy advanced to our Continental Line they received a well-directed and incessant Fire, but their numbers being superior to ours, they gained our Flanks, which obliged us to change our Position. We retired in good order about 50 Paces, formed, advanced on the Enemy and gave them a brisk Fire, which threw them into Disorder... We entirely routed the Enemy, and their retreat continued for upwards of 20 Miles. Our Loss is very inconsiderable, not having more than 12 killed and 60 wounded. The Enemy's Loss was 10 Commissioned officers & upwards of 100 Rank & File killed; 200 wounded; 29 Commissioned officers, more than 500 Privates, and 70 Blacks fell Prisoners into our Hands. Also, two field Pieces, two standards, 800 muskets, one travelling forge, 35 Wagons, upwards of 100 dragoon Horses, and all their Music. We fought with only 800 Regulars and opposed upwards of 1000 chosen British Troops. Such was the Inferiority of our Numbers our Success came from the Justice of our Cause and the Gallantry of our Troops."

From Nathanael Greene to George Washington
Camp on the Pee Dee, South Carolina, January 24, 1781

"Sir, I have the satisfaction to transmit your Excellency the copy of a letter which I this moment received from Brigadier General Morgan announcing the defeat of Lieutenant Colonel Tarleton's detachment. The victory was complete, and the action glorious. The brilliancy and success with which they fought does the highest honor to the American arms and adds splendor to the character of the general and his officers. I must beg leave to recommend them to your Excellency's notice and doubt not, but from your representation Congress will receive pleasure from testifying their approbation of Morgan's conduct."

From Lord Cornwallis to Lord Germain
Camp on Turkey Creek, Broad River, January 18, 1781

"My Lord, I think it necessary to transmit to your lordship a copy of my letter to Sir Henry Clinton, lest the exaggerated accounts from the Rebels should reach Europe before your lordship could hear from New York. This event was extremely unexpected; for the greatest part of the troops engaged had upon all former occasions behaved with the most distinguished gallantry."

***

People might say…

It's fitting Brig Gen Daniel Morgan age 44 routed his 27-year old junior Lt Col Banastre Tarleton…Never has a victory been more wanting to preserve the Revolution…When Cornwallis divides his forces to create a flying army following Maj Gen Nathanael Greene's move, American strategy is in the vanguard…Washington posting 80 horsemen behind the high ground was brilliant…American riflemen are ascending…It was high time Morgan took some wagons, though but 35, after the British seized nearly 300 between Charles Town, Camden, and Waxhaws…Charging bayonets is no longer a tactic excelled by the British alone…The Georgia-Carolina-Virginia militia provided a needed spark…Losing more than 400 British Legion will haunt Cornwallis for some time.

***

Commentary and background from our sources…

Morgan had marched to the northeast section of the Camden Precinct between the Broad and Pacolet rivers in South Carolina to form a junction with the militia and bring them under his command.

Cornwallis ordered Tarleton to intercept Morgan fearing any mischief that might delay the invasion of North Carolina. Tarleton proceeded with a corps made up of the Legion, a battery of the Royal Artillery, and a half dozen small infantry units.

Before battle Morgan surveyed the one square mile of cleared land used to fatten beeves before driving them to market. A veteran who'd fought alongside George Washington in the French and Indian War, he humbly walked it, dodging golden cow patties.

Tarleton's reputation for speed, stealth, and terror grew in two South Carolina battles where he helped Cornwallis to two major successes. A surprise attack at Monck's Corner cut Maj Gen Benjamin Lincoln's last escape route on the northern side of besieged Charles Town.

At Waxhaws between Camden, South Carolina and Cross Creek, North Carolina, Col Abraham Buford leading four-hundred Continental Army soldiers of the Virginia Line first refused to surrender to Lt Col Tarleton. When the British Legion attacked, the Continentals threw down their arms. In return, the Legion hacked sixty percent of Buford's force to death or near death. The engagement became known as the Battle of Waxhaws or Buford's Massacre.

# Map of Army Routes After Cowpens

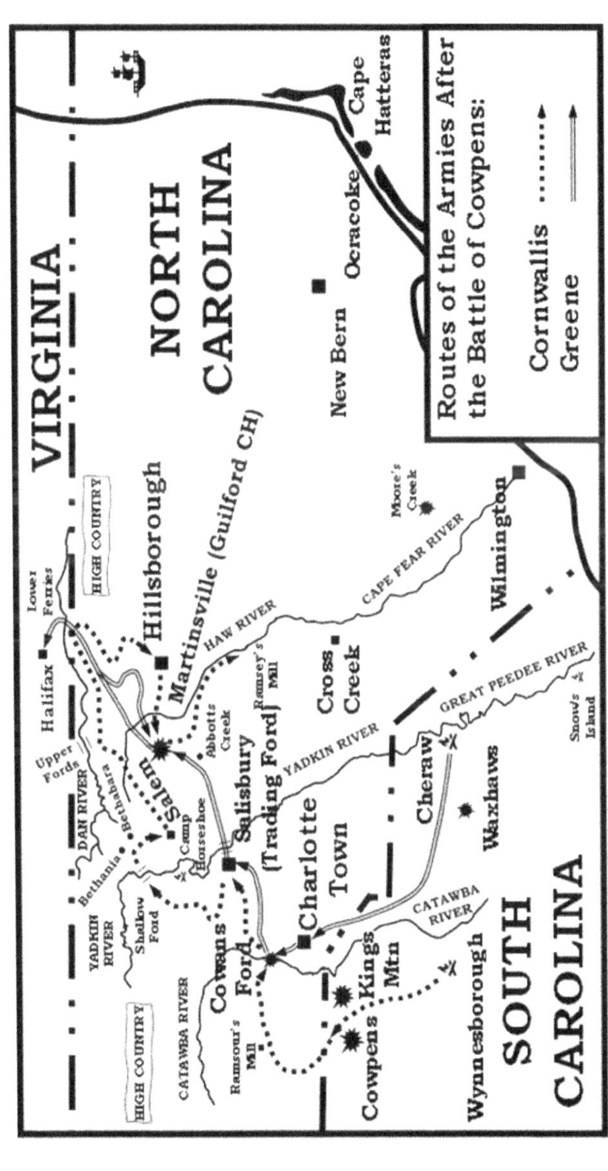

# Thirty-Nine ~ Second Invasion

— January 21, 1781

Maj Gen Leslie arrived from Charles Town and joined Gen Cornwallis. They marched north from Wynnesborough to near the border of North Carolina. In the backcountry just east of the Broad River they united with Lt Col Tarleton four days after the Battle of Cowpens and continued marching to Ramsour's Mill in North Carolina. The second invasion of the state had begun.

Humiliated by the Americans' unrelenting ardor, the lord yearned to catch Gen Morgan and retrieve his newly imprisoned forces. With Morgan camped fifteen miles east of the Catawba River at Charlotte Town, Cornwallis risked stopping four days to collect flour.

The lord sent for Tarleton to analyze the Cowpens blunder. Dealing with the vanquished junior wasn't going to be easy after defending him in post-battle communications to his superiors. Cornwallis had felt the explanation necessary, anticipating blame for sending the Legion commander instead of Maj Gen Leslie to contest Morgan.

Deflection and humor seemed the correct tone for Cornwallis to start the conversation in the dining room of a seven-room house taken for headquarters. "The Cowpens. What a bloody awful name for a battlefield. Never mind losing it. Who wants a stinking dung field?"

Tarleton dismissed the lord's tact and answered with his usual bravado. "I'll get revenge."

Cornwallis reverted to indiscretion. "Don't let me down."

Tarleton folded his arms and glared. "What can you do? You always tout my abilities. Who will believe I failed?"

Tarleton's insolence stung Cornwallis. "Don't insult me."

"I saw the letters you dictated to Captain Henry Broderick. You admitted no errors to your superiors. Why didn't you compel Leslie to reinforce me?"

The Lord intoned slowly and softly. "Get ahold of yourself."

"You nearly stranded me in the mires and swamps of the Broad River waiting for the reinforcements you promised."

Cornwallis leaned forward. "Your aggressiveness undermined you."

"You ordered me to push Morgan to the utmost." Tarleton calculated Cornwallis would neither speak ill of him publicly nor take retribution. "Don't even think of betraying me. I'll make a case to General Clinton or higher."

Cornwallis took a deep breath and exhaled instantly. He hung his head. In the polished surface of the table an image of Col Arthur Neal appeared. Didn't I fail to mobilize because of him? Greene isn't building a house. Neal's lost his mind. Can I believe anything he says?

Cornwallis stiffened against the back of the chair and pounded the table with both fists. "Forget Cowpens! From now on this army will fly. We'll reduce our baggage to what we can carry in our knapsacks and saddle bags."

"My Lord?"

"We'll mount the army and make it as nimble as the light infantry you lost at Cowpens."

"To chase the American general?"

"Our reputation depends on it."

"What about the wagons?"

"A dozen for hospital stores, salt, ammunition, and the sick and wounded. I'll burn the rest."

Wonderful. He's already planning for more casualties. "My Lord, that's a hundred carriages."

Cornwallis sneered. "Losing your wagon and lass bothers you."

Tarleton rolled his eyes. "The rum wagons?"

"Those too."

"My Lord, we have no prospects of obtaining rum or a regular supply of provisions for the soldiers."

Tarleton stared. The troops will pillage every private house and public place of hospitality. It hasn't been a year since the lord warned me over troop irregularities. We still had rum then.

***

Gen Greene had no more gotten the news of Cowpens than he served the officers Lady Martha Washington's cherry bounce and divided his corps again. He sent Brig Gen Isaac Huger with the main army of Continental infantry and artillery and all the heavy baggage up the roads beside the Yadkin-Pee Dee towards Salisbury. Greene flew with light troops to cover Morgan's movement and left a company to guard Camp Cheraw.

Cornwallis' pursuit of Morgan after Cowpens wasn't enough to confirm Greene's retreat strategy. But when the lord departed Ramsour's Mills heading east toward the Catawba River, there was no doubt Cornwallis had been hooked.

Greene couldn't believe his luck. Tarleton's pursuit of Morgan had been unexpected, but after prudent preparation for general warfare, the hero of Saratoga had urged his foe onto a perfect battlefield. The spectacular, incredible American victory at Cowpens had drawn Cornwallis into the chase.

Greene's corps joined Morgan's across the Catawba River at Sherrills Ford. In his first meeting with Morgan following the brilliant rout of Tarleton at Cowpens, Greene witnessed a giant man, one with a mind for battleground tactics. A man whose daring and prowess matched his intelligence.

***

Greene and Morgan sat on their mounts. Through field glasses Cornwallis watched helplessly from the opposite bank of the Catawba River, swollen and impassable from constant rain,.

"I'm impressed with the lord's stare," Greene said.

"He's certainly obsessed," Morgan said.

"Thanks to you."

"He must be seething."

Greene gambled the British general would long for the impossible. If Cornwallis remained hooked, a time could come when their armies would meet on the battlefield in general warfare more evenly matched.

"General," Greene said, "my appreciation for North Carolina's rivers grows."

Morgan nodded. "You can't beat a swollen river for keeping your enemy at bay."

"All we need is to keep these natural wonders between us and Cornwallis. Keep him on the chase and never let him catch us. He's burned his baggage. If we can get him far from British depots, we can turn on him when he's weak."

Morgan shifted uneasily in his saddle. "I'm of the opinion Cornwallis fully intends to make a push through this state in order to make a junction on the Roanoke or elsewhere."

"Let him come as long as he doesn't catch our rear or defeat our flanks. We can't let him circle us like Gates cornered the enemy at Saratoga." Greene cherished the accounts of Lt Gen John Burgoyne's surrender. "My God, your rifles made life insufferable."

Morgan doffed his cocked hat.

Meanwhile, Cornwallis came closer. Greene recoiled when he realized Royal artillery would have no problem raining cannon balls on their position. "If our friends knew our real situation they'd be mortified."

"I don't know. Washington is writing to the usual circle from the Hudson River saying he anxiously applauds the Southern army. Says you're studiously avoiding an engagement until you can draw together a greater force of militia."

"We'll press this retreat though from afar people will see it as a chase. Our meager flying army is ready for the most important consequences."

"Major General Baron von Steuben wonders whether Cornwallis has the capacity to figure he's being hoodwinked," Morgan said. "He doubts whether Cornwallis is a great general when these maneuvers prove him to be mad. How far can you lead Cornwallis?"

"I'm prepared to go as far as the Dan River over which we'll have our own supplies and reinforcements waiting."

***

The commander in chief of the Southern army ordered Morgan and his corps to hurry up the Salisbury Road to the Yadkin River crossing at Trading Ford. He stayed behind with the North Carolina militia, themselves ordered to defend the Catawba River crossing, reassemble, and march with him to Salisbury.

Early on February 1, 1781, a British detachment fired artillery and crossed the Catawba River at Beatties Ford, a ruse to draw the North Carolina militia. Meanwhile the rest of Cornwallis' army waded across Cowan's Ford six miles south and made a good landing.

Greene later received word the North Carolina militia had challenged the enemy at both fords. A militia detachment at the lower ford killed and wounded fifty or sixty then scattered when British light and grenadier companies emerged from the river and attacked. A dozen heroic militiamen including Brig Gen William Davidson lay dead after the onslaught. Though victorious, the British squandered precious time regrouping their fractured forces and chasing the rear of the Patriot militia.

Greene set off up the road to Salisbury. His black mare poked along, the road muddy from constant rain, but carried him steadily and surely in a small pack of militia forces who hoped Cornwallis wouldn't catch up before they crossed the Yadkin.

Miserable after the tragic news from the Catawba and conversation made difficult by sheeting rain, the men soon relied on their own company. Greene talked to himself at length, wondering if Maj Gen von Steuben had incorrectly identified the mad one.

An outsider should conceive me disheartened. Though the retreat is in force and the enemy has taken the bait, we have lost good men and allowed our pursuers to close the gap. But could anyone know my biggest worry? Between the lines of the Charlotte Town Gazette's big Cowpens story, the battle lasted less than an hour but consumed an abundance of ammunition. Without replenishment we'll blow the retreat and possibly the war.

I've apportioned the Marquis de Bretigny's gunpowder though lead is scarce. I'm depending on the Salem ammunition. Will it fall into the enemy's hands? The British army for the moment is too far away to touch it. That doesn't mean Loyalists won't try.

Hub, under the guise of Cornwallis, has established communication with Arthur Neal endeavoring to entrap him while getting the ammunition to safety. Will the Makers continue to hold their own against the Loyalists? Will Col Armstrong's regiment aid them? Can the Makers collect boats on the Dan in time? Can they usher the ammunition to Halifax?

On the second day of February and coming off a day's ride in the rear of his army, the general stopped at Elizabeth Maxwell Steele's ordinary in Salisbury. Wet, penniless, and begging for sustenance, he dropped into a chair and wrote to Quartermaster Edward Carrington.

"My aim is to draw the enemy to Virginia and thereby exhaust his provisions and in the meantime supplement our forces. We must prevent him from crossing the Dan. Therefore, I beg of you to spearhead the collection of boats at the Dan River ferries.

"We must possess enough musket cartridges to challenge the enemy in general warfare. I beg you to conduct the missions in and around Salem and get the ammunition across the Dan before the army crosses. Meet me February 10 at Guilford Court House for a council of war and tell me you've met the challenges."

Greene gave the message to an Express rider. When he turned around, the Patriot Mrs. Steele had brought him a meal and a small basket of gold and silver specie.

# Forty ~ A Special Convoy

Rumors drove central North Carolina citizens to seek hard news of the Battle of Cowpens and soon copies of the Charlotte Town Gazette spread up and down the Great Wagon Road and confirmed Morgan's victory. Brother Traugott Bach translated the story to German and directed the Salem printer to make copies for the town.

News of the Patriot victory lifted the spirits of the Moravians until they realized huge victories often spurred retribution. Cornered by anxious guests at Salem Tavern, Col Armstrong verified Cornwallis was pursuing Gen Morgan.

Armstrong said Maj Gen Greene left Camp Cheraw for the Catawba in an effort to get in front of the British army. That meant the war had leapt back into North Carolina. How long would it take before the combatants reached Wachovia?

*** 

Talk buzzed in the dining room of the Single Brothers House where Abe, Zeb, and George ate breakfast among Salem's boys and young men.

Zeb put a spoonful of porridge in front of his mouth. "My God, what am I doing here?"

"Wake up, Zeb. You're in the Makers company."

George paid no mind. Their conversation was unintelligible as usual.

"No, here in Salem again."

"Good. You're making progress. Now eat. We're needed at the brewery. We're lucky to get a respite from the war."

"You're not listening. When we leave Salem again, as we must, will the ladies come with us?"

"Is that what's bothering you?"

"Will I lose Yohanna?" Zeb put the spoonful of congealed porridge back in the bowl. "What am I saying? We're hardly on speaking terms. Still, the habits and manners we show each other stand for something."

"Don't say that."

"Why? I like Yohanna. What's wrong with me having feelings for her?"

"Nothing. I have feelings for Rahel. Forget things out of your control. Finish eating so we can get to work."

Zeb reflexively loaded his grumpy mouth until the pottery bowl scraped clean.

An old master brewer greeted the Makers at the Single Brothers Brewery, steepling his palms together as they entered a warehouse nearly emptied by the militia's presence. As they went to the various production stations, their help visibly eased the brewer's overwrought face.

George pumped wort from the mash tun to the copper brewing kettle. Zeb ground barley in the loft. Abe stacked wood under the hot water tank before firing the kettle.

As Abe threw split logs into the firebox, the tired brewer struggled below trying to empty the first-stage fermentation vat. "Brother Zeb!"

"Yes?"

"Have you finished grinding?"

"I'm tying the last bag."

"I beg you to pump out the first-stage fermentation vat for the brewer. First stir the beer with the wooden paddle and count the bubbles."

"What on earth for?"

"To make sure it's ready for final fermentation."

"Oh, alright." Zeb didn't see Abe's sneaky smile as he slogged to the vat.

Zeb leaned over holding a paddle. Putrid yeast vapor slammed his nose. "Oh my God!" A volcano threatened to erupt in his stomach.

Abe found Zeb bent over sick beside the vat.

"Brother Zeb, are you okay?"

Zeb looked up with a perspiring forehead and ashen face. "Just a moment." He pinched his nose and stood over the vat.

"What are you doing, my son?"

"I've yet to stir the beer and count the bubbles."

Abe's head lowered in humble regret. "Forget it."

"Why?"

"It was a lark."

Zeb covered his face. "What? You scoundrel." When his hand came down, a rosy glow replaced his sweaty, unnerved appearance.

Abe grinned. "Your mood is lighter."

"So, it is. Thank you."

***

Col Armstrong faced Traugott Bach. Normally staid in the company of the great Salem trader, the regimental commander had burst into Bach's study with anxious news. "Sir, the state militia has been called out."

Bach shot to his feet, alarmed at the possibility of losing the protection Salem had so dearly paid for. "Now?"

"I'm under orders to go in motion immediately."

"Your entire Surry County regiment?"

Armstrong nodded gravely. "I'll leave a platoon or company at most to watch over the ammunition and all of Salem town."

"What will you do with the Makers?"

"They're not under my authority. Captain Hawkins received orders to undertake a mission."

Salem's coerced affiliation with the Makers company concerned Bach. Mindful of his consent all but given to George Heider to marry Maria and Abraham's leading role among the Blacks, he didn't want to lose them. "Mission sounds dangerous."

"This is strictly confidential, sir. Hawkins will march his men outside of Wachovia and form a junction with a Patriot spy to lure a body of Loyalist dragoons with a decoy convoy. The gunpowder barrels we filled with dirt are going to be sent out on the road to draw out the Loyalists to capture Arthur Neal."

"I thought he'd left us alone."

"With Cornwallis on the march, we're afraid Neal will recruit energized Loyalists and menace the country."

"You mentioned a spy."

"He's called 'Hub'."

"That's the inner part of a wagon wheel."

Armstrong shrugged.

Bach folded his arms. "I want no further contact with Neal."

"Don't worry. Apparently, Hub has established communication and has Neal's confidence."

"Who's driving the convoy of fake gunpowder?"

"The Makers."

Bach shook his head vehemently. "Oh, no you don't. I don't want George Heider and Abraham put in danger."

"With all due respect, sir, they're General Greene's men now."

Bach looked at the wall then rounded back. "Why is it so important to get Neal out of the way?"

"We still have three wagons of ammunition needing transport to safety in Virginia. That's a real convoy Neal would love to seize."

Bach imagined the ammunition and his investment vanishing and cringed knowing he could lose his house and store.

# Forty-One ~ Besting

— February 2, 1781, Trading Ford, Salisbury, North Carolina

Greene and Morgan assembled their combined flying armies in Salisbury. Before crossing the Yadkin, Greene stopped to collect war materials stored in the Continental magazine. Rusted musket mechanisms caught the general's eyes as soldiers loaded them onto a wagon.

"Hold on, Private. I want to see one of those."

Greene examined a 1766 model French Charleville musket. Its .69 caliber bore matched the ones the Southern army used. Gunpowder residue blackened the end of the barrel. The rusted frizzen pulled back with resistance and the hammer wouldn't cock.

Greene snapped at aide-de-camp Maj Ichabod Burnet. "Muster all the regimental armorers here immediately."

When the armorers came, Greene ordered the corroded muskets overhauled.

"As soon as we decamp across the Yadkin, form fatigue parties and disassemble, polish, lubricate, and reassemble all seventeen-hundred guns. They must be perfect for the Virginia militia which I'm praying joins us."

"Yes, sir," the armorers clamored.

"All arms henceforth will be cleaned after action and kept dry in tents."

A sergeant protested. "These muskets will displace men from a dozen tents."

"The sixty soldiers can bunk with others."

***

The Yadkin River rose over the banks at Salisbury, so deep Greene's foot soldiers at the end of a thirty-five mile forced march from upper Charlotte Town found it impassable by wading.

At the horse ford the depth wasn't yet deadly for the cavalry and wagon drivers, but individuals would drown in the swift waters. Washington's anticipation of river crossings may have been intuitive but

Greene's decision to prioritize the ferries and position extra boats in advance was prophetic.

Ferry boats went back and forth moving the light infantry and dozens of camp followers to the east side of the Yadkin. As the operation ran into late night, the British vanguard approached Trading Ford.

Brig Gen Charles O'Hara arrived first. Ordered by Cornwallis to cross the Yadkin, the general witnessed a harrowing sight. Greene's forces were either across the Yadkin or enroute. They'd taken every vessel.

A rear guard of one-hundred Virginia riflemen and North Carolina militia countered British pistol fire from three Durham boats while feverish rowers plied the flooded river. They volleyed until safely across.

In the moonless night no one could see O'Hara's face turn red over the Rebel's unbelievable luck. When the rain ended, troops tore apart a broken down Patriot wagon and made a bonfire. In the light of the fire and emerging moon their enemy and the beaten up and muddy bank appeared.

There was no chance of British forces crossing. A scout informed the officers with creeping drama that as soon as the Patriots crossed the bulk of their forces, the waters rose unbelievably higher.

Including the ferries moored on the far side, the Patriots had secured all the boats. They'd scuttled some craft by shooting them with a half-dozen lead balls, piling them with large rocks, and pushing them into the river.

The Yadkin River proper was impassable to the two-thousand man British infantry and the three-hundred man Royal North Carolina Regiment. Neither would the mounted two-hundred British Legion nor baggage wagons and artillery cross at the deep, treacherous horse ford.

The Patriots' luck might run out if O'Hara's cannonade executed well. But the Royal artillery struggled to range correctly in the darkness. Those who'd never been under fire marched double time to safety when cannonballs at last jarred the ground behind their heels.

O'Hara sat mounted on horseback in early daylight. From a bluff he didn't need field glasses to apprise the topography of Trading Ford. Wide bodies of deep, daunting brown water straddled the rushing Yadkin River.

Shocked by the morass unseen the previous night, O'Hara instantly rode back to Cornwallis' headquarters situated in a house seized from a prominent Salisbury Whig.

O'Hara approached with caution. "Good morning, my Lord. Reporting conditions on the Yadkin."

Cornwallis pushed away a plate of fried eggs and bread when O'Hara relayed Greene's success. He threw down a linen napkin and fell back against the chair letting out a moan. "How did he do it?"

"Greene's body of infantry passed in the ferry's flat boats supplemented with a crude flotilla. His cavalry and wagons passed by the horse ford. When we arrived, the last Rebels had slunk away in Durham boats. Then the river and its banks overflowed with a sudden rising of the waters."

"What of my officers and men taken at Cowpens?"

"I've learned they crossed four days ago, my Lord."

Cornwallis twisted his face into a miserable knot. "Where are the boats now?"

"At rest on the other side or scuttled, my Lord."

"Where did the extra boats come from?"

"Apparently, Greene procured them ahead of crossing."

"So, boats will now await wherever Greene meets a river?"

"It might be worth keeping in mind, my Lord."

"Don't tell me what to keep in mind." The lord huffed. "Sudden rising of the waters?"

"A miracle smiled on the enemy."

"Next, you'll say the Patriots parted the Yadkin like the Red Sea!"

"It merely rose to permit their escape."

"Don't blame the water! You got there late."

For the second time Greene had upstaged Cornwallis at a major river crossing. Sorely recalling Washington crossing the Delaware on riverboats on Christmas day in 1776 with the Continental army, Cornwallis guessed only a thick book could document all the times Americans used rivers to their advantage.

It was too late to produce boats himself, but the lord had options for getting around the Yadkin River. He tarried at Salisbury resting and consulting with Loyalist scouts.

***

Major General Greene left Trading Ford heading northeast, putting room between himself and Cornwallis. His corps marched twenty miles northeast to the Quaker Meeting House at Abbotts Creek and halted to rest and secure scouting reports of Cornwallis' army in order to plan movements to lure the lord toward the Dan River.

Greene made headquarters at the house of William Spurgin, a Tory colonel away at muster. Privately he regretted the Tory's absence for the missed Patriot-Loyalist chat. Still, the colonel's Whig wife Mary Spurgin graciously opened her house to the general.

Nathanael Greene took pleasure in relating his long-term position held as Quartermaster General of the army but admitted leading military forces with the highest of honorable objectives pleased him more. He explained to Mrs. Spurgin a set of tactical duties inherent to a commander in the field.

Knowing the enemy's position was paramount. By the time Greene got to Abbotts Creek, Cornwallis would have moved out of Salisbury. The lord must cross the Yadkin River if he wanted to catch the Americans. But, where? It was possible the British were taking the route up to Shallow Ford where Maj Gen Gates had said the river was passable without boats.

"We need a good local scout."

Mrs. Spurgin removed a sated baby from her breast and gave Greene a quizzical stare. "May I recommend someone?"

"Of course, ma'am."

Spurgin held the baby face down on her shoulder and patted its back. "My son Johnny is a fast rider who knows the backcountry." The baby burped.

"Get him here. Hurry."

She went to the foot of the stairs.

"Johnny!"

Greene figured Johnny was a boy. After all, she was feeding his sibling.

The "boy" bounded down whisker-faced and strapping. The general sat down with Johnny at a large kitchen table and pointed to their location and Trading Ford on a map.

"Now, son, I'm going to lend you a fast horse. I want you to ride with one of my scouts down to Trading Ford. Find out the movements of the British army."

Johnny stood. "I can do that, sir."

"Hold on. If you don't see them in Salisbury, go ten miles north along the river and look for them."

"I understand, sir."

"One more thing, son. Take a squad of cavalry to the Horse Shoe on the Yadkin. The cavalry will destroy a set of flat boats at the crossing and return without you and the scout. Keep searching up the river."

Johnny rode off. Greene ordered his field officers to drill and condition the troops in the interim. Regimental leaders directed the infantrymen and cavalry to dry their musket cartridges in the open air, and clean and lubricate all the muskets including the ones collected at Salisbury. Then, following mock gun-loading practice, they would rehearse tactics and commands and have bugle, fife, and drum calls played until they knew the difference between "charge" and "retreat".

Greene proposed a hike to aide-de-camp Maj Ichabod Burnet to stir the blood in their legs after long days of near continuous riding. He interrupted the walk repeatedly to mention the terrain in terms of its goodness and advantage in battle. He'd been away from the field too long. Conceiving plans on his feet was more necessary than sporting.

Greene soon found himself weighing strategy. While I don't know where the coming battle will take place, general warfare with Cornwallis will occur here or somewhere else nearby in central North Carolina and possibly soon. Where to fight the British isn't strictly a decision in my control unless I can turn on them when I want.

Not that the field will be in Abbotts Creek, but it could be if I remained in place until Huger's corps arrived. The best I can do is to know my ground and prepare for the time when I'm blessed with enough support to let the battle fall.

Greene emerged from his thoughts. Johnny Spurgin and the scout approached.

Johnny told enthusiastically how far and where they'd gone to let Greene know he'd followed orders. He looked at the ground and told the general he hadn't seen the British army.

"You must ride again and make another search further west along the river. Get going! I need that information!"

# Forty-Two ~ Cornwallis Pursues

— February 6, 1781, Rowan County, North Carolina

A Tory sighted Maj Gen Greene's army at Abbotts Creek and passed the information to Cornwallis. Once scouts confirmed the presence of Greene's troops, Cornwallis aimed to jump ahead. If the Rebel general wanted to reach Virginia, he'd have to go through the King's men.

Cornwallis had no choice but to march around Trading Ford at Salisbury for a northward course plotted on Mouzon's 1775 *Accurate Map of North and South Carolina* through backcountry along a line ten miles west and roughly parallel with the Yadkin. He planned to cross the Yadkin at Shallow Ford and enter Wachovia twenty miles northwest of Abbotts Creek.

Cornwallis left Salisbury heading west. At Second Creek he turned north toward Wachovia and the Great Wagon Road which promised to put him in place to block Greene. More than practical, the route tantalized his mouth with designs of refreshment at Wachovia's settlements.

***

Two days after Cornwallis marched from Trading Ford, Capt Hawkins received an Express from Lt Col Carrington. "I will meet you in Salem on or before February 10. General Greene has called a council of war to meet that day in Guilford County. First, I must check conditions at the ferries on the Dan River. Loyalists are eager to capture ammunition. March the decoy convoy without delay."

Hawkins had two days. He gathered the Makers and a partial company of Surry militia detached by Col Armstrong. "Hub's messages posing as Cornwallis have apparently worked. Colonel Arthur Neal and his band of Loyalist provincials want the ammunition for the lord. We'll dangle the bait, draw them in, and make a capture."

Sgt Vinyard nodded along with Hawkins until the captain's last word. "What if we can't capture him?"

"Then Neal and the other Loyalists should be killed."

Vinyard smiled and nodded. "Very well, sir."

"To make sure Neal attacks," Hawkins said, "we've been ordered by Lieutenant Colonel Carrington to load the decoy barrels."

Zeb Mitchell raised his hand and didn't wait for permission to speak. "Barrels, sir? Why not boxes?"

Hawkins hushed Zeb with an outstretched palm. "What makes you think you can interrupt me?" Not seeing signs of Zeb's regret, he continued. "There could be anything inside the boxes. Barrels labeled as gunpowder are sure to get Neal's attention."

"Neal must know we made ammunition with the powder."

The captain's eyes menaced Zeb like the end of a gun barrel. "We're out of time." He turned to go. None of the men moved. "Load the wagons now! We need to be on our way."

***

Not long after the three wagon decoy convoy turned southwest on the Great Wagon Road at the crossroads of Bethania and Bethabara, Hawkins' body of troops came upon a man surveying land. He assured them they'd come to Shallow Ford in another mile.

Splendid music of water rippling over rocks filled the air as they approached. A hooded person on horseback left the woods and conducted his mount into the road. The convoy stopped. The Surry militiamen and Makers jumped down and cautiously met the stranger. The hood lowered and Sara McMurray introduced herself as Hub.

Zeb eyed her with a hundred questions. "You've addled me since Camp Horse Shoe. What brought you to do this?"

Sara threw a cool glare then grinned. "Glad to see you too."

He shook his head. "That's not fair. You were a bundle of nerves in New Garden."

"Before you left for Camp New Providence Maria gave me Arthur Neal's code book and letter. Until then I didn't know his name or how to find him. The gall of that man wrecking father's shop hit me in the face."

"It must have smacked you silly."

"I'll disregard that. When you and your Makers forces left, I saw no one else would come to father's aid."

"We're at war. You don't shoot guns."

Sara begged a rifle from the Surry militia and loaded it with ease. She aimed at a tree thirty yards away on the side of the road. "See that swelling redbud?" The rifle went off and split the thin, black trunk.

Zeb's eyes snapped open. He grinned, recalling her words back in New Garden. "There's nothing you can do that doesn't break something. Fine, Sister. Let's do this."

***

Zeb Mitchell sat on the floor of the middle wagon with Sara McMurray and George Heider in a space opened up by pulling back the canvas cover. The material flapped in a cool breeze made by the wagon's movement. Beside them lay eight Surry militia rifles loaded and begging to be fully cocked and fired at the enemy.

Soon a stilted conversation began.

Zeb poked George's chest. "George has also learned to be an expert gunner."

George grinned. "I expert gunner."

"Sometimes I think you speak broken English for laughs." Zeb stopped chuckling to admire the Moravian, fortunate to have a language barrier to cover fears they all felt. "But can George ever shoot. You should have seen the straight musket shot that wounded Arthur Neal. I'm looking forward to seeing what you two do with rifled barrels."

The decoy convoy wagons swayed and bounced on a base of slimy rocks sunken under a foot of frothy Yadkin River water as they left Wachovia at Shallow Ford and crossed into Rowan County heading south toward Old Mocks Field.

Sara had to climb down from the pedestal Zeb had put her and George. "Don't get your hopes up."

"Come on. Obviously, you've been practicing. Who taught you?"

"Thomas Bourne."

"My God, that Quaker boy fancies you."

"Don't be silly. He happens to aim guns well."

"And you just happen to be working hard to get back at Neal."

Her face tightened. "I'm not doing this to avenge father."

While Zeb hadn't obsessed over Sara's fright in New Garden, he wondered if she'd freeze up. But hadn't he been affected? "I'm sorry for that. You've been incredible as a spy. It should be enough that you arranged for Neal to meet us."

"You're not completely misguided. People are looking for retribution."

"What'll happen if the Revolution is won but the division persists?"

"I don't know, dear Brother. Let's win the war first."

The wagons halted. After a short stop so George and Sara could take their places under the cover and Zeb could take the driver's seat, they continued to the place of assignation. Another half-hour down the road Sara recognized a thicket near a path that crossed the Great Wagon Road. She rapped on the cargo box and Zeb halted on the verge.

Zeb jumped down. He glanced at the thick woods and couldn't imagine a lead ball passing. After grabbing a mallet and jar from the toolbox, he went to the right rear wheel and hammered the hub before wiping a handful of grease in the axle joint.

The pretense continued. He studied a wrinkled canvas cover in the center of the wagon along the side facing the woods. He untied the ropes and lifted the cover to reveal the entire center section of barrels. The cargo box at the forward and rear of the wagon remained loosely covered.

Twigs cracked in the woods. Zeb made nonchalant steps to the road side of the wagon. Crouched behind the barrels, he doffed his cocked hat and peered. The horsemen from Neal's detachment of the Royal North Carolina Regiment emerged from trees like rats through a holey wall.

A Loyalist jumped, from real or imagined movement in the wagon. Everything in time and space froze. Two Loyalist green jackets in front resumed their approach no more than fifty feet away. Five more Loyalists followed close behind them.

A barrel-bellied, ruddy skinned Loyalist with a bandaged left arm closed in last. He squinched at the wagon load and braved a shot that split the top of a barrel. "It's a Rebel trap!"

George shot and missed Neal. One of the forward Loyalists took a ball in his chest and dropped. Sara picked up another rifle.

Neal fired again and made a hole in the cover hiding George. Return fire strayed. The colonel crouched in the brush.

"Neal!" Sara cried. Another Loyalist popped out from behind a tree and leveled a pistol looking for a target. Sara killed him instead. Others continued approaching with muskets.

Hawkins wasn't visible but his voice rose from a funnel made from his hand. It sounded false and cheap but boomed and echoed from the leafless trees standing like pins crowded on a cushion. "Fire and this ammunition will go up."

It was too late. Rather than a warning they took it as a dare and kept coming.

Two more shots came from Sara's position in the front of the wagon. She reloaded and fired once more. The fire mounted when all the Makers and Surry militia joined her. Smoke obliterated the view of the woods.

The blue haze cleared and near silence returned. Across the woods horses pranced as the Loyalists threaded the undergrowth. Hoofbeats gathered into a mad, galloping din in a clearing on the other side.

Abe tore away to George. He shuddered when he pulled back the cover and found his Moravian brother lying still with closed eyes. When Sara and Zeb arrived, George woke and shook his head. The blackout was over.

Four Loyalists lay dead and one badly wounded. Enveloped in smoke and noise, the chaotic circumstances shrouded Col Arthur Neal's whereabouts. He didn't turn up in a search.

The Makers and Surry militia returned to Salem and unhitched the wagons. An hour later, they'd fed and cleaned the horses when a horse sprinted down Bethabara Street throwing clods of mud and manure.

The rider had come down from the upper villages of Bethania and Bethabara. He dismounted at Salem Tavern and gulped before crying the news. "Lord Cornwallis is coming up the Great Wagon Road heading for Wachovia!"

# Forty-Three ~ To Wachovia

— February 8, 1781, Forks of the Yadkin, North Carolina

At eight in the morning the British army stopped on the South Yadkin River, the last major tributary running east to the Yadkin River. They drank and filled canteens then marched north through Old Mocks Field before turning east onto the Great Wagon Road to Shallow Ford.

At four o'clock Cornwallis finally crossed the Yadkin River at Shallow Ford. The army forded at a wide and shallow section without incident and entered northwestern Wachovia. News rapidly spread of the British army's advance, though the lord appeared not to be in a hurry.

***

At noon on February 9, the troops under Cornwallis entered Bethania before falling down to her sister village Bethabara which lay above Salem. Long feared, Cornwallis no longer lazily passed in and out of Moravian reflections.

The enormous British army darkened Wachovia more than black clouds. Anybody who could leave did and the Great Wagon Road backed up with dozens of wagons filled with fleeing travelers.

***

Surry militia successfully flew from Salem. As they were inclined to hurry out of Wachovia, they headed north on the Great Wagon Road. Also known as the Carolina Road, the wide path ran between Bethania to the north and Bethabara to the south. It was a road meant for traveling.

The Makers, Sara, and the Salem sisters followed later but found themselves blocked in Bethabara traffic. They wouldn't soon make it up the Great Wagon Road past Wachovia to form a junction with the militia.

Carrying the aroma of beer production and still wearing Salem Brewery aprons, the Makers decided to take refuge at Bethabara Brewery. Blending in was easy but fraught with danger. They gathered outside wearing grave apprehension in their eyes as the Redcoats marched down from Bethania. They'd joined the North Carolina militia never realizing how close they'd come to British troops.

George Heider stood with the single brothers and watched the wretched soldiers. Maria, Sara, Rahel, and Yohanna had taken refuge at the bakery on the other side of the road where they too watched the British parade of soldiers, catching a glimpse of the invaders marching in two files.

George watched Maria standing idle and available. He fumed, imagining Bishop Graff coming along and seeing her wild and conjuring presence. The bishop would banish her beyond the Wachovia tract with the other wild creatures.

Maria admired the Redcoats. George dashed across the road between the British ranks to admonish her.

"You shouldn't be over here, Brother Heider." Maria wiped her floury hands. "I'm in enough trouble with my father."

"I didn't ask you to become a camp follower. Serves you right Brother Bach sent you to Single Sister service." Her eyes drifted. "Don't eye the soldiers!"

She motioned at the boys outside Bethabara Brewery. "They're gossiping at us."

"It's you, Sister. You have no right measuring up the enemy. Your place is in the bakery."

"We shouldn't be talking, Brother Heider."

"I gathered that, Sister. It'll be okay when the Savior blesses us with marriage."

"Don't get ahead of yourself. Our single brothers outnumber our single sisters." She watched the soldiers slapping their dirty soles on the road. "I feel sorry for those boys."

George turned icy. "Ridiculous."

The Great Wagon Road was muddy. It would worsen if the hungry soldiers kept drooling from aromas arising from the bakery and local houses where housemothers slow cooked stews for family meals. The smells might kill them without powder and lead.

"You can see how thin they are."

"Why do you think they're hungry?"

"Brother Heider, don't stare!"

"I know how you want to be looked at."

"How dare you? They don't want me. They want food. They want to go home."

"Look at their aggressive gait."

"They're shivering!"

George howled. "Probably drunk. Go back to work. You're meant for me."

"I'm not a young doe in the wild woods. You're no less conjuring than outsiders."

"Do you like Salem? Remember, the bishop sends unmarried women to Pennsylvania for Moravian marriage."

"Change or I will gladly go northward." Maria gathered the black and white checked dress from her feet and strode up the path and into the back door of the bakery.

*** 

The British storm upset life in upper Wachovia. Children who typically played in the yards found care and safety in schoolrooms while their mothers baked loaves of bread by the hundreds and cooked for the soldiers. When the British commissary general discovered Bethabara's flour mill, he ordered milling commence to replenish stocks.

Meat-starved Redcoats roasted venison foraged in nearby woods. When deer thinned, they harvested domesticated animals. Every free range chicken, goose, and duck landed in a pot. They demanded beeves to slaughter, sparing neither bulls needed to sire the next season's issue nor oxen used to plow the fields.

While meat roasted, the marauders returned to various stillhouses discovered in the woods and freely consumed the liquor. Cornwallis called for brandy and the Bethabara distillery obliged with a half-dozen casks.

Someone had set up tables and chairs outside the brewery and served mugs of beer and brandy at an impromptu fresh air tavern. A pompous Legion officer snapped his fingers to get the attention of Zeb Mitchell or Abraham Hellerschwarz for service.

Tarleton looked with curiosity at Zeb standing before him. "Are you German?"

Zeb sought George's broken English. "Yes...I mean ya, I German."

The British officer's eyes drilled with skepticism. "Do you know who I am? I'm Lieutenant Colonel Banastre Tarleton. 'Bloody' they call me."

Zeb froze.

"Prevarication galls me. You don't sound German. What are you?"

Abe watched the exchange with horror and came to Zeb's side smiling. "Don't mind him, sir. He's German-Amerikaner. Do you want something to drink?"

"Brandy, my good man. Make it a large one. Quickly before I'm missed."

Abe gave Zeb a wink and slowly uttered German. "Hans, bring the gentlemen a large brandy." Abe quickly bowed to Tarleton and followed Zeb to the brewer who had tapped a cask of brandy.

The brewer poured four inches into a mug. "There you are."

"Are you sure? That much?"

"We want the Englishman to drink well and be happy. Maybe he'll take to bed early."

Zeb grinned and left for Tarleton. After bumping into Rahel and seeing tears streaming from her eyes, he continued to Bloody Tarleton.

Abe came by her side. "What's wrong?"

"I thought we'd escaped. Will we never get out?"

He wrapped his hands around hers. "Hang on, dear. Captain Hawkins and Sergeant Vinyard have come around to Zeb and Sara's plan."

***

All the private houses of Bethania and Bethabara turned into hostels filled with officers and their servants. Soldiers, full of meat, bread, beer, and brandy slept outside. Lucky ones sheltered in makeshift tents while most wrapped in blankets  and slept in the yards.

The villages lay despoiled. Every scrap of fence and privy boarding went into camp fires sprouting all over. Moravians thanked God for preventing a conflagration from soldiers who, either tired or in near blacked out stupor, built unsafe fires without pits.

***

Lt Col Tarleton continued to enjoy Bethabara distillery's spirits late into the night and for the third time staggered, searching for a privy. Not finding one, he swayed down the street and pissed in a horse trough. His head spun as he hung onto the hitching post. Behind him a wagon rolled down the street. Pots tied to the sides clattered. He looked over his shoulder. The wagon had stopped.

A black man, who Tarleton faintly recognized, leaned from the driver's seat while watching a black woman securing iron cooking vessels to the side of the wagon with extra rope. She pulled herself up beside him and the wagon passed south through town in the gray light.

Tarleton mumbled and tripped in the doorway of Bethabara Gemeinhaus. Unbeknownst to him, Lord Cornwallis was out walking and heard the sounds and witnessed Tarleton go inside. He opened the door and found Tarleton swinging a sword at an imaginary foe.

Cornwallis bravely took the sword from Tarleton. "Why do you cause mischief everywhere I go?"

Tarleton stood up to the Lord. "Why did you destroy me?"

Cornwallis shielded his nose from the man's alcohol-infused breath. "Make yourself clear."

"You promised to give me aid yet left me in the mires and the Cowpens on my own."

"Fool. I told you not to rush into battle. Get over it."

****

Zeb helped Yohanna tie two sheep to the feed trough on the back of the wagon. One moment they stood side by side and the next faced each other. He leaned in and kissed her hair as she lay against him. She uttered one word and halted. A frown gave way to a sigh at their poor communication. They found each other's lips and briefly nourished their growing hunger, talking unnecessary.

All the mock refuge seekers tied implements and washboards to the sides of the wagons. They hid their weapons and dressed in rough clothes, making their appearance especially disheveled and grimy. Sara, Maria, Rahel, and Yohanna grew with child from rags balled and stuffed in their midriffs.

With new teams of sorry horses purposefully covered with fine road dust and harnessed in old leather they set off from Bethabara. Roughened with a wire brush and wiped with ashes, the wagons took on a gray, weathered look that broke Zeb's heart.

One by one, the Makers' wagons trickled to Brother Johann Stockburger's farm below Salem. No sound came from the four trumpets at Peter Yarrell's tannery while the Makers carried ammunition boxes from Brother Zillman's house.

Soon they turned around and trickled back to the upper Wachovia villages and got on the Great Wagon Road. Abe and Rahel had gotten there first and waited on the verge above Wachovia for the others to form a convoy with the militia.

British pickets had no reason to suspect anything. Except for travelers seeking safety from the siege befalling Wachovia, all was calm in the night.

Taking the last few miles through Bethabara and Bethania in three wagons concealing Capt Hawkins, Sgt Vinyard, James Gillies, and precious cargoes of musket ammunition, the fake pioneers clutched their hearts with worry. But they only had to stand their anxiety a bit longer until they reached the Great Wagon Road where the Surry militia platoon joined them with their two wagons.

# Forty-Four ~ Salem Tour

— February 10, 1781, Salem

In the morning, martial drumbeats preceded from Bethabara as the British army fell down Shallow Ford Road into Salem. They turned due east onto Hope Street, turned south on Bethabara Street, and halted in front of Salem Square under ribbons of wool dyed red in bloodroot.

Big and wealthy Salem, like the small upper villages, could do nothing. It couldn't keep out undesirable individuals and this was an army of them. British fans had hung the ribbons and now watched the parade. Though town folk met their loyalty with skepticism, they still dotted the street sides waving and shouting, "God save the King!"

Ever since the British brought hot war to the South by taking Charles Town, Patriots demanded to know Moravian political leaning. Now they might wonder if open allegiance to His Majesty the King would replace quiet patriotism.

After locals recognized the "Loyalists" as Bethabara residents paid to appease the British, Salemites whispered rebukes. Shouts of "Hurrah for Washington!" by a man using his best German-inflected English mimed a Whig to answer the false Tories.

For the safety of the town, two Salem fellows chased off the Washington devotee. Having false Tories and Whigs shouting over each other risked a fate worse than plundered foodstuffs. The crimson ribbons remained in a nod to reason.

After a raucous score of young, undersized fifers and drummers wearing red-faced blue frocks passed in the vanguard, large companies of grown infantrymen sporting red frocks marched by. Hordes of stout, beastly Hessian foot soldiers and riflemen stomped along next, the former wearing blue frocks and the latter green. Both German corps donned a mixture of pointed helmets and tricorns. Onlookers eyed the long mustaches sprouting from many of their faces and knew wild fighters had come to town.

***

That masses of British Regulars had come thousands of miles across the Atlantic to march thru Salem made the town stand. Up close, however, the Moravians pitied the soldiers donned in wrinkled and soiled uniforms. How could these thin, wasting soldiers who coughed and sniffled constantly, put such fear into the Colonies? The answer came in the great number of professional troops brought and the unforgiving determination they wore on their faces.

Awe of the marchers rose when another green-garbed German regiment marched by and thin ranks of green-jacketed dragoons of the British Legion cavalry followed, seated high on their mounts and kitted with gleaming swords. The big guns of the Royal Artillery brought every Moravian to their feet when ominous and ultimate, Lord Cornwallis, the man Moravians loathed in their heart, sauntered by on horseback amid a brigade of red-clad guardians.

Resplendent in scarlet, gold, and lace, the lord was the King's highest representative in the South. To their surprise, admiration radiated from his face as he viewed their town. Laid out neatly in a rectangular grid with buildings of good character, it seemed to him a tiny version of Philadelphia which he'd seized with Sir William Howe in 1777. Did Salem please him or was there something pernicious in his smile?

Though Salem had flirted with the Patriots, they'd kept their political views private. If there was a hint of collaboration the whole Wachovia tract could be at risk. Would the British run amok? Would a falling out of the Moravians with one combatant or the other lead to the British and Continentals using the settlement as a battlefield?

*** 

The soldiers exuded a great unedifying odor. Hopefully, once dismissed from their ranks, they'd march to the wash house.

The Hessians from the von Bose and Yager regiments searched for Salem Tavern. Respect and sadness overcame them as the squares of white stone marking the graves of the sleeping in God's Acre appeared between the wildflowers. They removed their pointed hats momentarily, turned, and retraced their steps.

They walked south on Bethabara Street and stopped at the splendid brick and half-timber Fourth House. The German architectural motif gaped their mouths and transported their hearts to the land of their fathers and mothers.

The Hessians met the owner who greeted them. "Wilkommen." Each soldier privately wondered if anyone would miss them after Cornwallis left Salem. The man took them next door to the Salem potter and bought them mugs before directing them to the tavern.

The British Foot regiments ventured out with packs on their backs south down Bethabara Street and found Single Brothers Brewery. Beer sloshed from oak buckets as lucky Redcoats hurried to the yard. While they stabbed kegs with bayonets, throngs of thirsty troops formed a proper English queue to wait their turn in the chilly air.

***

Lord Cornwallis dismounted. A man with long, queued black hair, pleasantly dispositioned face, and round jaw approached the general. Dressed in black except for a white neck cloth, he made a deep bow.

"I am Bishop Johann Michael Graff, your Excellency."

Cornwallis shuddered and motioned to aide-de-camp Capt Broderick.

"Welcome to Salem. A town whose name—"

"My good Bishop," Broderick interrupted, "General Cornwallis is a lord. He dislikes George Washington's mere title."

Well I revile "lord", thought the bishop. There was one Lord, but this was no time to give a Sunday school lesson. Graff bowed again and donned his black floppy hat. "My Lord."

Cornwallis nodded with approbation in his eyes. "Continue."

"Yes, my Lord. Salem is a town—"

"Are you the leader?"

"Will not a holy man do?" Graff folded his hands. "Oh, I see. You want to meet the chief shareholder, Brother Traugott Bach. He will return later today."

"You'll do for now."

"Salem derives from shalom, the Hebrew word for peace." The bishop counted nine men kitted out in swords and pistols surrounding Cornwallis. "Are these your officers?"

"Guards. My officers are still with their regiments." Cornwallis made a cursory glance around the street. "Where's Banastre?"

Broderick grinned wickedly. "He's gone to the tavern."

"I should have known. Fetch him!"

Maj Johann du Buy, a commander of Hessian forces allied with the British, joined Cornwallis in time to hear Graff utter German words with closed eyes and bowed head.

"What did he say?"

Maj Johann du Buy's facility with German and English made him essential in Cornwallis' army of troops speaking different languages. "A prayer, my Lord."

Cornwallis snarled. "I could see that. What did he say?"

"He asked God to bless the Carolinas with peace."

Cornwallis grumbled. "Ask him to bless me with a tour of Salem."

"My Lord," Bishop Graff said, "it will be a pleasure." He led Cornwallis and du Buy to a two-row buggy handsomely decorated with Moravian stars, tulips, birds, and German phrases in Gothic text.

Graff clicked his tongue and the vehicle rolled down Bethabara Street. Cornwallis touched the bishop's arm. "My good man, stop at the tavern first."

Lt Col Tarleton stepped out of Salem Tavern glowing from brandy and sauntered to the buggy. Cornwallis glared while he got in the back seat with Maj du Buy.

Graff turned the buggy north.

"Stop!" Cornwallis said.

"Yes, my Lord? What is it?"

"What's that?"

Graff followed Lord Cornwallis' finger. "Our Gemeinhaus. The place where town folk gather to worship the Almighty."

Cornwallis stretched his arm and pointed at a hollowed log from which water ran. "No, that."

"Part of our waterworks, my Lord."

Tarleton watched Graff go to the standpipe and cup his hands for a drink of water. He leaned forward and whispered in Cornwallis' ear. "What a change. To have come out of the wilds and find such industry."

Cornwallis sneered over his shoulder. "You've been drinking."

The junior officer evaded. "They make us look idle."

"Idle is a good change for *you*." Cornwallis scanned the town. "Philadelphia is bigger and sophisticated, but the Moravians have built a beautiful, civilized town in the middle of a backward province. Americans are going to get better. Is it too late to keep them down?"

Graff reboarded the buggy. "Pardon the delay, my Lord. Such a thirst came over me."

"You should thank God your pipes aren't made of lead like those of ancient Rome."

"We thank God for everything, my Lord."

"Has He taught you to avoid *all* uses of lead?"

The bishop replied with a pitch to make the Lord see the blasphemy of thinking God makes all decisions. "He has framed in our conscience the proper use of it."

The tour continued with Cornwallis' guards escorting the buggy on horseback. Graff announced every owner of a house or business preceded by the title *Brother* in an equality-minded way Cornwallis had heard often in America. The more Graff said it, the more Cornwallis wanted to vomit. Would the Bishop drop "Lord" and start calling him Brother Cornwallis? It was time the lord asked the tough questions.

"I've learned Moravians aid my enemy."

"Moravian brethren are pacifists."

"Are you keeping any secrets from your English friends?"

"We pay the three-fold tax to absolve our participation in the violence. We say oaths to neither side."

"That doesn't mean you don't provide aid."

"Our aid is promised to the suffering of the world." Bishop Graff trembled before God. He refused to do it before the man at the top of the British Southern command. "My Lord—"

I remain a lord, thank God! "Don't trouble yourself denying it, my good man. Open up and you won't be troubled."

Bishop Graff sighed with all his diaphragm. "Thank you, sir, um Lord. We stand in the middle while both sides bear down."

"Not the British."

No, not the British. Merely their Tory and Loyalist lackeys. "You are most correct."

"Then, who are you speaking of?"

"The Continentals have in fact imposed upon us," Graff fibbed. "We are weak neutrals who don't bear arms. What can we do?"

"Stop dodging. That's what. You have sympathy with the Continentals."

"My Lord, we are a nonaligned people. We cling to no power except God."

"You're selling to Greene's army. Sell to mine."

"What do you need?"

"Everything. Gunpowder, lead, food, and shoes."

"We can provide food and shoes. We have no gunpowder or lead." At least not discrete gunpowder or lead. For the sisters rolled it into ammunition.

Graff directed the buggy south, crossed over the Wach River, turned east, and drove for a mile before crossing over the Wach again to come up Bethabara Street. A cheer from the beer-drinking Redcoats at the Single Brothers Brewery rose in the distance as the buggy passed an unadorned barn spilling amber sap from recently cut wood.

Cornwallis touched Graff's arm again and the buggy stopped. The lord pointed his thumb behind him to the twenty-four-foot by thirty-foot structure while looking quizzically at the bishop. Graff had described every other structure in detail yet suspiciously avoided mentioning that one.

"What building was that?" Cornwallis said.

"Naught but an empty warehouse, my Lord."

"Go back and show me."

An uneven road surface—ruts of icy mud sliced down and across by wagons and teams and refrozen—rattled Cornwallis' bones. Bad roads bothered riders the world over. If the clever Moravians couldn't fix them, nobody could.

The carriage halted in front of a crude door having two planks wedged against it. They hung in slots nailed to the wall. Cornwallis directed Tarleton and du Buy to remove the planks and door.

Cornwallis put his head inside and sniffed.

"A disused store, my Lord."

There was no gunpowder, but the lord was sure there had been. The small warehouse reeked of boiled eggs. Spills of the black grains had mostly been removed from the earthen floor. A dead rat lay in sweepings.

Cornwallis got another whiff of the air in the room. "Sulfur!"

"My Lord—"

Cornwallis cut him off. "I get enough dissembling from my field officers."

Graff hung his head. Cornwallis sniffed again.

"This is a magazine for gunpowder storage or a laboratory for fashioning lead shot and gunpowder into cartridges. Did you do that for the Continentals?"

For a Bishop, Graff's response came out quite fabricated and he winced with regret. "Lead. For coffins, my Lord. Insufferable smallpox."

Cornwallis intoned as icily as the air. "My good man, I smell gunpowder. Where did it go?"

Graff made a thin, apologetic grin and raised his eyebrows. "To be honest, I too am wondering what happened to it."

Cornwallis inspected Graff's cunning eyes. "To be honest! Why must a Bishop evade?"

"If I permit myself to be accused of lying, and if we are to consider this term of reproach an injury, I shall not let it rest upon me."

"Well, don't martyr yourself."

Graff turned grave. "No, my Lord."

The empty building meant it was too late. Cornwallis rued not getting the ammunition. "Forget it. I can't dally with my enemy near." He motioned to Tarleton and du Buy to replace the door.

Graff suppressed a sigh. "Very well, my Lord. Please enjoy Salem's quarters, food, and spirits."

# Forty-Five ~ Attack

— February 10, 1781, Town Fork, North Carolina

Lt Col Carrington rendezvoused with the ammunition convoy just past midnight above Wachovia on the Great Wagon Road. Capt Hawkins, the Makers, Sara, the Salem ladies, James Gillies, and Surry militia gathered to hear him explain the route to the ferries at the lower fords just before the Dan River joins the Roanoke River in southern Virginia.

Hawkins watched Carrington remount. "What's to come, sir?"

"It depends on the council of war with General Greene in Guilford County. Whatever the outcome, depend on him to put Cornwallis twenty-four hours behind."

"That means I'll have twice the lead."

"You also have a priceless burden. I'll rejoin you soon."

"Of course, sir. I pray to keep a good pace and the musket cartridges safely ahead."

Carrington eyed the young bugler. "Master James, come along if you want to join up with Lieutenant Colonel Lee." The tug of the reins urged the horse into a trot. Carrington yelled over his shoulder. "Push your teams hard!" James Gillies raced on horseback down the moonlit road and caught up with Carrington.

***

Hawkins addressed the assembled convoy. "We're going to rest here at Town Fork for the night. We have horses to feed and groom and a camp to set up. Let's get to work so we can rest securely."

Sgt Vinyard didn't jump to the chores. "Speaking of secure. How are we going to arrange the wagons?"

"Colonel Arthur Neal worries you?"

"Exposing the ammunition will get us all killed."

"Do you expect him to bring an army?"

"Begging your pardon, sir, isn't clear thinking in order after the calamities we've seen?"

"Pretending we'll be in a little skirmish that will decide America's fate isn't clear thinking. Are you so vain?"

The sergeant glared at Hawkins. In flare light, seas of white surrounded Vinyard's brown pupils. "They could blow us away with one errant bullet."

"Would you have us firing on anybody who comes near? I don't want to go down in history for inciting a massacre."

"We've skirmished twice with the Loyalists already. Neal should be dead. Heaven help us if he comes at us again."

"I have no orders to kill Colonel Neal."

"That's not what you implied recently."

"Never mind. Be watchful but not savage. If we lose this ammunition, we'll answer to Major General Greene. If we butcher our enemy, we'll answer to God Almighty."

"All I want is to secure the ammunition for general warfare."

The convoy camped off the main road hidden in a copse of trees. Three pickets secured the outer perimeter and two guards watched over the camp premises. No dangerous beasts, Indians, robbers, or Loyalists would get past them without the camp waking. The party lay down for six hours of sleep.

***

Near daybreak the convoy camp woke to a picket warning of an intrusion. Capt Hawkins jumped to his feet and sent two men to the edge of camp to fire warning shots through the gray light in a show of force.

Sgt Vinyard bellowed at the ladies, "Get in the militia wagons and lay flat!"

Sara reached for a rifle. "Not me."

The sergeant threw her a stare. "Your death won't be on me."

"And yours won't be on me."

Everyone else except Maria, Rahel, and Yohanna grabbed a weapon and hurried to the defense.

Col Arthur Neal's reconstituted Loyalist force had found a narrow stone ridge with deep pools of water on either side leading to the Patriot's camp. Hidden in brush, the path had no guard. They couldn't believe the Patriots had allowed intruders to use an unseen approach.

The twelve Loyalists dismounted and crept along the ridge. A major engagement commenced when the men emerged and faced a fighting body. The Patriots had indeed guarded the causeway.

After a short conflict, Neal ordered his men to make a suicide dash into a thicket of pines growing full to the ground on the Patriot's right flank. Abraham volunteered to approach the grove and flush the enemy. He didn't expect a Loyalist would soon come to the edge of the boughs aiming a pistol.

A voice familiar to Abe yelled. "Nein! Hör auf damit!"

Abe's eyes never left the flinching Loyalist holding the gun. The man's green jacket matched those of his comrades. However, they wore helmets and he wore a sharply peaked hat that was slanted back on his head and sloped down to a visor brim.

The Loyalist lowered the pistol. Abe hadn't retreated more than twenty yards when a gun popped.

My God, they've hit George! Abe turned sharply. A man had approached on his side. It was George. His eyes gleamed and the rifle smoked.

"I thought you'd been shot." They ran back to the grove. Abe gazed at the dead man on the ground at the foot of the pine. "Well done."

George nodded. "My father has a similar hat. I took a chance the Loyalist would flinch at my German speaking."

Rahel ran to Abe and threw her arms around him but lost her grip when he shouted. "Get to safety!" She ran back to the wagons and hid.

Abe and George ran behind the grove and flushed out the remaining Loyalists who feigned a retreat to the causeway but took safety behind another thicket and turned their guns on the Patriots.

Eight Surry militia crouched behind thick tree trunks and barrels ready to attack. Armed with their accurate-firing rifles, Sara McMurray and George Heider flanked them.

While the Loyalists again left safety and courageously battled on open ground, the militia took their volley training to heart, simultaneously standing and cracking fire at the green jackets.

The Loyalists fell back without a third attack. With three of their men killed and four wounded, the Makers obliged the last five to retire. The Patriots took advantage. One of the enemy fighters got nearly across the causeway but fell to George's bullet.

The last four failed to escape. Two tried desperately to jump ahead and ran into their fellows. They all fell into one of the pools. Three swam to the edge and hoisted themselves out under guard. Neal floated upright revealing a bleeding socket where his right eye had been.

***

Yohanna Heider folded a large kerchief into a two-inch wide band and tied it as an eyepatch around Neal's head. Neal begged Maria for a prognosis. She said there was nothing left of his eye. He lay down and shut the other.

Sara and Zeb approached and stood over Neal. "Is he dead?"

Maria shook her head.

Neal opened his left eye.

Sara was silent. She glared at him with smoldering eyes then breathed deeply and exhaled the toxic bile that had been building inside.

Neal clenched his teeth and muffled cries escaped his mouth.

Yohanna threw her eyes on Zeb. "Brandy!"

Zeb instantly obeyed and hurried back with a jug and a cup. George followed.

"Danke," Yohanna said. She nursed the spirits to Neal. He took a gulp and shuddered and guzzled the rest.

Zeb sat down next to Yohanna. In the brief time he'd known her she'd been entirely selfless. Stopping the Loyalists made him feel glory, yet her call for assistance regaled him with joy. He relaxed behind a proud face. Life ahead, after the war, was something to anticipate. They'd forge divine assistance unto each other in a loving, obedient, and faithful marriage.

Yohanna warmed in Zeb's nearness. Without looking away from her patient, she spoke to George. "Zeb is the future I want."

George gazed at Zeb and replied to Yohanna. "He's a good man. You're making an excellent choice."

Zeb hadn't a clue how to translate the German, but he appreciated the context of his name and George's warm expression.

Sara broke the spell of camaraderie. "Why did you ruin my father's wagon shop?"

"For my King."

"Would the King give his right eye for you?"

Sgt Vinyard heard the conversation and approached.

"What are we going to do with him?" Sara said.

Capt Hawkins approached. "We'll take him up to Virginia to be imprisoned with the British captured at Cowpens."

Vinyard was sorry Neal lived. He threw disdainful eyes on the captain but broke a sigh. "Very well, sir."

"Who shot Neal?"

"Don't know, sir."

"Find out and I'll write the man—or woman—a letter of commendation."

The sergeant gazed at the captain with new respect. "Yes, sir!"

* * *

The unharmed Loyalists buried their dead under the watchful eyes of militia guards. Except for two wounded men unable to walk, they surrendered their horses.

Capt Hawkins freed everyone but Neal after they said an oath to defend the Revolution and gave up their arms. Sgt Vinyard tied Col

Neal's hands behind his back and ordered Zeb and Abe to place him on one of the militia wagons.

The convoy party quietly ate a breakfast of cornbread, bacon, and tea. Capt Hawkins surveyed his drowsy corps and followers. He couldn't give them anymore sleep but an explanation of what lay ahead and encouraging words was due. "We're taking the musket cartridges to the Continental magazine in Virginia. When the ammunition is safe, we'll gather boats at Irwin's and Boyd's ferries on the Dan River. We have little time. God be with us and look alive!"

Hawkins pushed the convoy, knowing horses never waver once they reach a steady gate. Whether large rocks or low-cut stumps riddled the road bed, the convoy wagons bounced and kept going, every bump magnified. For as long as the constitution of the horses, harnesses, and wagons held up, they'd run breakneck as much as thirty miles a day. Hawkins meant to maintain their lead.

They took twenty-minute intervals occasionally to rest the horses. A quick midday meal of bread, cold bacon, and beer at Speedwell Ironworks on Troublesome Creek sufficed. They returned to the road.

# Forty-Six ~ Council of War

Only days before, when Johnny Spurgin sighted the British army marching north along the western reaches of the Yadkin River, Greene set his army in motion and marched east to Guilford County. Cornwallis in turn mapped the Americans' fairly sideways movement to his right and found their position to be inconsequential. If Greene intended to repair in Virginia, his new position didn't show it.

Movement by the two armies had halted with Cornwallis staying in Wachovia and Greene dwelling in the Quaker Quarter in Guilford County. The lord, knowing the enemy's position, didn't see him getting away.

***

While the Makers-Surry militia convoy broke camp at Town Fork, the British marched out of Wachovia without fanfare. The British stay in Wachovia wiped any last Moravian sentiments of loyalty to the King.

The American army also marched. Gen Greene's suspicion that Cornwallis intended to cut off his northward route confirmed, he covered the last few miles to Martinsville where Guilford Court House stood.

Now that he left Wachovia, Cornwallis couldn't pretend the stasis had been anything more than a delay in a worsening fate. But now, Continental stores lay less than eighty miles away at their principal depot at Halifax, Virginia and would draw Greene like iron to lodestone. On the other hand, the distance to Cornwallis' principal depot at Charles Town had grown to two-hundred and eighty miles. A secondary British depot at Wilmington was two-hundred miles away.

It was Greene's turn to break for replenishment, a sustenance different to the lord's: A junction and council of war at Guilford Court House. The massive march beginning at Camp Cheraw one-hundred and twenty miles below in South Carolina was coming to fruition.

***

Greene arrived at Martinsville with his flying corps and discovered Brig Gen Isaac Huger encamped a few hundred yards behind the court house with the main army and baggage brought up from Camp Cheraw. Though Huger's route had been more or less direct and half the distance of Greene's, the majority of his forces marched on foot with a slow wagon train up from South Carolina.

Greene found Huger's quarters. He shook the South Carolinian's hand. "When did you arrive?"

"Four o'clock yesterday afternoon. Lieutenant Colonel Lee's Legion is south of here, two and a half miles this side of Bell's Mill. I thought it proper to halt him there until he received your orders."

"I shall invite him by Express. Who else is here?"

"Let's see. There's Colonel Kosciuszko. Captain John Smith of 1st Maryland came up yesterday with six-hundred shirts and three-hundred pairs of shoes. A militia quartermaster is on the way with three-hundred hogs. They're slow in their movements."

Greene snorted. "A hungry army awaiting would slow me."

Huger grinned. "Did General Morgan come up with you?"

"Yes. Took to bed with sciatica as soon as we arrived. He reckons to go home to Virginia."

"That will be a great loss. Speaking of losses, I haven't seen heaps of militiamen here. Only Colonel John Paisley of the Guilford regiment."

"I ordered General Stevens and his militia to Virginia with the Cowpens prisoners."

"The general shall be missed."

"No person commands a militia with more propriety."

"If we're going to beat Cornwallis, we'll need the militia," Huger said.

Greene sneered as he felt inward for a response. "I can't feed and clothe them just to watch them leave at the end of their short enlistments. They'll fight if I take them on when I need them."

"Don't wait until planting time. It comes earlier in Virginia than Rhode Island."

***

While Greene waited for the other field officers and their regiments to arrive, he walked the ground. A wagon train of the remaining stores amassed from Salisbury and other parts of central North Carolina was leaving Guilford Court House for safekeeping in Virginia under his orders. Only by keeping supplies away from Brig Gen Benedict Arnold and Lt Gen Cornwallis would Greene rest.

Brig Gen Isaac Huger and Col Paisley approached.

Greene swept his view over the mostly untouched land surrounding Guilford Court House. "This place is convenient to Virginia and her militia. I understand scores of soldiers and officers came here at least once after the Battle of Camden."

Dense woods covered the land, only breaking for a handful of small clearings, fallow or recently plowed for row crops. The landscape sloped down to the west from the courthouse where they stood. Two creeks and various ravines cut the site. A vale lay west of the heights.

"These woods," Greene said, "would be a perfect defense. Infantry could fight from tree to tree. The trees themselves will arrest the charge of cavalry or files of bayonets."

Col Paisley regarded Greene's interest. "You approve of this land."

"It has everything a commander could want. When I fell down from Philadelphia and first saw Martinsville, the potential for a battlefield offering crucial retreat lanes astounded me."

"This central part of North Carolina is loyal to the Revolution. A handful of Quaker settlements are near, New Garden being the closest. They're anti-war but won't stand in your way nor will the Moravians west of here. But here you'll find Whigs."

Greene studied the site around the courthouse again. He saw no white winter landscape, though a lead sky common to the Colonies at that time of the year hung over them. Intermittent icy rain replaced the snow Greene normally saw in February. "Winter feels strange here. I expect to see hints of growth on the bleak ground or hear croaking frogs any day."

The colonel mocked fanning himself. "You must be burning up in this weather."

Greene nodded emphatically and went to his marquee.

Paisley watched the general shuffle away. "I apprehend he'd make a stand if Cornwallis showed up today. Are we and the enemy so evenly matched?"

Huger shrugged. "Lieutenant Colonel Lee thinks Greene's united force, including five hundred militia he can call on, exceeds two-thousand three hundred. He estimates the army of Cornwallis numbers two-thousand five hundred including four-hundred provincials."

"You have to admire Lee. His cavalry, though smaller than the one Cornwallis converted from infantry, is rumored to be far superior to the lord's regarding size, condition, and spirit of the horses."

***

Greene opened the council of war sixty miles northeast of the Yadkin River crossing at Trading Ford. A week had passed. "The army is all the states have to depend upon for their political existence. By now, the Colonies are celebrating our success and the enemy's capital loss at Cowpens. Few have joined us, and those principally without arms or ammunition, but our provisions keep improving.

"Our army is so great an object with Cornwallis, and the reduction of the Southern states depends so much upon it, I think it highly probable he will keep pushing us."

"What are the risks if we continue the retreat?" Gen Huger said.

"Cornwallis will follow," Greene said with haste before turning grave. "He may push through Virginia. Perhaps he will unite with Arnold. Only militia reinforcement of our army can prevent that."

Lt Col Carrington dashed into the marquee. Revulsion of Benedict Arnold hung on the officers' faces. Greene nodded. "Are you well?"

"Well enough after shoe trouble with a poor horse. I just rode with James Gillies from Town Fork above the Wachovia tract where I met the Makers."

"We're discussing risks to continuing the retreat. Having our backs to the river and Cornwallis in our face is the one I fear most. Please report the boat and ferry situation on the Dan."

The Quartermaster stood. "The lower fords at Irwin's Ferry and Boyd's Ferry are seventy miles from here. I suggest using both to cross the Dan. Including the flats Makers company will bring down from Dix's Ferry to Irwin's, we'll have enough boats. The lord may opt for the lower fords. As long as we arrive a half-day earlier, we'll safely cross."

"Thank you," Greene said. He studied Gen Huger's eyes. "Did I answer your question?"

"Alright," Huger said, "what are the risks if we don't continue the retreat?"

"Cornwallis will oblige us to risk a general action. Again, there's little prospect of making an effectual stand unless reinforcements come from the militia. Among valuable lives, we shall lose our stores."

Greene clasped his hands with his palms at right angles in a sign of optimism. He gave Carrington an entreating glare revealing underlying anxiety. "Speaking of the Makers. Will they get the Salem ammunition to safety?"

Carrington shivered inside not knowing what might happen to the ammunition convoy. "Put your confidence in Captain Hawkins and the Makers. With a small body of Surry militia, pray they'll get the wagons over."

Col Paisley of the Guilford regiment motioned to speak. "Assuming the retreat continues, what will you do to keep Cornwallis at bay?"

"Preoccupy him with a seven-hundred man flying army split from the main army."

"Why break up the army again?" Huger said. "We're going to the same place."

Greene nodded to Col Otho Holland Williams. "Colonel Williams will lead Lieutenant Colonel William Washington's 1st and 3rd Continental cavalry, a detachment of light infantry under Lieutenant Colonel John Eager Howard, and Lieutenant Colonel Henry Lee's Legion. He'll also have a company of Virginia riflemen under Colonel William Campbell, a man who rallied his men to victory at Kings Mountain."

Williams stood and addressed Huger. "The detachment will harass and check the enemy's progress and give the slower troops and supplies an opportunity to retire across the lower ford without a general action."

"Thank you, Colonel."

Gen Morgan reached around his waist with both hands and massaged his back. "How do you apprehend the lord will respond?"

"Hopefully, by crossing the Dan at the upper fords," Greene said.

Morgan grimaced in pain. "Would Cornwallis go for the horse fords? That would take him away from our supplies."

"That's the purpose of Williams' flying corps. To draw him there. Of course, by now the lord must be thinking we own all the boats at the lower fords."

The council unanimously advised to avoid a general action and retire beyond the Dan River immediately. They adopted Lt Col Carrington's plan to cross at Irwin's Ferry.

Greene acknowledged the task ahead. "This retreat will wear us. Forced marches through rain and sleet over muddy roads hurt everyone's morale. May it hurt theirs twice."

# Forty-Seven ~ Bugle Boy James

Greene was *en marche*. Cornwallis put his own army in motion to the area west of Guilford Court House,  hanging on to the prospect of battle and freeing his men captured at Cowpens.

The lord didn't want Greene to flee without a fight. He consulted a Tory guide near Daniel Dillon's Public Grist Mill to learn the nature of the Dan River and the best way to enter Virginia.

"My Lord, cross at the upper fords."

"Why?"

"The lower fords stand where untold years of contours have led the Dan to the Roanoke."

"Have you seen the lower fords?"

"Yes, my Lord. They're deep in winter. Didn't you go around the Yadkin because the river was too deep at the lower fords?"

"I had no boats."

"Yet you crossed the Yadkin at the shallow ford into Wachovia *above* the forks. Don't you suspect your enemy has learned to cross at shallow fords?"

Cornwallis gauged the man with suspicion. How did he know the British route so well? He took a moment to reflect. "I must leave at once to get between Greene and the upper fords and not let him escape without a fight."

***

Lt Col Henry Lee left camp at Guilford Court House the morning after Greene's departure and led his Legion northwest to Bruce's Cross Roads to wait for Col Otho Holland Williams. There the flying army planned to throw themselves in front of Cornwallis and urge him to the upper fords of the Dan River.

Lee's horsemen took breakfast near the crossroads where a homestead appeared in a break from thick woods. Lee queried the owner's name and his politics. Charles Bruce showed himself to be a Patriot and offered hospitality. Lee sat at the kitchen table with two Legion officers and the owner while Mrs. Bruce's cooking tempted their noses.

A pony ambled up to the house and the rider, a nearby planter, dismounted in the front yard where a sergeant and five privates rested around a fire pit while bacon and eggs sizzled in a skillet. He threw the reins to one of the privates and banged on the door.

Bruce and Lt Col Lee stood in the doorway. Bruce's neighbor swallowed, drew a deep breath, and pointed southwest towards Dillon's Mill. "To horse, gentlemen. The enemy are at hand!"

Lee ordered the sergeant to fetch his horse from the main Legion bivouac in Bruce's woods at once and bring Capt James Armstrong and his horse. Lee eyed the neighbor's slow mount and told the sergeant to bring the bugler's horse.

Armstrong and the sergeant returned. Fourteen-year old bugler James Gillies followed in a tear, worried about his plundered horse.

Lee fired off instructions. "Captain, this is Mr. Bruce's neighbor. We're going under his guidance to discover if Tarleton's Legion is coming this way." Lee told the neighbor to take the bugler's nimble mare.

Damnation stirred in Gillies' eyes. Making the humiliation worse, Lee ordered the boy to take the neighbor's pony. Gillies was to ride with the scouting party, go inform Col Williams of the enemy's and Lee's positions, and rejoin the party.

***

Lee, Capt Armstrong, the neighbor, Gillies, the sergeant, and three privates laid crops on their horses. Armstrong scouted ahead but slowed and came to a rest to study the road. His stallion raised a lather and panted. The other riders caught up.

"I figure we've come two miles and still there's barely any hoof prints," Armstrong said.

The neighbor begged Armstrong to keep riding and a minute later they came upon a throng of cavalry riding under a British legion standard. They outnumbered the Patriots more than five to one.

Pistol fire erupted. Lee cried, "Retreat, boys!"

Lee's small detachment joined the main corps hidden in Bruce's woods. After Tarleton's dragoons rode by, Lee noticed Bugler boy James was missing but figured he'd gone to warn Col Williams.

***

Not only did the substitute pony poorly match the British Legion mounts, but the boy bugler had left his bugle and pistol tucked in a saddle bag on his horse. Somehow Gillies had pushed the neighbor's slow horse hard but Capt Miller and a sodden squad from the green-jacketed British dragoons passed Bruce's woods and overtook him. Miller ordered a man to pull the boy down from the pony. An interrogation ensued.

"What are you doing out here, boy?" Miller said.

"I'm a bugler, sir."

"I don't see a bugle. You're a little Rebel soldier."

"My bugle got left behind."

The dragoons laughed.

Miller dismounted and towered over Gillies. "Liar! Cavalry don't ride ponies." Gillies folded under Miller's knee.

Meanwhile, alarmed that Gillies hadn't returned, Lee gathered his cavalry and rushed to find him. In the distance he saw Gillies fall flat on the ground. The British captain swung a saber over and over while the boy begged for quarter.

Lee's corps charged and crushed the enemy who put up little resistance. Although Lee commanded his men to give no quarter to the British, they captured Capt Miller. Miller, hands tied and sitting on the ground, claimed he tried to stop Gillies' inhumane killing because he reviled Lt Col Tarleton's tactics.

Lee, fond of Gillies' bugle mastery and ability to recall and play any field music, hung his head. A young Patriot cavalry man was at his side. "Go fetch a preacher and some spades." Lee looked down on the captain. "Rogue! He was a boy!"

While Lee interrogated Miller and buried James Gillies, the main British army advanced. Lee forwarded Miller to Col Williams who in turn sent him on to Gen Greene.

A Patriot pistol shot in the sky warned the Americans to leave immediately. Lee mounted his horse. Before leaving, he looked at the dirt mounded over the grave in the Bruce family cemetery and mouthed a quick remembrance to the short life of Master Gillies.

When Cornwallis passed Bruce's Crossroads, he was outraged to see the British Legion still there. What had Tarleton been doing? Already the army was behind in its quest to catch Greene.

# Forty-Eight ~ Race to the Dan

— February 13, 1781, Irwin's Ferry, Dan River, Virginia

Lt Col Carrington and Col Kosciuszko hastened from Guilford Court House like Express riders. At Irwin's Ferry they found the Makers and Surry militia getting the convoy over the Dan River. After depositing the ammunition at Halifax, the Makers collected flat boats at Dix's Ferry and navigated them down to Irwin's Ferry.

In the meantime, not knowing when the army would arrive, the Makers and Surry militia rushed to collect other boats in the vicinity. They fashioned a pair of rafts and pine poles to maneuver them before building breastworks on the north side of the Dan for the militia to cover the crossing.

The Makers and Surry militia posted at the south bank of Irwin's Ferry waiting to assist the infantrymen. A dozen went a mile downstream to Boyd's Ferry to support the crossing of baggage wagons and artillery.

***

Above Bruce's Crossroads, Col O. H. Williams inclined his flying army west and threw them in front of Cornwallis who was making for the upper fords of the Dan. Taking the corps to be Greene's entire army heading to the shallow crossings, the lord hastened to apprehend them. At that instant, Greene, with the remainder of the army, marched rapidly northeast to Irwin's Ferry at the lower fords.

Williams used a gamut of tactics to prevent Cornwallis overcoming him. He pushed horses and men, rode in the gray light before dawn and after dusk, fell trees to block roads, burned bridges, and built false camps lit by dozens of fires.

Though the British Legion had given Williams an early lead by squandering time at Bruce's Crossroads, Lt Col Tarleton's vanguard could see Williams' rear guard at times. Lt Col Henry Lee pushed the cavalry hard to widen the gap. They gradually separated from the enemy. Whether it came down to their breed of horse or human determination, they had no time to deliberate.

Bone-chilling rain poured. The flying army rode horses while the main army slipped on mud in forced marches wearing worn out shoes or none down gloomy, icy roads. Occasional skirmishes took lives but more fell to fatigue and loss of sleep. At night dead tired troops wolfed down whatever rations could be found and fell to dreamless sleep beside fires because tents were in the baggage sent forward.

***

Reckoning time came on the march to the Dan River. While Cornwallis maintained his sights on the upper ford, Col Williams changed course downstream, swerving right to take the northeast road toward Dix's Ferry. The lord learned of the deceit and turned as well.

Tarleton in the vanguard closed in. Yet the Patriot flying army won the better part of a skirmish that ensued. Col Williams turned further northeast and again Cornwallis chased his foe.

After a final turn, Col Williams dashed to Irwin's Ferry fifteen miles downstream from Dix's. He rode his corps hard through the night hoping to steal a march before the enemy could detect the deception.

***

An unwelcoming void greeted the Patriot infantry at the two-hundred-foot wide crossing point at Irwin's Ferry where they gathered along the banks of the black, ice-cold Dan River to launch into the nothingness of mist and fog. It was mid-February. Greene, minus his flying forces, would soon be *driven* out of North Carolina.

Bobbing flat boats waited to take the army across. With a rear guard of artillery and rifles, Greene ordered the crossing to commence, assisted by the Makers. The first ferry boat filled with troops and began its journey under the power of a donkey pulling a tow rope. At starboard aft Sgt Vinyard sat watching a rope pay out from the south bank.

Soon the boat sagged at Vinyard's position. Greene, recalling George Washington's wisecrack to the hefty Col Henry Knox while crossing the Delaware, bellowed. "Shift your hindquarters and trim the boat." A moment of nervous laughter rose and fell.

At five-foot ten, Greene was generally taller than the average soldier. He straightened his gimpy right leg and stood statuesque on the prow of the ferry. Currents and eddies dampened fortuitously and he kept upright.

Greene's exhaustion worried Abraham Hellerschwarz. "Should you stand, sir?"

"I got my sea legs crossing the Delaware River with his Excellency George Washington. Anyway, I've been on horseback too long."

Reverence and awe registered in the troops' faces hearing the commander-in-chief of the entire American army cited with familiarity.

Zeb Mitchell sat forward with Abe. "Tell us about it."

The general raised a finger to pause the banter. He'd noticed the boat drifting. Then a sharp, precipitous lunge threw the vessel at an obtuse angle. Greene pivoted at his waist and all chatter amongst the men stopped. He bellowed to the south side. "Tighten the rope! Make it taut!"

Inspired by Greene's vociferous command, the entire boat joined in. "Make it taut! Make it taut! Make it taut!"

The boat moved straighter and swifter to the opposite bank.

"We froze on Christmas eve before the Battle of Trenton," Greene said. "An icier, wider river than this lay in darkness concealing danger. Even for our good health we didn't shirk our duty. We could have retired to a warm fire like the drunken Hessians, but we didn't and they caught *our* fire."

Silence pervaded the remaining journey. Greene stepped off first. "Makers, return and supervise the crossings!" After everyone but the Makers disembarked, the winch drums reversed, and the boat recrossed the river.

Long, flat batteaux. Durham boats. Canoes. Every craft for miles up and down the Dan joined the ferry boats. Soon the Dan resembled a trough of bobbing apples. Back and forth the boats made run after run.

Disaster struck once when a tow rope snapped and a ferry boat inched away downstream imperiling other boats. A wagon of provisions that should have crossed at Boyd's Ferry jumped the chocks and nearly rolled off.

Gen Greene took charge. "Boys! Don't lose that boat!"

The young soldiers, lightly clothed and shivering, hesitated to get into the freezing water.

"Are you afraid to get wet? Wash up in there. You'll smell better and drown the lice."

A soldier whispered, "So says the general who scratches his stinky body."

A brave group swam to the ferry boat dragging poles. The infantry onboard took the poles and braced the vessel to a halt in swift water until a ferryman tied a replacement rope to the prow.

Greene rewarded the men at camp with a hot meal of roast pork, reconstituted peas, and yeast bread baked in scores of Dutch ovens over open fires. A sutler sold Greene enough Virginia whiskey to serve every man a gill. Rumors spread through camp the general gave him a chit worth over fifteen-thousand Continental dollars payable by Gov Jefferson.

Every man who wanted one took a hot wash in a canvas bath house heated by a campfire. They exited clean yet more sweet-smelling from crates of French soap paid for by their regimental commanding officers. Afterward, a floral breeze infused the camp air. Each man guarded the fact it came from his own skin by casting humored aspersions on the next man. Good evening, my lady. Don't you smell lovely?

# PART III

# Forty-Nine ~ Late Again

— February 14, 1781, Boyd's Ferry, Dan River, Virginia

Predawn, Col Otho Holland Williams flew to the lower fords of the Dan River. The gap between his forces and the British widened throughout the day as he pulled the last measure of fortitude from man and beast.

As Cornwallis chased his enemy to the lower fords, he seethed at his inability to catch Williams. But he wasn't out of hope. While the enemy might have their boats, there was hope he could interrupt their passing into Virginia.

Williams, leading Lt Col William Washington's cavalries, Lt Col John Eager Howard's light infantry, and Col Campbell's company of Virginia riflemen, reached Boyd's Ferry in the afternoon. They took to waiting ferry boats while Lee's Legion defended the road and by dark all had gotten across. Lee and his corps then made the crossing.

Cornwallis' army arrived en masse at Boyd's Ferry six hours later, the last of his foe safely encamped on the opposite bank with their boats. The defensive breastworks designed by Col Thaddeus Kosciuszko stood empty and unscathed.

Reminiscent of the Yadkin catastrophe, the lord abandoned hopes of crossing and rejected going upstream to cross at the shallow ford. Though turning away shocked his army, the lord couldn't push his famished men any longer.

***

Cornwallis reached for the doorknob at Wiley's Tavern when a secretive exchange of voices arose nearby. An outrageous conversation took his breath. The words condemned and stung as the Lord waited outside the shack five miles south of Greene's crossing points.

Col James Webster, commander of the 33rd Regiment of Foot soldiers mocked Cornwallis. "Our intelligence was exceedingly defective, which, with heavy rains, bad roads, the passage of many deep creeks, and bridges destroyed by the enemy's light troops, rendered all our exertions vain."

Lt Col Tarleton added a democratic but treasonous explanation of Greene's triumph. "Every measure of the Americans during their march from the Catawba to Virginia was judiciously designed and vigorously executed."

Cornwallis let the knob go and walked around the corner. The bravura of the junior field officers vanished.

"Is that how you feel, Banastre?"

Tarleton twisted envy and praise for the American commander-in-chief upside down. "The Dan was stolen from us and there's no worse thief than a premeditated one."

Webster's awkward attempt to make Cornwallis forget his and Tarleton's banter failed. "Greene must think you've been thwarted."

"I didn't need to cross the Dan! I have North Carolina."

Tarleton went into emergency flattering mode. "Loyalists should laud the King's troops. The Continentals fled North Carolina in panic."

Webster glimpsed Cornwallis' delight. Perhaps he could risk a question. "My Lord. Why didn't you push on?"

"Unnecessary."

Webster and Tarleton glimpsed each other for a sign one of them had defective hearing. Who turned the lord against defeating Greene?

"The opportunity is favorable for recruiting the King's friends and acquiring provisions in Hillsborough, North Carolina."

***

Greene invited Brig Gen Edward Stevens to army headquarters in Halifax, Virginia. It had been a month since they'd conversed and tipped brandy. Greene kept mum that he'd requested Stevens' militia from Virginia Governor Thomas Jefferson in case of general war with Cornwallis. But he heartily mentioned the late chase.

"I believed Cornwallis would cross at the upper fords, come down, and catch us. Worse for him, the devil halted at the ferries."

"Who would have thought defending the crossing unnecessary?" Stevens guffawed.

"It proves how deranged the lord has become. He reaped no advantage from the chase."

A burp escaped Stevens, a reminder to eat slower in Virginia, more blessed with food. "Our work charting the rivers, building the boats, and fortifying the ferries paid off."

"When I heard Cornwallis had stopped four days at Ramsour's Mill to collect flour and beef and burn his wagon train, I took that as the signal he intended to strike." Greene angled his head to the side. "Yet he brought no fight."

"What's his game? He trembled the South. Now, all of a sudden, he's impotent?"

"Our crossing mesmerized Cornwallis. He's infuriated we have all the boats."

Stevens proffered his palms as if holding a tray. "He could have built boats or swam the river. He could have aimed cannons at the ferrymen and sued for passage."

"Perhaps he remembered he'd left the forts in Camden and Charles Town foolishly exposed."

"So, now it's time for Cornwallis to retreat."

Greene nodded and struck a pensive mood. "Maybe the idea possesses him that retreat isn't so inglorious."

***

Cornwallis' nominally superior forces abandoned Virginia. Before that, the possibility of general warfare reenergized Greene. Like his rigorous campaign to free up supplies for the Southern army, Greene set to recruiting and devising actions to better position himself for battle.

The general basked in glory and enjoyed a moment of public elation. Cornwallis was heading to Hillsborough thirty miles south. Whatever that meant, Greene couldn't relax. Though he continued to believe militias gave the Continentals a short-term boost, the thorns of feeding them and getting them to kill numbers of enemy stuck his side.

Recruiting momentum favored Greene. Broadsheets continued to advertise Gen Morgan's victory at the Battle of Cowpens and rumors of Cornwallis crossing the Dan to join up with Maj Gen Benedict Arnold persisted.

With the fight likely to occur in North Carolina, Greene needed their militia. Though he belabored that the Salisbury Brigade of the North Carolina militia dispersed at Cowans Ford, could he deny their prominence going back to 1775? And hadn't Brig Gen Davidson's killing alarmed them?

Every new man recruited to fortify his Continentals added to the day to day struggle to collect provisions, yet Greene humbled. He ordered Brig Gen John Butler to bring the Hillsborough Brigade of the North Carolina militia to Halifax, Virginia and he invited Brig Gen Robert Lawson to come with his brigade of Virginia militiamen.

Gov Thomas Jefferson responded to Greene's request for militia by ordering Gen Stevens' brigade of Virginia militia to Halifax. Hearing Greene's written plea for mounts, he impressed dragoon horses and outfitting for Lt Col Washington's 1st and 3rd Continental cavalry.

Luring Cornwallis to Virginia put South Carolina back in play and Greene quickly instructed the Partisans to take advantage. Francis Marion, newly promoted to brigadier general, received orders to harass the enemy west of the Santee.

Brig Gen Thomas Sumter, recovering from a musket wound, got orders to muster the militia in the Cheraw and Camden districts of upper South Carolina. Brig Gen Andrew Pickens, successor to Brig Gen William Davidson, heard orders to collect the Salisbury Brigade of the North Carolina militia and companies of South Carolina state troops and harass Cornwallis in conjunction with Lt Col Lee.

***

Greene had crossed into Virginia because his meager force couldn't stand a general battle. Now that he was there, he'd welcome Irregulars to supplement his Continentals who of late numbered near twenty-five hundred. Cornwallis could command an army of over three-thousand seasoned troops.

Enemy force estimation risked being terribly wrong. Cornwallis might have an even larger force. Despite Greene having newfound promises of enlarging his army, the lord felt promises too, especially recruiting and foraging. Which led him to the Loyalist stronghold at Hillsborough.

# Fifty ~ Loyalists and Provisions

— February 16, 1781, Halifax, Virginia

Maj Gen Greene invited the Makers to a meeting at his Halifax Court House headquarters to thank them for securing the ammunition. Lt Col Carrington and Capt Hawkins attended, the latter relating the ruses the Makers used to divert attention and flee Salem.

"I must say your company is refreshing," Greene said. "You're the most industrious and sober group of men and ladies I've ever met. Well-mannered and generous to the cause and quite possibly the saviors of the Revolution."

Murmurs of Maria Bach translating for George and Yohanna Heider and Rahel checked the general. "All set? I have another mission for you. I beg you to be my eyes and ears near Hillsborough."

Sgt Vinyard leaned toward Greene. "Will the platoon of Surry militia escort us?"

"No. Your party must be small and inconspicuous."

Vinyard screwed up his face. "I beg of you, sir, to know why we'd throw off so many muskets."

"To move quietly amid the enemy and dispatch intelligence respecting their motions." Greene studied their tentative expressions. "You'll honor the Revolution."

"Will Sergeant Vinyard and I wear our uniforms?" Hawkins said.

"There'll be no uniforms," Greene said. "The sergeant will be in the camp but I want you to stay here."

Vinyard allowed a sincere smile. "We'll miss the captain's leadership."

Greene panned the room. "Any questions?"

Zeb's face tensed. "We need to go home and get back to work."

"Because Neal has been stopped?" Sara said.

"Our enlistments are nearly done."

Sara sharpened her eyes. "Not yet, Brother."

"Father is going broke."

"You can't wait to marry Yohanna."

"That's not fair, Sara."

"Please," Greene said, "let's not argue."

A wide chasm of silence broke when Abe sighed. "We are brothers, Zeb. However, may I say the path to freedom and peace is yet fragile? After the war, your stepfather's pockets will overflow."

"Very well. I will fight for what I left behind and keep close that which I hold precious."

***

Hillsborough, one of the few major crossroads in the north central part of North Carolina, promised military succor and food for famished British soldiers. Once one of the seats of royal state government shared with Newbern, the territory held promise for recruiting Loyalist friends, though Maj Gen Horatio Gates made camp there after his defeat at Camden, South Carolina.

When Cornwallis reached the town situated along the River Eno, he repaired to the library in his headquarters at the estate of a Loyalist Presbyterian minister and prepared a proclamation inviting Loyalists to reinforce him.

The lord directed aide-de-camp Capt Henry Broderick to summon Lt Col Banastre Tarleton and Col James Webster from the cellar where they salivated as a butler displayed a wine collection.

Cornwallis produced the draft proclamation. "Read this while I meet with officials of the last Royal provincial government."

Tarleton and Webster sat down and read silently.

Cornwallis left for a waiting buggy. He climbed aboard and rifled through a stack of papers. ADC Broderick jumped in and sat down next to him.

"Remain with the carriage," Cornwallis said, "while I go back inside to retrieve something."

Cornwallis stopped outside the library door with sunlight pouring in from a window behind him. The voices of his field officers debating the odds of enlisting Loyalists emanated from the closed room.

"We've chased the Continentals," Webster said, "out of North Carolina. The Rebels are nowhere in sight. Won't Loyalists run to us?"

Tarleton shook his head. "They're afraid."

"No proclamation will flush them out?"

"They don't trust us. The King's troops have never made a serious effort to assist our allies in North Carolina."

The door thrust open and the doorknob caved the plaster. The officer's eyes fell on Cornwallis, tall and black in silhouette.

"Tarleton, you idiot," Cornwallis said. "I take your contrariness to mean the draft is perfect."

"My lord, I…"

Cornwallis plucked a marked up map of the environs of Hillsborough from a desk drawer and glared at Tarleton. "Notwithstanding the indifference or fright of the Loyalists at Hillsborough, we must entertain hopes of receiving reinforcements from the King's friends. Or do you wish to be outnumbered on the battlefield?"

***

Devoid of tents, the austere British camp on Hillsborough's Eno River resembled Camp New Providence's organized layout when Greene took command. Hoofbeats and creaking wheels from buggies and wagons swarming the streets spirited the mood of the army as hundreds of curious locals gawked. The Makers added their wagons to the hubbub. At ten in the morning, a pageantry to celebrate British victory in North Carolina began with the raising of the King's standard.

ADC Broderick ran from the printer with copies of Cornwallis' proclamation. He posted one and read it aloud to a throng of spectators:

"Whereas it is His Majesty's most gracious wish to rescue his faithful and loyal subjects from the cruel tyranny under which they have groaned for years, I have thought proper to issue this proclamation, to invite all such faithful and loyal subjects to repair, without loss of time, with their arms and ten days provisions, to the Royal standard now erected at Hillsborough, where they will meet with the friendliest reception. And I do hereby assure them, I am ready to concur with them in effectual measures for suppressing the remains of rebellion in this province, and for the reestablishment of good order and constitutional government."

— Charles Earl Cornwallis, Lieutenant General of His Majesty's forces.

The Makers came forward and pondered the wording. It posed a poor tradeoff to Loyalists. If North Carolinians wanted peace, the lord required them to secure it themselves and supply their own provisions and arms.

The civilian-dressed Makers stood among the crowd that parted to let a British officer through. Unmistakable in a feather-plumed black bearskin helmet, green jacket, and beige breeches stood Tarleton. Zeb, George, and Abe turned and shifted their attention to a "defective" wagon wheel.

Sgt Vinyard faced the lieutenant colonel and waved toward the proclamation. "To suppress the rebellion, shouldn't the lord defend the river, lest the Continentals recross?"

Sara spoke before Tarleton could answer. "The dread of violence and persecution prevent us from accepting this invitation."

Tarleton smugly nodded to Sara and Vinyard and left, his judgment of Loyalist fears confirmed.

The crowd groaned. Zeb approached a young man studying the proclamation. After a long admiration of the document, the apparent Loyalist murmured. "Cornwallis will cut the Rebels to pieces."

Zeb inched closer. "My mother stitched quilt panels from rags and stuffed them with wool. Is the lord so needled?"

Alarmed by Zeb's remarks, Sgt Vinyard yelled. "Zeb! Be gone!"

The Loyalist tugged Zeb's frock. "Greene's not a worthy enemy."

"You err thinking Greene falls below Cornwallis' stature."

"Greene is no bear. He runs like a lamb."

"Cornwallis couldn't bear defeat and took to retreat. He's learning from Greene."

"The Lord divided his troops and flew them to action."

Zeb gently pushed back Sgt Vinyard's tug. "Please. I have one last thing to say." He put his palms together and snapped them apart. "Let Cornwallis divide the meat from the peas on your plate. Don't complain of hunger because Greene ate your meal while the lord dallied."

After the exchange, the spectators, including presumed supporters of the Crown, trudged away.

***

Ordered to the neighborhood of the British army, the Makers camped outside Hillsborough near the Eno River where they discovered Thomas Hart's grist mill had been seized. Thirty Redcoats forced the mill to grind but they had no covering forces.

A kind Express rider took Sgt Vinyard's encoded message to Brig Gen Andrew Pickens. A day later, Pickens sent twenty calvary and twenty riflemen to attack the British body. A skirmish resulted in seventeen British killed and eight imprisoned and nine Patriot deaths. Cornwallis saw the initial forage of direly needed provisions in Hillsborough slip away.

Greene had been in Virginia nine days when he recrossed the Dan River reinforced with six-hundred militia under Brig Gen Edward Stevens. He aimed to energize Patriot friends and check Cornwallis from arousing Loyalists. Hearing his orders to harass Cornwallis heeded, Greene reported the news to George Washington.

The Makers learned from displaced local women that a large body of British troops had camped on the western road from Hillsborough. They consisted of Tarleton's Legion, half an infantry brigade, and artillerists towing two three-inch caliber bronze field pieces.

Subsequently, Col John Pyle, a prominent North Carolina Loyalist who responded to Lord Cornwallis' call for volunteers, came to the Makers camp and told Vinyard he was searching for Tarleton who'd requested Pyle to align with him and confront Greene's detachments. He asked Vinyard and his men to join his four-hundred Loyalist militia. The sergeant begged pacifism, turning him down.

The kind Express rider came for Sgt Vinyard's encoded message after Pyle departed. In the meantime, Tarleton sent Pyle a second request. With no reply, Tarleton's detachment failed to join Pyle's Loyalists.

Two American corps, concealed in woods, advanced on Col Pyle in the neighborhood of Holt's Plantation in Alamance. Lee's Legion proceeded with its infantry in the center and cavalry on the right. Militia riflemen under Pickens approached on the left, hidden so the enemy couldn't see the strips of white paper typically pinned to the hats of Patriot militia in the South.

Pyle took the Americans to be Tarleton's corps and sent two young countrymen to greet them. Lee sent one back with counter greetings and a request to let "Tarleton's fatigued troops" pass without delay to their camp.

Lee advanced with his cavalry following. When he reached Pyle, the Patriots were effectively opposite Pyle's column of mounted Loyalists. Pickens' riflemen still on the left fell back in reserve. Lee's men in their pale green jackets faced Pyle's men some of whom wore similar green jackets.

The moment Pyle and Lee shook hands, some of the Loyalists noticed Pickens' riflemen behind them among the trees and opened fire on Lee's men. Immediately a captain commanding the Americans down the line asked a captain in the line across from him to whom he gave his loyalty. When the man answered, "King George", the captain instantly struck him over the head with his sword.

Simultaneously the Patriots confirmed the strip of red cloth their opposites wore on their hats and, following the captain's example, sliced every Loyalist in sight, breaking and bending their swords. In less than a minute the attack ran along the whole line. Ninety-three Loyalists died in the melee. Col Pyle survived severe wounds.

***

No sooner had word of the bludgeoning reached the Makers than Sara found Zeb in camp packing his haversack. He avoided her gaze until he couldn't stand it any longer.

"I want out," Zeb said.

"You still miss father."

He threw his bag on the straw covered ground. He came face to face with her and grabbed her shoulders. "I want to get away from this war."

"It's too late. By now the Friends will have testified us out of the Quaker Quarter. We can't go home."

Zeb sat down on the straw and drew his knees to his chin.

"What are we going to do, Brother?" She wept and nudged him with a tear-drenched hand. "Zeb, talk to me."

He planted wistful but dry eyes on her. "Guess we'll have to fight our way through."

Sara convinced Matthew Vinyard to quit their mission. The sergeant messaged Greene explaining the camp's shock and begged to go west to the Quaker Quarter in Guilford County to forage on behalf of the army. Lt Col Carrington, responding for Greene, expressed understanding of their horror and excused them. Foraging was as important as intelligence.

But Carrington brought up their three-month enlistments expiring in early March and implored them as Patriots to agree to a one-month extension. They sent their agreement and chased the sunset up the Buffalo Road to Guilford County, not wanting to spend another night in Alamance with more horrific action possible.

***

Far afield of their supplies, the British hungered for basics. The Patriots usually foraged fresh food, especially milk, butter, eggs, root cellar vegetables, and dried fruit to supplement staples from Halifax.

The Makers returned from a day of farm to farm begging. After holding back rations of perishables for themselves, they gave their days' takings to a temporary army depot and returned to camp with fifty cloth sacks of weevil-infested flour gleaned from the land. The next day, Maria, Rahel, Yohanna, and Sara turned white from sifting all day.

Zeb approached the work party sitting on the ground. "My God, the war horrifies you. The blood has left your faces."

Zeb had stopped wearing his holey, irreparable wool stockings. When Maria translated Zeb's remark, Yohanna left a white handprint on his bare calf.

"Ouch!"

Sara laughed. "You deserved that, Brother."

Enjoined by the other three ladies, the merriment intensified and drew Abe, George, and Vinyard.

"What are you doing to Zeb?" Vinyard said.

Sara's eyes sparkled and the sergeant drew near hoping to hear her answer. "This, Matty." She printed his jacket sleeve with white powder.

Sara calling the sergeant by a nickname didn't escape Zeb. *We've all paired up. I wonder if everyone understands the changes we've undergone. In the midst of the most danger any of us has ever experienced, there is kinship and love.*

Zeb came out of reverie for a moment to see George and Abe getting their white handprints. The entire party fell into laughter. *How low had the world fallen? How high could it rise? It all came down to the Revolution's prospects.*

***

Not long after the Makers left Alamance, a skirmish arose near Clapp's grist mill on Beaver Creek, the site of a new British camp. The cleared mill premises served as a fine staging area for their forces. Woods to the north provided cover.

Col Otho H. Williams placed militiamen in front of British troops foraging three miles from their camp, hoping to draw them into an ambush. That early March day marked two long weeks since the Dan crossing and Lt Col Tarleton loathed the unending, deadly harassment. Alerted to Patriot dragoons in the neighborhood, he ordered his men to form and advance along a narrow road and wait.

Meanwhile, Williams' detachment of six hundred, composed of militia and Lee's Legion, advanced in three columns through thickets bordering the defile. Seeing Tarleton's infantrymen, they laid down a heavy fire and received a heavy response. The Patriots killed a Redcoat captain and sixteen privates. The British killed nine Patriot militiamen.

***

Another affair occurred days later when Cornwallis' army crossed Alamance Creek heading north to shadow Greene and the main army. The British van under Col Webster and Lt Col Tarleton sought to surprise Col Williams' detachments at Reedy Fork Creek and ambush them in front of deep water damned at Adam Weitzell's grist mill.

Col William Campbell, commanding the militia for Pickens, posted in advance, placing pickets south of Reedy Fork Creek to block a British onslaught. Heavy fire forced the Patriots to ford the creek for safety. Then the riflemen, veterans of Kings Mountain, rounded back to the mill and a school house atop a hill and picked off Redcoats wading across the mill ford.

Sick of their men falling wounded and drowning, the British ceded the main ford and crossed at the horse ford. Their heavy fire forced Williams' corps to retreat. Both sides sustained thirty casualties.

Cornwallis repaired west to the southern end of Guilford County in search of forage and security. Greene crossed the Haw River above the northern end of the county and retired to Speedwell Ironworks on Troublesome Creek to gather his forces and secure stores hauled from Virginia.

It had been three weeks since Cornwallis retreated from the Dan. The British, self-deprived of their baggage wagons and afar from supply depots, hadn't gained markedly in provisions or reinforcements. They happily left the supposed Loyalist land having suffered Greene's calculating and stealthy insurgency from Hillsborough to Alamance, not unlike Gen Marion's destruction in South Carolina.

# Fifty-One ~ Rally Forces

— March 14, 1781, Speedwell Ironworks on Troublesome Creek, North Carolina

The armies had been within shouting distance for a month during four skirmishes in the area west of Hillsborough. Not to discount killed, wounded, and captured, but the half-hearted and phony fighting did little to settle scores.

Maj Gen Greene's reluctance to fight a general battle still nagged Cornwallis. But Greene's dour outlook eased as reinforcements arrived. His growing army subsisted on provisions Commissary General Davie continuously foraged and ordered by the wagonload from Halifax Court House in Virginia to the camps. Less than bountiful, the provisions just met ration requirements.

Cornwallis' forces hungered after taking the war to North Carolina and chasing Greene to Virginia with most of their provision wagons left behind in flames. Charles Town's supplies lay too remote. The nearer port of Wilmington, North Carolina tempted the lord and he weighed going there against the unfinished business of meeting Greene for general war.

While Greene headed west for camp at Speedwell Ironworks on Troublesome Creek a half days' march north of Guilford Court House, Cornwallis foraged at a Guilford County plantation then revisited Dillon's grist mill, effectively moving parallel to his enemy.

With two depleting wagons of provisions and a handful of cattle the lord marched twelve miles south of the courthouse to the forks of the Deep River in search of provisions. His new position near the Cape Fear Road kept open his option of retreating to the coast.

The British camped near the Quaker Meeting House and helped themselves to the flour and meal produced at Mendenhall's Mills. A party of fifty privates led by an officer worked the site until exhausting the wheat and corn.

***

Greene received more reinforcements. Brig Gen Robert Lawson led six-hundred Virginia militia and brigadier generals John Butler and Thomas Eaton brought a thousand more soldiers from the North Carolina militia. Greene could now field forty-five hundred troops against Cornwallis' newly estimated twenty-two hundred. He sobered knowing his Regulars numbering fifteen-hundred full-time professionals were less competent to the business of battle.

From Speedwell Ironworks Greene fell down with his army to Guilford Court House at the village of Martinsville. It had been a month since they first crossed the Dan.

Rain had been falling for two days but high pressure blocked a cold front that might have brought snow. Before leaving camp, Greene ordered all weapons cleaned and lubricated, and muzzles stoppered to keep them dry.

Regimental officers distributed cartridges before the march. Militiamen got four to six rounds. Regular infantry and riflemen got twenty for their muskets and rifles. Cavalry received twenty for their pistols. Any ammunition found on the battlefield would be fair game.

Each man carried a days' rations. Ammunition and provision stores remained under guard at Speedwell Ironworks.

At the battleground Greene toured the site with his officers, Commissary General Davie driving them in an open wagon westward starting from Guilford Court House. After one-and-a-half miles they crossed Little Horsepen Creek. Davie turned around to approach from the west as Cornwallis would.

"We're looking up the great road as it heads east to Hillsborough," Greene said.

"The Quakers call it New Garden Road to advertise the location of their meeting house," Brig Gen Butler said.

"Understood, but for the pilgrims among us, let's settle on the more general name Salisbury Road." The battleground loomed. "Stop here, General."

Greene stood and panned his right hand before a crop field.

"We're favored by the features of this site. Seeing our formation, the enemy must march down Salisbury Road and spread his forces left and right to match ours. To reach us, Cornwallis must cross a ravine made by Little Horsepen Creek and plod across that plantation field." The owner had plowed a portion, leaving red clay exposed and muddy from recent rains.

Lt Col William Washington, a hero of the Battle of Cowpens, assessed the clearing and the land beyond. "It's a large battlefield."

"Bigger than Cowpens?"

Washington nodded. The battleground measured more than a mile deep and a half-mile wide. Thick woods hemmed the plantation clearing and covered nearly all the land to the courthouse. "I understand you'll have three lines of formation."

Greene nodded.

"Reminds me of Morgan," Washington said.

"He gave me the idea. We'll form two lines of militia to give the British hell before they reach the Regulars."

Col Otho Holland Williams took off his hat and scratched his head. "Three formations on a mile-long field. That's a long way between lines. How will they support one another?"

"The First Line will fall back to assist the Second Line, and both will fall back to assist the Third Line."

"Nice plan." Lt Col John Eager Howard also fought heroically at the Battle of Cowpens. "The British will be exhausted if they reach the Third Line."

"That's the design," Greene said.

The party climbed back on the wagon. Greene instructed Davie to drive slowly to give him time to explain the plan while the landscape unfolded. The others sat on empty half barrels, bouncing and swaying as the wagon rolled up Salisbury Road.

"The cleared ground comprising the First Line is eight-hundred-yards across. So wide by my calculations," Greene said, "Cornwallis will have to commit every troop to close ranks and keep his flanks covered. Nevertheless, the British will be dangerously exposed. Their infantry will face a rail fence protecting our militia—"

Davie interjected. "That old fence will protect whom?"

"Granted, it's not a breastwork," Greene huffed, "yet it will give the militiamen a place to balance their muskets."

"Which militia will take the fence?" Brig Gen Stevens said.

"North Carolina's."

"General, I can put my 1$^{st}$ Brigade of Virginia militia on one side of Salisbury Road," Stevens said, "and Brigadier General Lawson can put his 2$^{nd}$ Brigade on the other side."

"The Virginia brigades will take the Second Line where the woods begin. We'll flatter the home militia with the first pick of the enemy."

Brig Gen Eaton's eyebrows arched. Brig Gen Butler, who shared leadership of the North Carolina militia, looked to the heavens.

"I'll explain myself more when we get to the woods." Greene touched Davie's arm. "Please continue."

They drove up Salisbury Road to the edge of woods looming beyond the First Line.

"The Second Line begins here. Thickets on either side of the first two lines will conceal riflemen and companies of infantry who'll pick off exposed Redcoats. Cavalry will also stage there, ready to fly to the enemy's rear as he moves downfield."

"If we get out of the woods," Washington mumbled.

"There's a clearing before the Third Line. It's not the big Cowpens feedlot, but I hope you'll find honorable action."

Brig Gen Stevens coughed. "You'll put the Virginia militia here?"

"Hot fire will soften the Redcoats before they get to the Regulars. Your gallant experience holding off the British at the Brandywine retreat is appropriate for the Second Line."

Stevens bit his lip to contain a smile and felt thankful Greene didn't mention the Battle of Camden where Virginia's militia fled, followed by North Carolina's. He hoped his oft-spouted warning against abandoning the line would honor Virginia.

"Thickets behind the Second Line and on either side of the field," Greene said, "will impair bayonet fighting in which the British still excel against Irregulars. The large tree trunks will cover us as well. Further back—drive on, General Davie—the terrain rises and various ravines will constrain British momentum.

"Salisbury Road bisects the entire site, allowing free movement of our troops and artillery. Guarding it will confine the British to our fire and the entangling thickets."

They came to the foot of the thickly wooded Third Line, the final defensive point. The battleground had steadily risen. The elevation to the left, north of Salisbury Road, stood seventy to ninety feet above Little Horsepen Creek at the battlefield's start.

Guilford Court House rose along Salisbury Road. Though a lower elevation, it was still high ground for the battlefield. In front of the Third Line ran Hunting Creek, preceded by a fallow field receptive to cavalry attacks.

Greene pointed to the high ground. "We'll have Regulars and artillery posted up there. If the enemy elects to climb the terrain or circle it to take the rear guard and seize the escape route, they'll face our experienced soldiers and two large guns. These wooded heights are a natural fortress.

"Should we need to withdraw, Reedy Fork Road near the foot of the courthouse and behind the Third Line will take us to Speedwell Ironworks and Virginia."

Davie saw the battlefield in terms of architecture. The treeless First Line resembled the beginning of a long manor house drawing room. Salisbury Road might be a runner down the center leading to the Second Line midway. An armoire on the left rear wall could be the heights of the Third Line. Through a back door would lay Reedy Fork Road much like a narrow hall set crosswise.

"General…General Davie. What are you thinking?" Greene said.

Davie threw off the daydream. "I was trying to envision the field."

"General Greene," Lt Col Washington said, "will the lord come?"

"Cornwallis may be weak yet he's no less aggressive. He won't pass this opportunity to fight before complete hunger drives him to Wilmington. The place to fight him is here. If not Guilford Court House, where? Possibly down Salisbury Road at New Garden or further southwest at Deep River. Cornwallis will soon get intelligence that we're at Guilford Court House. My arrival lays down the challenge."

***

Lord Cornwallis sat in his Deep River headquarters contemplating how best to counter Greene. He quashed thoughts of retreating. He hadn't hounded Greene this long and far only to high tail it to Wilmington. Would he march to the Rebel general or await his advance?

It had to be the former. Cornwallis didn't relish defense. The lord had once derided the idea of upstart colonials attacking his forces in New Jersey, but George Washington validated his offensive courage by defeating British-allied Hessian forces at Trenton.

While musing that Greene hadn't overplayed his hand until now and probably wouldn't do so, ADC Broderick rushed in carrying hot intelligence. Greene's army stood ready at Guilford Courthouse joined with thousands of North Carolina and Virginia militia, Virginia Regulars, and recruits for the Maryland Line.

***

Greene wondered if Cornwallis had received the leaked plan. Had the lord accepted the challenge? To avert surprise, Greene met with Lt Col Henry Lee and ordered a test.

"Gather your Legion of horsemen and light infantry with detachments of Virginia and Guilford County militia and Colonel William Campbell's Virginia riflemen. Go down Salisbury Road toward New Garden Meeting House. Should the British seek general warfare, they'll come up that route."

Cornwallis needed to scout the enemy as well. He notified an advance guard headed by Lt Col Banastre Tarleton's Legion of cavalry, the Hessian Yager and von Bose infantry regiments, and British infantry of the 23rd Regiment to prepare.

Lt Col Lee sent a lieutenant and party of dragoons to the area near Deep River Meeting House to further ascertain British army intentions. They discovered a deployment at two in the morning.

The lieutenant sent a terse message to Greene at Guilford Court House: "MG Greene, a large body of horse are departing from Deep River Meeting House."

Thirty minutes later Greene read the lieutenant's dispatch with delight. Guilford Court House would be the field. He immediately messaged Lee: "Lieutenant Colonel Lee, place your corps on Salisbury Road halfway between the courthouse and New Garden Meeting House. Take your breakfast no later than four o'clock and await the British vanguard."

The movement heard earlier at the British camp was merely essential baggage sent to safety in case of the lord's retreat. The actual advance started at four a.m. when Tarleton's corps broke camp without taking breakfast and marched in the van.

The narrow cut of Salisbury Road confined British infantry to march in two files forcing Tarleton to come up less than apace. As his corps neared New Garden Friends Meeting House musket fire erupted from nervous British and Patriot pickets clashing a half-mile up the road.

The skirmishing alarmed Lee. Then, when his lieutenant returned from the spying mission, enemy horse leisurely tailed. Lee retreated slightly with his Legion. Tarleton's vanguard approached, thinking the Patriots were fleeing.

Tarleton ordered an attack but only a few Americans in the front ranks took a blow in the close lane. Lee ordered a counter-attack, telling his men to trample the enemy under their mounts. The horn sounded and the riders urged their horses into a gallop.

The nearest section of British Legion dragoons dropped with their horses and fell dead or prisoner. Tarleton ordered a retreat down an adjacent road. Lee, feeling the road would round back at New Garden Meeting House, planned to ambush Tarleton by continuing down Salisbury Road.

Lee hadn't forgotten the murder of Master James Gillies. He rode with every exertion the horse would give, then halted and waited. Tarleton's corps didn't appear. Instead, the sound of slow, creaking wheels arose. Out of the pre-sunrise gray light a wagoner reined his team.

"Excuse me, sir," Zeb Mitchell said. "Do you know the way to Speedwell Ironworks?"

Lee studied the young man and the two companions sitting on either side of him. George Heider rose in the cargo box behind them and rubbed his eyes. "Who are you?" Lee said. "Why are you going there?"

Matthew Vinyard stuck a hand in front of Zeb. "I'm their sergeant. We're in the Makers company of the militia. We want to deliver forage to the commissary."

In the next few moments, a handful of bellowing cattle under the whip of a horseman crept up Salisbury Road behind the wagon.

"That must be our supper."

"Tis, sir," Vinyard said.

Lee glared at Abraham Hellerschwarz. "What are you doing away from home?"

Abraham heard the implication. "Sir, I volunteered with my master's permission."

"Do you have a note from your master?"

Abraham pointed to Zeb. "Private Zebulon Mitchell is my master."

"Is that so, Private?"

Zeb withheld his outrage. "Um, yes."

"Stay on Salisbury Road. In four miles you'll be at Hoskins' Farm where Greene has the army encamped. At Guilford Court House, another mile further, pickets will direct you to the ironworks."

Zeb commanded the horses, "Gee up!" Once they'd gone a hundred feet, Zeb raged at Abraham. "Stop calling me your master."

"It worked."

"Why can't you lose your yoke?"

"Were it that simple."

"In my company you're not a slave."

"You're one man."

"After the war—"

"Don't say that. There's no hope for me and my people."

Zeb looked up to the sky. "I beg forgiveness."

Lee's horse overtook the wagon. "Hold on, son! Leave one man to conduct the wagon. The other three will join us with arms."

Abe translated the directions for George before climbing down with Zeb and Sgt Vinyard, each carrying a musket.

Lee quickly forgot the waggoners. In the breaking sunrise, files of Redcoat infantry rising up Salisbury Road would soon counter him in front of the Meeting House. Their feet pounded the road in a roar like unrelenting, rolling thunder. Could it be the whole British army?

# Fifty-Two ~ Battle Erupts

— March 15, 1781, Friends Meeting House, New Garden

There would be a less vulnerable time to swallow. Worse than the sight of Lt Col Tarleton leading eager British and Hessian infantry was seeing his new bugler so near the enemy. Lt Col Lee signaled retreat. The bugle boy sounded it well. Lee wheeled his cavalry from a chase of lead balls. His horse threw him.

Though alarmed by the precise movements of the British foot troops reloading, Lee gently rubbed his horse and remounted. Lee's infantry and riflemen rallied for action, marching toward the British infantry with their arms at the ready.

Lee nodded and the bugler responded. Charge! Chaos of musket and pistol fire, gunpowder smoke, and clashing swords followed as the adversaries fought in the developing daylight with the meeting house a backdrop.

Pacifist Quakers came out of their houses and watched from a safe distance as the shocking melee unfolded. Amid pounding musket fire and screaming men spitting blood someone rang a handbell. Twigs rained down from a great oak tree next to New Garden Friends Meeting House after a poorly aimed volley from the British infantry. Quaker onlookers backed further away before Virginia riflemen fired their own volley.

Twenty minutes later the battle drifted a quarter mile south of the meeting house. Tarleton raised his cavalry sword as a musket ball hurtled toward him. Though spared of death, two fingers hewed from his right hand and fell into the lane. He rode away seeking treatment. A young woman in black clothing hailed him from the meeting house.

Smallpox carried by soldiers passing through the Quaker Quarter had victimized dozens of locals with fever, red rash, and blisters. Nevertheless, Sara McMurray was sure hostilities would break out and disregarded the contagion. She towed Maria Bach, Rahel, and Yohanna Heider with her to New Garden Meeting House to try and save lives.

Tarleton went inside. He was dusty, pained, and as green as his jacket. Sara paid no mind to a trail of blood dotting the wooden floor. His sword hanger was empty but a saber wouldn't have mattered. She invited him to sit and pressed a flask of brandy into his quivering left hand.

"Drink this, sir, and turn your head."

She dressed the wound by packing cotton on the finger-stubs and snugly wrapping one of her father's soft, absorbent neck cloths repeatedly over the cotton and around the hand. She brushed fresh sweetgum sap on the end of the cloth and stuck it to the dressing.

Before setting his arm in a rag sling, she held a cold, wet cloth against his forehead sprouting sweat from the shock.

Tarleton started for the door but stopped and turned. "Thank you, dear lady." As he gave her a deep bow, he recognized the young woman standing before the proclamation in Hillsborough. The registration in his eyes gave way to the pain coursing through his hand and he stepped away.

Sara followed him out the door watching as he caught up with the British dragoons. Only then did she feel her father's presence. While the battle in their neighborhood saddened most the Quaker community, Michael McMurray seethed.

"You shouldn't have been alone with that soldier."

"He was bleeding."

"Nursing a young man is not for thee, a young unmarried woman. Let your mother do it."

"He needed help!"

"That's no excuse."

"Blame your King who sent him."

"Don't take that tone with me, Daughter."

"How can you still like the Crown?"

"It's not a matter of liking the legitimate authority."

A young American soldier disoriented and shaking stepped from behind a tree across from the meeting house. He looked at the Quakers with the eyes of a hunted animal and furtively stumbled down the lane alone. Moments later two Redcoat infantrymen carrying bayoneted muskets ran in the direction of the pathetic soldier.

Cries erupted from the side of the meeting house. "No! Please don't!"

The bayonets whispered as they plunged into flesh and the Redcoats grunted from their exertions. Piercing howls turned to cries as the Redcoats fled.

Sara and her father ran to him. Blood pumped from the boy's brutal wounds. When his eyes became vacant, the red flow abruptly changed to a seep and stopped altogether. She turned ashen, closed her eyes, and said a prayer.

***

Though humiliated by the nasty injury, Tarleton rebounded to lead his corps. Mortal losses accumulated until both sides retreated, drained of energy.

Lee inquired his aide's count. "What have you seen?"

"We have dead and wounded infantry and riflemen including a Virginia militia captain and half his company. We have an infantry lieutenant down. Between twenty and thirty of their guards, dragoons, and yagers are dying or wounded," the aide said, pointing to a pile outside the meeting house.

Tarleton's infantrymen, British in red frocks and tricorns and Hessians in blue frocks and steepled hats, resumed their attack. Lee hollered. "Retreat! Leave the dead and dying on the field."

Lee's corps fled, passing the Meeting House and going up Salisbury Road a mile where a lane veered off northwest to Daniel Dillon's grist mill and Bruce's Cross Roads.

Lee ordered the corps to halt and stand their ground. All action stopped and the men happily caught their breath and reloaded. Lee used the ceasefire to dispatch his aide to the courthouse to warn Maj Gen Greene of the near fighting and British pressure.

As the aide galloped up Salisbury Road, Lee yelled "charge" which the bugle boy seconded. A hearty roar came from Lee's corps and they attacked. Unbeknownst to them, the enemy's forces had increased by the 23rd Regiment which Tarleton had called up from reserve. Now, Lee fielded six-hundred. Tarleton matched him plus two-hundred fifty.

***

For ten years Quaker Nathan Bourne had worked two large corn fields along Salisbury Road. Over the preceding week Patriot and British army foragers had ravaged Guilford County planters. Losing six horses, six oxen, two milking cows, a beef cow, bins of grain, chickens and ducks, plows, a wagon, and a buggy ruined Bourne.

Nathan's fifteen-year-old son Thomas snarled at the action from behind a rail fence. He gripped a half-cocked long rifle, pulled back the frizzen, and held it. Into the pan he poured a little gunpowder from a horn and let the frizzen spring back in place. He poured an amount of powder down the barrel that experience taught him would send a shot flying fifty yards. He dropped in a lead ball and a wadded piece of paper and rammed the charge.

With the rammer back in its holder Thomas fully cocked the hammer, laid the long muzzle on a rail, and shook his wide-brim black hat until it fell to the ground. Curls tumbled over his collar as he searched through the fence for an authoritative man, someone who may have directed the farm's plunder. It didn't matter what party they belonged to.

Somebody outside the faith had wronged the Bourne family. Disownment was out of the question. A primary Quaker Rule of Discipline—Quakers gather with fellow Quakers and each reform from their trespasses lest they receive disavowal as heathens and publicans—didn't work on non-Quakers.

Though young Thomas looked eastward, low gray clouds tamed the sun. He spotted a Redcoat captain, whose gold facing buttons ran in pairs, mounted on horse. Thomas squeezed the trigger. The frizzen sprang and the flint sparked the pan. The powder in the pan flashed hot and bright before his aiming eye and the butt of the rifle bucked into his shoulder. Out of the muzzle came sharp gunfire.

The British officer stood in the stirrups and ordered his bugler to call charge just as the lead ball accelerated down the grooves of Thomas' rifle and left the muzzle with a precise spin. The officer slumped dead on the mount's neck. His light infantry, seeing a stream of gun smoke above the fence, scattered fearing more shooting. Master Bourne reloaded.

The killing of the officer doubled British determination and led to the heaviest fighting of the morning. Though waking early to march, weariness didn't quell their zeal to kill and wound Patriots.

Lee wanted his corps to be fresh for the larger battle sure to take place later at Guilford Court House. He called for a final retreat and the corps marched up Salisbury Road. When the British yielded, the Battle of New Garden was over. Tarleton and Lee sat on their mounts at the head of their forces. Henry Lee nodded to Banastre Tarleton and they urged their horses to a meeting in the lane.

Tarleton admired the quality of Lee's stout, active horse as it pranced regally toward him. Lathered in sweat, it's measured breathing and bright eyes showed it to have weathered the excitement well and remained a battle steed of the highest condition.

"Sir, you are an excellent horseman," Tarleton said.

Lee offered conciliation to his opposition mounted upon a smaller horse. "Because of this superior Virginia horse."

"There is no victory for either of us."

"The disgrace of defeat would have been extreme," Lee said. "My corps will depart. I only ask that you care for my wounded men."

The feather in Tarleton's black leather helmet scraped the air while he motioned with his reins-holding left hand. "My pleasure."

Lee touched his helmet, turned around, and ordered the troops to march in two files to Guilford Court House.

***

From the side of the road Michael McMurray glared as companies of weary soldiers strode north along Salisbury Road. They'd soon pass him. The Quaker wainwright shook his head in disbelief, trying in vain to fathom the depths of civil anguish Guilford County had fallen.

When companies of the 1st Regiment of Guilford County neared, the beautiful, youthful faces of the local boys tore his heart. His blood pressure jumped and he turned his gaze when he counted Zebulon among the marchers.

McMurray looked again and squinted. It was Zeb's usual proud countenance. The same look baby Zeb wore the day Michael married Olivia. The expression he showed the world when he first stood and walked. The look Olivia often described as a mature, competent man breaking out of a boy's body to achieve his aims.

Embarrassment reddened McMurray's cheeks and blood rushing through his brain broke sweat on his forehead. Only a deranged person would march for that twisted, perverted army. My precious son is a battlefield hunter! My God, why? "You're a fool!"

With Zebulon marched Abraham Hellerschwarz and Sgt Matthew Vinyard. Although a sneer emanated from the sergeant, neither Zeb nor any of the other frazzled militiamen reacted. The parade continued like clockwork. What happened to this world? What good comes from Zeb having triumphed today if he's done evil?

McMurray stumbled homeward hanging his head. He stopped and braced against a tree; his heart riven with despair. Zeb will surely die against the King's army. He will lie forgotten in a miserable grave. Tears streamed as he made near silent murmuring. "Oh, my son! I've forsaken thee!"

# Map of the Battle of Guilford Court House

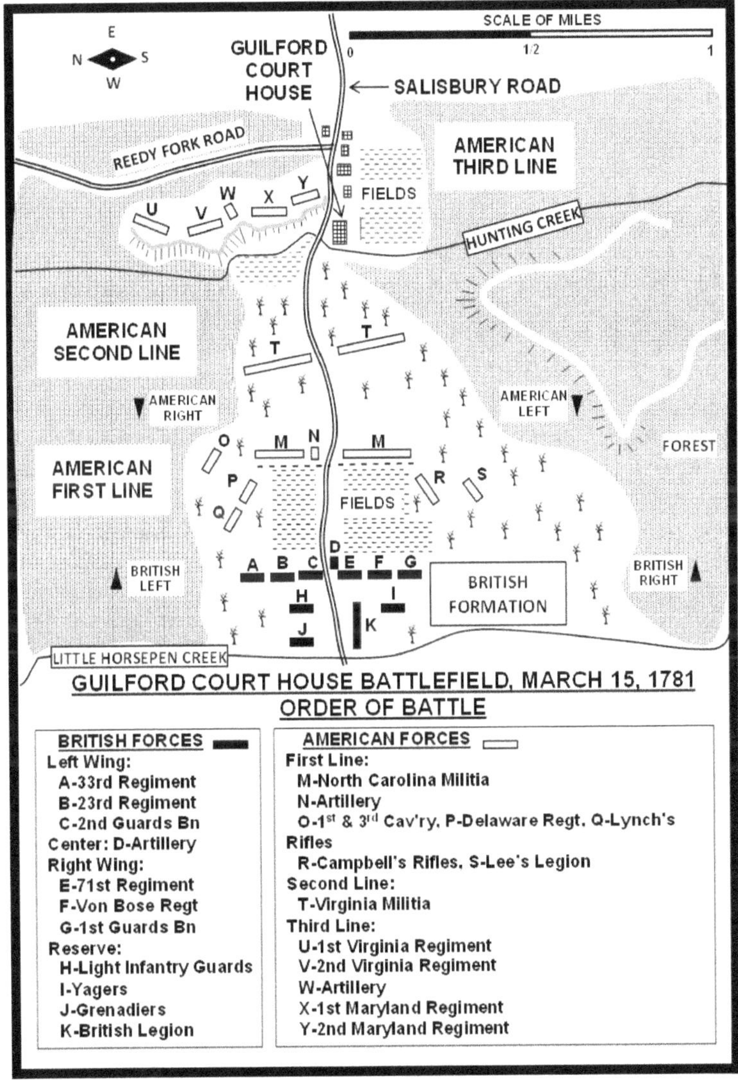


## GUILFORD COURT HOUSE BATTLEFIELD, MARCH 15, 1781
### ORDER OF BATTLE

# Fifty-Three ~ The Day Has Come

— March 15, 1781, Guilford Court House Battleground, The First Line

Pvt Zebulon Mitchell observed the signs of nature all around the battleground. From the moss on the trees to the shadows, he figured the time was somewhere between noon and one o'clock. While days and months normally meant little to a young man, he sensed the date would be significant.

Zeb hoped to live to see the end of March nineteen years hence his birth. Two years after that, he'd no longer be bound to his father. In the meantime, Michael McMurray claimed the proceeds of his labor. As for war wages, McMurray didn't want them, not that the state had money in their chests.

All morning as Patriot soldiers warmed by campfires made around the First Line, talk centered on whether a general battle would arise out of the Battle of New Garden. The consensus was a battle where they sat would eclipse the one fought in the early hours and it would be the hardest fight they'd ever know.

While Zeb mused about his rights as an individual man and citizen of the United States if the hopes of the Rebellion came true, Maj Gen Nathanael Greene trotted out to the First Line on a feisty black mare and dismounted in the middle of the North Carolina militia formed up along the eastern side of Joseph Hoskins' split rail fence.

Except for the Makers company, the militia stared. Most had never heard of the commander-in-chief, never mind seeing the man with two silver stars sewn on his shoulders. They noticed his tricky knee wobbled his gait. A hobbled commander in critical need of a victory seemed ominous.

Still, a grand general who had the Revolution weighing on his success, sought their company. Everybody acknowledged his authority, offering poor, unsophisticated salutes or silent, rigid salutations by standing at attention.

"At ease." Greene panned the hundreds of teens and young men. "I've put you up front to scare the enemy." Nervous laughter. "Sorry, I didn't mean for that to be funny. Don't discount yourselves. If the lord's army numbered five, you'd be two."

Greene borrowed a musket and laid it over the top fence rail so the muzzle pointed west from whence British fire would come. "This fence is most advantageous for raw troops not used to the shock of battle. The rails will steady your muskets and block the enemy's shots."

Zeb sized up the fence, a barrier to befuddle deer coming from the forest edge to feast on sweet kernels of corn. The gray wood, rusted nails, and gaps between the rails made him suspect the fence might not be as valuable as advertised. Greene, glimpsing Zeb's doubt, took off his black cocked hat fringed with gold and wiped his brow. Zeb buttoned his lips.

"Does everyone know what a volley is?" Greene said.

A volunteer spoke from a face pitted with smallpox scars. "All of us firing at the same time."

"A volley will make this field hell for the Redcoats. At once it will take down scores of them." Privately, a substantial portion of the young militiamen thought the sophisticated Redcoats might know the technique. "Why do we fire in volleys?"

The volunteer spoke again. "Because you never know where a musket shot might go. One musket might miss."

"Excellent, son. Missed shots will hit others. The spectacle of hundreds of guns firing will halt them in terror no matter the overall accuracy. Remember, a volley is everybody shooting at once. Wait for the signal, 'Make ready! Take aim! Fire!', from your commanders. They're checking the distance. They'll know when to fire."

Gen Greene pointed to the flanks. "You won't be alone out here. On your flanks sharpshooters will watch over you with rifles. Still from each of you I want at least two shots."

Greene studied the cross-section of North Carolinian men. Whites. A smattering of Blacks. Irish. Scottish. Germans. First and second generation with harsh accents. Scads of planters and the odd sawyer, blacksmith, wheelwright, and shoemaker.

"Why are we here?"

The volunteer clammed up not to overdo it. Zeb raised his hand. "To decide our future for ourselves, sir!"

Greene nodded enthusiastically. "Absolutely. Any other opinions?"

"We're protecting our families," an older man said with passion.

"Okay, boys. Stand firm and do what you can. Remember, I want at least two shots fired in volleys. Listen to your commanders."

***

Lt Gen Charles Cornwallis reached the battlefield. After he established headquarters at the home of ardent Patriot Joseph Hoskins—a man who fled Chester County, Pennsylvania four years prior when the lord helped Sir William Howe seize Philadelphia—Cornwallis would parade his troops east up Salisbury Road to the battlefield.

The lord's sagging eyes attested to the long, tiring march Greene had wrought. The adventurous quest was over and it had come down to this one day. The British have come to take North Carolina back into the fold of Royal authority. It has always belonged to the Crown and I intend to humiliate the Patriots with a great victory.

Cornwallis, loosely surrounded by a squad from the Brigade of Guards watching for any threats to his security, sized up the enemy and battlefield with unaided eyes and through a field glass.

"Are there thousands?" Cornwallis said to ADC Capt Broderick.

"May I offer an estimation, my Lord?"

Far on the Second Line the first high notes from the fife of Maj Ferguson Taylor of the Virginia militia interrupted Cornwallis' concentration as the song *Soldier's Joy* began. The lord frowned at the music and answered Broderick.

"Certainly. Do I ever mind your opinion?"

"Em…no, my Lord. Perhaps one thousand militiamen stand. The space between the woods can't be more than twelve-hundred yards. That would leave—"

"Broderick, I know mathematics."

Cornwallis looked downfield. Civilians lined the edge of the field. A dozen first and second line fifers gradually joined the Fife Major and drummers added tempo until the music amassed into a wall of sound.

The lord covered his ears and yelled to Broderick while motioning with his head to the spectators. "There may be one-thousand militia, but hundreds of women and children wave and throw kisses. God, look at the pumpions." He blared down a speaking trumpet made with his hands. "Why don't you eat and drink while your sons and fathers and brothers die?"

From the periphery Cornwallis saw traveler wagons trying to come up Salisbury Road from whence the army had marched.

"Find the quartermaster and tell him to block the road with the hospital wagons."

"Yes, my Lord."

***

Earlier, Guilford County's high sheriff warned off the public anticipating the violence as if it would be a mere flogging. The crowd returned to the dubious boundary of the battlefield when he departed to guard the courthouse gaol crammed with friends of the King.

Quakers mostly stayed away. If talk amongst the spectators was true, they'd stayed home threshing wheat in their sheds under state order to pay their share of the war expense.

Camp-following women hoped a young man on the First Line would look their way. Militiamen, unlike Regulars, could steal away after a battle no matter which army won. Though financial straits meant the boys had no wages, they might bring scraps of food or a tin canteen of rum saved up for trade in a secluded candle-lit shed. The maidens curtsied and smiled at their fanciers. Cornwallis, feeling the burn of a particularly relentless stare, stole a look and shuddered at a mouth of green teeth smiling from the wrinkled face of a poor, old wretch.

Sara McMurray sat on a log with Maria Bach, Rahel, and Yohanna Heider supporting their Makers assembled on the First Line. The men, formed up sleepy-eyed and solemn from the early morning battle, listened to an officer decorated with gold and attended by staff.

Sara, Yohanna, and Rahel watched and privately cheered and fussed over their men. Their worries, diminished since the skirmishes in Orange County, returned. The prospect of marriage was in the offing if the boys could get through this battle.

Sara wanted to be out there with Sgt Vinyard. She'd lent him the Surry rifle broken in from the fight against Arthur Neal. Matthew assured her he'd kill Redcoats.

Yohanna held out hope this would be Zeb's last encounter with a life-risking battle. Their time had come. It didn't matter if they lived in Salem or New Garden. The only thing important was marriage and consummating it with love and children.

Maria's hoped-for fiancé and Yohanna's brother was missing from the company. Had the British captured him in the Battle of New Garden?

Three-hundred yards behind Cornwallis' right heel, ten-year old Jonathan Jessop, the son of Thomas Jessop who farmed property south of Salisbury Road sat on the ground and finished a simple sketch. Remarkably, the boy captured the essence of the skirmish at New Garden in the early hours.

Master Jonathan learned about the Battle of New Garden from rumors shot through Martinsville. He drew the British and American lines facing each other in the "Great Battle" that was to come, as he noted it, and a mass of soldiers clashing their swords and taking the conflict to Guilford Court House proper.

To Maria's and Yohanna's relief, Pvt Heider came running onto the field and joined the Makers company standing south of Salisbury Road on the First Line of the Americans. Kept behind after delivering the wagonload of forage, he'd been rerolling damaged musket cartridges.

The leather straps of twelve cartouche boxes full of cartridges slung over George's shoulders. He kept four cartridges for himself and prayed to use them all. Having passed out ammunition along the line, he joined Zeb, Abe, and Matthew behind the fence.

With enough pageantry to crown a monarch, all the British drummers, fifers, and Highland bagpipers produced a glorious sound that made the Patriot musicians stop playing and listen. The British paraded their regiments down Salisbury Road waving the combined crosses of Britain's St. George and Scotland's St. Andrew emblazoned on the King's Colors.

Cornwallis gazed through moist eyes at the Union Flag and smirked at the Americans. Of the small number of militia companies that hoisted them, their shoddy standards paled in comparison. He dismissed a flag that suggested a union of the colonies.

The Colonists have no idea what constitutes a united nation or a flag of one. I plan to celebrate the spoils of victory by planting the King's standard firmly in the ground of the last ramparts held by the stinking Rebels.

Listless in the cold, calm air, the flags heralded the coming carnage. Spectators lost their cheer and filed away expecting the festive atmosphere to plunge into gravity. A battle promised a victor and scores of dead and wounded.

Not to let the Patriots feel their spectacle lacking, Lt Col Lee rode up to the First Line brandishing his sword, marred with lines of dried blood spilled at the Battle of New Garden.

Pvt Abraham Hellerschwarz gathered with the Makers company on the far left American flank as safe from the artillery as Capt Abercrombie Hawkins reckoned necessary. He got Pvt George Heider's attention with a poke in the ribs.

Leaning to speak above the roaring British music, Abe told George something he'd overheard earlier on the First Line. "That's 'Light Horse Harry' Lee. The Legion leader we saw this morning."

George shrugged.

"You don't know who he is?"

"I missed all the action this morning," George said.

Abe gave George a friendly fist in the side. "No, three weeks ago. He tricked the Loyalists into thinking he was Lieutenant Colonel Tarleton and cut them to pieces at Pyle's Massacre in the Stinking Quarter."

"Don't talk like that. You're inviting a horrible fate."

"Ha. Cornwallis doomed us when he marched onto this field."

Lee read from a piece of paper. "My brave boys! Your lands, your lives, and your country depend on your conduct this day! I gave hell to 'Bloody' Tarleton three times this morning and I'll give him more of it before night!" He rode along the line of militia acting in a great rage for battle and told them it would be sufficient if they'd stand to make only two fires.

# Fifty-Four ~ Cannonade

The British army marched to the field. Six-hundred yards from the First Line, the files turned left or right depending on Cornwallis' orders and started the process of dressing shoulder-to-shoulder. Successive regiments marked by their standards would take their places until a wall of British military opposed the anxious Americans.

First, a column of Royal Artillery marched under Lt John MacLeod. Next came Col James Webster commanding the left wing brigade of the 23rd and 33rd infantry regiments. Maj Gen Alexander Leslie, Cornwallis' second in command, brought up the right wing brigade of the 71st Regiment of Foot, and Regiment von Bose.

Reserve forces stood ready comprised of the 1st Battalion of the Guards and the Light Infantry of the Guards. As well, Brig Gen Charles O'Hara commanded the 2nd Battalion of the Guards, Yager Riflemen, and companies of Grenadiers. Tarleton's British Legion followed behind in column on Salisbury Road.

Cornwallis couldn't plumb the depths of the American order of battle, though on the First Line the Patriots lived up to their reputation of leading with their least experienced troops. Obvious from their civilian clothing, militia lined up and facing him covered the field between the woods skirting the First Line. Yes, they wear black tricorns, but Regulars don't wear rough brown hunting frocks or go shoeless.

He extended the tubes of a pocket telescope and observed. A Rebel corps of observation on Cornwallis' left, overflowing from the edge of the woods far north of Salisbury Road, revealed themselves to be Regulars. Capt Robert Kirkwood led two companies of Delaware "Blue Hens" infantry who wore short blue frocks with red facings.

Col Charles Lynch's Bedford Riflemen and Lt Col William Washington's Continental cavalry accompanied the Delaware troops. The stern-faced riflemen, resembling their long and thin weapons, dressed in a variety of rough, backcountry garb. Their faces volatile and eager like chambered gunpowder.

The calvary donned uniforms, both regiments in high black leather helmets and buff breeches. The 1st wore white jackets and the 3rd blue and each had wrapped the legs of their horses with cloth for protection against sharp tree limbs and brush in the close quarters of the woods.

The lord looked past his right flank situated far south of Salisbury Road. Another Rebel corps of observation. Lee's Legion, the devils who bloodied my men and maimed Tarleton this morning, wore split pea green jackets, poor replicas of the British Legion's verdant fabric. We'll soon meet you devils up close. Just you wait.

Nearby Lee's Legion, the companies of Col William Campbell's Virginia Riflemen menaced the lord from their cold, ragged faces. Like Lynch's corps, the tall, thin backwoods men practiced their aim down long, narrow barrels growing out of their faces. The woods being sparser on that side of the field seemed opportunistic for a special thrust of Cornwallis' army.

Somewhere beyond the sacrificial militia and small units of Regulars, Cornwallis sensed Greene's brigades of Continentals lay unseen. Despite Loyalist scouts leaving the lord with no idea of their configuration or whether they'd dug breastworks, surely they lay beyond.

Like Jonathan Jessop, the battlefield mystified Cornwallis. Past Little Horsepen Creek and the rising plowed field, the vast woods kept a secret. Greene has done himself proud picking a brilliant field. I can hardly wait for the chaos to begin and attack his Regulars.

***

In making their formation, the Redcoats marched to Little Horsepen Creek on the western border of the battlefield. North Carolina militia on the First Line hushed and gazed wide eyed at the processions. Banners of red dipped as companies marched down the far bank of the creek bed. Up the near bank, the Redcoats elevated again.

Subtly, the First Line of militia at Salisbury Road parted to allow the passing of artillery. When a pair of six-pound brass field pieces came forward and rested, the line restitched. The center-forward placement of the 1st Continental Artillery commanded by Capt Anthony Singleton attached to the Virginia Line told Cornwallis they'd come down Salisbury Road.

What's at the back of this terrain that Greene seeks to protect? Of course! Guilford Court House and the route to the American camp which the lord knew from reconnaissance to be Speedwell Ironworks on Troublesome Creek eighteen miles to the north. The lord's eyebrows arched in appreciation of the depth and logic of the battlefield.

All eyes rolled to Capt Singleton, ordered by Maj Gen Greene to check the British army. Though two deadly cannon muzzles dared them, Redcoat columns continued to take the field, issuing companies into the single line forming across from the Patriots. The captain ordered the gunner to oversee a salvo, never waiting for the line to complete.

"Load and ram!" The loader matross placed the powder end of a gunpowder-sabot-ball cartridge in the muzzle and rammed it into the breech.

"Prime!" The vent matross pricked the bag of gunpowder with a priming wire down the touch hole and inserted a fuse.

"Make ready!" The matross drummer beat an anxious roll to alert the gun crew and frighten the intended targets.

"Fire!"

A matross lowered a burning cord of twine held at the end of a linstock safely away from his body and touched off the fuse of the first cannon. The gunpowder in the fuse ignited and reached down to the breech. The cannon boomed and rolled back two feet after throwing a six-pound ball with a great exhalation of fire and a whistling arc.

The matross fired the other cannon repeating the hell fury. He took three paces back and stuck the pointed non-working end of the linstock into the ground and came to attention awaiting orders.

Deployment of the British formations turned chaotic as troops bolted for cover in the woods lining the sides of the field.

Cornwallis ordered Lt MacLeod to respond and he readied two three-pounder Royal Artillery cannons. Artillery crewmen loaded the cannons and aimed at the militia near the center of the First Line. The Americans dashed left and right. When the Royal Artillery gunner yelled "Fire!", MacLeod's cannons boomed and the first rounds landed on the evacuated First Line and destroyed part of the fencing.

Pvt Heider took his hands away from his ears and looked up to see Lee riding hard, determined to dodge a cannon ball. The Legion commander shouted. "You hear damnation roaring over all these woods! After all, they're no more than we!" He galloped to safety on the American left flank.

Meanwhile, the teams at Singleton's cannons prepared for another salvo by disposing themselves to a series of actions designed to kill masses of Redcoats while avoiding accidents and thereby preserving Continental lives.

The stout sergeant gunner maintained meticulous discipline to ensure the dousing and removal of any burning material still in the muzzles and vents to prevent the next gunpowder charge exploding prematurely. He barked orders, watching the matrosses keenly as they cleared the cannons.

"Clear the vent!" the Gunner said. The vent matross worked a length of wire in and out of the touch hole.

"Worm and Sponge!" The vent matross plugged the touch hole to rob it of oxygen while the wormer matross successively worked a corkscrew and a moist swab down the muzzle. They prepared the second cannon.

Capt Singleton ordered another battery salvo. British troops marveled at the muzzles throwing red fire. They glimpsed the whizzing iron balls and guessed where they'd land or how far they'd skip over the ground.

Singleton and his counterpart knew any range was possible. After recoiling thrice on the sloped field, MacLeod's cannons pointed higher and their trajectories ran deeper. By the time his fourth volley came, balls flew over the First Line and assaulted the Virginia militia on the Second Line.

Capt Hawkins watched MacLeod's crews dipping their cannon muzzles. "Take cover!"

Confused by the order, George watched the other boys and knelt on the ground. MacLeod's fifth volley struck boulders in front of the First Line and threw splinters of granite into his face. Singleton answered MacLeod by traversing his cannons to the corners of Cornwallis' line and throwing more salvos.

Though the cannonading was more galling than purposeful, the deafening noise aroused Guilford County. Residents for miles around, including Michael McMurray, stopped to listen.

McMurray ran from the wainwright shop and hastened to the battlefield on a lively chestnut filly. He stopped to redirect Continental baggage wagons trying to find their way to safety at Speedwell Ironworks and tore away to the field. McMurray waved his arms in futile anger at the combatants when he spotted Sara and the Moravian ladies and shooed them away.

Less than a half hour of cannonading ended. A dozen men lay dead or wounded. The action softened the resolve of the British infantry and North Carolina militia and gave each side time to reconnoiter their enemy. Cornwallis, given cursory knowledge of the field by Loyalist guides, learned the two lines his forces would need to push through.

Useful intelligence came after the First Line militia parted to avoid the cannon fire. The Second Line consisted of militia minus corps of observation. The cannonading cost the lord, however. A young lieutenant of the Royal Regiment of Artillery, himself the gunner of the British three pounders, fell dead.

# Fifty-Five ~ Clashing on the Field

Artillery fire over, Cornwallis resumed regimental deployments. When a complete red banner stretched across the field in front of the First Line, he commanded field officers to take quick advantage of the Irregulars. They bellowed a command meant to bleed the Americans, revealing their pleasure to oblige.

"Fix bayonets!"

Sgt Roger Lamb, a twenty-four year old Irish veteran, attached a bayonet to the end of his musket in precise coordination with fellow troops of the 23rd Regiment. Patriots on the north side of Salisbury Road shivered at the sight, feeling frightfully diminished as the seventy-five inch spear-guns momentarily towered in front of the Redcoats. Lamb waited with fellow Royal Welch Fusiliers for instructions from Col James Webster who was riding to the front.

"Charge!"

Lamb and his company burst into a smart march with arms charged. The militia of the First Line rested their muskets on the rail fence. Bravery wasn't widespread, but not all North Carolina militiamen feared action. Lamb recoiled, seeing them taking aim at his regiment with the nicest precision.

The Fusiliers halted at two-hundred yards. Both parties surveyed each other, musing the decisive moment with awful suspense. A militia colonel taunted the 23rd, "Come on, you Lobsters!"

Another militia colonel posted behind the tall stump of an old tree. Pvt William Beck, a boy who'd nearly served at the Battle of Camden, spotted him over his shoulder. I suppose elders have rights, but bayonets are coming and we have no trees to interrupt them while my commander takes protection. He intends to ride behind the Second Line and, Dear Mother, let us die. God, save us.

***

South of Salisbury Road the faultless marching of the bayonet-ready 71st Foot led by Maj Gen Alexander Leslie horrified Capt Hawkins. The Redcoats have struck terror in my boys. My God, look at that. They're eyeing paths from the field and the battle hasn't started.

He watched the boys, their knees wobbling as they stood. Their fire would be useless.

"Boys, kneel if you must! Thereby lose your shakes and keep a straight mark. Aim at their knees and listen for my command!"

The 71st Highlanders advanced professionally, disregarding the muck of the late plowed field. Hawkins would order fire when the enemy passed two bare trees one-hundred yards from the fence. Two-hundred yards and coming. Dear God, let the shivers rattling through my men ease in time.

Hawkins looked around the line for reactions and admired Sgt Vinyard's determined glare on the enemy. Lucky Redcoats wouldn't get his ball.

Vinyard had come off the spying and foraging mission with his Makers squad. How they'd gotten on the battlefield Hawkins didn't know, having lost contact. With too many men in the backcountry resisting the fight with the Crown, their presence brought confidence to his chest.

Hawkins motioned to a British captain driving his men with a drawn sword.

"Sergeant Vinyard! Can you take him down?"

Vinyard patted the Surry rifle. "Watch me!"

"Let him come within fifty yards!"

At that instant Gen Greene's aide-de-camp Maj Burnet visited Hawkins.

"Vinyard!" Hawkins yelled in the noise of marching Redcoats and commanders motivating their militia.

"Sir?"

"General Greene orders me to the courthouse to rally the men in case of defeat! Take my place!"

"Yes, sir!"

The enemy closed in to one-hundred fifty yards. Bright red frocks. Red and white argyle stockings from their knees down. Blue woolen bonnets. Occasionally a Black Watch kilt.

Vinyard gave the awaited commands. "Company! Make ready! Take aim!"

Drums rolled in a tense thunder preceding a lead downpour.

"Fire!"

Forty other regimental commanders all along the First Line repeated the command. British boys in tight, mechanical formations fell, crying for their wounds or hushed in death. Smoke like filthy cotton smothered the field.

Abraham Hellerschwarz stood resolute by Vinyard. He could hardly believe it. After the North Carolina militia delivered their first fire, the British line seemed like knubby canes in a harvested Salem cornfield.

Vinyard didn't volley with the company. Wearing Sara's brown ringed, golden knit wool cap that perfectly kept the hair out of his eyes, he steadied his rifle and looked down the barrel. He squeezed the trigger and the 71st Regiment captain fell dead. Vinyard gave Abe a rueful shrug.

Another captain commanding a 71st company couldn't quell the gruesome poetry chanting in his mind. In our advance the Americans covered by the fence reserved fire until we came within thirty or forty paces then opened a most destructive bloody hell fire. Too many of us dropped on the spot. Heaven will quake when it opens its arms.

The 71st Foot lost a quarter of their line to gunshot death and injury. The ones still standing halted or backed up. Their intrepid commander Leslie admonished the ones taking cover on the ground to get up. He told all to march. From thirty yards away, they gave a close round to the North Carolina militia, reloaded, and fired again.

Leslie screamed the dreaded command. "Charge bayonets!"

Accompanied by a shrilling drum roll, the Highlanders extended their muskets vertically at arm's length. Gleaming bayonets pricked the sky. After rotating them ninety degrees, the 71st Foot wailed banshee cries and charged the weak split rail fence. They opened fire, thrust their spikes, and the North Carolina militia gave way.

***

Webster rode in front of the 23rd Regiment on the north side of Salisbury Road and inspired them with a commanding voice. "Come on my brave Fusiliers!"

The musketeers rushed forward amidst the enemy's fire. Havoc overcame the Americans when the 23rd volleyed.

Answering fire on the 23rd Regiment came from Capt Robert Kirkwood's Delaware Regiment, Col Charles Lynch's Rifles, and Lt Col William Washington's Continental cavalry on the right flank of the Patriots. The 33rd Regiment took fire as well and jarred Webster to action. He swerved his advancing formation to the left under a shrieking voice and drum roll.

"Regiment—Left oblique!"

The regiment wheeled left forty-five degrees and marched until it lay before the American right flank.

"Regiment—Right oblique! Regiment—Forward march!"

The regiment turned and proceeded toward the Americans nearest the woods. As the horde came, Brig Gen Thomas Eaton directed his body of North Carolina militia to the right to assist the flank.

Tarleton eagerly watched Webster's regiment marching for the Patriots with the steadiness and composure of a field surgeon. The order and coolness of those troops advancing across the open ground, exposed to the enemy's fire, cannot be sufficiently extolled. Webster's left flank, now moving through the protection of the woods, is no less gallant. Nor are the enemy easily provoked, allowing Webster's men to arrive before giving their fire. Shooting pain prevented Tarleton from raising his right hand in a fist.

Support drawn from the militia to the American right flank hit the 33rd Regiment hard and brought the aid of the 23rd Regiment. Consequently, and unseen by Patriot officers, the center of the field opened for exploitation.

# Fifty-Six ~ First Line Panic

Butler's and Eaton's jaws dropped as scores of their North Carolina militia broke and retreated. The sight from the Second Line disgusted Brig Gen Edward Stevens who surmised they'd suffered no less than the Redcoats. He hoped to escape humiliation. He'd placed guards behind his line with orders to shoot every Virginia deserter.

Lamb of the 23rd Regiment with unequalled curiosity marveled as the militia made a general retreat. Though we're driving them from their ground, they're conducting their retreat with order and regularity. Never should they quit, yet they gave us a fight before leaving the field.

Tarleton couldn't forget the Continentals' sudden about face at the Battle of Cowpens that turned deadly. The North Carolina militia turning their backs sickened him. Is this also a trick? It was impossible to warn Webster the militia would retreat ten yards, turn, and give fire. His voice would never carry.

***

On the Patriot left flank Lt Col Lee espied the breaking militia. Red-faced from anger, he rode past them and shrieked over the din. "Go back to the line! I'll set my horses on you!"

A humiliated militiaman unknown to Lee glared at the Legion leader, elevated and high minded upon his horse, letting others like his humble mount do the hard deeds. Would you come down here and fight?

"Fight, man!" Lee bellowed. "The Revolution wasn't won in Boston."

Lee galloped to safety while inexperienced militiamen threw down muskets, cartridges, and all other accoutrements and high tailed to the rear. The bravest militia stayed and continued to fight, but whole companies of lads plainly done with their position on the front line against the Regular forces of the Crown couldn't abandon the field fast enough.

One militiaman saw the eyes reproaching him for tossing his musket. He picked up the drum of his company's dead musician and found sticks knocked from the odd tree by a cannon ball and started beating the taut circle of leather. He hung his head in embarrassment.

The sound was far from music and his uniform, not the blue-faced red frock of a militia drummer, was all wrong. Who was he fooling, dressed in a hunting shirt?

He didn't see in that tumultuous moment the ghost of red paint showing through the thin blue topcoat recently painted over the drum's shell. Nor did he know the drum had once belonged to a drummer in a company of the 71st Regiment of Foot who fell at the Battle of Cowpens.

Virginia militiamen in the Second Line laughed and tormented the fake drummer. "Three-month boy, you're going to jail! You'll swing for desertion!" An opening between two regiments in the Second Line appeared and he barreled through it. When he stopped running and bent over to catch his breath, thick woods engulfed him. After deep gulps of air, he started again, flying from the carnage and noise.

***

Capt Singleton's hope of high-spirited Regulars and militia holding the line faded under the British shifts. After the center of the field lost support, he ordered crews of the 1st Continental Artillery to harness the teams and pull the cannons up Salisbury Road toward Guilford Court House. On his rear came Redcoats flooding up the road.

A squad of the 71st regiment attacked the artillery but Singleton and his men fought back. The Patriot matross who'd been firing the cannons turned his linstock around and used its sharp end as a spontoon to hold off bayonets until the rest of the gun crew loaded their muskets and volleyed. The artillery remained secure in the road, blocking the enemy.

***

South of Salisbury Road the 1st Battalion of Guards took hits from the Patriot left flank's steady fire. Lee's Legion of cavalry and light infantry and Col William Campbell's Virginia Riflemen eagerly took their pick of targets from the woods. Cornwallis watched the overwhelming display with aide-de-camp Broderick at his side.

Though he expected accurate-firing riflemen from the Americans, Cornwallis little appreciated there would be so many or they wouldn't need to line up like musket men. Mouth agape, he watched the riflemen work independently, quickly reloading and making themselves small by laying on the ground behind rocks and logs. Broderick spoke Campbell's name with a sneer.

Cornwallis fumed as he eyed Campbell ordering pot shots. Why don't we have more rifles? Major Patrick Ferguson, brutally murdered with his Loyalist militia at Kings Mountain, South Carolina in October, had held a patent on a breech-loading type! His model holds a bayonet and the Rebel types don't!

Just as the situation for Col Chapple Norton and the 1st Battalion of Guards on the far right couldn't deteriorate more, Leslie assisted and the British pushed back the American riflemen. Butler threw his body of North Carolina Militia to the left to assist Lee and Campbell. Again, the center of the field gashed and the 71st and von Bose regiments bled through to assault Stevens' brigade.

***

The 71st, with the support of Norton's 1st Battalion of Guards, volleyed at the militiamen who turned left to aid their flank. Vinyard and his gritty, small Makers company answered them as best as they could while British powder and lead threatened their charmed lives.

Theory annoyed Matthew Vinyard. In a perfect state our guns can fire three rounds a minute. In live action a soldier is lucky to get off a round every couple of minutes. Petty things reduce a man's concentration: reloading under fire, aiming, or sucking deep breaths because your messmate and friend perished by your side minutes ago.

Vinyard's Makers company dwindled and those remaining ran low on ammunition. The sergeant tossed his men extra musket cartridges. Zeb half-cocked the hammer, bit off the end of a cartridge, and pulled back the frizzen. He filled the pan with powder and let the frizzen snap back. He dumped the remaining powder into the muzzle and the ball surrounded by the cartridge paper then rammed the charge. The ramrod broke after two rattles.

He compacted the lead and paper against the powder with a found rod then fully cocked the hammer. Worried the squad had abandoned him, he frantically aimed at the Redcoats and got a good aim on a 71st infantryman struggling to unjam his musket and return fire.

Zeb fired and missed his foe, instantly regretting taking advantage. He turned under heavy fire to abandon the First Line and discovered he hadn't been alone. Sgt Matthew Vinyard was down on one knee with a neck wound trickling red and a shattered leg. He motioned to Zeb. Save yourself. A bayonet drove Zeb away.

Twenty-three year-old Vinyard, a four-year veteran of North Carolina militia service, had never gone down in action. Was he nothing to the enemy soldiers wearing red frocks and Black Watch kilts and trews coming to crush him underfoot and uttering all but intelligible English?

Zeb ran for safety. It was the last thing the sergeant would see before falling on his back wheezing blood and air through the neck hole as events all around whirled out of control. A pair of wishes chased by turns in his mind. For the health of Sara. For one of the Scottish soldiers to shoot him out of pity or revenge.

The last of the North Carolina militia ran behind the Virginia militia line. Campbell's Virginia riflemen stood and swept the British in swift fire. The 1st Battalion of Guards formed and came down upon the riflemen in columns twelve and sixteen men deep. Their rapid fire and bayonets compelled the Patriot left flank to evacuate to the Second Line.

***

Lee's implication that Patriots equaled Redcoats echoed in Zebulon Mitchell's mind. He'd believed it until he heard the elitist "three-month boy" taunt suggesting some Patriots excelled other Patriots.

Although Zeb had a taste of death when Arthur Neal's Loyalists tried their utmost to kill the Makers and steal the Salem ammunition, nothing could have prepared him for the present carnage. The intensity of fighting over the past two months had snared him, Abe, George, and Matthew before they knew it.

Zeb chafed at the Virginia militia and protested their pettiness with his eyes. Why are you uncivil to your fellow Americans? You stood behind us while we suffered two months of pent up Redcoat rage. You're a small-minded, ungrateful lot. We softened up the lobsters!

How could you forbid the North Carolina boys from retreating when they could barely stand from shaking? In the confusion that was the First Line, nobody will know the whole truth. Is there no hope humanity in deference to young souls everywhere will judge them fairly? We're small spokes in large, cynical wagon wheels.

I declare the leaders stood us up like peculiar straw men in a fallow corn field. We got off one or two fires. We don't need your damnation, approbation, sympathy, or laughter. None of us militia or Regulars have learned through trials how to stare back calmly at the muzzle of a gun. We took the fire and gave fire sometimes without mercy and made the path of the Redcoats a bit harder. I reckon we did what the general asked.

The day Yohanna and I become proper lovers eludes me. Will I get off this field alive? George bleeds and I have no idea where he and Abraham are. My God, what will I tell Sara?

# Fifty-Seven ~ Defensive Nerve

— March 15, 1781, Guilford Court House Battleground, The Second Line

Lt Gen Cornwallis had exploited the sluggish Americans who'd waited hours for his approach by dispatching infantry as soon as the cannonade ended. His optimistic moves against the First Line quickly turned defensive as the North Carolina militia unleashed a thundering volley.

The North Carolina fusillade ended and an unspectacular number of the militia reloaded. Cornwallis had repeatedly witnessed this stage of battle in the Colonies. Green frontline Irregulars would seize up at the sight of British bayonets, fall into disarray, and fly.

Col James Webster and Maj Gen Alexander Leslie had wheeled their forces into the flanks to hush the expert rifle and musket men, sending them retreating to the Second Line. The next stage of battle would begin with a thousand North Carolina militia erased from the field.

North of Salisbury Road—on the Patriot right flank— Capt Robert Kirkwood's Delaware "Blue Hens", Col Charles Lynch's Bedford Rifles, and Lt Col William Washington's 1st and 3rd Continental cavalry braced for another onslaught of Webster's 33rd and 23rd.

South of Salisbury Road—on the Patriot left flank—the corps of Col William Campbell's Rifles and Lt Col Henry Lee's Legion horse and light infantry readied for Leslie's 71st Regiment, Regiment von Bose, and the 1st Battalion of Guards to come again.

***

The remaining battleground epitomized the North Carolina backcountry. Hills covered with a thick forest of oak, hickory, and pine and a few old fields awaited the British forces moving toward the American Second Line a thousand feet beyond the first. To Cornwallis' left, north of Salisbury Road, the land rose steadily then reached into thickly wooded heights a half-mile away. There must stand his goal.

South of Salisbury Road, thinner woods looked promising to infantry penetration but for a wooded ridge slowly rising to a plateau on the far right of the Second Line. Not knowing whether the elevated woods continued to the court house or dropped off prior to it bothered Cornwallis. British corps equal in strength and superior in experience could crush militia in the first case. In the latter case a small, stealthy corps of militia might take deadly advantage.

Cornwallis admired Maj Gen Greene's foresight in choosing the mysterious field. The lord wouldn't have made the successive lines so distant from the First Line. Too remote to get support. No wonder the North Carolina militia failed. He guessed the distance between the Second Line and the Continentals was as far and grinned.

***

Constituting the Second Line, a brigade of Virginia militia formed on either side of Salisbury Road. Brig Gen Robert Lawson led the 2nd Brigade north of Salisbury Road. Brig Gen Stevens led the 1st Brigade south of Salisbury Road. Both Lawson and Stevens had commanded Regulars before. That didn't stop them commanding Irregulars in Nathanael Greene's extraordinary need.

Lawson and Stevens learned from telescope gazes on the distant First Line and the cannonballs that not long ago inched their way. Great plumes of smoke along the edges of the woods apprised them of Cornwallis' assertive attack of the flanks. News of the First Line's terror came in the eyes of the North Carolina militia.

The Virginia militia line parted here and there to let through the breaking North Carolinians. Lee observed the First Line militia continuing to bleed away and galloped to Stevens.

"General, I beg of you to close your line to the fugitive militia!" Musket explosions in the distance and twelve-hundred prattling Virginia militiamen swamped Lee's voice. "They're making a bad impression on your boys!"

To the ranks of Stevens' and Lawson's fresh, young militia had come Regulars who at the end of their enlistments joined the militia as substitutes, draftees, and volunteers. Rather than impressionable, Stevens considered them leaders and he wasn't alone in saying so.

Brig Gen Daniel Morgan counted on the presence of veterans on a battlefield. "Among the militia", Greene read in Morgan's letter before recrossing the Dan, "will be found a number of old soldiers". It was these experienced troops Morgan referred to auspiciously in the same letter. "If they fight, you will beat Cornwallis; if not, he will beat you."

Now, Stevens bristled at Lee's lecture and shouted over the din. "I've instructed my brigade to receive the retreating North Carolinians!"

Lee's puzzled stare pinned Stevens. "You told your men to let them through?"

"I told my men the First Line could break!" Stevens raised his voice over the incessant noise. "Would you rather my men be surprised and panic as well?"

"What will you do when your own men run?"

Stevens restrained himself with steely nerves. "My brigade knows that behind them are snipers with orders to shoot any Virginia man who runs!"

"They flew at the Battle of Camden!"

"They won't retreat until ordered to do so! Unlike the North Carolina men I saw running subsequent to your watery orders!"

The upbraid stung Lee. He rode up next to the general close enough to weave the horses' manes. "You urged Gates on at Camden."

"It was too late to retreat," Stevens said.

"You chucked your boys over for Gates. He was predisposed to do battle. No wonder you threaten your boys. Your word means nothing."

Stevens sat still on his mount bothering no more with the lieutenant colonel. "I'll take my leave, sir," Lee said, "but not before giving you credit for restoring your militia and coming to Greene's aid."

Stevens shook his head momentarily at the bold Legion leader's manner of mixing poison and sweetness and got back to conducting his brigade.

***

As the First Line took fright, Maj Johann du Buy's Regiment von Bose and Col Chapple Norton's 1st Battalion of the Guards ordered fixed bayonet companies to the rising ridge south of Salisbury Road held by Surry riflemen assisted by a group of North Carolina militia. Intending merely to block the Surry-North Carolina makeshift corps to allow the 71st Regiment to advance, they'd severed them from the Second Line, driving them far south and threw them under the command of Campbell's corps.

Campbell's men wanted no part of British bayonet butchery and, still feeling triumphant after the Battle of New Garden, took to trees or lay on the ground to make a keen aim. No position impeded their ability to fire and rapidly reload their rifles. Quickly, they and the Surry riflemen repulsed Regiment von Bose and the 1st Battalion of the Guards.

***

Near the south center of the Second Line stood the Augusta and Rockbridge County regiments of the Virginia militia under orders to prevent the 1st Battalion of the Guards and Regiment von Bose turning the corner and getting in the rear of Stevens' line. Elements of the two county militias broke from the hot fire of the 71st Highlanders on Stevens' line and joined the Campbell and Surry riflemen.

Pvt Sam Houston was one of the Rockbridge County militiaman breaking away. A tall, dignified, square-shouldered man, he took duty as seriously as a fiery Sunday morning preacher. The cheerful twenty-three-year-old patted a foolscap diary folded in his pocket. He planned to record the days' events in post-battle candlelight.

The way I will remember the battle is to say how the day started. We often paraded on the rainy ground in the morning. I hoped to keep my papers dry, so the camp fire was welcome. Though the weather cleared, my journal might yet soak in red rain.

We heard our light infantry and cavalry down near the First Line begin firing on the enemy and immediately fell into our ranks. The North Carolina militia ceased firing and our brigades stood ready.

We marched to the left wing. Armed with their muskets and bayonets the Redcoats came nigh and close firing began near the center and soon spread along the line. We made a volley and the enemy charged again. Maj Alexander Stuart ordered us to take cover behind trees.

****

The Second Line's maturity surpassed the First Line's owing to the former Regulars among the militia. They had no fence rails on which to rest their muskets. Past the corn field and standing amongst a scattering of trees, Virginia's formation had none of the Carolinians' linearity and appeared to number far fewer.

A growing number of fighters supported the Second Line. After Webster and Leslie quieted their weapons on the First Line, the Patriot corps of observation had fallen back to Lawson's and Stevens' flanks. Zeb Mitchell, Abraham Hellerschwarz, and George Heider ended up with Lawson's men north of Salisbury Road after crossing the field.

Zeb arrived last looking much different than the blithe man Abe and George met on the summer day nine months earlier in Salem. His mouth had blackened from biting off cartridge ends. The life in his eyes had nearly burned out. No need ask how he'd fared on the battlefield.

His story before the battles was common with all the young men who'd renounced home and family for a cause. The Moravians might find redemption. He wouldn't. As a Quaker, he was damned. Guess we'll have to fight our way through. How could he have been so glib?

The field was noisy and confused. Another attack on their lives was forming. Zeb wanted to grieve and explain the details of Sgt Vinyard's last stand, but there was only time to say he'd gone to God on the First Line.

Redcoat officers tapped their cocked hats with their swords. "Charge!"

Musicians beat their drums or blew across the mouth holes of their fifes. The music grew from a feeble, unorganized start into a resonating electric current sharp enough to make Ben Franklin's hair stand up. The Second Line braced with their muskets pointed at the British commanders on horseback and their respective forces marching quick time and yelling. "Huzzah!"

# Fifty-Eight ~ Holding the Line

As Webster's 33rd Regiment neared the woods north of Salisbury Road, Brig Gen Lawson decided to annoy its  flank. He ordered Col John Holcombe's Regiment of Amelia, Charlotte, Mecklenburg, and Powhatan counties in the middle of the 2nd Brigade of Virginia militia to advance. The initial shift got the attention of Washington who joined his cavalry with Lynch's riflemen to enlarge the attack.

When the 33rd and 23rd infantries closed in, the Virginia militia emerged from cover of trees and dales. The young and old men brought a deadly volley. Instead of puncturing Rebels with honed carbon steel bayonets as they'd hoped, the Redcoats scattered and retreated. The Patriots withdrew to their trees.

The British had a wealth of experience dealing with Irregulars who often got their backs up but soon lost their nerve. Virginia's militia brought exceptional resolve in great numbers of veteran soldiers. British forces found themselves in unfamiliar and uncomfortable defensive warfare.

***

Dense, gray musket smoke hung above the field. Maj St. George Tucker in Holcombe's regiment shook his head as he glimpsed at the half-circle view downfield. The battle is raging, and I can't see or comprehend the activity except in the area of my command. A cannonade of half an hour ushered in the battle and now it's all muskets and Lynch's rifles.

Our friend Maj Henry Skipwith posts on the left with his battalion in the express direction of the shot and holding his post during a most tremendous fire with a firmness which does him honor.

Col Beverly Randolph's regiment holds the ground on my right, so I find perfect security except for occasional shots knocking on my tree. To the right of Randolph the Kirkwood-Lynch-Washington corps of observation take and give a tremendous fire. Lynch's riflemen shoot and reload with amazing speed.

It's a sight to see, but something doesn't feel right. The faces of my brother Patriots, having a great advantage of tree cover and a night of rest, are complacent. They're woodsmen well acquainted with the deer, bears, and other creatures in their camouflaging coats. But the British in open fighting might bravely brandish their bayonets and kill us.

***

Stevens observed plumes of smoke rising over the treetops far south of Salisbury Road. That and the thinness of the Redcoats meant a portion of the opposing formations had disengaged from the main battle.

The corps of Campbell-Lee veered south of the ridge lying on the American left flank of the Second Line. It had been their intention to line up with Stevens' brigade, but du Buy's Regiment von Bose and Norton's 1st Guards cut them off along with the Surry riflemen, putting them farther south of Salisbury Road than they should have been.

Campbell directed his rifles to take careful aim and shoot von Bose's troops passing by. The Hessians fell back, perplexed by the accuracy of the rifle fire. Then fates reversed. The riflemen, whose muzzles had no bayonet mount, saw the von Bose bayonets coming close. Campbell's men fell back, still loading and firing on their pursuers with a destructive fire.

In response to the onslaught of bayonets, Lee swept in with his horsemen and joined Campbell. Though von Bose asked for it, necessity alone united Campbell's rifles and Lee's bloody swords. It didn't take long before Regiment von Bose and the 1st Brigade of Guards themselves united to repulse the Patriots.

Because the Patriot left flank preoccupied von Bose and the 1st Brigade of Guards, Stevens might fare better. But he'd be embarrassed if the 71st Regiment made a hole through his 1st Brigade of Virginia militia. Cornwallis would run through it and quickly oppose the Third Line. Stevens ordered his regiments to up their fire on the 71st Regiment and the companies of Virginia volunteers tendered their spirit.

Col Peter Perkins' Pittsylvania Regiment answered with a withering volley on the 71st Regiment, the multiple of any First Line volleys. Pvt Henry Ingle shook his head at the fallen Redcoats. He could have walked for a hundred yards and not touched the ground. After the dreadful slaughter, the British retreated and reinforced and came again, killing American boys with equal brutality.

***

Holding forth on the north side of Salisbury Road, Lawson took the opening provided by the Patriot core of observation to try and stall Webster's 33rd and 23rd. The British left flank flailed. Cornwallis instructed ADC Broderick to dispatch an order to Brig Gen O'Hara to support Webster's right with his 2nd Brigade of Guards.

Cornwallis eyed Tarleton who nearly jumped in anticipation of action. "Remain in reserve should the militia be stupid enough to throw down their arms and retreat into the clearing. With all these muskets and thick woods, I want my cavalry compact and safe."

Tarleton sighed internally for the dwindling hope of instructions and fawned before moving to the rear to sulk with the Legion.

Meanwhile, Cornwallis viewed the action on Webster's left where Lynch's rifles and Kirkwood's muskets kept a warm fire on the 33rd. Threatening again, the British had to counter the Patriot right flank. Cornwallis surveyed the reserves. The Yagers and the Light Infantry of the Guards remained idle near the Royal cannons on the road.

"Tarleton!" the lord screamed.

Tarleton trotted his horse to Cornwallis and bowed.

"Give word to the Yagers and the Light Infantry of the Guards to attach themselves to Webster's left."

Tarleton let a moment of injured pride invade his heart as Broderick waited beside Cornwallis. If not for losing so many of the British Legion at Cowpens, the ADC might be the one rushing with the order.

***

On the Patriot's left, elements of the 71st Regiment broke off and headed in the direction of Regiment von Bose and the 1st Battalion of the Guards. Apparently, the gallant fight in the flank of Campbell-Lee so consternated the British right only a combined opposition would suffice.

Internally, Stevens thanked the corps of observation for taking enemy eyes off his militia. Any help stopping the enemy or weakening them for the Continentals was welcome. Virginia's militia kept its head and took occasional shots from the British right flank. Now and then they held their fire as the momentum shifted.

Virginia militiamen made a braver and stouter resistance than the North Carolina men. The line containing Lee drifted far south of Salisbury Road. Heartened by the lieutenant colonel's men who drew the enemy further from him, Stevens found room to mindfully direct his four regiments.

***

Legendary for ruthless, tight ranks, British infantry halted in the face of a heartier foe on the north side of the field. The 33rd and 23rd regiments had swept North Carolina militia off the field like a new broom. But the landscape ahead through the woods, while fragmenting Patriot firing lines, would deflect British spikes.

British regiments entered a forest of scattered light where shadows made hulking adversaries waiting in the periphery and tree limbs leveled like muskets. Black, leafless trees shattered regiments into smaller units exposing them and impairing their attack. The Redcoat infantry reduced from a thundering herd yelling "huzzah" to individuals quietly delving.

From all points of the Kingdom, the lads had come on the promise of a heftier pay packet, but the present abuse reduced the bargain. They'd marched twelve miles at daybreak to counter Lee at New Garden. With battle putting little priority on subsistence and flour stores depleted, their miserable stomachs panged. On their own, vulnerable, and losing the cohesion of company, regiment, and brigade, their internal strength sapped as well.

Tarleton returned from the errand, loathing the woods. Worse than impeding the British infantry, they kept his cavalry out.

Lamb of the 23rd Regiment found opportunity. Trees break lines of men into intervals, smashing their hopes of a front equal to the enemy. Out of inexperience, fear, or lack of orders the Americans defend the tree line, declining to use gaps in formations to chase their prey. I shall pursue.

# Fifty-Nine ~ British Success

Though the British stalled on the Second Line, keeping them from the Continentals looked impossible to Lawson's and Stevens' Virginia brigades.

North of Salisbury Road, British discipline and reserves tamped down Patriot glory. Webster rallied the troops in conjunction with the Yagers and Light Infantry of the Guards on his left and the 2nd Battalion of Guards on his right. He drove tree-by-tree slamming a wedge of individual muskets and bayonets between Lawson and the Kirkwood-Lynch-Washington corps of observation.

After Lawson's veterans thrice thwarted the enemy's attacks, Webster had had enough. He used the din of covering fire to allow the reserves to secretly pour in and conceal themselves. Oddly the British fire halted. The Patriots reloaded their calm weapons and listened. A fifer's first few notes of *Yankee Doodle* disarmed the militia. The sprightly notes shifted. Charge! The Redcoats rose and ambushed their prey who returned a panicked, unfocused volley and hastily retreated.

***

The contest between the Virginia militia and the British front culminated. The 71st Regiment slogged through woods as thick as pudding on the south side of Salisbury Road and fully engaged Stevens' brigade of Virginians. North of Salisbury Road, the 23rd reached Lawson's line. All the while, O'Hara's 2nd Battalion of the Guards drove fresh infantry up the middle and broke through.

No less gut-foundered than their comrades, 2nd Guards pushed to have the battle finished. Their desire partly rested on O'Hara's leadership and partly on a hunger for victory having nothing to do with raising flags. Dead and abandoned Rebels meant a chance to search pockets and haversacks for scraps of meat and bread and flasks of rum.

Exposed to the flanks of the incursion and driven through the middle, Lawson wavered in the confusion and held ground where he could. Although Washington's cavalry detected O'Hara's push and circled around, helping was impossible. Deep woods stymied the cavalry and the onslaught of Lawson pressed on.

***

The cannonade seemed long ago, but its effects lasted. Both the First Line and Second Line of militia had withdrawn safely away from each side of Salisbury Road, but when the cannon fire ceased, the militias fanned out. The men closest to Salisbury Road remembered balls flying down the road and shied away.

Maj Skipwith's regiment, formed north of the road, wheeled reinforcements toward Lawson's flank which struggled with Webster's 33rd. Sgt Lamb of the 23rd spotted the move and ordered his company into an unorthodox formation, the type of quick, meticulous maneuvering that distinguished the British from the Americans. They formed into a single file perpendicular to Lawson's line and advanced like a jolt of lightning through a gap in Skipwith's thinner formation and reached the rear.

Maj St. George Tucker, who commanded in the regiment to the right of Skipwith, was too far away to stop Lamb's spearhead or signal Skipwith's line. The Redcoats turned the corner.

Finally, Tucker got through to Maj Skipwith. "Hank, they're in our rear!"

Lawson's line already oozed militiamen on the right and Lamb's action threw the remainder of the formation into confusion. Scared troops broke off in retreat.

"Halt! About face!" Skipwith yelled along with every officer from colonel to captain.

Disobeying their officers endeavoring to make them return to the line and engage the enemy, all three of Lawson's regiments instantly broke off without firing another round and dispersed like a flock of frightened sheep. Connection of the American corps of observation and the 2nd Virginia Brigade ceased.

Lawson became the first to lose the Second Line and abandon the field. His militia flooded to the rear of Stevens on the south side of Salisbury Road and continued east toward Guilford Court House and the woods on the south side of the village. Those not fortunate to flee found themselves surrounded. They threw down their muskets and offered their hands to the smoke tarnished sky.

Never was Lamb prouder of the undying prowess and skill of the British soldier. Our disadvantage in numbers is perhaps the most extreme in this battle. Nor have we ever fought with such determination. We came lean from hunger and cold marching whilst you lolled and burped by warm fires. No force, not even you lot fighting like rats, will overcome the British empire.

***

At the same time, south of Salisbury Road, the 71st regiment received the order to charge Stevens' brigade and run them down in the forest.

Mimicking Cornwallis burning baggage at Ramsour's Mill to convert his army into a flying corps, the Highlanders threw down knapsacks, canteens, and everything else in their kit not deadly that could weigh them down or catch on trees and underbrush. Musicians threw down their drums and fifes and picked up loaded muskets abandoned by Americans.

Maj Gen Leslie pressed forward with the 71$^{st}$ arrayed in a wide front to cover Virginia militia and took an advantageous position up the middle of the battlefield. Stevens deserved credit for blocking Leslie's superior regular soldiers so well and long. Cornwallis, seeing Leslie's performance, wanted badly to turn back the calendar to mid-January and march Leslie by force through the swampy muck and mire of South Carolina and onto the field at the Battle of Cowpens in time to rescue Lt Col Tarleton from Brig Gen Morgan.

O'Hara took a musket ball in his thigh then Stevens too in eerie sympathy. Confusion accelerated. Aware of 2$^{nd}$ Virginia passing in the rear, 1$^{st}$ Virginia slowly lost its will and hope of resistance. Stevens, wounded and without a mount after he lost his horse to a shot, ordered a fifer to call retreat. So ended the brave resolution of the Virginia militia to support their line and force the British to retreat or suffer before reaching the Continentals.

* * *

Stevens' men lifted him onto the saddle of a replacement horse, and he joined the retreat on Salisbury Road toward Guilford Court House. Surrounded by aides and guards, Maj Gen Greene came down the road from the east. He eyed the blood seeping from Stevens' leg.

"Let's get you to the medical tent."

Greene came alongside and the pair of generals trotted up the road. Stevens mustered strength and put on a brave face. If not for the bloody leg, no one in the tiny village of Martinsville would have suspected the wound.

They passed the Third Line. Regiments of watchful Continentals peered at them from defensive nests. Greene asked about the battle, more to distract him than to retrieve information.

"Today was a vastly different situation from the Battle of Camden."

"How so?" Greene said.

"Camden was a rout. We lined up against the British. The sun had no more lit the sky than they charged first yelling 'Huzzah!' and firing. My men threw down their arms and fled followed by the North Carolinians. The Maryland Line momentarily held but Tarleton swept in to hack them to pieces. The Regulars retreated and the battle was over."

"How was your action today?"

"We gave them a warm reception and kept up a heavy fire for a long time as did the corps of observation under Washington and Lee. The enemy gained their point by superior discipline, experience, and reserves. Yet this battle isn't over."

***

When the Second Line dissolved, the Makers sought medical treatment for George Heider. They located the field hospital where an ivory rectangle of linen hung as a flag of truce from a pole fashioned out of a short leaf pine.

They left the dreadful battle to go inside the white canvas walls where they found Zeb's mother Olivia, Sara, and the Salem ladies attending the wounded. The tent's falsity of refuge quickly revealed itself by wailing men and blood which was everywhere.

"Mom!" Zeb said.

"Keep your voice down. Are you hurt?" Olivia said.

He shook his head. "George is."

Olivia cleaned George's eyes and found no lacerations. The blood came from three cuts on his forehead.

"Zeb. You and Abe leave George. Doctor James Wallace will suture his cuts."

Zeb and Abe passed Greene, helping Stevens enter the tent.

Stevens declined the mug of brandy Sara handed him. Dr. Wallace probed the hole in the general's leg looking for damage and a lead ball. Stevens' eyes shot open overflowing with tears. "Brandy!" he yelled.

Wallace pointed a bloody pair of forceps at Stevens. "Good boy. You're going to need it."

The alcohol didn't take away the pain but made the general less concerned with it as Wallace removed the ball and sutured the hole.

"Well, sir. I couldn't find any major blood vessel damage, so you get to keep your leg for now."

"Why, thank you, doctor," Stevens sloshed.

Outside the tent sporadic gunfire started up followed by squeaking gun carriage wheels as teams pulled Capt Singleton's six-pounders up Salisbury Road.

# Sixty ~ A Separate Battle

Terrain past the Second Line challenged the British army anew. Besides thick woods and undergrowth, Hunting Creek, vales, and steep hillsides further divided and encumbered their progress. Wing commanders attempted to regroup their units and learn the position of the Continentals.

Meanwhile, clashes of Regiment von Bose, the 1st Battalion of the Guards, and elements of the 71st Regiment with Lee's Legion and Campbell's rifles and militia persisted far south of the Second Line. Cornwallis detested the separate, sternly maintained battle. None of the King's remote troops could fight the Continentals until they unpinned themselves.

***

Rockbridge and Augusta militiamen and Surry riflemen became so deadly to Regiment von Bose that Norton rushed to aid the Hessians with his 1st Battalion of the Guards. Ultimately, a combined volley of the von Bose and 1st Guard's muskets overpowered Campbell's corps and drove them further south where they hunkered down.

Campbell's riflemen had retired deep into the forest a quarter of a mile southeast of their first position. They established ground and made it so hot a company of 1st Guards daring to finish them retreated in great disorder. Cornwallis, weary of Campbell's audacity, came riding to the fore rallying the 1st Guards. Seeing the lord immobilized when his iron-gray horse fell to a ball, the 1st Guards abandoned the area lest they catch a shot. The lord bolted on another mount.

***

Norton and du Buy received dispatches from an irritated Cornwallis demanding they finish Campbell's corps. The regimental leaders designed a vice to crush the riflemen, the jaws being von Bose and the 1st Guards. But a blunder wheeled von Bose past Campbell to the side of the Guards. Campbell's rifles and muskets laid on a heavy fire. When the 1st Battalion of Guards formed a covering party to relieve the Hessians, Lee brought the Legion to their rear and turned the vice against the British.

Campbell ordered the militia to cool their muskets and allow the riflemen to fire three volleys into the trees. When no British answer came, the tactic seemed effective. However, Norton hadn't retreated. He and his men kneeled on the ground listening and waiting for the riflemen to reload en masse. Directly after the last volley, 1st Guards charged their bayonets. The riflemen and militia made a speedy retreat.

In the other direction the bayonets and muskets of von Bose parried Lee's horsemen who found their swords slicing trees more often than enemy troops in the close quarters of the woods. As the Legion ebbed, the Hessians lost interest and funneled their weary troops with the Redcoats into a single file and marched away leaving the Legion and riflemen bereft of targets.

The 1st Battalion of the Guards and Regiment von Bose rested and marched northeast hoping to support the 71st Highlander Regiment on the Second Line when thick woods broke their files. Empty deer hide cartouche boxes littering the ground meant Rebel militia ammunition had run low. They wormed through the woods hoping to catch the enemy in a close skirmish.

The Rockbridge and Augusta militia had jettisoned the boxes while executing orders from Campbell to form a ring around 1st Guards and Regiment von Bose. They made their way to the hill on the Second Line and stumbled upon a small wayward company of the 71st Regiment under Capt Tavis Burns before the 1st Guards and Hessians caught up.

Bayonets mattered little in the thick woods. Militia dashed from one tree to another and fired irregularly so the British line never knew whether to pursue their front, flanks, or rear. After three charges, the militia surrounded the Highlanders. But, during militia pot shots, calls made by the 71st bagpiper attracted 1st Guards and von Bose.

Regiment von Bose and the 1st Guards closed in on the Rockbridge and Augusta militia and assumed they and the 71st could squeeze the Patriots. As the British rescuers approached the rear of the militia, the bagpiper played retreat instead of the expected charge.

With his company hemmed in, Capt Burns' music had been a warning to 1st Guards and von Bose to avoid the menacing militia. His warning came to naught as they continued their pursuit. Rockbridge and Augusta heard the brush whispering behind them. They turned and threw down a suffering volley.

Regiment von Bose and 1st Guards reversed only to face Campbell's rifles. "Charge!" Col Norton yelled. Rather than fighting, the British ran through Campbell's men.

***

Virginia militiamen continued their massive retreat. Making their way through thick woods, remnants of the Pittsylvania Regiment of Stevens' 1st Brigade of Virginia militia under the command of Col Peter Perkins marched in two quick-stepping files. East of the Second Line, Capt Angus Mackenzie's company of the 71st Regiment tracked them in a parallel course thirty-yards away.

The enemy cut off Pittsylvania's rear ranks and peeled away three privates and marched them back to the Second Line with bayonets in their backs before the regiment caught on. Perkins halted the regiment and rotated them about face. Mackenzie's company approached like madmen. Perkins turned the regiment again and retreated.

When Perkins' regiment cleared off, Mackenzie's company returned to the British rear.

Mackenzie screamed at the captured militiamen whose sweat tracked their dirty faces. "Dozy Rebels! After we defeat General Greene, you're coming with us!"

One of the privates threw a puzzled face. "Where?"

"To the prison ship *HMS Pack Horse,* a nice big schooner lying at Wilmington."

"How can we be your prisoners? We're subjects of the King."

"Shut your gob!"

"Has George given up on us?"

"You'll get your answer on the *Pack Horse* once you see wharf rats climb the tending lines day and night…" The captain hesitated as though collecting more rags to stitch in his tale. "…and feast on wounded Rebels. You'll be begging for your mother and wishing you'd died right here."

***

Lt Col Banastre Tarleton's right hand throbbed as he watched the battle from the British rear. His horse bayed and ambled uneasily as hundreds of guns cracked the air. He speculated his chances of getting into the battle. Seeing no sign from Cornwallis, Tarleton mumbled to himself. As victory favors neither army, my dragoons will stand fast. But, damned Rebels, let your side take the upper hand and I will enter.

Rockbridge militiaman Sam Houston mulled how he'd record events in his quarter. We pursued them two-hundred yards to the top of the hill on the Second Line. When we got there, they stood their ground and we retreated to our original position. We repulsed them again and for the second time they made us retreat to our first ground. On our third advance we took their fire and didn't retreat until we fired sharply on them. We made them retreat a little.

Houston's description too modestly described the dramatic surrender of Capt Burns. For, under the watchful eyes of a line of riflemen, the company of British infantry stood at attention in a parade of two files in ranks of sixteen and waited until a bagpiper came to the front. Dressed in a Black Watch kilt the piper exhaled into a leather bag until a foundation of reedy music started up. An eerie melody played as he uncovered and covered the finger holes of a wooden tube while his company followed him down the ridge. At the bottom, the 71st Highlanders grounded their arms before the awed militia.

# Sixty-One ~ The Continentals

— March 15, 1781, Guilford Court House Battleground, The Third Line

Cornwallis had every right to imagine a less certain end to the battle as he closed in on the Third Line. American Irregulars had given him spirited action, twice holding a wide breadth of land. Despite overcoming two lines, the next obstacle loomed in the form of thick elevated woods full of the most experienced and freshest American troops.

***

Salisbury Road continued to snake through the center of the battleground which itself yet unfurled eastward. Maj Gen Greene posted the majority of the Continentals on the Third Line north of the road. Farthest north or left from Cornwallis' perspective, Brig Gen Isaac Huger's Virginia Brigade assembled atop the highest elevation. South of Huger, and still in high woods, braced Col Otho Williams' Maryland Brigade.

Next south and hugging the north edge of the road lay Capt Singleton with the two six-pounder cannons pulled up from the First Line. They guarded the log-constructed Guilford Court House.

Huger's Virginia Brigade consisted of two regiments. Col John Green's 1$^{st}$ Virginia took the northern part of Huger's position and Lt Col Samuel Hawes' 2$^{nd}$ Virginia took the southern part.

Capt Ebenezer Finley of the 1$^{st}$ Continental Artillery attached to the Maryland Line took a position on the left flank of 2$^{nd}$ Virginia aiming a second pair of six-pounder cannons down the hill.

Williams' Maryland Brigade also consisted of two regiments. Col John Gunby's 1$^{st}$ Maryland took the northern part of Williams' position and Lt Col Benjamin Ford's 2$^{nd}$ Maryland took the southern part. 1$^{st}$ Maryland, the first Continentals likely to see action from Redcoats coming up Salisbury Road, was the vanguard of Greene's Continental defense. Besides protecting the courthouse, Singleton's cannons partially defended 2$^{nd}$ Maryland's left flank.

***

Cannonades and musket volleys blasting across a clear expanse opened the battle. Of late scattered gunfire of individuals and smaller corps amongst thickening forest brought the action to the edge of the Third Line.

Cornwallis' regiments, after losing as many as a third of their forces in severe action with the militias, still had momentum. Desires of avenging their fallen drove them to the Continentals.

Breaking through the Second Line hadn't come easy to Sgt Roger Lamb and the 23rd Regiment. For a considerable time they'd taken cover behind trees to avoid a galling fire from the Virginia militia which executed a braver and stouter resistance than the North Carolinians.

Not to dismiss British prowess, the Virginia militia retreated in droves having burned through their ammunition. A mixture of alert Patriots and lost, wounded, and stunned stragglers fell back to the last stage.

Lamb observed an American officer fleeing and darted after him. Before he caught up with the Rebel, an odd beat pelted his goatskin knapsack next to his neck. He took cover behind a tree. Not one yard away, from the direction of the gunfire, lay a dead Guard. Lamb dared a furtive glance. Though a small body of young Virginia militia drew up to take cover behind a pair of green rhododendron shrubs to his left, he remained protected. He knelt and took his lifeless comrade's cartridges and musket.

The sergeant reloaded both muskets taking care not to advertise he had two guns. He fired one musket into the shrubs. The rhododendrons trembled yet returned no fire. Either the militiaman had no ammo or froze in fright. Lamb fired the other musket. Shortly the lucky militiamen cleared off, baffled that a musket man could fire two quick rounds.

Daylight turned gray as dark clouds rolled in and the woods thickened beyond the Second Line. While the extra trees offered cover, they changed battle dynamics. Battalions broke down into companies and companies broke down into squads. Bayonets did no good and musket fire ebbed as lines of sight among the tree trunks declined. Only smaller formations acting alone in close communication would sustain the strength and effectiveness of the British army. Sgt Lamb's rank rose in importance.

He huddled on the ground behind the root ball of a massive fallen tree with three men of the 23rd regiment. Remaining pockets of the 23rd positioned themselves close by behind tree trunks, shrubs, ravines, large rocks, and other fallen trees. Lamb bracketed his party toward the Third Line going from one hiding place to another and recognized other groups in the 23$^{rd}$ doing the same. He'd never fought on a larger battlefield and reckoned the ominous quiet to the east meant the Continentals awaited.

Lamb peered over the edge of the roots. Wooded heights rose beyond a fallow corn field north of Salisbury Road. He decided the eminence must be the Continental Third Line. He looked for colorful clothing and listened for man-made sounds but the landscape revealed nothing. Amidst gurgling Hunting Creek and a crow's hoarse cawing, the elevated forest was quiet.

Suddenly the feet of a hundred men came up behind and to the right of Lamb, pounding the forest floor in two files. Bursting through the front, the 2$^{nd}$ Battalion of the Guards, presently commanded by Lt Col James Stuart in place of injured Brig Gen Charles O'Hara, reached the corn field. O'Hara wore a pained expression as he straggled up on horseback one leg of the white breeches more scarlet than his coat.

The 2$^{nd}$ Guards crossed the field and skirted south of 1$^{st}$ Maryland. They crossed the creek, stormed up the hill, and attacked a gap in Williams' Maryland front where the 2$^{nd}$ Maryland Regiment perched. Their spontaneous vigor mesmerized 2$^{nd}$ Maryland. Stuart soon reached the north-south Reedy Fork Road cutting through the woods behind the Continentals. The 2$^{nd}$ Guards had gone straight through 2$^{nd}$ Maryland.

Meanwhile, elements of the 2$^{nd}$ Guards supported by squads from Leslie's 71$^{st}$ and Webster's 23$^{rd}$ took Capt Singleton's two six-pounder cannons. Noise from the Highlanders' approach up Salisbury Road had panicked Singleton and the gun crew. Too late to spike the vent holes, they jumped behind a copse of red cedars.

* * *

Greene paused his mount on Reedy Fork Road in the rear of Col Green's 1$^{st}$ Virginia Regiment. He looked south through a field glass and shuddered at the commotion arising behind 2$^{nd}$ Maryland at the end of the Third Line. Voluminous blue musket smoke settled to reveal Redcoats. That 2$^{nd}$ Maryland allowed 2$^{nd}$ Guards through the south flank of the Third Line created a critical situation.

Sure the 2$^{nd}$ Battalion of the Guards would take the entire Continental rear and ally with Redcoats in the forward area to surround the Third Line, Greene ordered a fifer to sound retreat. In the clamor and low visibility of musket fire arising all around, either none of Greene's field officers got the message or in their zeal to defend the Third Line didn't acknowledge it.

The general dispatched aide-de-camp Maj Ichabod Burnet and two captains to relay the retreat order on horseback to the commanders. Burnet and one captain returned amidst ceaseless noise and smoke.

"Well?" Greene said.

"I couldn't find one commander," Burnet said. "They'd always dashed off just as I got there."

The captain repeated Burnet's claim. Five-minutes went by and the second captain, a gaunt thirty-year old man, rode up grimacing from a musket wound in his leg.

"How am I supposed to find anybody with a battle going on?" The captain pointed over his shoulder in the direction of the smoke and noise. "I couldn't find one fifer willing to play retreat."

Greene ordered the uninjured captain to usher the injured one to the hospital tent. He turned to Burnet. "Inform Brigadier General Huger I'm ordering Colonel Green to cover a retreat then find Green and tell him to bring 1st Virginia to the edge of the woods here by this road at once and stand by."

***

Brig Gen Huger had gotten the Maryland and Virginia Regulars safely up from Camp Cheraw, South Carolina to Guilford Court House before leading them to Virginia and back. Two-hundred-and-fifty miles later it came down to the battle of Guilford Court House. He was about to lose half a brigade for retreat duty.

The "Hell-fired Blues" 2nd Virginia Regiment—survivors of the bloody Battle of Waxhaws in South Carolina ten months earlier—fell under the command of Lt Col Hawes, now a five-year Virginia Regular in the war. In front of him Finley's two six-pounder cannons poised forward of the line. Green's 1st Virginia covered his right flank.

Pvt Lewis Griffin shivered in his short, thin blue jacket. He perversely wished for 2nd Virginia to find action for it might stir his blood which was freezing up on the wooded height. Before the sky grayed, Griffin had hoped sunlight would carry through the bare trees and provide relief, yet the rays hadn't broken past the tree trunks.

Below, Col James Webster guided a corps toward the Continentals. He'd broken through the Second Line north of the 23rd Fusiliers to find thinning woods and the clearing. Soon he scanned the wooded heights. With information given by pickets, he'd strung together loose forces of his 33rd and 23rd regiments, Yagers, and Light Infantry Guards into a regiment and shifted them south. Webster waited momentarily and ordered the troops to cross Hunting Creek and slowly, quietly scale the heights at the center of the Third Line.

Brush cracking under the enemy's feet covered the racket of Regulars atop the ridge who cocked their muskets. Griffin's line lay quiet and still as the Redcoats ascended a sudden sharp angle of the hill, inching closer, and gaining height. Hawes waited for replies to dispatches he'd rushed to Gunby of 1st Maryland to the south and Green of 1st Virginia to the north pleading for help.

# Sixty-Two ~ Humbled

Col Green held his tongue. If he spoke, the resultant humiliation and anger at Greene's order to protect retreating forces might threaten his Continental army commission. He'd commanded men at war since the start of the Revolution. Fifteen minutes earlier the first close volleys assured him that 1st Virginia would soon see action. He never expected Gen Greene to pull him.

Green reluctantly led 1st Virginia to the rear. He received a dispatch from Gen Greene who heard of the colonel's displeasure and rode horseback out of the woods to the general for a private meeting.

"Something bothering you, Colonel?"

"I'm honored you chose my regiment to guard the retreat. Might not another regiment be more eligible?"

"No commander is more sober." Greene spoke to the colonel's persistent anger. "I can see this order upsets you. You don't relish an order distinctly inglorious."

"No, sir. I don't."

"Nor did I enjoy retreating to the Dan nor seeing 2nd Maryland taking a beating moments ago."

"No, sir."

"Will you wait until the next battle?" Greene was losing the present battle. Would there be another one?

Green's hesitant nod sufficed.

"Be patient, Colonel. You shall have the first blow next time."

Green broke a grin. "I'm holding you to that, sir."

***

Encouraged by 2nd Guards, Sgt Lamb waited five minutes then signaled a 23rd Regiment fifer to play a recognition call. Upon hearing the communication of Lamb and the fifer, piecemeal units of the 23rd girded for action.

"Fifer! Assembly!" Lamb yelled. The fifer played the call repeatedly and members of the 23rd raced to Lamb's position. Soon three partial companies assembled. Taking overall command in lieu of higher officers, a second-lieutenant messaged Webster to the north offering support. Webster told him to wait for a signal and lead the 23rd past Hunting Creek and up the hill to attack the Virginia Regulars.

***

Col John Gunby sent Lt Col John Eager Howard with three 1st Maryland companies to assist Hawes' 2nd Virginia. Green begged off to guard the retreat with 1st Virginia. Capt Robert Kirkwood's Delaware "Blue Hens" and Col Charles Lynch's Bedford Rifles, who'd taken 1st Virginia's place on the northern edge of the Third Line, answered Hawes' call.

Webster's 33rd teetered at the crest of the hill and received a stunning volley from 2nd Virginia and its allies. His south flank took bayonets from 1st Maryland.

The 23rd Regiment fared worse, coming under volleys from Finley's two six-pounder cannons sitting in front and south of 2nd Virginia. The salvos alternated such that the Redcoats never got their feet planted or found cover. The second-lieutenant died in agony and a captain fell wounded.

Webster hobbled in the arms of two privates with a gruesome knee wound as the regiment retreated from the hill. They recrossed the creek and clearing and found security in the thick woods to count casualties and rush a dispatch to Cornwallis.

***

Hawes thanked the Delaware "Blue Hens" and the Bedford Rifles for saving him and they returned to their places on the northern end of the Third Line. Howard and the 1st Maryland companies returned to their positions with their bayonets dripping blood. While helping 2nd Virginia, 1st Maryland received a message from Col Otho Williams who said 2nd Maryland might not hold much longer from the marauding 2nd Battalion of the Guards.

Gunby of 1st Maryland peered down a telescope through gaps in the woods and confirmed Williams' fears. Howard, second in command to Gunby, learned 2nd Guards had crept up Reedy Fork Road behind his companies of 1st Maryland. He rode to inform Gunby. Chaotic fire rang out all around their meeting.

"Colonel!" Howard said. "The 2nd Guards have broken the corps! They're covertly massing behind us! I don't think we can hold this ground!"

"Order your companies to load and turn! Let 2nd Guards follow then turn and fire!" Gunby's face tightened in anger. "Advance and fire some more!"

Howard recognized the situation as mysteriously similar to one in the Battle of Cowpens. Detachments of the Maryland-Virginia line under him had misunderstood his call in the din. He wanted them to change their front. Instead, they retreated from overwhelming numbers of 71st Highlanders. Howard yelled, "Halt! About face! Fire!" Deadly shooting stunned the Scots. They froze.

Lt Col William Washington's Continental cavalry and Andrew Pickens' militia seized the opportunity to squeeze the panicked Redcoats from each side in a double trap and snatched victory from Lt Col Banastre Tarleton at the Cowpens. Howard dreamed of another huge opportunity.

Gunby's horse took a ball in the head and wailed before dropping to the ground. Pinned under his mount, Gunby shouted to Howard. "Take command!"

Howard rode back and gave 1st Maryland its orders. The 2nd Guards advanced and made two volleys. When 1st Maryland retreated, the Guards celebrated. "Hail, King George!" After taking ten steps, 1st Maryland turned and charged with their bayonets and a lead volley. The 2nd Guards volleyed wildly and retreated.

Zeb and Abraham had fetched George from the hospital tent. They watched with him and other militiamen near Guilford Court House from a safe distance anticipating fireworks as the British met the Continentals on the Third Line. Though George detested the British hailing their king, the close quarter fire of 1st Maryland on the 2nd Guards wrought morbid fantasies in his brandy-drenched mind.

Chaos ran amok as some of the frightened 2nd Guards' stumbled into the rear of Huger's Virginia brigade and scampered back to their regiment upon hearing movement. Huger's alarm went up as well. With the enemy at the back door, how long would it be until the Redcoats encircled the Continentals?

***

Minutes before, Greene had moved south on Reedy Fork Road behind the Third Line and watched the action down Salisbury Road. He was looking west at Guilford Court House, Hunting Creek, and the cleared cornfield that fronted the Continental's positions. He saw Washington spot 2nd Maryland reeling from the 2nd Battalion of the Guards' heavy attack.

Luckily for Washington another company of 2nd Guards had assembled in a long vulnerable formation of double files in the clearing. His 1st and 3rd Continental cavalry could ride alongside and fell them like rotten fenceposts before they had a chance to mount a multi sided bayonet defense.

Free from observation duty alongside Lawson's militia, Washington indulged his imagination, recalling the wide-open feedlot of glorious Cowpens.

"Bugler, call charge!" Washington yelled.

The cavalry woke to a full-throated horn and followed Washington with their sabers held high and galloping headlong to the rear of the 2nd Guards. Washington rode out of a copse leaning into the neck of his horse as it leaped a ravine then cut past the head of Leslie's 71st Regiment into the space between the files of the 2nd Guards celebrating their action on the Third Line. Continental cavalry thundered close behind and brought down troops in the near file. A second line of dragoons hacked the other file of Redcoats.

A pitched battle of dismounted Continental Cavalry dragoons and 2nd Guard's infantry arose. Nicknamed "Peter", Pedro Francisco, Washington's most notable cavalryman swung a long broadsword at the enemy who felt the giant blade pounding their sabers. They took stinging cuts, never finding an opening.

Redcoats soon regretted daring the six-foot eight, two-hundred-and-sixty pound Portuguese man. When the dragoon's sword rested, Francisco had cut down four of the 2nd Guards and left the clearing bloody from end to end like his sword.

# Sixty-Three ~ Ruthless Fighting

Maj Gen Greene's worry over the 2nd Battalion of the Guards dropped like a rock. He admitted the early retreat call was panic. Notwithstanding the scare of 2nd Maryland, all regiments held. The entire line had not collapsed and the intrepid efforts of 1st Maryland and Lt Col Washington's cavalry became self-evident.

Fresh reports of Brig Gen Stevens escaping death while making a gallant stand on the Second Line further heartened the commanding officer. The notion of battlefield evacuation quietly withered. None of the doughty commanders heeded it. Why not let the Patriot warriors have their day?

Though he'd chosen the field and analyzed its present state, Greene took nothing for granted. While reconnoitering the action he passed within thirty paces of an enemy body. Fortunately, aide-de-camp Burnet discovered them and guided Greene through thick woods to the Patriot line.

***

The din paused and Sgt Lamb examined his location. He'd become separated from the 23rd Regiment again. Joining them was nigh impossible with the enemy passing through the clearing fronting the Continentals. It was time to fall back to safety.

Lamb gasped when he noticed Cornwallis riding alone across the open ground. Past the lord, a large Continental cavalry officer mounted his horse while eying Cornwallis. Unaware of the danger, the lord awkwardly rode a dragoon's mare whose drooping saddle retarded his progress.

Lamb ran to Cornwallis and furtively panned the area before half-cocking his musket.

"Sergeant! What are you doing?"

"My Lord, I must caution you." Lamb nodded toward the menacing dragoon, oblivious of the Continental calvary leader's identity. "If you pursue that direction, he may cut you to pieces if not capture you."

Lamb loaded his musket and took hold of the bridle to redirect Cornwallis' horse. He pointed toward a gathering of red forming in tall brush. "There, my Lord, is the 23rd Regiment in the skirt of the woods." Lamb grabbed the reins and guided Cornwallis to safety.

Cornwallis, under cover of the 23rd Regiment, rode up Salisbury Road to gain intelligence from the commotion between the foot of 2nd Maryland's evacuated precipice and the courthouse. He stopped at Capt Singleton's cannons, now in British possession.

***

Washington's attention turned to the hubbub among Maryland's 1st Regiment. They'd no more retreated behind Continental cavalry than Lt Col Howard turned them about face and shouted an order. "Fix bayonets!"

Washington would join Howard in another attack on the 2nd Guards as soon as the Marylanders deployed. He pulled back hard on the reins to settle his horse rearing at the action all around. Before him a young dragoon on horseback slashed at the air fighting an imaginary enemy.

"Private, come here!"

Washington wasn't yet thirty-years old, tall and thick. Though kind and cherubic, his face now inspired more fright than fight. The younger dragoon approached.

"What are you doing?"

"Killing Redcoats, sir."

"Cutting like a mad horseman will expose you long to the enemy's muskets."

Washington sat straight in the saddle holding the reins in his left hand. From his right hand a saber extended at forty-five degrees.

"Fix your saber and ride. Let your momentum and horse do the work. Brace as blade collides with flesh. Be swift and spoil their shot."

Washington motioned to companies of Redcoats regrouping opposite 1st Maryland.

"Are your pistols ready?"

"Yes, sir."

"Cover my left flank while I cut the 2nd Guards to pieces!"

***

Both 1st Maryland and 2nd Guards brought heritage to the battle. Remnants of their encounter in the New York campaign yet flowed in their veins four-years on. For 2nd Guards who threw chaos into the American line on Long Island or 1st Maryland who guarded the American army retreating from Brooklyn Heights, the legacy was personal.

Now that the 2nd Guards rolled over 2nd Maryland and 1st Maryland turned and volleyed furiously at the 2nd Guards, they wanted to destroy each other.

***

Howard cried "Charge!" and 1st Maryland attacked the 2nd Guards on the ground between the courthouse and the position evacuated by 2nd Maryland. Washington charged Lt Col Stuart with a saber, but the Guards' commander took a life-saving dive. Capt John Smith of 1st Maryland hounded the shaken Stuart with laughter. The Guards-Maryland bomb was lit.

Without regard to the bayonets and swords clashing all around, Lt Col Stuart and Capt Smith approached each other on foot daring and proud, remembering from a previous encounter their vow to end their next meeting in blood.

They charged with fury. Lt Col James Stuart's small sword wielded lightly in his hand. He swiftly sliced across his foe's space, closing in. Smith evaded repeatedly and brought a heavy saber down on his foe's head. Smith fell from the exertion face down on Stuart's lifeless body. Simultaneously, a pistol ball grazed Smith's head. An instant later, the bayonet of Smith's personal guard pierced the heart of a Stuart devotee.

An all-out melee ensued. Infantry from both sides thrust bayonets at each other and officers wielded ringing swords against their counterparts. Washington's dragoons dismounted and joined the fight using sabers, guns, and bare knuckles.

Lt John MacLeod entered the open ground with his two three-pounder cannons. Cornwallis, seeing the tragic loss of Lt Col Stuart and the riot, decided to stop it at all costs. He gave the artilleryman a strange order. "MacLeod! Prepare grapeshot salvos!"

Brig Gen O'Hara, wounded and resting on the ground near the 2nd Guards, exclaimed. "My Lord, the fire will destroy our men!"

"We'll endure the necessary evil!" Cornwallis yelled.

MacLeod's matrosses rolled the small bronze cannons into place. After the powder bags, they loaded each with a case of grapeshot. MacLeod sighted along the cannons and adjusted the elevation of the muzzles to put the grapes dead on the fighters sparring in the brush twenty yards away.

Cornwallis nodded to MacLeod who shouted "Prime!—Make ready!—Fire!" to the gun crew.

Called "grasshoppers", not for their oxidized green hue, but for their retrograde leaping, the cannon-ettes jumped backwards. Hardly innocuous, they each fired nine eight-ounce iron balls in a destructive wide pattern.

"Upstart colonists!" Cornwallis echoed the grasshoppers. "We are the British Empire!"

When the fracas ended, 2nd Guards retreated and Patriots regained Singleton's cannons. Redcoats and Rebels covered the ground unhurt having thrown themselves down seeing the cannons lit.

Washington and the Continental cavalry withdrew, followed by 1st Maryland. O'Hara, though grievously wounded, rallied the 2nd Guards and elements of the 71st. Unburdened by 1st Maryland, he contemplated his next move.

***

Except for small parties of Americans and British murmuring as they removed their wounded to medical help, quiet fell on the clearing. Lt Col Tarleton watched from horseback two yards from the British commander. Cornwallis caught the sound of gunfire and lifted his eyebrows. Fighting had become limited to the area far south of Salisbury Road.

"My Lord, the Legion awaits."

Through a telescope Cornwallis observed the action four-hundred yards away. Maj Gen Leslie grimaced as the 71st Regiment exchanged fire with the Augusta and Rockbridge County militias. Maj du Buy's Regiment von Bose engaged Lt Col Henry Lee's Light Infantry and Col Norton's 1st Guards parried Col Campbell's rifle fire.

Cornwallis replied irritably, "I'm well aware of that." I'm also aware this fawning idiot is of little use. Never again will his mutilated hand wield a saber.

"My cavalry is ready to charge."

Cornwallis took the glass away and groaned at the obsequious junior. "The Americans are retreating. Take a squad to Leslie and determine the general intelligence on our right."

# Sixty-Four ~ Waning Battle

Remote battle south of Salisbury Road raged in thinning woods amenable to accurate fire. Leslie had collected loose numbers of the 71st Regiment on Salisbury Road and retreated to escape the withering fire of Maj Stuart's Augusta and Rockbridge County militias. Norton's 1st Battalion of the Guards, believing the Hessian Regiment von Bose adequate to the contest, inched north to Salisbury Road as well.

Lee ordered reserves to cover his retreat to join Washington's dragoons moving against a large body of well-armed Tories formed at Guilford Court House ready to claim the prize. When the Washington-Lee corps approached, the Loyalists fired their guns, and took shelter behind, inside, and under the structure among the piers. The Patriots withdrew.

***

Pressed by Lee's light infantry, Regiment von Bose withdrew and followed Norton, presently marching the 1st Guards near the heights which Stevens' Virginia militia once held on the Second Line. Lee returned from the courthouse and ordered the Legion's foot soldiers to hold Regiment von Bose. He departed and returned with his horsemen who circled Norton's 1st Guards like cattle and drove them back with von Bose.

Having rounded up 1st Guards and doused von Bose's fire, Lee appraised the enemy under control and left it up to Campbell and Stuart when they would join the retreat. Lee led the Legion to Guilford Court House to help guard the better part of Greene's forces retreating.

Absent Lee's farewell or full intelligence of the Legion's final retreat, Campbell indulged a captain with his humiliation. "Where is Lee going?" The captain took a hit by a fresh ball and stared with plummeting life. "Lee! Return at once!"

Lee's Legion went up Salisbury Road and joined the masses of Americans moving down Reedy Fork Road. Among them many of the cavalry marched having abandoned their horses. Some beasts, wounded and dying, littered the ground. Others meandered in spooky gloom.

***

At the separate battle far south of Salisbury Road neither obstinate side reckoned to quiet their guns. When a cease fire came, some riflemen continued to fire. The 1st Guards and von Bose volleyed over their heads and persuaded a halt.

Col William Campbell and Maj Alexander Stuart decided to retreat. On their way to Reedy Fork Road, in a state of confusion reminiscent of Pyle's Massacre, the Americans fell for the blue Hessian uniforms of von Bose. "Liberty! Liberty!" Houston cried to the Germans to check their friendliness. When the dumbfounded Germans ignored the signal, the Americans charged and fired until the Hessians retreated.

Tarleton arrived at the remote battle. The pain of his throbbing hand had worked up his face into a contemptuous sneer as his cavalry charged the Americans. A thinner forest greeted prime British Legion dragoons whose raised sabers cut down Maj Stuart's Augusta and Rockbridge County militias. Before abandoning the riflemen and militia to the retreat, the British Legion captured Stuart and released British prisoners.

Rockbridge militiaman Sam Houston looked back on the two-and-a-half-hour battle wondering, of all the action, what to put in his journal. We drove the British back three times and they compelled us as often to retreat before the bayonet. We are sore tired. The militia is scattering. Firing has long ceased all around us and presently the British Legion is coming our way!

***

In the hospital tent erected by Guilford Court House, not fifty yards away from the main fighting, Olivia and Sara McMurray and the Salem ladies nursed brandy until the wounded could swallow no more. Soon the haziness restored their courage. Surgeons extracted lead shot when they could. Where the flesh hung from the bone, they amputated the ruined limb and threw the lower part into a wheelbarrow brimming with bloody hands, arms, feet, and legs. They trimmed the remaining bone and stitched healthy, whole flesh over it.

For patients too far along to wait the effects of alcohol, surgeons shoved wadded rags between their teeth and lashed them to a door borrowed from a house in Martinsville before sawing away a destroyed limb. The lucky rolled their eyes in wild torment at the bone saw and obliged the surgeons with unconsciousness that lasted the surgery.

***

Col Webster, knee bandaged but his 33rd unbroken, resolved to avenge injured and dead. He instructed the Yagers and Light Infantry Guards now under his command to head up the ridge far north of Salisbury Road and attack Capt Robert Kirkwood's Delaware "Blue Hens" and Col

Charles Lynch's Bedford Rifles. He ordered The 23rd Regiment to take Capt Finley's artillery.

"Charge!" Webster's troops again advanced across the clearing, down and up the banks of Hunting Creek, and scaled the wooded heights. The 23rd Regiment held back until Webster's muskets volleyed. Finley wanted to turn the two six-pounders on Webster's 33rd but their high position risked killing Continentals. Before he could aim downhill, the 23rd came up and took them.

Pvt Lewis Griffin's brother suffered a traumatic thigh wound from a musket ball. Lewis had only cringed in sympathy when Huger took a wound while rallying his men on horseback. The general hoisted a sword and a shot came. The sword fell in his lap and Huger with keen poise drew a handkerchief, wrapped his hand, and moved on.

Huger was the last American field officer engaged. On the verge of entrapment, he ordered a retreat to Reedy Fork Road. Anyone not seeing the Virginia Line's earlier action may have reckoned they withdrew at the first threat of action, such being the effect of isolated fighting. They exited with order and dignity knowing they'd checked the enemy.

# Sixty-Five ~ Retreat and Repair

— March 15, 1781, Guilford Court House Battleground, Retreat

Maj Gen Greene ordered fifer Maj Ferguson Taylor to signal the army's departure. Fifers wearing blue-faced red frocks that marked them as non-combatants joined the retreat call, urging their companies out of the woods to complete the parade that had been forming on Reedy Fork Road.

Col Green's 1st Virginia Regiment lined the road to cover the regiments assembling their weary, battle-thinned ranks. Informal roll calls returned horrendous yet quite believable counts of killed and wounded. Names gushed from the lips of their comrades. Who took the highest losses? Those on the Third Line could rightly claim that ignominious title.

Lt Col Edward Carrington saw the overall assembly far from complete. He pulled his assembled Makers company out for instructions.

A militiaman from another unit had barely overheard Carrington's orders and called out. "Hey. Where are you boys going?"

"Taking prisoners to Halifax gaol. Then, I reckon we're going fishing."

"Fishing?"

"We've been ordered to catch fish."

In the morning wagons would carry them from Speedwell Ironworks for a month of service in Virginia after delivering British prisoners taken at the battle.

The Roanoke River teemed with alewives, bluebacks, and other herring migrating upstream. Commissary General Davie planned to smoke and salt a thousand barrels of kippers for Greene's army, facing an over-foraged land and a growing season barely showing green sprouts.

A disturbance broke out behind the court house. A Highlander whose face puckered in teary anguish strode toward the parade bearing a musket. He picked out a tall young man twenty feet away in the

Makers' formation. He and Zeb exchanged fateful glances before the Redcoat raised his musket.

The Highlander pressed the trigger with a sweaty finger. The flint pushed the frizzen out of the way but failed to raise sparks and ignite the primer charge in the pan. The Redcoat adjusted the flint with fury, quickly aimed, and fired.

The blast brought everything to a standstill. Seconds later, fellow Redcoats held the Highlander miscreant.

Greene cautiously walked his horse to the Makers.

Carrington met the commanding officer. "Sir, a rogue fired on the Makers. Private Mitchell took a shot in the belly."

Militiamen crowded around the fallen soldier. In the moments before the man expired Abe held his hand and wiped drops of blood from his comrade's face.

Greene hung his head. "My God…the Quaker. His patriotism was key to the Makers saving our ammunition. Otherwise, we couldn't have fought today."

Three men helped Abe carry the bloody body by the arms and legs to the hospital tent. Gen Greene shook his head to dislodge the shock of seeing Zeb at one quarter holding the lifeless body's left arm.

No matter how the body jerked as the bearers tramped fast over brush and uneven ground, George wouldn't awake. Zeb examined the limp, muscular body. He eyed Abe through teary basins. "This is my fault."

"No."

"I fired on that Redcoat on the First Line and missed. He wanted revenge."

"Don't blame yourself."

Zeb sobbed while pouting and shaking his head. He wiped the tears with his free hand. "My God, I once couldn't wait to see George fire a gun."

"We both encouraged George."

Zeb's face tightened. "If only this land wasn't so divided."

"Free your anger. Would you dishonor George?"

"No. No, of course not." Zeb sniffed the moisture from his nose. "George will always be my gentle brother."

When the bearers arrived at the hospital tent, the women instinctively looked toward them making quiet, individual evaluations trying to decide in what order they would treat another man.

George's face betrayed his late cheerful countenance. Olivia, Sara, Yohanna, and Rahel at last fathomed his features before gasping and bowing their heads with gushing eyes. Prayers passed their lips and they resumed caring for their patients, though torment etched their faces.

Olivia glimpsed at Abe and Zeb. She gazed at them, hoping to ameliorate their shock with stoic pause. She folded her hands under her chin and nodded a somber face.

Sara resumed wrapping a British soldier's amputated limb. She spoke with guarded anxiety without looking up. "Oh, Abe…My God, we have lost George." Tears fell beside her lips. "Where's Matty?" She noticed her mother's curiosity, turned formal, and bawled. "Sergeant…Vinyard."

Abe pursed his lips and closed his eyes. "On the battlefield." He instinctively spoke German. "Auch er ist tot."

Sara froze. "What?"

Yohanna tenderly caressed Sara's side. Sara returned the gesture.

"I'm so sorry," Abe said.

***

Capt Singleton waited at the southern end of Reedy Fork Road near Guilford Court House. He was a troubled man, feeling sorry for the fate of his artillery. Most of the dray horses lay dead. Despite great odds against getting his two brass field pieces to camp, he opposed leaving them as spoils of war.

Singleton weighed his fortune. Cornwallis must be planting the King's Colors where Huger made the last stand. Capt Finley's two six-pounder cannons remained up there.

Gen Greene responded to Singleton's request for towing power by shaking his head. "Leave them. We have a long march ahead and our horses are precious."

"We have men. Colonel Henry Knox brought fifty-nine cannons three-hundred miles to Boston."

"Our march is twenty miles," Greene said. "The men would die pulling them. Knox had oxen and sleds and icy ground." He put a hand on Singleton's shoulder. "Don't worry, Captain. I'll send for replacements from our stores at Prince Edward Court House in Virginia." Ordering up new cannons would have been fantasy in December.

***

The Battle of Guilford Court House was over. Green's 1st Virginia Regiment joined the assembly and the Americans marched toward Troublesome Creek. Gen Greene looked back. Redcoats surrounded the courthouse. Loyalist prisoners freed from the gaol gathered and cheered as flames licked the log house of the court clerk.

Only four o'clock, dusk had come. The sky rumbled as rain drenched the warriors. With torches to light the road the parade gained speed from the battleground without note except for a minor skirmish when a body of Tarleton's horsemen showed themselves in the rear at a Haw River bridge.

Cornwallis countermanded his order that a detachment of British Legion pursue the Americans. A vast number of American and British remains lying on the field necessitated manpower to bury them.

Cold driving rain fell. The army marched another mile and halted to take refreshment and collect stragglers.

Elements of Augusta and Rockbridge Virginia militia regiments attached to Campbell elected to stop. Worn out, Sam Houston and his fellow militiamen let the parade proceed up muddy roads in darkness to Speedwell Ironworks without them.

Houston's band rested at a layby on Reedy Fork Road. Their lot, including sick and badly cut individuals, camped around fires, made cornmeal and bacon cakes, and sheltered under blankets.

***

Moments of quietude and exhaustion attended the marchers. While those still shocked blotted out the horror, others attempted to untangle each side's every move and countermove to assess the validity of tactics.

Roused from contemplation, Gen Greene, riding with Lt Col Lee and Commissary General Davie, evaluated the battle. Light from the torches agitated in his eyes. "Word is, the Carolina brigades of militia neglected to take advantage of their position, but fled—"

"The greater part of them, without giving more than one fire," interjected Lee, "let the enemy attack the Second Line."

"Could I have but seen the Virginia militia gall the enemy with their volleys."

"Let me be your eyes," Lee said. "It was an incessant fire which lasted for a considerable length of time. Superior discipline at length prevailed."

"As the commanding officer, the Virginia militia deserves my warmest approbation. Generals Stevens and Lawson with all the officers under them did themselves great honor."

"You did well today if you consider no general ever commanded worse troops than those which form your present army."

Davie had had enough. "I must disagree if you mean North Carolina's militia."

Lee spared Davie no honor. "Carolina's militia was no better today than at the Battle of Camden."

"That battle wouldn't have been lost, sir," Davie said, "if the Virginia militia hadn't initiated the retreat."

"Gentlemen. Don't bicker. Let the commanders of the brigades answer for themselves. Allow the same privilege to the officers of the corps comprising those brigades. I never ordered the militia to retreat."

The flickering of Lee's eyes indicated he'd moved on to a new topic. "Well, I'm of the opinion nothing is left for us but to imitate the example of Scipio Africanus."

Davie's horse continued straight as he turned to Lee. "Scipio Africanus?"

"The general of the Roman Republic who put down Hannibal the great Carthaginian. Scipio Africanus threw away conventional tactics such as placing militia first. He made gaps in formations to let the enemy charge through."

"Letting the enemy through is foolish."

Lee eyed Davie. "Give the enemy a gap to rush through in narrow files straight into a body of militiamen who in their nature desire to trap animals."

Davie shook his head. "I don't see our forces using such sophistication."

"It works another way for enemy forces. A company of Webster's 23$^{rd}$ came in a wide front upon Lawson's brigade, changed their geometry by ninety-degrees, and attacked with a single column of men deep through  Skipwith's Regiment."

"What happened?"

"Lawson's line broke and retreated in panic."

Greene got back into the conversation. "Even crude tactics shine if executed well. That comes from good leadership. The failed Third Line tactics are my fault."

"You couldn't have known the situation of the entire field," Lee said.

"I knew it when the 2$^{nd}$ Battalion of the Guards blew a hole through the Maryland Regulars on the Third Line."

"You have no regrets, General. In my view, we evenly drew the enemy in battle. Only the final retreat to preserve the army gave Cornwallis the field."

"If I'm honest," Davie said, "Gen Stevens' brigade and 1$^{st}$ Maryland fought the whole battle."

Greene furrowed his brow. His mount's neck made an outline in the low torch light. "Yes, and it's over. The retreat and the battle."

Lee gazed at Greene in the gloom. "Are you surprised by our stand?"

"Call me deranged if I say otherwise. Three months ago, in Charlotte Town, I could but wish to stand as well as we did today. I never believed such a thing would be possible."

"That's what I thought when we almost didn't make it across three rivers," Davie said. "The impossibility made it thrilling."

Greene nodded. "Just the fact we walked away today intact save for our poor losses is monumental. Whatever we can achieve in the future to maintain our honor, I don't know."

"What will you say in your report to General Washington?" Lee said.

"That we lost." Greene glared thru the gray at Lee's and Davie's disbelief. "It's true."

Davie laughed. "I'm glad you'll be writing to him. No one believes your little lies in person."

# Sixty-Six ~ Renewed Outlook

— March 15, 1781, Speedwell Ironworks on Troublesome Creek

Greene's defeated army repaired from the bloody fields and woods of Guilford Court House to Speedwell Ironworks in cold, cleansing rain. A fast rider rode ahead to alert the commissary to ready a hot meal they'd been preparing since morning.

Roast Beef! Famished soldiers answered the drums and fifes and came running with their mess mates to take heaping tin plates. They formed two serving lines and resumed their stories about the shots they'd gotten off before making it off the field alive.

Quality food surprised the troops as they beheld tender, fresh beef roasted on an open pit. For the first time in a week, they didn't have to choke down salty, stringy beef. They ate delicious beans and fluffy bread. Thank God for bacon and brewery yeast.

Gen Greene walked among the troops stopping to thank individuals for their efforts. For two hours the wounded and stragglers returned from the field. When mess finished Greene ordered regimental drummers and fifers to muster the men for roll call. Assembly! Captains throughout the camp head-counted their companies.

The Makers company formed before Capt Abercrombie Hawkins and Lt Col Edward Carrington. The captain pained in humiliation. "Sir, I have but twelve men mustering."

My men went nervy before the first charge. Some fled without giving two shots. They were scared. But didn't the dead and wounded feel scared? Didn't other militiamen lay their muskets on the rail and shoot up their cartridges?

Hawkins tread lightly. With the fog of smoke still in his eyes and scores of muskets yet deafening, it would be easy to forsake his men. Hadn't they prepared boats for the crossings and delivered the ammunition under threat of death?

"Where are the others?"

"Twenty-three mustered for battle. Private Heider and Sergeant Vinyard are dead and two others have serious wounds. Seven are missing."

Between the Virginia and North Carolina militias, seven-hundred and sixty-eight missed roll call, five-hundred and fifty-two from the latter. Rather than captured, Maj Gen Greene assumed they went home to kiss their sweethearts and eat their mother's cooking.

***

"Troublesome" seemed unfair for a creek that provided water and mill power. It better characterized Speedwell Ironworks where Joseph Buffington tinkered with every combination of fire, materials, and methods but failed to purify the local grade of iron ore. Finding his process either too simple or uneconomical, the Quaker admitted failure and let the furnace fall into disuse.

Gen Greene understood Buffington's frustration having worked with iron as a blacksmith. Indeed, the army had been through a purification process. They toughened with reinforcement in troops and ammunition but, like Buffington's product, they broke.

The day after the battle, Greene prepared the army for a second stand, ordering them to clean and lubricate the muskets and wash their bloody bayonets and swords. Then bathe, clean and repair their uniforms, make shoes out of leather provided by a tanner who carried away the fresh beef hides, and wait for action at short notice.

Meanwhile, the general wrote to George Washington explaining why the Battle of Guilford Court House had been unsuccessful. Victory was certain had the North Carolina militia fired more than once or twice before retreating.

Greene laid down the quill. Is my harsh judgement of the North Carolina militia necessary? If I put myself in their place, would I see a difference from other militias? All over the Colonies soldiers, especially the Irregulars, deserted. The Continentals of the Pennsylvania Line recently mutinied.

Why would my militiamen quit? They are at the end of their three-month terms and I have no money to offer extensions. I can't feed and clothe them properly. Smallpox has broken out. Loyalists took the oath to defend the revolution yet they can't kill the British. Plowing season is coming up.

What would have made them stay? The experience of pride fighting for independence. To get a proper discharge and thereby keep their pension. Do glories mount higher than preservation of life?

Greene set aside his feelings and continued the letter by telling how he had fainted after the battle owing to excessive fatigue and anxiety. To sum up the long six weeks since leaving Camp Cheraw and post-battle relief, Greene wrote he'd at last taken off his clothes and bathed properly.

Done with the necessary dispatch to Washington, Greene wrote to his dear wife Catharine. After expressing his love and loneliness for her, the letter moved to the battle and Cornwallis who he said still needed a sound beating to make him leave North Carolina. He also responded to an earlier letter in which Caty expressed a desire to come down. He said with quill strokes so hard the ink bled the idea didn't sit well with him. She had no concept of the shocking devastation south of Virginia. What would make him happy? An honorable end to the war and life on a farm with his little family.

***

Greene learned over the next few days his troops had killed or wounded one-quarter or more of British forces present at Guilford Court House including one of every three officers. That compared to American losses of less than ten percent overall. Quite possibly the militia had softened the British.

Though Cornwallis won the field with half as many troops, he took much greater losses. Greene shot off an account to Governor Jefferson. "Our loss is very trifling, not more than 300 killed, wounded, and taken; that of the Enemy's, from a variety of circumstances and the best intelligence I can get, is at least six hundred."

The general gave the letter to the Express rider when intelligence came that Cornwallis was decamped at Ramsey's Mill on the Deep River ninety miles southeast. Greene, hoping for a second general battle, ordered two days' rations of meat, flour, and beans drawn and cooked immediately ahead of a forced march. He allowed the men a gill of rum.

The army assembled by regiment, companies lining up in four tight files to proceed swiftly. Soldiers stepped to the drum cadence and the formations crept away with order and discipline as a unit taking their mission with gravity and purpose. The feet of three-thousand men touched the muddy road and lifted, making perfectly timed kisses.

Maj Taylor started piping the strident patriotic tune *Chester* in the vanguard of the march. Fifers down the assembly made out the notes above the mass of marching feet and mimicked him. Notes in plentiful volume reached the expanse of the marchers and lifted morale like bird chat.

Somebody shouted an order from the back of the parade to the front to open the files in the center for field officers to advance on horseback. As if hewn by a giant sword, two files of North Carolina militia moved to the left and two moved to the right. Had they not moved over, the sight on the verge might have gone unnoticed. A body hung from a tree with a note pinned to its frock. Upon large slate outcroppings nearby sat ten backcountry men.

"Halt!" Brig Gen Thomas Eaton yelled.

Companies stopped in a succession of reactions that produced two waves that reached the van and the rear. The drums and fifes hushed. Ranks parted to allow Eaton to ride up near the body.

Eaton summarized the paper's content. "They caught and elevated this man for his deeds as a Loyalist." More evidence terror in the South was the most brutal and personal in the colonies. "Forward—March!"

The parade accompanied by the drums and fifes soon fell back in standard time and distance between the ranks. Gen von Steuben would marvel seeing the men marching with *Blue Book* precision.

Greene detached with a small party for a stop at New Garden Meeting House while the army marched south down the spine of Guilford County. He handed his pistol and sword to ADC Burnet before going inside.

Rank wounds and spicy brandy punched his nose. It was the smell Greene had equated with hospitals since the Battle of Boston. Olivia McMurray pointed to the minister kneeling at the side of a wounded young man.

Greene cleared his throat. "Minister, may I have a word?"

The plainly dressed Quaker minister rose. "Yes?"

"I'm General Greene. Thank you for aiding the men wounded at Guilford Court House. I beg of your humanity for the continued relief of their suffering."

The minister offered somber umbrage. "We don't believe in fighting or wars, but we shall do all that lies in our power to relieve their pain."

"Quakers have been called enemies to independence. What do you say?"

Irritation flared in the minister's eyes as he restrained himself. "We make no distinction as to party and their cause."

"I respect you as a people and shall always be your protector. This is no religious dispute, but one for political liberty without which you cannot enjoy free exercise of your religion."

The discussion had reached the point typical of exchanges between Quakers and non-Quakers. The minister folded his arms, held his ground, and guarded his temper. "It was the British who guaranteed our free exercise of religion."

"They excite your apprehensions respecting free worship. You would neither have religious liberty nor property could the enemy succeed in their measures."

"We lost liberty and property before Cornwallis came to North Carolina."

"To pay for the war." The minister's petulance irked Greene. "Don't you want the war to end?"

"Of course."

"There's one way to end it."

The minister cracked an icy grin. "Indulge me."

"War will end when the people are united."

"We find it odd you and Cornwallis united to stage a battle in our quarter and throw us the wounded. As for war, negotiation and patience can prevent it. It's up to the Colonies to respect English governance."

Greene shook his head. "Do not be deceived. I shall be exceedingly grateful if you contribute all your power to relieve the unfortunates here. Doctor Wallace will point out the things most needed. He's ready to receive donations."

"In our present situation, we can't do as much as we would like. The state has lain much upon us in taxes and penalties, and of late Patriots and Loyalists plundered our quarter."

Greene rejoined the army. The parade turned east at Deep River and paralleled the waters to their junction with the Haw River. At Ramsey's Mill on the Deep, the British army was escaping down the Cape Fear Road to Wilmington. In the river lay the remains of a destroyed makeshift bridge. Hundreds of tree trunks floated downstream like the products of lumberjacks to sawmills.

To a rearguard Redcoat officer Greene shouted. "I'm not chasing *you*!"

# Sixty-Seven ~ Grieve the Heroes

— March 18, 1781, Guilford Court House, Martinsville, North Carolina

Quiet distinguished the hospital tent at Guilford Court House from its former role. The canvas box where selfless doctors and nurses had worked feverishly to save lives served as cold storage for dead heroes.

Sobbing mourners waited outside to claim their boys, among them the loved ones of George Heider and Matthew Vinyard.

Olivia broke the silence. "We can do naught but lightly mourn, for death is inevitable. War which by itself is a sin stole life from young George and Matthew."

Michael McMurray held Olivia's hands. "God gave them to the world as a reminder of how battle is absolutely contradictory to the prophet Isaiah who said that nation shall not lift up sword against nation and neither shall they learn war anymore."

Abraham placed a hand over his breast bone. "I'm not wise to Quaker beliefs. Moravians believe the hand of God protects. What...I must be careful asking this...do you believe? Did God leave them unprotected for a reason?"

"Mankind left them unprotected," Olivia said, "as our cost of war."

Zeb put a hand on Abraham's shoulder and looked into his eyes. "Please, don't take this wrong. Quakers rely on their personal relationship with God to do what He commands. He doesn't allow us to sit idle while he does the work."

"How can you say that? *You* didn't do as God commanded," Michael said.

"I did as He commanded. He told me to exercise tender care of you by fighting the British to secure your wagon business from their predatory merchants."

McMurray tilted his head, taking in Zeb's point. "Maybe so. The greater command was to seek peace. You erred in taking sides."

"Please, let us not be as divided as this land," Olivia said. "We can't blame Zeb for not attaining a sufficient level of conscience with God."

Michael lightly kicked the ground. "I couldn't stop him with a labor of love."

"Please, dear. The elders let the battles happen."

Michael gave Olivia an obedient nod and rested his eyes on Zeb. "Our disagreement reached the point where I could only censure you. It was painful."

"I encouraged George and Zeb," Abraham said.

"Don't blame yourself," Zeb said. "I shouldn't have let the spirit of party influence me."

"You're my son. I cringed at your enlistment, but I should have made peace with your decision."

Maria took Yohanna's hand gently. "She has lost her brother and I have lost my intended." They came closer and stood before Michael and Zeb. Olivia, Abraham, and Rahel gathered beside them. "Anger fell upon the land. It pulled us all into the abyss."

"Let's not forget the fallen." Sara had been apart, staring at the tent and couldn't contain her aggravation. She came near the group. "Aren't you concerned for Matthew and George who died in battle so that you could freely criticize each other?"

"We are, daughter," Olivia said.

"Even though their deaths resulted from partisanship?"

"I've talked to the minister. He won't deny Matthew and George interment in the meeting house cemetery. He'll properly record the burials as any Quaker's."

"That's a kind gesture as George and Matthew are far from home and need a resting place," Abraham said.

Olivia addressed the Moravians. "Normally, we don't allow the burial of others not in communion with Quaker beliefs. The unusual circumstances temporarily remove any resentment of the combatants and their different faiths."

Sara shook her head lightly. "Are you not listening? They fought on the losing side. I'm afraid no one will view them honorably."

Michael side-hugged Sara. "In war, both sides lose, though your concern is admirable."

Olivia's eyebrows moved in recognition of Sara's concern. "My darling daughter, I now see your true feelings. We don't judge Matthew's decisions in life. Only honor his soul. The irritations won't easily fade. May we all remember Matthew and George with joy."

***

Michael, Zeb, and Abraham nailed the covers to seal George's and Matthew's remains which they'd gently lowered into the boxes. The pounding ended with a hush that endured the loading of the coffins onto the wagon and a slow march to the McMurray home in New Garden.

Yohanna, Maria, and Sara strolled behind the McMurray homestead wordlessly hand in hand sharing their shock. They found flowering redbud branches to lay on the coffins to begin the wake of George and Matthew.

The ladies knelt with their heads against the fresh, bright pine and said prayers to go with George's and Matthew's souls to God. Abraham, Zeb, and Michael repeated the sendoff.

The McMurray's shared their home with the Moravians. Overnight, grieving erupted like a rainy, wailing storm that wetted their eyes and stirred their thoughts as powerfully as gales. In the morning the mourners stared from red, empty eyes and quietly ate breakfast.

***

Oak trees stood black and striking on the perimeter of the cemetery at New Garden Friends meeting house. Friends had dug dozens of graves. Once they finished a handful of six-sided wooden coffins, wide at the shoulders and narrow at the feet, a series of simple burials commenced.

With Quaker propriety the ceremony progressed, offering nothing to beautify or ease the horror. Neither mourning clothes, music, singing, or preaching. Solemn pauses preceded and followed the internments.

With the graves closed, it was time to say a last goodbye. To the boys and to the local challenges that wrought their deaths. Doubts about the Revolution ended. It was time to move on to the next battle and the next battle until the war ended in victory for America.

***

Abraham panned the burial ground. "This cemetery is similar to God's Acre in Salem with its small, square markers."

Numb and blank-faced, Michael gathered Abe was speaking and added, "We'll soon allow simple monuments."

"George was a simple, gentle man," Abraham said. "He wanted to see the world outside of Wachovia. He didn't want to take sides or kill his fellow man. He wouldn't have betrayed an escaping slave."

"As for Matthew," Zeb said, "he took his role seriously and found a place of leadership in this awful war. Over time he accepted the differences of Abraham and George being small."

"They're home now," Michael said.

Yohanna, Sara, Olivia, and Maria left to board the wagon. Michael McMurray broke the silence. "I suppose there's hope the war won't bother your militia while you fish on the Roanoke."

"I'm coming home directly after fishing," Zeb said.

Michael smiled at Rahel who lightly leaned onto Abraham. "Will you both return to Salem?"

Abraham looked to the wainwright with a keen inquiry. "I beg to ask you a question first. Are you aware of the proclamation General Cornwallis made after the battle?" He translated for Rahel, who wouldn't leave his side.

"He claims a signal victory over Americans that will restore order and good government. General Greene also made a proclamation of sorts when he stopped at our meeting house before passing through."

"Oh? What did the general say?"

"America can protect religious freedom by guaranteeing political liberty. He also asked the Quaker Quarter to aid the wounded."

"Between Cornwallis and Greene, who do you believe?"

"The words of warriors bother me. What's your opinion?"

"I'm a black man. Order and good government are pleasant words, but only political liberty can pull out problems by their roots."

"Will you leave Salem?"

"I did when I enlisted…Oh, I see. Blacks never escape and make it alone. I know no one outside of Salem except for you folks."

"I know few people outside of New Garden."

"Where is this conversation going?" Abraham said. "Did I miss something?"

"Olivia and I are going north of the Ohio River and west of Pennsylvania to settle. Will you and Rahel come with us?"

Abraham's jaw dropped. Rahel tugged his frock and begged him to translate. He placated her with a gentle shove. "Is it possible?"

"If we're careful."

Stunned, Zeb extended his hands and chopped the air. "Excuse me, father. You never told me." He folded his arms. "I caused this. Didn't I?"

Rahel disregarded Zeb's petulance and begged for a translation. Michael's offer pleased her so much she practically leapt into his arms. He blushed and returned her hug.

"Aren't you taking me? What about Sara? Why Ohio?"

McMurray gazed at Olivia sitting on the wagon across the cemetery. "I can no longer show my face at the meetings. Perhaps I don't want to."

"My God, you'll leave the Friends. I shouldn't have taken the oath."

"Their power over me is gone. I renounce the Rules."

Abe lifted his eyes and shook McMurray's hand. "Alright, Rahel and I will get married and go with you when Zeb and I come back from the Roanoke."

Zeb gazed at his stepfather. "You can't stop me from going with you." He pulled a deer antler ring from his pocket. "Or stop me from getting married." He ran to Yohanna.

***

Rejoicing amidst warming spring weather, Wachovians stirred outdoors. Planting time had come. Corn and oats would soon shoot up and green the barren Wach valley. The kitchen and apothecary gardens would come back where the militia had camped.

News of the battles at New Garden and Guilford Court House came to Salem by word of mouth from Surry militiamen straggling home. Moravians praised God for His protecting hand. Wachovia had not experienced so much quiet in over a year.

Moravians donated rags, meal, and brandy to the Quakers in New Garden caring for the wounded soldiers. Cornwallis was rumored to have gone to Wilmington with his ailing army and Greene was heading to South Carolina to try and crush the entrenched British captors.

The battles in Guilford County would let off the pressure keeping the people at odds. Wachovia hoped to grow in the wake of its assistance in the war effort.

Bishop Graff pondered the flower of Salem's future returning. George Heider and Maria Bach would wed and start a family. He hoped to promise Yohanna Heider in marriage to a Moravian. Brother Meyer needed Abraham and Rahel in the tavern.

Graff recorded the events of the previous day in the Salem diary. Hoofbeats and creaking wheels came from a horse and cart as a boy drove root vegetables up to the Gemeinhaus. The bishop blotted the entries and closed the book.

END

# Premise

Dear Reader,

The genesis of *Zebulon's Oath* came to me after I viewed the grave of Private William Beck, a Revolutionary War soldier buried in Winston-Salem, North Carolina. Beck was fifteen years old when he fought on the First Line at the Battle of Guilford Courthouse in present-day Greensboro. He served seven months total as a Private in the North Carolina militia. When I found his war pension application on revwarapps.org, his story struck a chord of fascination in my mind.

I researched the pension applications of other soldiers and soon found myself digging through the documented history of the Southern theater of the war. This was during the early weeks of the Covid-19 epidemic and libraries were closed. Thankfully, I found plenty of primary sources online.

Greensboro was my home at the time. After I walked the preserved Battle of Guilford Courthouse battleground, I could have kicked myself for taking it for granted. Ultimately, I discovered the skirmishes in South and North Carolina were more than romantic colonial history; the British Army hobbled into Yorktown and succumbed to the American colonies because they had been weakened in the South.

I was born and raised in Michigan and don't remember being taught about the Southern Theater. I took for granted that the Revolutionary War started in Boston, slogged through Philadelphia and New York, and ended in Yorktown. I don't begrudge the North as they suffered long under the British before the war fell to the Southern colonies.

The stalemate finally broke when the Patriots rallied in North and South Carolina and that fact is too little celebrated. Hopefully, more Southerners, especially the youth, will claim their Revolutionary War heritage as the history continues to emerge.

I have mainly left the huge Patriot victories at the battles of King's Mountain and Cowpens for further writing. Undoubtedly, those magnificent meetings were the beginning of the British demise. My story looks at the nearly two months of movements and skirmishes of the British and American forces in North Carolina and culminates with the Battle of Guilford Courthouse.

During my reading of the history of the Revolutionary War in the South I found a recurring theme involving a "race" or "chase". While I learned that the British pursued American forces from Charlotte, North Carolina to Virginia, I wanted to know why the redoubtable British never caught them. My hope was to illuminate the facts of the "chase" in the context of a compelling story.

This book contains many basic historical facts of the American Revolution in the Southern Theater. But not all of the facts. My tale is one interpretation of the unfolding of events. To have included every historical nuance that occurred between the Spring of 1780 and the Spring of 1781 would have taken too many pages for one novel. There are countless details ripe for alternative plots should historical fiction authors desire to present them.

For the fiction I wove around the history, choosing to concentrate on the lives of typical local inhabitants in central North Carolina, especially in the places we presently call Greensboro (Martinsville in colonial times) and Winston-Salem (the Wachovia settlement and its towns of Salem, Bethabara, and Bethania in colonial times). Among the settlers of Greensboro I follow the Quakers. In Wachovia I follow the Moravians. These two groups were notable as being among a few North Carolina brethren congregations opposed to the war on religious grounds. The majority of the state's citizens generally identified as Loyalists or Patriots and neither were opposed to war.

There are hundreds of facts related in this story. Though I diligently reviewed and linked each one to a source document, I am obliged with heartfelt thanks to correct any narrative in error that you the reader may find.

David R. Dowdy

# Chapter Notes

The following notes are intended to 1) help the reader better understand certain real and imagined events and characters, and 2) explain slight changes to the history made with artistic license.

Chapter 1

I opted to change Traugott Bagge's surname to Bach to emphasize Germanic names common to the Moravians.

Chapter 2/7

Nearly every item about the North Carolina Moravians came from their extensive official diaries (see "Records of the Moravians in North Carolina" in Selected Bibliography).

Chapter 3/5

We don't know if the British ever lost wagons of gunpowder by ambush. We know Maj Gen Gates ordered Francis Marion to destroy ferry boats on the Santee that otherwise the British might have used. We also know Marion and his militia waited for the British in the early morning on swampy ground near Nelson's Ferry just after the Gates' defeat at Camden to capture a convoy taking one hundred and fifty American prisoners to Charleston.

Chapter 4/6/19/20

The history of the North Carolina Quakers is sparsely documented. I took inspiration for their lives and beliefs from Quakers living in Pennsylvania.

Chapter 8

Abraham is based on a real slave named Abraham who came to Wachovia during an earlier period.

Chapter 12

Finding a population of Loyalists and getting them to fight on his side was a make or break situation for Cornwallis.

Chapter 13

The dramatization of George Washington and his bond with Nathanael Greene is essential to understanding each. Their thoughts in the letters they exchanged bring their supposed dialog to life. I used this method to create realistic conversation whenever possible.

Chapter 15

To understand the outcome of strategic events in revolutionary North Carolina one must understand the pressure Cornwallis felt and his capacity to execute in the face of significant yet guarded communication from his hierarchy. Clinton's statement about Cornwallis' ability to speedily march all over the South came later than this book's timeline.

Chapter 16

The singlehanded brilliance of Nathanael Greene's decision making is startling. He always seemed determined to make the best results from meager information and material prospects. Greene probably didn't ride to North Carolina in a fancy carriage.

Chapter 17/18/29/31

The British transferred gunpower seized from the Americans at Charleston to their fort at Camden via Nelson's Ferry which happened to be a place wholly insecure due to the threat of Francis Marion's Partisans who preyed on convoys. Ammunition wasn't entirely in short supply to the Continental Army of the South.

Lt Col Edward Carrington wrote Maj Gen Gates on October 13, 1780 about the arrival of sixty thousand musket cartridges at the Continental magazine at Taylor's Ferry in Virginia. Getting ammunition to the field was challenging. Lt Col Carrington remarked in letters that wagons were in short supply. Letters requesting powder from the North Carolina government agencies showed a high degree of anxiety over dwindling supplies in the field.

Exact amounts of ammunition on hand at the Continental's storehouse in Salisbury aren't known. A large holding of gunpowder in Charles Town remained in a secret location; it couldn't be transferred.

In Salem a place for making ammunition was erected and two wagons of gunpowder came from the Salisbury storehouse to be rolled into ammunition (source: Moravian Records). I fabricated the story about confiscating the powder from the British at Nelson's Ferry and Traugott Bach selling it to North Carolina.

I wrote that ammunition was removed from Salem while the British slept there. In reality, finished ammunition was rushed to safety from Salem before Lord Cornwallis passed through during the race to the Dan. Whether Loyalists put the gunpowder and ammunition under existential threat is not known but attack would have been conceivable.

Finally, I brought forward the date when Benedict Arnold raided Richmond to put a fine point on Patriot gunpowder needs.

Chapter 22

Like Zebulon and others, Rahel is a distillation of many people. Many women like her feared daily interaction with authoritative men, the soundings of war magnifying her fright. Still, strong people in desperate times rise to their inner strength as she did.

Chapter 25

Makers company have a basis in a dozen artificers given to Greene in Philadelphia. The fictitious Makers celebrate the real non-combatants who supplied the American army.

Chapter 26

Zebulon does what he must but breaks the sacred Quaker rule against speaking oaths. Sergeant Vinyard is based on Capt Arthur Forbis.

Chapter 27/38

The battles at Kings Mountain and Cowpens should be seen as the beginning of the end for Cornwallis and British hopes.

Chapter 28

I refrained from using current locale names. Two name changes occurred after the war. Greensboro, the location of Guilford Courthouse, was once known as Martinsville. That name didn't become official until 1785, so I brought it forward. Winston-Salem derived from Salem.

Chapter 30

There will always be champions of a moral cause such as Gov Abner Nash and others (ex. Traugott Bach and Col Christian Febiger) but they are often overlooked, even forgotten. Which is a shame because they are real, heartfelt characters.

Chapter 34

Correspondents at the time of the revolution made it clear hunger in the field was real. Back then, foraging was as common as people today making a trip to the grocery store. Except colonial soldiers had to do it every day. Our marketing is usually a guaranteed proposition whereas our ancestors often came up short. I tried to balance British and American hardships against the fact that the armies somehow existed and progressed, scraping by in a manner that befuddles us.

Chapter 39/41/42/48/49

While Greene got Cornwallis to chase him is self-evident, documents detailing how that strategy was executed don't exist. Nor do many documents show how boats were procured and built for Greene's retreat. This is my attempt to fill in the missing pieces.

Chapter 44

I altered the history of Cornwallis in Salem. He and ex-Governor Josiah Martin met with Traugott Bach (Bagge) the town's leader. I omitted Martin and Bach and substituted Bishop Graff to change the military theme to a view of Moravian and American technical progress such as the water system and munitions laboratory. I also wanted to point out that 1) brotherhood devalued aristocracy, and 2) American audacity to split morality down the middle in time of war could be counted on.

Chapter 47

A true story. Bruce's Cross Road is now called Summerfield.

Chapter 51

My description of ammunition distribution is speculative. Greene didn't have an unending supply but he was supplied well enough to commit plentiful cartridges to a crucial battle.

Chapter 52

Banastre Tarleton lost two fingers in the Southern Theatre, either at Cowpens or the Battle of New Garden. I chose to present the injury happening at the latter. The source information leans toward it.

Chapter 53-65

I took some artistic license with the execution of battle scenes, especially the tit-for-tat scenes on the Second Line south of Salisbury Road. The overall movements happened. Unfortunately, details are sparse.

# Bibliography


1.   Records of the Moravians in North Carolina, Vol IV, Adelaide L. Fries, Raleigh, 1930
2.   The Carolina Quaker Experience, Hinshaw, Dexter, Michigan, 1984
3.   Thesis: Good Wares And Modest Manners, the Salem store entrusted to merchant Traugott Bagge, 1775-1800, Lola Langdon Culler, Interior Architecture, UNCG, 2009
4.   Clinton-Cornwallis Controversy, Vol II, by Benjamin Franklin Stevens, London, 1888
5.   Memoirs of the War in the Southern Department, Vol. I, Henry Lee, published by Bradford and Inskeep, Philadelphia, 1812
6.   Sketches of the Life and Correspondence of Nathanael Greene, Vol. I, William Johnson, Charleston 1822
7.   A History of the Campaigns of 1780 and 1781, by Lt Col Tarleton, Dublin, 1787
8.   Supplying Washington's Army, Center of Military History United States Army, Erna Risch, Washington, D.C., 1981
9.   King's Mountain and Its Heroes, Lyman C. Draper, Peter G. Thompson Publisher, Cincinnati, 1881
10.  The Writings of George Washington, Vol XII, Jared Sparks, Boston, 1839
11.  The Artillerist's Manual, by Maj F. A. Griffiths, Seventh Edition, London, 1856
12.  A Sketch of the Life of Brig. Gen. Francis Marion, William Dobein James, 1821
13.  Rules of Discipline of the Yearly Meeting of Friends, For Pennsylvania, New Jersey, Delaware, and the Eastern Parts of Maryland, Philadelphia, 1888
14.  Faith and Practice of the North Carolina Yearly Meeting of Friends (Book Of Discipline), 1956
15.  Nathaniel Greene Strategist of the American Revolution, Thayer, New York, 1960
16.  Life of Nathanael Greene, George Washington Greene, Vol III, Boston, 1864
17.  The Parliamentary History of England from the Earliest Period to the Year 1803, vol. XXI, London, 1814
18.  Southern Campaigns of the American Revolution, The Journal of the Southern Campaigns of the American Revolution, Vol. 1, No. 2, October 2004
19.  Major General Nathanael Greene: Study in Leadership Culminating at the Battle of Guilford Courthouse, Gerald J. Krieger, Journal of Military and Strategic Studies, Vol. 20, Issue 3, 2021, ISSN : 1488-559X
20.  Old Salem Historic District, National Historic Landmark Nomination, United States Department of the Interior, National Park Service, drafted October 2016
21.  History of Wachovia in North Carolina, John Henry Clewell, New York, 1902
22.  First Census of the United States, North Carolina, 1790
23.  Brothers in Bondage The Moravian's Struggle with the Institution of Slavery, by Dr. Jon F. Sensbach, Tar Heel Junior Historian, North Carolina History for Students, (ISSN 0496-8913), Volume 51, Number 2
24.  Common Sense, Thomas Paine, Little Blue Book No. 50, edited by E. Haldeman-Julius, Haldeman-Julius Company, Girard, Kansas, 1920
25.  The Revolutionary War Sketches of William R. Davie, Edited by Jeffrey J. Crow, Raleigh, 1976
26.  Southern Campaigns of the American Revolution, The Journal of the Southern Campaigns of the American Revolution, Vol. 3, No. 2, February 2006
27.  General Joseph Graham and His Papers on North Carolina Revolutionary History, William A. Graham, Raleigh, 1904

28. Faulty Linchpin of a Failed Strategy, A Thesis, by William Paul Burke, College of William & Mary Arts & Sciences, 1988

29. The Loyalist Regiments of the American Revolution 1775-1783, by Stuart Salmon, PhD Dissertation 0020749, University of Stirling, 2009

30. The Life of Nathanael Greene, Major-General In The Army of the Revolution, Simms, William Gilmore, ed., New York: George F. Cooledge & Brother, 1849

31. The Life of Nathanael Greene, Vol. I, George Washington Greene, New York, P. Putnam And Son, 1867

32. The War of the Revolution, Ward, New York, 1952

33. The Continental Army, Center Of Military History, United States Army, Robert K. Wright, Jr., Washington, 1983

34. The Writings of Benjamin Franklin, Vol. I, Albert Henry Smyth, ed., New York, The Macmillan Company, 1905

35. History of The Religious Society of Friends Called by Some The Free Quakers in the City of Philadelphia, Charles Wetherill, Philadelphia, Printed for the Society, 1894

36. A Complicated Scene of Difficulties: North Carolina and The Revolutionary Settlement, 1776-1789, Dissertation by John R. Maass, M.A., The Ohio State University, 2007

37. Negro Population 1790-1915, Washington Government Printing Office 1918, Kraus Reprint Co., New York, 1969

38. Martha Washington, An American Life, Patricia Brady, Penguin, New York, 2005

39. Documents of the American Revolution, Vol XVIII, Edited by K. G. Davies, Irish University Press, Dublin, 1978

40. Documents of the American Revolution, Vol XX, Edited by K. G. Davies, Irish University Press, Dublin, 1979

41. Correspondence of Charles, first Marquis Cornwallis Vol I, Edited by Charles Ross, p. 80, London, 1859

42. Regulations for the Order and Discipline of the Troops: Regulations for the Order and Discipline of the Troops, by Maj Gen Baron de Steuben, Styner and Cist, in Second-street, Philadelphia, 1779

43. The State Records of North Carolina, Vol XV, Edited by Walter Clark, Goldsboro, 1898

44. Memoirs of the American Revolution, by William Moultrie, Vol. I, printed by David Longworth, New York, 1802

45. Letter from Christian Febiger to Nathanael Greene, Lowcountry Digital Library, The Charleston Museum Archives, 1780-11-07

46. Ammunition Supply in Revolutionary Virginia, The Virginia Magazine of History and Biography, Donald E. Reynolds, Vol. 73, 1965

47. The State Records of North Carolina, Edited by Walter Clark, Vol. XIV, Winston, NC, 1896

48. A Treatise on Gunpowder, Firearms, and Artillery, by Alessandro Vittorio Papacino d'Antoni, translated from Italian by Capt Thomson, London, 1789

49. Thomas Jefferson, Richard B. Bernstein, Oxford University Press, New York, 2003

50. The State Records of North Carolina, Vol XX, Edited by Walter Clark, Goldsboro, 1902

51. Wesley's Standard Sermons, Vol I, Edited and Annotated by Edward H. Sugden, Lamar & Barton, Agents Publishing House, Richmond, 1787

52. The Quakers In The American Colonies, Jones et al, London, 1911

53. William Byrd's Histories of the Dividing Line Betwixt Virginia and North Carolina, William Byrd, With Introduction and Notes By William K. Boyd, Raleigh, 1929

54. Map Guide to American Migration Routes, 1735-1815, William Dollarhide, Heritage Quest publisher, Bountiful, Utah, 1997

55. Revolutionary Anecdotes of the American Revolution, by Alexander Garden of Lee's Legion, printed by A. E. Miller, Charleston, 1828

56. Governor Abner Nash, Address by Joseph. G. De Roulhac Hamilton, Raleigh, 1909

57. New Lloyd's List No. 1227, December 26, 1780; New Lloyd's List No. 1243, February 20, 1781

58. David Rumsey Map Collection, Virginia. S. Lewis del. Tanner sc., published by John Conrad & Co., Philadelphia, 1804

59. The State of South Carolina From the Best Authorities, by Samuel Lewis, 1795, Fairfield County Genealogy Society,

60. Kosciuszko, A Biography, Monica M. Gardner, Charles Scribner's Sons, New York, 1920

61. History of the Great Iron Chain, Military War Museum, New York, 1900

62. The Battle of Guilford Courthouse, by Charles E. Hatch, Jr., Office of History and Historic Architecture Eastern Service Center, Washington, D. C., July 1971

63. A New American Biographical Dictionary or Remembrancer, Fourth Edition, Thomas J. Rogers, Published by Samuel F. Bradford, Philadelphia, 1829

64. Cowpens, Downright Fighting, The Story of Cowpens, by Thomas J. Fleming, Division of Publications, National Park Service, U.S. Department of the Interior, Washington, D.C. 1988

65. The Campaign of 1781 in the Carolinas, by Henry Lee, published by E. Littell, Philadelphia, 1824

66. A British Orderly Book, 1780-1781, Edited by A. R. Newsome, The North Carolina Historical Review, 1932

67. The Reluctant Partisan, Nathanael Greene's Southern Campaigns, 1780-1783, Justin S. Liles, B.A., Thesis Prepared for the Degree of Master of Arts, University Of North Texas, May 2005

68. A History of Rowan County North Carolina, by Rev. Jethro Rumple, Published by J. J. Bruner, Salisbury, NC, 1881

69. A Treatise on Brewing, by Alexander Morrice, Fourth Edition, published by Sherwood, Neely, and Jones, London, 1810

70. An Illustrated Encyclopedia of Uniforms from 1775—1783, The American Revolutionary War: An Expert Guide, by Kiley, Kevin F., et al, Published by Lorenz Books, United Kingdom, 2008

71. North Carolina 1780-'81, Being a History of the Invasion of the Carolinas, by David Schenck, published by Edwards & Broughton, Raleigh, 1889

72. Whigs and Tories, The North Carolina Booklet, by professor W. C. Allen, Capital Printing, Raleigh, 1902

73. John Mitchell, Fife Major, Virginia Militia in the Revolutionary War, 1913

74. The State Records of North Carolina, Vol XVII, Edited by Walter Clark, Goldsboro, 1899

75. The Life and Character of the Reverend David Caldwell, by E. W. Caruthers, printed by Swaim and Sherwood, Greensboro, NC, 1842

76. State Records of North Carolina, Vol. XVII, Edited by Walter Clark, Goldsboro, 1899

77. The Annual Register for the Year 1781, London, 1782

78. Correspondence of the American Revolution (to George Washington), edited by Jared Sparks, Vol III, Little, Brown, & Co, Boston, 1853

79. Pyle's Defeat, Deception at the Racepath, Carole Watterson Troxler, Alamance County Historical Association, Graham, North Carolina, 2003

80. An Answer to that part of the Narrative, by Earl Cornwallis, London, 1783

81. Guilford Courthouse National Military Park Cultural Landscape Report, by John Hiatt, Guilford Courthouse National Military Park, Greensboro, North Carolina, 2003

82. The Battle of New Garden, by Algie I. Newlin, North Carolina Friends Historical Society, Greensboro, 1995

83. Battles of the United States, Vol I, by Henry B. Dawson, Johnson, Fry, and Company, New York, 1858

84. The Magazine of American History, Edited by John Austin Stevens, A. S. Barnes & Company, New York, July 1881

85. An Original and Authentic Journal of Occurrences During The American War, Roger Lamb, Wilkinson & Courtney, Dublin, 1809

86. Interesting Revolutionary Incidents and Sketches Of Character, Rev. E. W. Caruthers, Second Series, Hayes and Zell, Philadelphia, 1856

87. Sketches of Virginia, Historical and Biographical, by William Henry Foote, second edition, J, B. Lippincott & Co, Philadelphia, 1856

88. Colonel John Gunby of the Maryland Line, by A. A Gunby, The Robert Clarke Company, Cincinnati, 1902

89. The Drummer's Instructor, by J. L Rumrille and H. Holton, Packard and Van Benthuysen, Albany, 1817

90. Desertion in the American Army During the Revolutionary War, Graduate Thesis by James Howard Edmonson, Louisiana State University and Agricultural & Mechanical College, 1971

91. Letters By And To Gen. Nathanael Greene With Some To His Wife, George H. Richmond, New York, 1906

92. The Stoughton Musical Society's centennial collection of sacred music, Da Capo Press, New York, 1980

93. North Carolina in the Revolutionary War, Phillips Russell, Heritage Printers, Charlotte, 1965

# Internet Bibliography With Links


1.  Mouzon, Henry, and Robert Sayer And John Bennett. An accurate map of North and South Carolina... London, Printed for Robt. Sayer and J: Bennett, 1775. Retrieved from the Library of Congress, www.loc.gov/item/gm71002153/
2.  http://www.elehistory.com/amrev/SitesEventsTroopMovements.htm
3.  Price, Jonathan, -1822, et al. To David Stone and Peter Brown, Esq.: this first actual survey of the state of North Carolina taken by the subscribers is respectfully dedicated, Philadelphia: Printed by C.P. Harrison, 1808. Map. Retrieved from the Library of Congress, www.loc.gov/item/2011593508/
4.  https://founders.archives.gov/
5.  A Size Roll of Noncommissioned Officers and Privates of Virginia, http://revwarapps.org/b81.pdf
6.  What'll Thou Have: Quakers and the Characterization of Tavern Sites in Colonial Philadelphia, Northeast Historical Archaeology, Vol. 35, Article 24, John M. Chenoweth, 2006, http://orb.binghamton.edu/neha/vol35/iss1/24
7.  https://www.merionfriends.org/quaker-plainness
8.  North Carolina Quakers in the Era of the American Revolution, Master's Thesis, Steven Jay White, University of Tennessee, 1981. https://trace.tennessee.edu/utk_gradthes/1227
9.  http://firearmshistory.blogspot.com
10. https://www.revolutionarywarjournal.com/ferry-boats-of-colonial-america/
11. Trent River Flatboat, University Of North Carolina at Chapel Hill, retrieved from https://ancientnc.web.unc.edu/colonial-heritage/by-time/antebellum/trent-river-flat-boat/
12. Tarleton: Before He Became "Bloody Ban" by Michael Schellhammer, https://allthingsliberty.com/2013/01/tarleton-in-new-york/
13. www.moravianchurcharchives.org
14. https://www.oldsalem.org
15. https://mesda.org/exhibit/plan-of-salem/
16. "Rules by Which a Great Empire May Be Reduced to a Small One, 11 September 1773," Founders Online, National Archives, https://founders.archives.gov/documents/Franklin/01-20-02-0213
17. https://www.ncpedia.org
18. http://revwarapps.org
19. https://www.mountvernon.org
20. https://www.daviecountync.gov/DocumentCenter/View/489/History-of-Davie-County-Presentation-PDF?bidId=
21. Skipwith Revolutionary War Letters, downloaded June 22, 2023 from https://egrove.olemiss.edu/skipwith/4
22. The Race to the Dan Begins, The Crossing of the Dan, The American Revolution, The Southern Campaign, author unknown, 2020, retrieved June 21, 2023 from: http://oldhalifax.com/Crossing/CrossingPage3.htm
23. Pension application of Mattias Swing S7669, downloaded August 12, 2023 from http://revwarapps.org/s7669.pdf
24. Notes about Scotch-Irish and German Settlers in Virginia and the Carolinas, by William Lee Anderson III, 2018 http://www.elehistory.com/gen/ScotchIrish.pdf
25. Decoding British Ciphers Used In The South, 1780-81, Journal of the American Revolution, Ian Saberton, June 6, 2019,

www.allthingsliberty.com/2019/06/decoding-british-ciphers-used-in-the-south-1780-81/

26. Origin of the Hand Salute, US Army Quartermaster Museum, https://qmmuseum.lee.army.mil/research/vignettes/origin-of-the-hand-salute.html

27. Charleston Museum Collection of Revolutionary War Letters, https://lcdl.library.cofc.edu/lcdl/catalog/lcdl:64139

28. Small Arms Across Three Wars, A History of Small Arms in America's Wars, American Battlefield Trust, https://www.battlefields.org/learn/articles/small-arms-across-three-wars

29. Pension Applications of the Guilford County, NC Soldiers of the Revolutionary War, Southern Campaigns Revolutionary War Pension Statements & Rosters, http://revwarapps.org/

30. The King's Broad Arrow And Eastern White Pine, Northeastern Lumber Manufacturers Association, https://www.nelma.org/kings-broad/

31. North Carolina Slave Code of 1715, https://www.ncpedia.org/anchor/growth-slavery-north

32. https://ncgenweb.us/guilford/wp-content/uploads/2012/05/GuilfordCourthouseByJessop.jpg

33. https://www.wikitree.com/wiki/Jessup-321

34. https://www.flaginstitute.org/wp/uk-flags/union-flag-history/

35. https://spycurious.wordpress.com/tag/kings-colours/

36. Joshua Fry and Peter Jefferson, A Map of the Most Inhabited Part of Virginia, 1755, Document Bank of Virginia, accessed June 18, 2023, https://edu.lva.virginia.gov/dbva/items/show/59

37. The Online Institute for Advanced Loyalist Studies, British Legion Biographical Sketches, Infantry Officers, downloaded August 22, 2023 from http://www.royalprovincial.com/military/rhist/britlegn/blinf1.htm

38. Battle of Hart's Mill, Marker G-122, North Carolina Department of Cultural Resources, downloaded July 9, 2023 from http://www.ncmarkers.com/print_marker.aspx?MarkerId=G-122

39. Battle of Clapp's Mill, Marker G-111, North Carolina Department of Cultural Resources, downloaded July 9, 2023 from http://www.ncmarkers.com/print_marker.aspx?MarkerId=G-111

40. Battle of Weitzell's Mill, Marker J-37, North Carolina Department of Cultural Resources, downloaded July 9, 2023 from http://www.ncmarkers.com/print_marker.aspx?MarkerId=J-37

41. Beloved Possessions, The Liberty Cap, A Greensboro family's surviving link to the Battle of Guilford Courthouse, By Jim Dodson, O Henry Magazine, 2021, downloaded July 26, 2023 from https://www.ohenrymag.com/beloved-possessions/

42. The Age of Firearms, a Pictorial History, by Robert Held, Harper, New York, 1957, pp. 150-153; The Ferguson Rifle: A Revolutionary Weapon, Institute of Military Technology, downloaded July 27, 2023 from https://www.instmiltech.com/the-ferguson-rifle-a-revolutionary-weapon/

43. http://www.historyofparliamentonline.org

44. Fragment Shows Captive Caledonian Warrior Wearing Tartan Trews, The Scotsman, 2012, downloaded 07/26/2023 from https://www.scotsman.com/arts-and-culture/earliest-depiction-of-scottish-tartan-discovered-on-roman-statue-1598796

45. British Tactics and Conflicting Strategies in Executing the American Revolution, by Adam E. Zielinski, American Battlefield Trust, 2023, downloaded July 27, 2023 from https://www.battlefields.org/learn/articles/british-tactics-and-conflicting-strategies-executing-american-revolution

46. http://historicalfictionalightintime.blogspot.com/2012/06/patriot-prisoners-and-prison-ships.html;
http://americanfounding.blogspot.com/search/label/Pack%20Horse

47. John Green, 2023, https://www.arlingtoncemetery.net/j-green.htm

48. British Brigade of Guards in the American Revolution, Revolutionary War Journal, by Harry Schenawolf, June 8, 2013, downloaded August 5, 2023 from https://revolutionarywarjournal.com/british-brigade-of-guards/

49. Escape From New York, by Norman Goldstein, Historynet, 11/1/2016, downloaded on August 5, 2023 from https://www.historynet.com/escape-new-york/

50. Many Were Sore Chased and Some Cut Down, Fighting Cornwallis with the Rockbridge Militia, by Odell McGuire, December 1995, downloaded August 7, 2023 from http://rockbridgeadvocate.com/odell/guilford.htm

51. https://egrove.olemiss.edu

52. Troublesome Iron Works, North Carolina Office of Archives & History — Department of Cultural Resources, 2008, downloaded August 10, 2023 from http://www.ncmarkers.com/Markers.aspx?MarkerId=J-16

53. Ramsey's Mill, Moncure, North Carolina, in Chatham County, Historical Marker Database, downloaded August 11, 2023 from https://www.hmdb.org/m.asp?m=218157

Dave Dowdy lives in picturesque and historic North Carolina, often musing on the state, a place rising to action in the late stages of the Revolutionary War.